THE SCOT & THE SORCERESS

CLAIRE DELACROIX

DEBORAH A. COOKE

The Scot & the Sorceress
By Claire Delacroix

❦ Created with Vellum

BLOOD BROTHERS

A MEDIEVAL SCOTTISH ROMANCE SERIES

The sons of a notorious mercenary should never have met...but now that they are sworn allies, the Scottish Borders will never be the same...

1. **The Wolf & the Witch**
(Maximilian and Alys)

2. **The Hunter & the Heiress**
(Amaury and Elizabeth)

3. **The Dragon & the Damsel**
(Rafael and Ceara)

4. **The Scot & the Sorceress**
(Murdoch and Nyssa)

∼

DEAR READER

The Scot & the Sorceress is the fourth and final book in my *Blood Brothers* series of medieval romances, in which the heroes are all sons of a notorious mercenary. This is the story of Murdoch, who has sworn vengeance upon the Silver Wolf for the death of his foster father, and Nyssa, the healer with the hidden past who has taken refuge at Kilderrick and sees Murdoch's merit.

Murdoch, of course, is the warrior who killed Jean le Beau and the series opened with his perspective at that mercenary's funeral. He also was raised at Kilderrick so was not pleased about his childhood friend, Alys, accepting the Silver Wolf as her husband. In a way, Murdoch is the voice of dissent among the villagers, many of whom are likely to have some mixed feelings about Maximilian. He's not inclined to compromise and I, like Nyssa, admired how he adhered to his principles—though Nyssa has an ability to turn things around so Murdoch sees them in a new light. Murdoch's emotional journey is the larger one in this story, but that's often the way when a character who was a villain in an earlier story becomes the hero in his own book. I find such characters challenging and interesting to write—and it's only fair that if love conquers all, sometimes it has a bit more of a challenge.

With the final book in a series, there is always a long list of details to be resolved. I like all the familiar characters to have their HEA, for example, so you'll be glad to know that Royce meets his match. I also like to have cameos from the other couples in the series, and we need to see their children—you can expect to see Amaury and Elizabeth, as well as Rafael and Ceara, appear in **The Scot & the Sorceress**, along with Alys and Maximilian, of course, to ensure that Murdoch and Nyssa have their happy ending. It's also a bit sad to finish up a series and wave farewell to the characters we've come to know and love. Finale books are bittersweet projects, for sure. I'm really happy with this one, even though it's much longer than I anticipated, and I hope that you enjoy it, too.

The Scot & the Sorceress, like the other three books in the series, is available in ebook, trade paperback and a hardcover collectors' edition. I'm planning to create collector hardcover editions in 2024 of all four books in this series, along with new cover illustrations and a map (! I love maps!) so watch my website for news about that. You'll be able to get these new editions early, signed and with series swag in a campaign at Kickstarter. Watch my website for news about that.

You can, as always, find additional resources on my website. There is a list of characters in the series, which is updated after each book. I have a Pinterest page for the series—there's a link on the *Blood Brothers* tab on my website—which is a work-in-progress and will give you a glimpse of my inspiration. There are also a number of blog posts, linked on each book's landing page, about my research for the series.

And of course, you can sign up for my medieval romance newsletter, *Knights & Rogues*, to receive an alert when I have a new release, and to hear my news as well as any special offers or sales. There's a link on my website under the *Newsletter* tab. You can also follow me at many portals—those links are on the *About Claire* page.

Until next time, I hope you have plenty of good books to read.

All my best

Claire

CHAPTER 1

Kilderrick, Scotland—January 10, 1377

$\mathcal{M}$urdoch Campbell was caught between his loyalties. He had fulfilled half his sworn quest for vengeance but completing the task would mean injuring Alys Armstrong.

The choice was to keep his pledge to avenge the past and sacrifice a former friend, or surrender his sworn word and his honor.

'Twas a conundrum, to be sure. There was naught Murdoch valued more than his vow.

Murdoch told himself that 'twas Alys who erred in this matter, for she had come to love the Silver Wolf whom Murdoch was sworn to kill. If she had to pay the price of her folly, he should not blame himself.

Strangely enough, that argument, which had been compelling two years before, had lost its lustre.

He must keep his vow –regardless of the cost. Of what merit was a man whose pledge was worthless?

But Alys would be devastated and he could not ignore that. He had known her almost all his life.

Murdoch had been raised by Rupert Campbell, the castellan of Kilderrick and the man he had long believed to be his father.

Murdoch's mother had died when he was five. The Lady of Kilderrick had delivered a daughter to her lord husband a mere two years later. Though the lady died soon after, the daughter, Alys, and Murdoch soon became allies in all manner of mischief. There had only been her nursemaid Morag to fuss over them and all of Kilderrick to explore while their fathers tended to the holding, each in his own way.

In those days, when he had a measure of ale, Rupert would suggest that Murdoch's future might be as Laird of Kilderrick himself. The castellan was not alone in believing that Murdoch and Alys might one day make a match, or that their friendship might become more.

All changed when Murdoch had seen sixteen summers and Alys a mere nine, when the son of Jean le Beau attacked Kilderrick at the mercenary's demand. Maximilian de Vries, known as the Silver Wolf, had not been much older than Murdoch, but he had been shaped by battle into a weapon in his own right. Both laird and castellan died in the fire that destroyed the keep that night—as had Murdoch's conviction that Rupert was his blood father. Rupert had told him the truth before insisting that Murdoch run to Rowan Fell to warn the villagers. They had argued fiercely, to Murdoch's continued regret, for he had not wanted to leave Rupert alone.

By the time Murdoch returned, Kilderrick was consumed by fire, crumbling to ash and Rupert was dead. Morag had secreted the injured Alys in the forest, to use her healing potions upon the young girl, and the Silver Wolf had departed, undoubtedly to crow of his triumph to Jean le Beau and gather some reward.

It had been seventeen years since young Murdoch had stood over the smoking ruins and vowed to exact vengeance from Jean le Beau and his son the Silver Wolf. He had left Kilderrick and all he knew. He had trained as a warrior, labored with mercenaries and fighting men, spent years honing his skill, earning his way with his blade, and saving his funds until the moment for vengeance was ripe.

Jean le Beau had met his destiny two years before, but the Silver Wolf now held Kilderrick—and was wed to Alys herself. Their match had been made by force, despite the objections of the lady, but Alys subsequently declared she loved the fiend.

Loved him.

Murdoch had not truly believed it possible, given the losses she could attribute to that man. He had thought her enchanted or beguiled, perhaps afraid—though the Alys of childhood had been fearless. In his skepticism, Murdoch had allied with Alys' former betrothed against her husband.

That scheme had failed.

Now, Alys and the Silver Wolf had a son, and the Silver Wolf, as the new Laird of Kilderrick, gained the support of more people with every passing day. Truly, the sun shone upon the villain. The king granted favor and power to the former mercenary; his comrade and half-brother Rafael commanded the nearby Barony of Gisroy; his half-brother Amaury was Warden of the Marches on the English side and Lord de Beaupoint, a powerful holding of his own. Instead of gaining his rightful due, the Silver Wolf went from success to success.

While Murdoch was nigh diminished to a wild man of the woods, the Silver Wolf built a rich future. Alys, it might be said, had chosen aright.

But hardship had tempered Murdoch's will like iron on the forge. He would complete his quest—and he would do so by destroying all the Silver Wolf held dear.

First, would be the child. Spawn of a villain, the child could have no good future. 'Twould be a mercy to end the babe's days early before his heart was turned black by his father's wickedness, before he was compelled to follow in the Silver Wolf's rampaging path.

Second, would be Kilderrick. It had burned once and it could burn again. It had also been rebuilt once, and could be rebuilt again—finer, better, with a more honorable laird.

Third, would be Alys, if she insisted upon keeping her husband's side. Murdoch paced over this, but he could not shirk the price of keeping his word. And truly, Alys had already betrayed all they both knew to be of merit. He could not let sentiment obstruct his course. Alys was united with the villain and Murdoch could not save her from the import of that.

Fourth and finally, would be the Silver Wolf's own life. The cur might be content to die then, when he had been cheated of every advantage and lost all that he believed to have merit.

'Twas the perfect scheme for vengeance, and one that would make his enemy suffer most.

Murdoch knew he had need of an ally, one within Kilderrick, to see his scheme succeed. He was not so fool as to believe he would find a willing one.

Nay, someone had to be coerced.

As the new moon approached, Murdoch knew who it had to be. Alys' friend, the seer and wise woman, went alone to the Ninestang Ring each new moon after the high quarter day. She was predictable. She was vulnerable.

She was beautiful, though that was of no import at all.

Murdoch Campbell had no qualms in using whatever resource came to his hand.

The seer would suffice.

Vengeance would be his and soon.

'TWAS A FOUL NIGHT, cold beyond compare. Nyssa wished she did not feel obliged to seek a portent. Instead of lingering in the warmth of Kilderrick's hall or even the solitude of her chamber, she slipped through the gates in darkness, resenting her customary task.

Of what merit was a portent? Did her occupation matter to those around her? Did her visions make a difference? Since the nuptials of her companions—or more importantly, the arrival of their children— she felt dissatisfied with her life.

But no seer bore children. Nyssa knew that well. The choice was one or the other, for as soon as a seer experienced a man's touch, the visions abandoned her. Without the sight, she would be like any other woman; worse, she would be surrendering her gift for fleeting pleasure.

She squared her shoulders and set out for the Ninestang Ring alone but for Dorcha, who took flight as soon as they were through the gates and followed her.

She told herself it would not take long.

The wind tore across the heath with such fury that the raven could not keep close. He was cast from the sky by the brutal wind, swept behind Nyssa time and again, even forced to the ground. She retraced her steps and bent over the bird, offering her hand, and he seized her fingers with his claws, his feathers fluttering and his head hunkered low. Dorcha was not a small bird, but this wind was too much for him. He cawed, as if in complaint that she had left the keep at all, and she smiled that he sounded to be insulted that the elements should abuse him thus.

"Aye, *you* would have the sense to remain sheltered," she said and held him against her chest as she trudged toward her destination. She felt his beak against her throat, cold and hard, and the flutter of his pulse beneath her sheltering hand. The grip of his talons on her other hand was tight. He was a little warm, his feathers as soft as silk, and she felt honored by his trust.

But then, she was a healer. All manner of creatures came to her for solace.

Cold rain began to slant from the sky when she was halfway to the stone circle, striking her shoulders so hard that the drops could have been pellets of ice or small stones. Dorcha ruffled his feathers and made a quorl against her throat but Nyssa did not turn back.

'Twas the night of the new moon, the first such since the high quarter day, and her visit to the standing stones was due.

Indeed, the wild weather echoed of her fears. Something was awry and dire possibilities swirled in her dreams. She feared that a glimpse into the future would offer little consolation, but she had to know for certain.

Two years before, Nyssa had foreseen an insatiable wolf, and the notorious mercenary Maximilian de Vries, known as the Silver Wolf, had arrived to claim Kilderrick shortly thereafter. He claimed its heiress forcibly as his bride, thus convincing Nyssa that he was the predator of her vision. But she had been mistaken. Maximilian had become the protector of both Alys and Kilderrick, while the wolf in Nyssa's dreams still howled for blood.

Of late, Nyssa had dreamed of that the wolf devoured the moon, then hungered for the sun. She had dreamed of a wolf that destroyed all that came within its reach, a wolf that devoured more when all around it was a wasteland—a wolf that would never be sated.

Nyssa also understood that only she could stop him. Only a healer could halt a hunter, but that did not diminish her dread of their encounter.

Of late, she had seen a light in the distance at intervals as if someone kept watch upon those at Kilderrick and guessed that the 'wolf' she feared was a man in truth. He would be a man whose heart was shadowed, a man so bent upon his own objectives that naught would stand in his path, a man who would wreak evil upon this land.

'Twas the task of a healer to mend the wounded, even one so damaged as this, but what could she offer such a foe? She knew she was fated to defend all she loved from this fiend, and though she feared failure, Nyssa could not shirk her destiny. Failure would be simplest, in truth, for success might come at a higher price than she might prefer to pay. The ravening wolf of her dreams might meet her this night and claim his due.

Still, she went. One of her first lessons had been that fate could not be denied.

Nyssa wore men's garb on this night, taking after the choices of her friend Ceara. Her chausses were dark and her boots high, wrought of sturdy leather. A dark tabard was belted over her chemise, and she had wrapped a dark cloak around herself. She might have been as one with the shadows, save for the fair length of her braid. The wind drove against her face and whipped at her clothes, compelling her to narrow her eyes and trudge onward. She knew the path so well as her own name, but it seemed further this night to the standing stones.

When Nyssa stepped into the stone circle, her eyes widened in surprise. There was usually a quietude within the circle of stones, a tranquility that settled her agitation, but on this night, there was a maelstrom swirling within the protected space. The wind cast loose leaves against the stones, prompting them to swirl and dance. She was shocked by the hum of discord, as if the stones themselves wished to cast out an intruder.

They could not be allied against her!

Nay, there was another within the circle, shrouded by darkness. She took a step toward the middle of the circle, scanning the shadows ahead. Dorcha craned his neck, evidence that he, too, sensed another. When she halted, Nyssa heard a step, despite the wail of the wind, and her heart stopped.

Dread rose in her throat as a silhouette separated from the stone opposite her, the great leaning stone that was her destination. It was a man, larger and stronger than she, a man she could not recognize in the darkness. He carried something that she could not see clearly, a cluster of twigs that was roughly circular. Though it did not look like any weapon she knew, she did not trust it—or him—a whit.

"The seer," he said in Gaelic, his voice husky, approaching with menace.

Nyssa retreated a step, recognizing his voice. He was Murdoch Campbell, the half-brother of Maximilian, the man who had betrayed Alys. "Leave me be," she said, wishing she had a measure of Ceara's boldness.

Murdoch laughed, a cruel sound and one of confidence. "Not before you aid me." He snatched for her with his free hand with remarkable speed.

"Nay!" Nyssa cried and Dorcha cawed, struggling in her grasp. She released the raven and the bird dove toward Murdoch, talons outstretched as it flew toward his face. She raised a hand and whistled, not trusting her adversary, but Murdoch plucked the bird out of the air with unexpected agility.

In that moment, she realized that Murdoch carried a spherical cage, one wrought of vines and twigs.

He had planned for this encounter.

"Nay!" she cried again, even as the raven screamed outrage. She darted toward Murdoch, as Dorcha struggled, biting and scratching at his captor, but the larger man easily evaded her. Within two heartbeats, the raven was secured within the device, his efforts to gain freedom utterly futile.

Murdoch lifted his hand before himself, the cage swinging from his fist over Nyssa's head. "You *will* aid me," he repeated, his assurance so complete that it gave Nyssa a chill.

"Wretch," she whispered.

7

"I am that," he agreed readily.

She remembered him well even though he was shadowed on this night, remembered the auburn curl of his hair, the fullness of his beard and the steady blue of his gaze. She remembered the size and the strength of him, the resolve he showed in battle, and dread chilled her very blood. He was larger than she was and a skilled warrior, a man whose presence sent a curious thrill through her.

She reminded herself that he was wicked beyond all and that she should be terrified of him. Aye, Nyssa had no evidence that Murdoch possessed a heart at all.

She would never forget his betrayal of Alys, his alliance with that woman's former betrothed to see the Silver Wolf killed, a plan that would have resulted in Alys' own eventual demise. Nyssa shivered, though she had known of the evil in men long before that incident.

On this night, Murdoch wore a short dark cloak, though his hood had fallen back. She could barely discern the length of plaid wrapped around his hips and over his shoulder beneath the cloak, his tall boots, the gleam of daggers on his belt. How many weapons did he carry? She had no doubt he knew how best to use them all. Her treacherous heart leapt and pounded.

"Do not injure Dorcha," she whispered. "Whatever you desire, the bird is of no import."

"To the contrary, you hold the bird in affection, which makes it an asset to be used."

"Nay! Dorcha is a living creature, a life to be honored."

He spat on the ground. "It is a tool." He took a step closer and she felt the weight of his will bent upon her. "A pawn. A cause for negotiation." Murdoch spoke softly, reasonably, which made him all the more terrifying. He halted directly before her and drew his knife, the blade glimmering even in the darkness, and Nyssa's heart stopped. "You will aid me, seer, or the bird will die."

Nay!

Dorcha tried to peck at him, but the vines were woven tightly together, the gaps so small that he could only get a single talon through the gaps. Though the sphere was of good size, it was not big enough for the raven to flap his wings. He struggled and pecked at his

8

prison, to no avail, and Nyssa was sickened by the sight of him so confined.

"You will have to release him to kill him," she said softly.

"Nay," Murdoch replied readily. "I can hold this cage beneath the waters of the stream. I can stab my knife between the vines, slicing the bird to ribbons in increments. I can break the cage against the ground by pummeling it with rocks." Nyssa was horrified that he had already considered this so thoroughly. "I do not have to release it to ensure its demise."

"Such wickedness," she whispered. "Such evil. Your heart cannot be so dark as this." She reached a hand toward the cage, but he lifted it beyond her reach. "Whatever you desire, there must be another way to achieve it. There is no need for such cruelty..."

"Nay, there is not. If you aid me, I will release the bird." Murdoch shrugged and smiled a little, as if there was nothing to find troubling about his proposition. His eyes gleamed and she feared him to her very marrow.

He was evil. He was the ravening wolf, and he held Dorcha captive.

Nyssa's innards quivered with outrage but she stood tall. "What do you want of me?"

"I want the Silver Wolf dead, but first I want him destroyed."

Nyssa held her tongue, unable to envision Maximilian at such disadvantage.

Murdoch swung the cage, much to Dorcha's indignation. Each cry of frustration from the creature tore at Nyssa's heart.

Doubtless the cur intended as much.

"You think me unlikely to succeed," he said in that dreadful calm voice. "I hear as much in your silence. You believe I am doomed to disappointment." Murdoch shook his head. "But you err, seer. I will triumph because you will aid me. My prospects have changed with this encounter, just as I intended." His tone turned taunting. "Can you not see our shared future through your witching stone?"

Nyssa did not want to look through her stone. She did not want to avert her gaze from this fiend. "But how will you triumph?"

His voice dropped to a whisper. "Bring me the child," he said and Nyssa gasped aloud. "On the morrow, at sunset, to this very place."

Nyssa was appalled. "But you cannot injure Michael! He is innocent, a mere babe."

"And his father has sufficient guilt for two." Murdoch shook the cage and Nyssa took a step closer at Dorcha's caw of dismay. "You have until sunset, seer, and not one moment longer."

"But I cannot do this…"

"Find a way." He reached into the cage and pulled one of Dorcha's tail feathers so that the raven squawked, then offered it to her. It gleamed obsidian between them and she did not know whether to accept it or not. Murdoch smiled, which did not make him look less fearsome. "Or this will be all you have of the bird."

Nyssa was afraid and she was angry, but she also despised how he strove to terrify her. She refused to surrender even that much to him. She would feign boldness. She reached out, her chin high, and plucked the feather from his grip. Their fingers brushed in the transaction, his sufficient warm to send an unwelcome thrum through her, one that heated her beyond expectation. He smelled of fury and violence, his gaze simmering with an anger she knew would never be satisfied.

Yet there was something else, something softer that she could not name.

And the touch of his hand reminded her that he was a man, with a man's appetites. Could she use them against them? Might that be his weakness?

On a whim, Nyssa pulled the witching stone from her pouch and lifted it to her eye, her posture defiant. She viewed Murdoch through the round hole. Sure enough, she saw a wolf before her, a grey wolf with cold eyes of silver blue, a wolf that did not so much as blink.

A predator, and not one known for its mercy.

Nyssa might have shivered but in that moment, but her vision changed. She suddenly saw a woman running ahead of her. Her hair was long and loose, as white-blond as Nyssa's own. Her sleeves were rolled up, revealing the blue marks on her forearm, so many more than graced Nyssa's arm. She laughed as she ran through the shallow water, the silhouette of a familiar keep rising in the distance, seemingly from the very waves. And when she turned back to look over her shoulder, offering her outstretched hand to Nyssa, the sight of her face sent grief stabbing through Nyssa's heart, with a vigor that left her trembling. She had only a glimpse of the merry green eyes that were both familiar and lost, then the vision faded to swirling mist.

She lowered the stone and found Murdoch before her, his expression wary, even as wolves howled in the distance. Her heart was in her throat and her mouth was dry. Elsa!

"Do you see death, seer?" Murdoch demanded, folding his arms across his chest as he surveyed her. "Or an angel of justice?"

"Neither," she said with heat, declining to share her vision with him. Truth be told she was shaken by it. The healer within her was touched – and astonished that she could feel any compassion for this warrior who threatened her pet and her friend.

But her vision meant that Nyssa understood. Grief drove Murdoch Campbell. Grief and sorrow, just as grief and sorrow for the loss of Elsa tinted every waking moment of Nyssa's life. Grief was better than evil intent, though the results could be similar.

His heart might not be completely black.

Did it matter?

Could she save Dorcha and the Silver Wolf by healing Murdoch in time?

"Do you see your future?" Murdoch demanded. "Do you see the price of defying me? For your bird will be but the beginning, seer, upon that you can rely. You come to these stones alone at regular intervals. I have watched you. I know your ways. I will see you harnessed to my will, regardless of your own."

Nyssa took a step back, disliking that he had planned for this encounter. He had stalked her as a hunter followed his prey. He had taken note of her weakness in her affection for Dorcha and had planned to exploit it. How long had it taken him to weave the cage?

How had she not sensed his malice and anticipated his scheme?

How could she foil him?

She strove to listen to him as one who also ached with a loss.

"If you betray me," he continued darkly. "I will not only find you but I will ensure that you can never betray another again." He leaned toward her. "Trust me in this, seer."

There was sufficient menace in his words to turn her blood cold, but Nyssa heard the anguish beneath his fury. She reminded herself that his own wound drove him to injure others.

The realization emboldened her as little else could have done.

"Why?" she demanded. "Why do you desire that the Laird of Kilderrick pays this price?"

"He is not the rightful Laird of Kilderrick, no matter what he claims. He killed the true Laird of Kilderrick in that man's own chamber."

"But that deed is not yours to avenge. Alys, the laird's sole child, is content to have Maximilian as her spouse."

"Alys is a fool beyond all expectation," Murdoch said bitterly. "She is beguiled by pleasure and luxury, deceived as to her husband's true nature."

Nyssa held her tongue, not believing that for a moment.

He stepped closer. "He razed Kilderrick, turning it to a ruin, cheating Alys and I of our home."

"And he has rebuilt it, finer than it was before." Nyssa reached out to touch Murdoch's chest with her fingertip, astonished even by her own audacity. How much of his manner was bluster? She felt the need to test the depth of his wickedness. "These may be his crimes, but I ask the root of your hatred for him."

"You must know it," he said with heat. "He killed the man I knew as father, and for no just cause. He took Rupert Campbell's life, just as Jean le Beau shamed my mother and left her with child."

"With you."

He bowed his head.

Jean le Beau was his father, then, as Maximilian had suggested, and they two were half-brothers. "Is that why you killed him?"

"He deserved no less for his crime against her."

"You avenged her and now you will avenge your father, as well."

"What else would any son of merit do?" he demanded.

Nyssa shook her head sadly. "Aye, because the solution to violence can only be more violence. There is the thinking of those like Jean le Beau."

Aye, 'twas the solution of warriors, in Nyssa's experience, and one that few would dispute.

Save a healer like herself.

"I will see them both avenged, if it is the last deed I do!" His voice rose at this and Nyssa took a step back, wondering whether he would strike her in his fury. His fists clenched, one on the cage and the other on his dagger, and his eyes blazed. "Save your trickery for another, seer. I will not be turned aside."

The wind swirled between them for a moment, even the bird falling silent as Nyssa decided how far to press him. She played a dangerous game and she knew it, but she could not leave the matter be.

"But what then?" she asked softly. "What will you destroy after the Laird of Kilderrick is ruined?"

"I will see him *dead,* not merely ruined. I shall spit on his corpse."

"And then?" she persisted. "What future is there for you, if all that consumes you is a thirst for vengeance?"

Murdoch faltered, frowning as he took a step back. "That is of no import..."

Nyssa interrupted him with resolve, knowing she had glimpsed a doubt within him. "It is of every import! What if your quest means that you become like Jean le Beau?" She raised a hand and pointed to him. "What if that fiend's evil survives in this world because of you? Is that the legacy you would leave, the same scar as Jean le Beau?"

"I am not his son!" Murdoch roared.

"Aye, but you are, by your own admission."

"I will not be his son!" His eyes flashed with fury as he lunged toward her, jabbing toward her with the knife. "And I will not bargain with you. Flee, witch! Do my bidding by tomorrow night or fear my price!" He shook the cage and Dorcha croaked and fluttered helplessly.

Nyssa retreated a step and found herself outside the circle of stones. The wind raged around her and the clouds churned overhead, as if Murdoch's fury was shared. She heard the howl of those wolves in the distance, but when she looked into the Ninestang Ring again, it was empty.

There was no sign of Murdoch Campbell.

Even the wind stilled.

He might never have confronted her, but Dorcha was gone.

Save for the single ebony tail feather in her grasp.

Nyssa turned the feather, her consternation rising. Dorcha was captive and imperiled, and 'twas her fault. She had to save the raven, but she could not sacrifice the laird's son to do as much. She could not choose one over the other, yet saw no way to save them both.

Yet.

The rain fell with even greater vigor so she pivoted and walked briskly back toward Kilderrick. The land around her seemed still now, but watchful all the same. There was no sound but the pounding of the rain upon the ground. She was certain that she could feel a malevolent gaze upon her. Did Murdoch follow her? Would he assault her before she reached the keep? Nyssa kept her pace, refusing to run, refusing to grant him the triumph of knowing she was afraid of him. She did not like the sense of being prey.

But she dared not fear him, lest trepidation make her err. She would respect him and his power, but she would not cower before his threats. Wolves devoured those who fell before them. She had to heal the rapacious wolf somehow.

Lives depended upon her success.

Nyssa could not fail.

MURDOCH WAS LIVID, though his plan had been executed to perfection.

How dare the seer suggest that he was like Jean le Beau? Never had a man been less admired by Murdoch, and never had there been one so opposite in his choices. The very notion was outrageous. They were as dissimilar as two men could be.

'Twas true that Jean le Beau had been a warrior, as Murdoch was, but there the similarity ended.

Murdoch pursued justice. He was on the side of righteousness. Jean le Beau had cared naught for justice, seeking only his own pleasure and satisfaction, following his own violent whim. That man had no care for others, no moral measure, no concern with good or evil. The Silver Wolf was the same, the very echo of his sire.

Murdoch, in contrast, avenged two foul crimes.

The Silver Wolf deserved to pay for his deeds, even if he had lately pretended to reform his ways. Laird and castellan were still dead, Alys was still scarred, and even though the Silver Wolf had rebuilt Kilder-rick, that did not mean it had never been destroyed.

There could be no other resolution than the elimination of the Silver Wolf. Murdoch's quest was justified and it was right.

Aye, neither Jean le Beau nor the Silver Wolf would have undertaken any quest on principle alone. There had to be coin or advantage to be gained for either to show interest in a deed.

Slaughter had been Jean le Beau's choice, though he had never cared a whit for justice.

There was the distinction. Murdoch sought vengeance for those who had been cheated by the old mercenary. He cared naught for his own advantage—that was why he was impoverished and living in the woods.

His was a just war.

Despite the merit of his own defense, Murdoch's resolve wavered at the seer's question. What would he do once his quest was completed? He could not say. For seventeen years, he had not thought beyond his quest. 'Twas the goal for which he strove, every moment of every day—there was no future beyond its completion. Perhaps he had suspected he might die at the task, but he had never considered what he might do afterward.

What had she seen through her witching stone?

He was curious beyond all. His mother had been convinced of the power of seers, and old Morag had not been without her gifts. He told himself that once justice was served, his path would become clear, but it seemed a thin proposition.

Murdoch was restless that night in his refuge and the raven was a poor companion. The bird croaked quietly as if muttering to itself about its plight.

He reminded himself that he had no patience for the entreaties of any creature. He forced himself to recall that it was just a bird. But those notions did not stop him from feeling sympathy for the creature. He had no fondness of being confined himself.

"Should she keep her word, you will be flying free soon enough," he bade the bird gruffly. "At least you are out of the deluge." The rain was falling in earnest, drumming on the thatched roof of the hut that was his sanctuary. He hung the cage from a hook at one end of the loft and settled onto his pallet at the opposite end. He was wet from the rain and chilled to his very bones, plus he wanted to keep his distance from the bird. Though it was dark, he knew the creature watched him.

He felt his solitude on this night and indeed, a measure of loneliness. A quest for vengeance was a solitary task, to be sure.

The seer's question did compel Murdoch to consider his choices. He would not linger overlong at Kilderrick once his quest was complete— the keep would never fall to Murdoch's hand, as once Rupert had hoped it would. Even if the son was dead, the Silver Wolf had a veritable army in residence and doubtless one of them would assume the lairdship in his stead. Alys might insist upon administering the holding alone.

That removed his final doubts. Kilderrick must be burned again.

Perhaps Alys would die in the fire. If so, Murdoch would not have to look into the eyes of his childhood comrade when she breathed her last.

Murdoch would not consider the task of killing the infant. Nay. 'Twould be best done quickly and not pondered overmuch. He reminded himself of the debt owed to him by the Silver Wolf. He shivered in recollection of that man's mother, who he had met at Château de Vries at the funeral of Jean le Beau. Ice had to run in that widow's veins, for her gaze was cold and her manner yet more frosty. He would have wagered that Lady de Vries possessed no heart. The Silver Wolf had been doomed from conception, perhaps.

Perhaps his own mother's kindness was what made Murdoch less able to follow the lead of Jean le Beau.

"She is wrong about me," he told the raven, which made a sound that might have been interpreted as skepticism—if a bird could express such a response.

With sudden clarity, Murdoch saw the seer again, so fair and ethereal. His hand rose to the middle of his chest where she had touched him, as commanding as a queen, as beautiful as a vision. She might not have been real, but he knew she was.

As real as her questions and the doubts they stirred.

The weight of her fingertip had burned, fairly boring a hole through his boiled leather jerkin to touch his heart with unfamiliar fire.

'Twas better not to think of it—or her.

He moved to the small gap he had made in the wall of the hut, peering through it. Naught. He could discern only darkness. The rain fell with such vigor that he could not even hear the trickle of the stream that he knew was half a dozen paces away.

The seer's name was Nyssa.

Nyssa. Murdoch whispered her name, savoring the feel of it on his tongue.

He had watched her since the arrival of the Silver Wolf's party at Kilderrick years before, fascinated by her grace and beauty. There was a woman to prize beyond all others. She ran like a doe, light on her feet and quick. Her hair was often loose, blowing like a golden cloud. Her eyes were as green as the sea in a tempest and he was glad he had not been able to see her more clearly on this night. He might not have dared to challenge her thus, to be so crude and blunt. Her beauty awed and humbled him—indeed one glimpse of her had convinced him that beauty was a weapon oft underestimated.

She could slay him with a glance, this one, and he had to ensure she never knew it.

Nay, he had to arm himself against her.

He was still amazed that she was so fearless. He could have done her great injury, and without much effort, yet she had not fled. Could she have summoned lightning to smite him? Murdoch would not have been surprised.

Worse, she had questioned him, nurturing uncertainties he had not known he possessed.

And she had not retreated, even when he had smelled her fear.

She was unlike any other person he had known. She awed him. Old Morag had been a healer, but she had never had the power and presence of this one. She had never prompted the conviction in Murdoch that she could read his very thoughts and discern his secrets. Her gaze had never been so steady, so piercing.

She had never reminded him that he was a man, with desires other than vengeance.

Worse, this seer made him doubt the merit of his cause.

Her spell was a potent one, and he was snared within it.

The bird croaked and Murdoch recalled that its plight had prompted the seer to challenge him. She would do much for others, this seer, and a part of him hated that he would use that against her, making her a pawn in his own scheme.

He bowed his head, fearing that Rupert would not approve of such an ignoble deed.

Murdoch knew he should draw out the agony of the Silver Wolf's suffering, but he dared not grant the that man any opportunity to retaliate. He had to strike quickly, each blow falling in rapid succession, to succeed against his foe.

To succeed despite his own doubts, before they gained supremacy.

By the end of the week, the Laird of Kilderrick had to be dead.

And what then? The question echoed in his thoughts, a query with no good reply, and one that could not be silenced. She was as good as a weapon in the Silver Wolf's grasp, though one that worked in mysterious ways that could not be readily defeated.

Murdoch knew he would never sleep. Instead of considering his future once justice was done, he found himself wondering what it would be like to touch a woman like Nyssa.

To kiss her.

Not to force his desire upon her, but to have her come to him willingly.

Aye, to be seduced by her.

The very possibility stirred an agitation and a need within him, responses that had no place in his quest. Murdoch strove to push them from his thoughts. He had been chaste for years, to keep his focus, and this was not the time to falter.

The seer was not a woman who would ever come to him.

He would never know the splendor of her touch.

She strove to beguile him, and he should not let her succeed so readily.

His musing was interrupted by the sound of ponies. He sat up, listening, certain he must have erred. 'Twas too foul a night for a company to be abroad and dark, too, with the moon new.

But the sound persisted and grew louder. It was a veritable herd of ponies, at least a dozen of them, then he heard the lowered voices of men, too. It made no sense. Murdoch left the caged bird behind. Once at the portal, he peered into the night without satisfaction, then left his sanctuary to learn the truth about the arrivals.

Who came to Rowan Fell in darkness and secrecy—and why?

CHAPTER 2

*N*yssa hastened her steps as the gates to Kilderrick loomed ahead. She was unsurprised to find Royce still standing sentry. The rain drummed steadily against the stone walls, turning them slick and gleaming. The clouds were so dense overhead that there was not a star to be seen and a mist gathered in the valley where once the Compagnie Rouge had camped. The masons had returned to the south for the winter and she could smell the fires from Kilderrick village beyond the keep, though it was lost in the fog. On a night such as this, the larger and more distant village of Rowan Fell might have been in another realm.

She was wet beyond belief, the rain having fallen in torrents after she left the standing stones. Her heart was heavy with fear for Dorcha and her innards twisted with her lack of choices.

How Nyssa hated to feel powerless. Her throat tightened in recollection of the last time, when Ceara had come to her aid, but her friend could not help her now. Ceara was wed and with child, as well as in residence at distant Gisroy.

Nyssa missed her bold companion more than ever on this night.

This was more akin to her first encounter with helplessness, alone, and she did not savor the reminder a whit. Aye, that should have taught her all she needed to know of the treachery and lust of men.

She was a fool and then some to acknowledge any allure in Murdoch Campbell.

Royce stood at his first impression of movement, his hand falling to the hilt of his sword. Nyssa knew the moment he recognized her, though he was but a large figure framed in the portal, for he grunted and leaned upon a stool again. His hands were busy and she guessed that he was carving while on duty.

Royce was a former mercenary who had accompanied Maximilian to Scotland and remained as one of that man's most steadfast followers. He was an enormous warrior with a long beard, his dark hair hanging to his waist. He also was missing one eye and part of one ear, though neither seemed to trouble him much. He favored silver rings and wore one on almost every finger. As Nyssa drew near, she saw that he was whittling with his knife.

"What news of future days?" the former mercenary demanded. There was humor in his tone, and Nyssa knew he did not believe in anything he could not hold within his own grasp. Her visions were but a fanciful tale to him.

Nyssa looked at his work once she stood out of the rain, curious as ever. He deftly carved a wooden spoon, as he had many others, but this one was smaller, with a loop on the handle.

"Clouded," she said simply and he flicked a glance to her face. "The weather was so foul that I could not see clearly."

"That is unlike you. Where is Dorcha?"

"I let him fly," she lied.

"On a night such as this?" Royce's heavy brows rose. "He will think you no good guardian, to be sure."

Nyssa caught her breath and averted her gaze.

"Aye, you lost him in the wind," the mercenary guessed, sympathy in his tone. How did anyone imagine that he was not perceptive? "Fear not, Nyssa. The wild creatures have their ways. Doubtless he will be on your sill in the morning, seeking a morsel of meat after his ordeal."

"Doubtless," Nyssa said, though she knew it would not be so. She shook the rain out of her cape and shivered. The cold within her would be dispelled by no fire. She recalled the resolve in Murdoch's voice and shivered again.

"Sit for a moment before you retire," Royce invited. "It will be chilly within at this hour." He lifted the spoon. "And I would have your counsel. Is it too ornamented for use?"

He offered an excuse to linger and Nyssa knew it. There was a kindness in Royce that many overlooked and which she found endearing, perhaps because it was unexpected in a man who appeared to be so rough. She sat beside him, glad of the heat of his small fire in the guard's chamber and examined the spoon. It was less than the length of her index finger, but ornamented with leaves, with a spiral carved in the bowl of the spoon itself. "I think it is lovely. Have you a recipient in mind?"

"For the boy," he said gruffly, apparently unable to meet her gaze. As she watched a dull flush rose on the back of his neck. "He will not be able to grasp a larger one as soon as he might prefer." Now it was Royce who averted his gaze, shy of showing his affection for Maximilian and Alys' son.

"You are a good friend, Royce." Nyssa gave him a nudge and he flicked a look her way.

"Anyone else would do the same."

"But no one else has done the same, or even considered the matter. But you are right: Michael will want to do for himself as soon as he can. It is his nature."

"He is Maximilian's son."

Hearing the admiration in his tone, Nyssa studied the burly warrior. He was armored in chain mail with a sword and a dagger hanging from his belt. His helm was set aside while he worked, but she had seen his speed in battle before. "Would you teach me to fight with a knife, Royce?"

His sidelong gaze was bright. "Nay."

"Whyever not?"

He stood, setting aside his work, and lifted his hands. "Assault me," he invited.

A test. Nyssa drew the knife that Alys insisted she carry, and lunged toward Royce, knowing full well that she would have little chance of doing him injury. She was right. In the blink of an eye, he had caught her hand and twisted her arm behind her back. He held her captive against one wall with her own blade against her throat. He had resolved the threat before she had even gathered her thoughts.

"Be glad the blade is small and dull," he said.

He released her and returned to his seat, offering the hilt of the blade to her before he picked up his carving again.

"So easy as that?" Nyssa asked.

Royce smiled. "Were it my own choice, you would have a guardian not a knife. I would even remove that one from your belt."

Nyssa exhaled and sat beside him again. "I could learn."

He shook his head, resembling a woeful bear more than ever. "You have not the nature to do injury to others. When you carry a blade, all you do is provide a weapon to your foe, whoever that might be."

"You will not teach me, then?"

He shook his head again. "'Twould be futile." He wagged his blade at her. "I will, though, accompany you whenever you leave the keep alone."

She eyed him with curiosity. "You never suggested as much before."

He winced. "'Tis a strange trade you have and one I cannot trust overmuch. I am wrought too simple for such portents and visions."

Nyssa smiled. "You did not wish to visit the Ninestang Ring at night."

"What man with his wits about him would? But this night is a foul one and you should not have gone alone." Again he shook his blade at her. "Next time, tell me of your scheme and I will go with you."

How strange that a man who had no belief in the unseen would sense that she had been imperiled, or be fearful of entering the stone circle at night. But then, Royce's ability to anticipate danger had been honed over the years. Perhaps his sense was the culmination of many small observations, ones he was not aware he had made.

"Thank you, Royce," Nyssa said simply and he grunted. She rose to her feet and took a candle from the store in the gatehouse, lighting it from his fire, before continuing into the quiet keep. He had spoken aright: it *was* cold. The stones emanated a chill that was damp and penetrating, and Nyssa found herself shivering again.

"The bird will return," Royce called after her softly. "Do not lie awake and fret for him."

But Nyssa would.

She could not lie again to Royce, though. Dorcha would not return unless Nyssa found a way to ensure as much.

What could she do?

EAMON, the sheriff of Rowan Fell, was arguing with his wife, Jeannie. The simple truth was that their situation had become desperate. The Silver Wolf had reclaimed Kilderrick after the lairdship had been empty for fifteen years. In those years, Eamon had dutifully collected the tithes and taxes, and sent the appropriate portions to both king and bishop. He had also exacted fees from villagers for minor offenses, though he had no right himself to hold a court. He told them all that he acted for the laird they did not have, and truly, he had been more fair than Robert Armstrong, the former laird and Alys' father.

At first, Eamon had saved the laird's portion, but over the years, he had become increasingly accustomed to considering it his own. The Silver Wolf's claim of Kilderrick had almost perfectly coincided with Eamon having spent the bulk of the coin he should have saved. Worse, it had not been spent on items that could be sold, save for Jeannie's pewter plates. Eamon liked a good dinner and he liked his ale. They had bought vittles aplenty and had only their plump bellies to show for it.

The Silver Wolf had demanded the coin that should have been saved for him, and there was little argument that could be made against him. His demand was right and just—if impossible to meet. The terrible thing was that this hardened mercenary had been gracious: he had given Eamon to the end of the first year after his arrival to raise the coin, then had granted him another delay, to the end of the subsequent year. In but a fortnight, the laird's first court of the new year would be held on the full moon, and Eamon knew he had to surrender every penny owing to the Silver Wolf or pay the price. There would not be another reprieve.

It had been a fair sum of money. Eamon still had gathered less than a fifth of it. There were not so many honest ways for a man in his position to raise funds. Some villagers had made gifts to him, preferring that he remained sheriff over another named by the Silver Wolf. He had sold Jeannie's pewter plates, a matter of considerable contention in their small household, and she had sold most of the eggs from the past year. Their belts were tighter, to be sure. It was not nearly enough, but Eamon had been preparing to face his reckoning.

Jeannie, evidently, had not.

"He is a good boy," she insisted again.

"Cedric is not a good boy," Eamon retorted. "He has never been a good boy. He was wicked from the day he was born and now that he is a man—" He exhaled at even the thought of this and flung out his hands. "Now there is naught to restrain him."

"Nonsense! My cousin taught her son right from wrong..."

"So, he has the wits to know when he sins. It does not stop him, Jeannie!"

"He is her only son. He is a good boy!"

"He is a man who was overly indulged as a child, who believes that his own desire is the only thing of import, and that no price paid by another can be too high for him to claim it. *That* does not make a good man!"

"You are simply envious of him. He has a horse not a pony. He has..."

"He will have no welcome in this abode with his stolen horse."

"Stolen? How dare you say as much to me? We speak of my cousin's boy..."

Eamon fixed her with such a look that she fell silent. "How many times did the witches at Kilderrick interrupt his returning party of reivers?"

"I cannot believe..." Jeannie began, but she had lost her bluster.

"You *know* that he leads a party of reivers," Eamon insisted. "You *know* that they rode south through Liddesdale at intervals and you know that I chose not to intervene, for the sake of your kin."

Jeannie tossed her head. "You could never have stopped them. A dozen young men against you?" She scoffed in a way that did little to assuage Eamon.

"I am sheriff, Jeannie, and I bid you remember that."

"Not for much longer." Her eyes narrowed and she turned to look pointedly at the two spaces on the wall where she had previously displayed her pewter plates.

Eamon frowned. "You should not have invited him."

"And what is your solution?" Her tone turned mocking. "Will you ask the Fae for the coin? How else will you gather it in a fortnight?"

He shook his head. "I will face the reckoning of the Silver Wolf and hope for his mercy."

Jeannie made an exasperated sound and shook her head. Eamon was saved from her reply, for the sound of horses came from behind their small house.

"How many?" he demanded but Jeannie was gone.

Eamon followed her with reluctance to the door of their hut that gave a view to the creek that ran toward Kilderrick keep, where the gorse shaded the stream. A company was hidden in the shadows there with their horses and ponies—a company of rogues to Eamon's thinking—and he disliked that they so outnumbered him. There had to be the full dozen of the villains, just as mentioned by Jeannie. Half a dozen shadows slipped from the gorse and strode toward the hut, each of them wrapped in a dark cloak and moving like mist over a river.

A shiver of dread slid down Eamon's spine.

Jeannie smiled and fussed over the leader when he reached the door. She kissed the cheeks of Cedric, who was taller and broader than Eamon as well as half his age, while the others ducked into the door. They brought the smell of wet horseflesh and wet wool, as well as the cold of the wind. There was a wicked glint in Cedric's gaze, which did not bode well for any change in his nature. He was accompanied to the hut by five other men, who stood in silence to watch and listen. One threw back his hood to reveal blond hair and silver eyes, as well as a gaze so assessing that it made Eamon shudder.

"Well, Cousin?" Cedric demanded, his manner jovial. "Shall we ride?"

"Ride?" Eamon asked, his gaze flicking between Cedric and Jeannie.

"It is akin to asking the Fae for favor," she said, her tone defiant. "But more inclined to good result."

"Aye, by choosing precisely what you prefer," Cedric said, then laughed along with his companions.

"You mean to go reiving again," Eamon said with belated understanding.

"We have changed our route, but we have not stopped. Are you with us this night or not?"

"I cannot go reiving," Eamon insisted. "I cannot *steal*. I am sheriff of Rowan Fell!"

Cedric smirked. "I had understood that *stealing*, Cousin, was the cause of your current predicament. Or is it not called theft when you take the laird's due for yourself?" He turned to his fellows. "Shall we ask the Silver Wolf for his judgement of his dishonest sheriff?"

His companions chuckled and nudged each other at this, save for the blond one, who solely watched in silence. That one might have been a hawk, the way his eyes glittered, and Eamon did not doubt he would rip the heart from any who betrayed him.

"Eamon? Have you lost your courage?" Cedric taunted and the blond one smiled at that. 'Twas not a kindly smile and Eamon averted his gaze. The way the company remained at the threshold told Eamon that they had no intention of lingering. They rode south this very night and would depart within moments, with or without him.

This opportunity had to be seized or lost forever.

Jeannie gave him a hard nudge. "Go," she said. "Fetch your cloak."

Theft and survival, or honor and death. The choice, placed in such bald terms, was simple.

"I have no fine mount," Eamon said, though his heart was not truly in the protest. "My pony is older and would not keep the pace."

"But we have ponies aplenty to bear our spoils," Cedric said easily. "What is one more with a saddle if it means another blade to our side?"

Eamon caught his breath at the suggestion of battle and bloodshed, but his own blood would be shed if he could not pay the funds to the laird. He was well aware of Jeannie's bright gaze upon him.

Perhaps the bold truly did seize the prize.

Perhaps he might find her a pair of pewter plates.

"I will fetch my cloak and boots," he said, and Cedric's hungry smile flashed.

~

As the company of strangers rode west from Rowan Fell, a cluster of shadows against the night, Murdoch flattened himself against the ground at his vantage point. He had retreated to the opposite bank when light had shone from the door to Eamon's hut. With no trees or rocks to hide behind, he had dropped to the bank. The water seeped into his garments, but he was already wet. He could not see the riders clearly enough to identify them, but they had definitely stopped at the sheriff's abode. There had been a glimmer of light as the door opened and another when they had departed, neither of which could be mistaken.

Murdoch was certain there was one more in their number when they left.

He recalled the steaming horses and ponies, left in the rain by the stream while some errand was fulfilled—or a companion gathered. There had been at least a dozen of them, only half saddled. The riders moved like young men and they had come from the north. Murdoch guessed their business. The valley of Liddesdale had long been used as a conduit for reivers, which was why Alys and her companions had demanded a toll to pass the ruined keep. The Silver Wolf had established a formal toll on the road that ran alongside the river.

It made sense that the reivers had simply chosen another route, one beyond the bounds of his reach. The road from Teviothead to Longtown through Langholm passed to the west of the Silver Wolf's holding, sufficiently distant to avoid his interference, at least most of the time. It was a larger road and busier which increased the risk, but riding at night would minimize any challenge. Dispersing some of their gains en route might encourage others to look away. They could retreat so far as Hawick or Galashiels to comparative safety after each raid.

As for their destination, Murdoch would wager, with the vigilance of the new Lord de Beaupoint to the south of the Solway Firth and the Baron of Gisroy to the east, that they would have to ride further south or east to find easy spoils.

But why would the sheriff of Rowan Fell himself join the foray? Murdoch was not overly impressed by Eamon's honor or integrity, so 'twas simple to guess. Perhaps life as sheriff was less comfortable than once it had been, now that there was a laird at Kilderrick.

Murdoch smiled, wondering whether his observation might prove useful in future.

Then he thought of the seer and recalled her pet bird, and returned to his refuge with purpose. If the bird was injured before he met her again, Murdoch knew he would have no hold over her.

Indeed, he wondered whether he truly had one now.

A BABE'S cry rent the air as Nyssa reached the upper floor of the shadowed keep, and she guessed that Michael dreamed. She heard Alys stir, that woman's voice sleepy as she spoke to her husband. Maximilian's reply was a low growl, then Alys laughed lightly.

"I will get him, Alys," Nyssa said. She shed her wet cloak as she approached the cradle. When the light of the candle fell upon the infant, Michael put his fist in his mouth, his eyes wide, but he quieted at the sight of her. There were tears on his cheeks and she whispered soothingly to him. Her heart twisted at his vulnerability, and she lifted him into her arms with a tight throat. He was blond with eyes of blue, like his father, a healthy child who was already tall for his age.

Not Michael. She could not bear to be a part of such a travesty. She rocked him and murmured to him, unable to keep herself from trailing her fingertips across the soft fair hair on his head. He was so fragile and precious, and deep within her that yearning for more grew a little more vehement.

What was it like to have a child? Even if Nyssa surrendered her gift, she was unlikely to have a son, but still, she wondered. She could imagine that a child would give completion and reason to a person's life, a sense of accomplishment and pride.

She had no reason for such discontent, though the yearning was not readily dismissed.

"He is well?" Alys asked in a whisper and Nyssa turned to find her friend close beside her. Alys' dark hair was braided into a single plait and she wore a linen chemise that fell past her knees. Her boots were lined with fur, and her scar was softened by the shadows of the candlelight.

"Perhaps a bad dream," Nyssa said quietly, offering the boy to his mother. She watched Alys kiss her son, listened to the infant's gurgle of satisfaction, and smiled when Alys cradled him close. His eyes were already closing, his fist locking now on the neck of Alys' chemise. The gazes of the two women met and Nyssa was glad of her friend's happiness.

How could she do aught to compromise it?

How could she abandon Dorcha?

Alys frowned a little after her gaze flicked over Nyssa's wet clothing. "You went to the stones? In this weather?"

"It is the new moon after the high quarter day." Nyssa lowered her gaze, hiding her thoughts.

Should she confide in Alys? If she did, Maximilian would be roused and told the tale this very moment, his men would be mustered and Murdoch would be hunted. He had been hunted before without success, and she did not doubt that he would blame her for any such outcome.

Dorcha would die, and Nyssa could not bear that prospect.

Such a confession might make Maximilian vulnerable, as well. Men died at the hunt, whether by accident or deliberate intent, and Murdoch might have planned for Maximilian's pursuit—just as he had planned for her arrival at the stones this night. He had built the cage to snare Dorcha, and there was no telling what trap he might have planned for the Silver Wolf.

Nay, there had to be another solution.

Alys waited in silence, rocking her son. "You must have seen something that troubled you," she said finally.

Nyssa shrugged. "I have told you of the wolf I see," she said, striving to keep her voice light.

"And you have seen it again?"

She nodded, then shrugged again. "Perhaps it is a dark fear of my own and no more than that."

"What fear could you have? Are you not secure here at Kilderrick?"

Nyssa chose to keep her secrets. "I did not willingly leave all I knew behind, Alys. You must have guessed as much."

"Then the wolf is a man," her friend guessed.

"I think it might be a man and a warning, both." Nyssa turned away, intent upon retiring though she doubted she would sleep. At least she would not have to deceive her friend.

"Perhaps you should take a companion when next you visit the stones," Alys said.

"Royce has just offered as much," Nyssa said, then glanced back. "In three months, after the next quarter day, all will be resolved," she said with confidence. "There will be no need."

Alys nodded agreement and Nyssa took the candle to her own chamber, sparing a backward glance from the portal. Alys was still watching her, Michael sleeping as she swayed with him in her arms. They made a sweet sight together, Alys' cheek against her son's head, and Nyssa's mouth went dry. She wanted to pull out her witching stone and look at the pair through it, but Alys was watching her with concern.

Nyssa's chamber seemed larger and emptier than she knew it to be, and much colder. She lit the brazier then went to the window, missing both Dorcha and Ceara. She would have welcomed Ceara's blunt counsel on this night. Doubtless that woman would have suggested a clever deception of some kind. Nyssa's thoughts did not run in such directions. The rain was beating down with vigor, the darkness almost complete, and Nyssa felt the hair on the back of her neck prick as she closed the shutters against the night.

Would Murdoch ensure that Dorcha was sheltered from the storm? She hated that she did not know.

She was undressing when she felt the weight of the witching stone still in her purse. On impulse, Nyssa returned to the window, opened the shutters and lifted it to her eye. Within the circular hole of the stone, the rain fell just as hard and the night was just as dark.

Then Nyssa murmured the old charm, the one she had not had a chance to utter at the Ninestang Ring this night. Her mother had taught it to her when she had chosen the stone for her, and the feel of it upon her tongue always made Nyssa yearn for former times. Given her glimpse of Elsa earlier, the words felt weighty on her tongue. How she missed her bold sister!

But there was no point in wishing for the past to return. Her home was at Kilderrick now.

It took an endless moment, but the view through the stone gradually changed. It swirled as if a wind gathered there, spinning as the view seldom did. Suddenly it stilled and she knew she peeked into another realm. She recoiled at the sight of the wolf when he turned his cold gaze upon her and bared his teeth, but she did not lower the stone.

Nyssa was glad she did not, for another wolf joined him. A smaller wolf of a darker hue of grey, one that nipped playfully at the larger one and wagged its tail, as if to play. The wolf Nyssa knew was clearly intrigued—he watched the other intently, then began to follow it, seemingly with reluctance, then with greater enthusiasm. Did the large wolf mean to injure the smaller one? Nyssa could not bear to watch if so, yet she could not look away. Despite its obvious disadvantage, the smaller wolf was persistent and fearless. When the larger wolf pounced upon the smaller one and it slipped from beneath his weight to circle him again, Nyssa understood that the new arrival was female.

The large wolf's fury was distracted by desire. He had no intention of injuring this smaller one. His desire was for some other deed.

Sure enough, the wolves coupled. Nyssa might have lowered the stone then, but she was glad she did not. For when they were done, the pair lay down together, the large wolf vigilant and protective as the smaller one curled against him to sleep. He nuzzled his newfound mate and his tail wrapped around her, his gaze cool when he looked again at Nyssa.

And she understood. The ravaging wolf could be *tamed* by desire.

The image within the stone swirled and dispersed, but Nyssa's thoughts were spinning even before she lowered the stone. The vision suggested that she was not without power in this exchange. Did Murdoch find her alluring? She had sensed the heat within him when she had touched him, to be sure. Could his desire be used to tame him?

Could she offer herself in exchange for Dorcha's freedom?

The very notion was troubling. The price would be high and there was no telling the potential of success. She did not fully trust this vision and wondered at her doubts.

Perhaps because the path was perilous. Perhaps because Murdoch was as unpredictable as a wolf.

Perhaps because she was afraid.

Not all wolves were tamed by desire. Her father had not been and the man chosen to wed her sister had not been. They remained predators and killers, both of them, though Nyssa could not dwell upon what had been. She had to consider the challenge of Murdoch and believe in her success.

Could she invite the touch of a warrior like Murdoch? Did she dare? She had doubts aplenty, but she sat in the darkness, considering that her past had shaped her purpose just as Murdoch's had done.

They had common ground in their grief and loss, in the fact that much had been stolen from them both. Would a shared sense of loss make them allies? 'Twas true they had chosen different paths, for he was bent upon vengeance while she chose to begin anew. Could she persuade him of the merit of her choice?

Perhaps one kiss would bolster her conviction, divert Murdoch's thirst for vengeance and ensure Dorcha's release. Nyssa did not consider herself a temptress, though she knew men oft believed otherwise. What if her power was that of physical temptation in this exchange?

She was not at all convinced of her success in this endeavor, but for the sake of Dorcha and Michael, Nyssa would try.

Elsa, she knew, would have succeeded with ease and that encouraged her as little else had done.

THE SEER WOULD NOT COME.

Murdoch's conviction grew steadily. He had slept poorly, his dreams filled with nameless threats that left him agitated. She had cast a spell upon him, to be sure. He waited restlessly for the day to pass, increasingly certain that the seer would not keep her word. He did not truly wish to kill the bird.

He told himself he would do what had to be done. The seer had the choice of saving the bird.

The raven watched him with bright eyes from within the cage, never seeming to blink, and Murdoch recalled all the tales he had been told of such creatures as a child. He was not fearful of witches and Fae, but this bird had an aura of animosity and Murdoch began to fear the practical considerations of releasing the raven.

Would it set upon him and peck out his eyes? Would it claw and scratch him? Murdoch had never feared a mere bird before but this one's malevolent glare concerned him. The bird's view was not undeserved, after all.

Ravens, it was said, understood the speech of men. They were harbingers of death and guides to other realms. His mother had called them corbies and insisted they saw the secrets hidden in the hearts of men.

Murdoch was keenly aware of the bird's vigilant stare.

Perhaps it would be better if the seer did not come.

Perhaps he would kill the bird either way.

He shied from the prospect even though he had made the threat. 'Twas one thing to kill a man who had never done a kindness in his life, like Jean le Beau, and another to kill a trapped bird for no good purpose. It was not as though he would eat the meat.

Nay, not of a corbie. He was not so desperately hungry as that.

The bird cawed softly, bobbing its head, the sound making his flesh creep.

The seer's words repeated in his thoughts like an endless refrain. She unsettled him, though, with her steady gaze and her soft challenge.

He would not even call her by name, for that would only increase her hold over him. Murdoch had a healthy respect for witches and their spells, thanks to his mother.

The bird, perhaps predictably, had a similar effect upon him. He hunted for meat all the time and thought little of it, but this creature eyed him so that he might have held a child captive.

Save no child could have such cunning in its dark gaze as this bird.

How could the day take so long to pass? Had the seer cast a spell upon the day itself, to tether him to an endless moment of torment?

Murdoch would have liked to dismiss the notion, but the rain fell steadily and the light did not fade, making him wonder at her skills. The day lasted an eternity, which was not how matters should be at this time of the year.

To his relief, the rain stopped finally and a pale sun emerged from the clouds, just in time to sink toward the horizon.

'Twas time.

Murdoch trudged back to the Ninestang Ring, uncertain what to expect. To think that he had believed the seer to be predictable. He carried the bird, now so silent and still that twice he checked that it still lived. When they reached the stones, he put a finger through a gap in the woven branches, intending to stroke its feathers and perhaps console it. The raven bit him with vigor, hard enough to draw blood.

That gave Murdoch little encouragement of the results of its release.

He would not think about the boy's demise.

He sat with his back against the greatest stone, letting its chill slip into him, the cage on the ground beside him and his knife in his hand. He suspected the seer would deny him one way or the other. If she came and refused him, he would have to kill the bird before her eyes. He had sworn to do as much and would not relent.

How he tired of feeling like a cur.

If she did not come, he would have to deliver the bird's corpse to Kilderrick somehow.

And then what? Her question haunted Murdoch, making him doubt the objective that had consumed him for half of his life. What would he do once he was avenged upon the Silver Wolf?

There would be no future for him at Kilderrick, not after his goal was achieved. He had no close kin who would welcome him, no bonds to any other holding, no prospects in his homeland at all.

What *would* he do?

He could, perhaps, join a company of reivers, like the one that had visited Rowan Fell the night before, but Murdoch had little taste for lawless thieving. He had never met a thief he could trust, while, oddly, he had known many mercenaries whose words were their bond.

He supposed he would return to the Continent and sell his blade, ending his days in his trade as a mercenary.

How did that make him different from Jean le Beau?

The bird made a curious sound, as if it laughed at him, and Murdoch felt his agitation rise.

Suddenly the hair prickled on the back of his neck. He looked up and blinked in astonishment to find the seer before him. He had heard nothing, not the whisper of a footfall nor the crack of twig. He was a hunter. He was attuned to his surroundings. No one surprised him with their sudden appearance.

But the seer was there, where no one had stood a moment before, and Murdoch had not heard her arrival.

Seers were witches, he reminded himself and his wariness redoubled as he rose to his feet.

CHAPTER 3

*T*he seer stood in the middle of the Ninestang Ring, her fair hair blowing loose. Murdoch could only stare. She wore a kirtle dyed a deeper blue than could be wrought with woad, a sapphire as rich a hue as the sky just before the stars appeared overhead. The garment was tightly laced to her sides in the French style, revealing that her figure was more feminine than he had realized. That unwelcome desire stirred within him, his gaze darting over the wide girdle of golden embroidery that emphasized her waist. There was more embroidery upon the hems of the sleeves and of the robe, around the neck, all serving to make him more keenly aware of her delicate femininity.

And her beauty.

She might have been a different woman than the one he had watched, one more confident in her allure and intent upon using it. 'Twas more than her change of garb. There was an assurance in her posture and a directness in her gaze that he had not noted before.

She knew her effect upon him, to be sure. Was she a maiden? He had always assumed as much but now he wondered.

And he wanted.

Aye, Murdoch had been chaste too long and she had guessed. She would use his weakness against him. Temptation of the most fundamental kind would undermine his quest completely, unless he kept his wits about himself.

Even knowing all this, Murdoch stared.

The seer was utterly still, her pale gaze fixed upon him, her expression inscrutable. Perhaps she granted him time to appreciate her. No man with blood in his veins could do aught else. She was so perfectly wrought that she might have been a vision, not a woman who drew breath. She might have come from the king's court, or the realm of the Fae. Was she truly before him? Or was her appearance some manner of enchantment?

Belatedly, he realized that her arms were empty. She had not brought the child. Anger shattered his desire. How dare she defy him? Did she not fear the price?

Murdoch seized the cage and stepped toward her, brandishing his dagger. "Where is the babe?" he demanded.

"Where he belongs," she said, her words soft and low. Her voice was deeper than that of many women, rich and melodic, the kind of voice that might lull a man to sleep.

Or one that might beguile him forevermore.

"Where?" he barked, refusing to be seduced.

"He sleeps in his mother's arms," she added, stretching out a hand for the cage as if she expected him to relinquish it for naught at all.

The bird cawed and flapped.

Murdoch retreated. "There is no cause for me to surrender the bird," he said. "You have not done as demanded."

"And yet, you will not injure him, for you know as well as I that he is innocent." Her confidence shook him as it should not have done.

"I will," Murdoch began, but he heard the uncertainty in his own voice.

The seer stepped closer, serene as he was not.

She halted close before him, her eyes full of stars, her lips ripe and lush, her breast so close that he might have caressed it if his hands had not been full.

He opened his mouth to argue again, but she laid a fingertip across his lips, silencing him with a gentle touch—and it must be said, a measure of surprise.

"You will not," she insisted with a conviction that he wished was undeserved. Her gaze was unswerving. "You burn to avenge a wrong done to you, but you are not yourself wicked."

He stepped away from her, his lips burning. "You cannot know that."

"But I do. I believe in your goodness." She glanced downward, laying that fingertip on the side of his blade. He followed her gaze, watching as he let her turn the blade aside, feeling like a man in a dream. He then sheathed it, as if that had been his intention all along—though in a corner of his thoughts, he marveled at her power.

She was a sorceress, but he was only too willing to be charmed.

"I believe in your merit," she whispered and Murdoch frowned at the lump that rose in his throat.

"You should not."

"I must. I am a healer. It is my task to name the wound and then to mend it."

"You know naught of me."

"I know you grieve," she said simply, her gaze knowing. "I taste it in your words. You have lost all of import to you. Grief is a wound that cuts deeply and bleeds long. But vengeance will not cure it."

"What does then?" His question was harsh, despite his curiosity.

"Mercy."

The very suggestion was absurd and proved that she strove only to disarm him. "You know naught," he said with impatience and retreated. "You would forestall me and deceive me..."

"Never," she said with such ardor that he fell silent again. She lifted her chin, as if steeling herself for some task and he wondered whether she was as indomitable as she appeared. "I have something you desire more than the death of the bird," she whispered and lifted one hand to cup her own breast. Her pupils were large and dark, her gaze so compelling that Murdoch thought he might drown in her eyes. He was like a man struck to stone for he could only stare.

And burn.

He recalled then with utter clarity how long it had been since he had been with a woman, how long it had been since he had pursued that earthy pleasure and satisfaction. His body grew taut with need, suddenly aware of the lack, and his gaze swept over her, his appreciation undisguised. She took his hand in her other hand, her skin so soft that Murdoch could scarce believe it. She lifted his hand as if he had no power over it himself and he could only marvel that she so readily reduced him to this.

To his astonishment, she placed his hand upon her breast, then cupped her own around it, holding it there. He caught his breath and felt her do the same, as if she was as affected as he. What a notion! Their gazes locked as he savored the curve in his hand, the pulse of her heart beneath his palm. He was certain she would smite him or retreat, but she stood, her own gaze simmering as he cautiously slid his thumb across her. Her eyes darkened, like a sea before a tempest, and her nipple tightened to a taut bud beneath his touch. The hint of her rising desire was all the encouragement he needed. His mouth went dry as he brushed his palm across her breast and caressed her. So lush and sweet. So beautiful.

So tempting.

"Call me by name," she invited, her voice husky. "And I will surrender a kiss."

A kiss! A kiss was both more than Murdoch could imagine and less than he desired. A kiss from an enchantress. What would be the price?

He feared that even if the cost was his soul, he would pay.

He swallowed, watching his own hand move lightly across her, feeling her nipple harden yet more beneath the cloth. He pinched it, rolling it between finger and thumb, watching her lips part in a gasp. He felt her arch her back, saw her catch her breath, felt the leap of her pulse. He frowned, wanting that kiss with a ferocity that shook him. But calling her by name would grant her a power, one he sensed but did not fully understand. He watched his own hand, awed, and felt his resistance crumble.

He *wanted.*

"My name," she insisted.

"Nyssa," he whispered, the sound as seductive on his lips as the feel of her was beneath his hand. He shook his head. "Though I know not your origin." He dared to meet her gaze and his heart leapt when she smiled.

"I never utter it, so in this, we will both be bold." She smiled a little and his chest tightened at the sight, at the prospect of her confidence. "I am Nyssa Sutherland," she whispered, as if surrendering a secret. It made sense that she was from the north, where the warriors were fair of hair and light of eye. "Say it," she urged, lifting her hand to his cheek. The soft caress of her fingertips against his face was a pleasure beyond expectation and Murdoch's chest tightened with vigor. "You will not taste what you refuse to name."

There was a wisdom in her demand, for he could not pretend that she was simply a woman, a stranger or a whore. She was the seer, the enticing woman he desired beyond all others, and his throat worked before he did her bidding.

She was *Nyssa*.

"Nyssa Sutherland," he said, his voice hoarse, then raised his gaze to hers. He was not surprised that she smiled, but he did not expect the heat in her eyes.

Could it be that she wanted him?

She smiled a little more, as if amused by his thoughts, and moved so close that her breasts were against his chest. His hand followed the slender strength of her, landing upon the back of her waist and fitting into the indent there. She felt so right pressed against him, so perfect.

"Murdoch Campbell," she said as if his name was an invocation. She framed his face between her palms and he was snared, powerless just because of her touch. Her gaze slid over him as if he were the marvel and he scarce dared to breathe as she studied his mouth.

She seemed to steady herself, then leaned against him fully, her breasts pressing against him and the scent of her skin inundating him. In one smooth move, she rose to her toes, slanted her mouth over his and kissed him.

The deluge of sweetness seared Murdoch's very soul, stirring a need so primal that it could not be denied. He felt as if a butterfly had graced him with a touch. He tasted uncertainty in her caress and feared to frighten her, then sensed a wonder that echoed his own.

She could not be innocent!

But if she was, her trust was even more humbling. Murdoch slowly angled his mouth over hers and when she did not move away, he deepened their kiss. His other hand rose to cup her nape like the treasure she was, and he invited her to meet him touch for touch. Her hair twined over his fingers like silk. He could feel both her softness and her strength and he was honored beyond all that she had invited his caress. A heartbeat later, she trembled, awakening a protective urge he had forgotten, then against every expectation, she kissed him back.

Murdoch was lost with that single kiss, a kiss that fueled his desire to a fever pitch, a kiss that promised more than he had ever imagined would be his to claim, a kiss that could not be denied—and one he did not wish to end. Her trust in his honor and her vulnerability reminded him of the warrior he had been raised to be. The cold edge of his fury, the hunger that had driven him almost as long as he could remember, began to dissolve.

There was only Nyssa and her alluring kiss. He did not care if her embrace carried him to oblivion. He would follow and gladly.

Murdoch heard the whistle of the bolt too late to move from its path, and pain flared immediately from his earlobe. He felt the sudden and warm flow of blood as the bolt seared a line of pain through his hair.

His reaction was immediate and primal. He cast the cage from his grasp as he flung the seer behind himself.

He drew his dagger and sought their assailant, prepared to defend her to his last.

MATTERS WENT awry so quickly that Nyssa could make little sense of what happened. She was confused by the power of Murdoch's touch, no less by the wild longing it awakened within her. She felt that she had only been half-alive before his touch seared her very soul, his kiss beckoning her to an experience she wanted to share with him.

Then the bolt whistled past her ear, and something warm spilled onto her hand. Her heart leapt in terror as he pushed her out of harm's way. She saw the cage fall from his grasp and seized it before it struck the ground, even as Dorcha screamed in protest. Murdoch swore and lunged past her with his dagger drawn, and she realized belatedly that there was blood upon her hand.

Someone attacked them!

But Dorcha had to be freed. Nyssa could not see the fastening on the cage in the darkness, but she found it by touch. It was a heavy lace, knotted and threaded through the lashed branches. She worked the knot with her fingers to loosen it even as she glanced back.

A familiar figure had bounded into the circle of stones, a crossbow in his grasp. Royce roared and fell upon Murdoch with gusto, leaving the crossbow and drawing a dagger. The pair of warriors exchanged blows then grappled for supremacy, grunting as they battled back and forth across the circle.

Finally, the knot gave way beneath her fingers. Nyssa heard Royce grunt at the impact of a blow as she unthreaded the lace. Someone fell heavily to the ground in the same moment that she released Dorcha, but Nyssa had no time to look. She had to reach into the confinement of the cage to pull the raven free of the tight space, but he did not linger in her grasp. Dorcha soared skyward with a triumphant beat of his wings, crying with satisfaction at his release. Nyssa's heart leapt at the sight of him against the night sky.

Murdoch swore again and she glanced over her shoulder to find him staring up at the bird, a scowl upon his brow. His hands were braced on his hips, Royce lay insensate behind him, and Murdoch's displeasure was clear. There were dark stains upon the ground as well as blood on Murdoch's temple and shoulder from the crossbow bolt. Nyssa was horrified. It was her fault that Royce lay so still, for he must have followed her to defend her.

And this was his reward.

All the same, her senses were alive from Murdoch's kiss, the taste of him on her lips, her nipple taut and an unfamiliar warmth in her belly. She felt that she had suddenly become aware of a pleasure previously unknown, one both potent and seductive. She wanted more and the truth of that shook her, even as she stared at Royce, regretted her part —and yet simmered for Murdoch.

One kiss and she had lost her wits.

"You had no right to free the bird!" Murdoch bellowed at her.

Nyssa was too agitated to choose her words with care. This was his doing! "You should not have caged Dorcha."

"You should not have betrayed me," he replied with equal heat, taking a step toward her. "Was this your scheme? Were you in league with this warrior all along?"

"Nay! I did not know that he followed me. How dare you injure him?"

He shook his head, his eyes narrowing. "You did not bring the child. You contrived a plan to betray me instead. You distracted me apurpose to grant him opportunity."

"I did not!" Nyssa replied. "You should not have kissed me."

"You should not have invited my touch." He pointed a finger at her. "I knew 'twas too good to be true. I should have realized that you meant to trick me."

"I am no liar, sir."

"Just a witch."

"A seer," she corrected, feeling suddenly aware that she was alone with this unpredictable, enticing man. She wondered what it would be like to feel his hands on her bare skin, to kiss him again with greater confidence, to let him take what he would of her, and her knees weakened.

She was a fool, to be sure, but she could not look away from him. If she was to surrender to a man and lose her all, 'twould be a vigorous warrior like Murdoch Campbell she would choose, to be sure.

Nyssa wondered whether she would even regret such folly.

He waved a hand. "Call yourself what you will. You cast spells."

"I have no such power," she retorted. "I see. That is the sum of it."

"And now you deceive me in this," he said with displeasure. "Have you no affection for the truth?"

"I only tell the truth!"

"I was a fool to taste your kiss." He wiped his mouth with the back of his hand as if the embrace they had shared was unsatisfactory.

Nyssa knew it had been a marvel, and one that muddled her own view of this warrior, so his gesture enraged her.

"And I was twice a fool to invite it," she retorted, recalling the well of sorrow she had tasted within him. "It is grief that drives you and sorrow that blinds you."

Murdoch moved so close that she could see the consideration in his eyes. His gaze roved over her and she was keenly aware of his distrust. Nyssa held her ground, striving to hide her trepidation. "'Twas an error indeed to let you so beguile me. Have you stolen my soul now, witch? Will you ever surrender it? Or will I dream of you forevermore?"

Nyssa felt her lips part, then close again. She had to drop her gaze from the intensity in his eyes. "I cast no spells," she whispered.

"I would argue that, for I am as enchanted as a man could be." His voice was low and echoed with a wonder that prompted Nyssa to meet his gaze again. They were a fiery blue, his gaze so hot that her heart clenched.

She shook her head mutely, not wanting to believe in his desire—yet desperately wanting him to desire her in return. "You grieve," she said softly. "That is no spell."

"And who would not be grieved?" he asked, his voice husky. "My mother shamed, the man I knew as father struck down defending his laird, my home razed to the ground. And for what end? So, the Silver Wolf could prove he was of the same ilk as his father?"

"As *your* father."

Murdoch grimaced. "A single act may create a child, but it does not make a parent. Rupert was my father." He made to turn away and she could not bear the loss of his attention.

"Yet if you avenge yourself upon Maximilian, *his* son will have no father. Is this how you would be remembered?"

His expression was guarded when he eyed her anew and his voice dropped low. "Your threat is empty, seer. No one will remember me, upon that you can rely." Murdoch started to turn away, but Nyssa reached for him, her fingertips landing upon his arm. The healer in her could do naught else. He looked down at her hand, then flicked a hot glance her way.

"Turn away," he said softly and it was only when he raised his dagger that she knew what he intended to do. "There is no other course. Not now."

"Of course, there is," she insisted, fearing for Royce. "There is always a choice. You could use your skills for justice. You..."

He scowled and shook off her touch. "It must be thus."

"Nay, it must not be..."

45

"Aye." Murdoch was still staring at her, as if he could not tear his gaze away from her, and that was key to his downfall.

"Nay," she argued in the same moment that Royce moved.

The mercenary lunged toward Murdoch with a power that proved he was not as injured as Nyssa had feared. Royce seized Murdoch by the ankles and felled him like a great tree. Nyssa saw Murdoch's astonishment as he fell. There was a crack as Murdoch's head struck the hard ground. Royce loomed over his opponent, fists raised to pummel him, then lowered his hands.

He shook his head and exhaled. "He will trouble no one for a while."

Nyssa fell to her knees beside Murdoch, feeling that she was responsible for his injury, however unwitting her contribution had been. "Is he dead?"

"Sadly, no." Royce unfurled a length of rope and bound Murdoch's ankles together with grim efficiency. He glared at her, chastising her as he secured his victim. "And I thought you a woman of wit. What madness persuaded you to meet him alone, and garbed as you are? No man with blood in his veins could have denied the temptation you offer. How could you kiss him?"

Nyssa knew Royce would not understand so remained silent.

"And then what, Nyssa? What was your intent?" He knotted the rope around Murdoch's wrists. "To welcome this villain between your thighs? To what purpose?"

"He is alone and grieving. He is not wicked."

"He is an enemy of Kilderrick," Royce corrected her tersely. "And you had best prepare yourself for the laird's disapproval for your actions. Where will you go when he casts you out for faithlessness?"

"I am not unfaithful to the laird!"

Royce shook his head, then hefted Murdoch to his shoulder. He grunted beneath the other man's weight, then gave her an intent look. "I wager that Maximilian will not agree." He bent his knees with care to pick up his crossbow without dropping his burden. He began to march toward Kilderrick, clearly expecting her to follow.

Nyssa hesitated only a moment before she did.

"You should have told me of your intention," Royce scolded,

evidently hearing her steps. "You should not have come to meet such a villain alone."

"But he wanted me to bring Michael to him," she said, trying to explain. "He intended to kill him."

"Better and better," Royce muttered. "You might have told someone of that or asked for aid."

"He would have killed Dorcha."

"And so, you dressed to entice him, kept the meeting and kissed him. Nyssa, Nyssa, there are times when your understanding of the world seems meagre, for all the wisdom you possess."

"I had to free Dorcha," she insisted.

"But the plan needed to be more robust than that. Once the bird was free, how would you escape the man?"

Nyssa did not reply to that, because she knew that Royce would not find her strategy persuasive. She knew the sorrow within Murdoch though and she knew she could heal him. She believed that his animosity toward Maximilian could be dismissed without violence, but she feared now that the matter could end only one way.

Maximilian would not be merciful to any man who had threatened his child, especially since Murdoch had conspired against Maximilian before. Once he had let Murdoch live out of consideration for Alys' past friendship with him, but that was unlikely to happen again.

Yet, she did not want Murdoch to die. She recognized also that there was a response within her to his pain, one more profound than she had felt before. She wondered what price she would pay to see him healed.

Or to see him freed.

In the night, on the moor, she considered that knowing Murdoch's touch and healing his wounded heart might be worth the sacrifice of her gift.

Then she dismissed the very notion as whimsy. That price was too high, to be sure.

And yet...

Royce was sufficiently vexed that he would not leave the matter be. He continued to grumble even as they approached Kilderrick. "Witless! I never expected as much from you. Ceara, aye, she would hurl herself at any obstacle without a thought for consequences, but you were always more cautious." He granted her a look. "I thought you *sensible.*"

"I am sensible," Nyssa insisted. "He is injured. I am a healer so strove to heal him."

Royce shook his head as if despairing of her.

"There is merit in Murdoch," Nyssa argued. "He cast me behind himself when you appeared. He protected me."

Royce laughed, though it was not a merry sound. "He protected his own prize, Nyssa. Do not imagine otherwise. That he did not wish to be disturbed while he despoiled you says naught good of his nature."

Nyssa felt her lips tighten. 'Twas clear that Murdoch would have no fair hearing—and truly, they were all mercenaries with blood on their blades. She did not appreciate the distinctions as much as Royce evidently did.

"You should let me tend his wound," she said as the shadow of the keep loomed ahead.

Royce scoffed. "You need not fear that he will have to endure a scar overlong. Leave it be, Nyssa. Murdoch Campbell will not survive the week and we all will sleep more soundly for that."

That was precisely as she feared. Nyssa set her lips and marched behind Royce, wondering what she could do.

Royce had not said his all as yet, though. "And use your good sense," he bade in an undertone. "Abandon your defense of this one, lest the shadow of his guilt be cast upon you." He gave her another intent look, then continued through the gates.

Nyssa knew she was right about Murdoch, but how could she aid him? Maximilian's justice would likely see him dead by midday on the morrow.

Perhaps Alys could be stirred to mercy and thus to intervene on her former friend's behalf.

"THREE DAYS AND NIGHTS?" Alys demanded of Maximilian in the solar, her low voice doing little to disguise her annoyance of her husband's decision.

How could he be as harsh?

"I invite you to recall that he meant to kill our son," Maximilian replied, his words so tight that she doubted he could be swayed. He cast his tabard aside with a gesture, not troubling to fold it with his usual care. Aye, he was furious.

She was not calm herself.

"But cruelty resolves naught," she insisted, unsurprised when he turned on her with flashing eyes.

"Alys!" He seized her shoulders, his gaze boring into hers. "I understand your concern. I know he was a childhood friend. But he means to kill our son for no cause beyond vengeance. He declared as much to Nyssa."

She frowned, unable to argue with that. "His father was a good man. You cannot be certain how many in Kilderrick find his view sympathetic."

"*Our* father was a wicked man," Maximilian corrected. "But I believe you about Rupert Campbell. He was loyal and valiant, to be sure."

"But..."

"Alys," Maximilian murmured, lowering his voice to an entreaty. He was no less intense in his manner, but she met his gaze, knowing he would explain. "Three days will not kill him. He will have water and food."

"Then why..."

"Because I must soften his resolve. He must have time to recognize the consequences of his path."

"And repent of his choice," Alys guessed.

Maximilian's lips drew to a taut line and he averted his gaze, then met hers steadily again. "How else could I ever release him? I will not imperil Michael and worse, I suspect that the death of the boy is not his sole goal." His steady gaze invited her to make a conclusion he found obvious.

Alys caught her breath. "Not that. Not you, as well. He would not do as much to me." Her voice faded in memory of what Murdoch *had* done.

"I remind you that he summoned your betrothed," Maximilian said, showing his characteristic bluntness. "He would have seen you sacrificed then, Alys, in his quest for vengeance. That urge can only be stronger now, for he desires to avenge himself upon me and knows of my love for you."

"What do you mean?"

Maximilian almost smiled. "To best torment a man, you destroy every item he desires in succession, and then you kill him when he has no reason yet to live. There was a time when I would have done the same."

Alys frowned.

Maximilian bent to look into her eyes again. "Do not show Murdoch a mercy he would not grant to you, Alys."

"You cannot be certain," she protested but her conviction of Murdoch's good nature was shaken and she knew her husband heard as much.

"And yet, I must be certain. I will not risk my greatest prize." He pressed his lips to her forehead in a chaste kiss, then drew her into his embrace, his fingers sliding into her hair. As ever, she was both comforted and aroused by his touch, by the smell of his skin and the heat of his body against her own. "Three days and nights, Alys," he murmured into her ear. "'Tis his opportunity and we can only pray that he seizes it."

Alys closed her eyes, understanding that Maximilian would not suffer Murdoch to live otherwise. She thought of the boy she had known, the way he had laughed, the pride of Rupert in his son's every achievement and she felt cheated by how he had changed. Murdoch would not even listen to her, so great was his anger against Maximilian.

"Will a shorter time not achieve the same end?" she asked finally. To her relief, Maximilian considered the possibility.

He pulled back so he could look into her eyes and his own gaze was searching. How she loved that he heeded her views and her under-standing of Kilderrick. "You think there are others who blame me for Rupert's death?"

Alys shrugged. "He was a good man."

Maximilian nodded, his eyes narrowed. "We shall compromise then. Two nights and a day. He will stand before me on Tuesday at noon." He lifted a finger as he looked into her eyes again. "But not a moment before."

"I like your compromise," she said and surrendered to his embrace again.

"And I like my lady's support at court," he said into her hair. Alys smiled as she leaned against him, then prayed that Murdoch would have the wits to seize the opportunity he was granted.

She could not see any other way this dispute could be peaceably resolved.

She would talk to Murdoch this night and hope that his view could be swayed.

MURDOCH AWAKENED in a darkness so complete that he could not doubt his location. This had to be the dungeon of Kilderrick, for no night could be so black. There was muck beneath his boots and a smell of dampness. Mercifully, he was not cast on the floor of the dungeon, but had been dropped against the stone ledge built against one wall.

He ran his hands across it, remembering Robert Armstrong's insistence that a measure of comfort would make confinement more horrendous to a prisoner. On such logic, the former laird had not starved his captives, but had granted them a tiny measure of the food from the hall each day. A taste was sufficient to awaken a yearning, and also enough to make a man aware of how ravenous he was. A mouthful of water made one notice the rage of thirst. And these minute measures of apparent kindness only made the prisoner endure longer, not just by offering a bit of sustenance but by feeding hope in the face of despair.

Aye, Robert Armstrong had been a fiend, but the Silver Wolf made the same choices. 'Twas no good reflection of the new laird that he could be like the former one.

The great stone ledge was dry and there was even a straw pallet upon it. Murdoch doubted there were vermin within it, or even rats in the dungeon itself. The dungeon was located beneath the high square tower of Kilderrick, carved into the earth below the keep's foundations and lined with stone. It had no drain, and solely one exit—the trapdoor by which Murdoch had undoubtedly gained admission, high over his head, so high that no man could reach it alone. It had not changed since he had been a boy, though much of the keep had been rebuilt.

Of course, the dungeon, of all the original construction, should be the part to survive. Of course, the Silver Wolf would make use of it, as well.

Murdoch's temple burned and he felt crusted blood on his earlobe and in his hair. The wound had not been tended but it would not kill him. A superficial injury, doubtless by intention. He felt a grudging respect for Royce, his strategy and his aim.

He would not think of the beguiling seer, or the way she had stirred his senses. It was not for him to possess such a woman, and he should have known as much. She had tricked him, no more than that, aiding Royce despite her insistence otherwise.

She had done it for the bird.

He admired that, though he would never admit as much aloud. It took a certain kindness to defend one weaker than oneself.

And what of him? He paced the width of the chamber, feeling the walls with his hands, gaining a sense of the space. Would he be executed or would the Silver Wolf leave him to starve? Murdoch suspected that the new laird was not one to let matters linger. Had he been a man to wager, he would have bet upon a public execution and soon.

Perhaps there was something fitting about his demise being at the hand of the favored son of Jean le Beau. Perhaps it was appropriate that Murdoch die here at Kilderrick, just as Rupert had.

He sighed and leaned his head back against the wall. Perhaps he should be glad that it would all come to an end. He had been driven by his need for vengeance for so long that he could not imagine being without its insistent burden. He had been vigilant and alone for so many years that it was a relief, in a strange way, to be imprisoned, with no choice in determining his own future.

Perhaps he would fall asleep in this place and never awaken. He stretched out on his back on the pallet, resigned to his fate, only to be suddenly blinded by brilliant light.

The trapdoor had been opened, far above him. At first, he saw only the light, then he was able to discern a figure on either side of the lantern. That it was a woman made Murdoch rise to his feet, as surely as if Rupert stood beside him. *Always show courtesy to a lady.*

Who came to him? Alys or the seer? Murdoch knew who he most wished to see.

Another kiss would be folly to request, but he yearned for it all the same.

"You were always an impulsive fool," Alys said, her voice little more than a whisper.

"Not I, my lady," Murdoch replied. "You were the one to follow your inclination without regard for the consequences."

"Yet though we have this in common, our alliances are in opposition. Why, Murdoch?" Her voice broke a little. "Why would you wish to kill my son?"

Murdoch's throat tightened. "Not your son, *his* son."

"But we speak of the same child. How could you plan such a betrayal, when we have known each other so long?"

Murdoch did not believe her to be blameless either. "How could you wed the Silver Wolf and welcome him, Alys, given all he has done?"

"Maximilian is a better man than I believed."

Murdoch held back his reply. Her measure was her father, who had been a selfish rogue. Any man, to Murdoch's thinking, save Jean le Beau, would do well by the comparison.

"And you are better than this," she insisted.

Something in her tone prompted Murdoch to look up. He realized then that there was another person there, one that remained mostly out of view. His heart leapt. Did the seer come to him? Was she the one who watched and listened but did not speak?

Had she brought Alys to talk to him?

"If you repent of this and apologize, Murdoch, Maximilian may be swayed," Alys continued. "Though I cannot swear to it."

"He will not be swayed," Murdoch said with confidence. "And if he is, he is more of a fool than I guessed."

"How so?"

"He forgave me once, and here I am yet, bent upon his destruction."

Alys caught her breath. "How can you refuse to see all of merit that has happened at Kilderrick?" she demanded.

"How can you hold *him* in any estimation?" Murdoch asked roughly and watched her straighten with disapproval. "How can you share his bed, Alys?" He raised his hands. "He burned Kilderrick. He killed both of our fathers, and yet, you *welcome* him." He could not keep the disgust from his tone. "You cannot believe him blameless. You are not so witless as that."

"Men change," she said with heat.

Murdoch shook his head. "Nay, they do not. Their tales change. Their lies change. Their goals may change, but in their essence, men do not change. Pray, Alys, that your husband never sees you as an obstacle to his goals, for I can predict your fate in that instance."

"Maximilian is not thus!"

Murdoch turned away from her, knowing she would not be convinced of the truth before it was too late.

"Even now he grants you two nights and a day to consider your course, when he could see you executed immediately. He is not without compassion!"

Her claim was a jest. The Silver Wolf possessed no compassion, but Murdoch would not argue with her.

The silence grew between them. Murdoch could not lie about his hatred for the Silver Wolf. He could not ask forgiveness of the man who had cheated him, he could not set aside his own quest, and he would never swear fealty to his sworn enemy.

He understood this meant he would die and soon.

"If you were released, what would you do?" the seer asked softly and he flicked a glance upward. Just the sound of her voice made his heart leap.

"You know what I would do."

"Even if doing otherwise ensured your own survival?"

"'Tis of no import. There is naught else to do but keep my pledge."

"Of course, there is," she said with a disgust he thought undeserved. "You might prove yourself a worthy son of Rupert, instead of the unwanted get of Jean le Beau."

Those words stung, for there was truth in her accusation.

She continued before he could reply, her voice sharp. "You might fight for honor and justice, swearing your blade to those who change their realm for good. You might defend widows and orphans, as the knights pledge to do. You might defend Kilderrick, the place you love most, or a woman who captured your heart." She leaned forward and the lantern gilded her features, as if an angel looked down upon him—and this angel judged him sternly. "You might find a future instead of mourning the past, Murdoch Campbell, and then you would *never* be forgotten."

He blinked but she retreated, vanishing from view just when he might have answered her appeal.

Alys waited, her manner expectant.

"I have sworn an oath," Murdoch said wearily. "I cannot break my vow."

"It has been a long time since Kilderrick burned."

"Seventeen years, but not all objectives are easily won. That does not mean they should be discarded for the sake of convenience."

Alys looked down at him for a long moment. "I fear the result of this, Murdoch."

"I do not, Alys," he said quietly, wanting to reassure her. "I know what my end will be."

"And still...?"

"And still. Of what merit would be my life if my word became worthless?"

She sighed audibly, shook her head, then stepped back. The trap door dropped back into place and a bolt shot home, leaving Murdoch in darkness once again.

Once again, the seer's words haunted him with an unwelcome persistence.

What if he could be Rupert's son, instead of the bastard of Jean le Beau?

CHAPTER 4

*N*yssa could not sleep after Murdoch's interview with Alys.

She was furious with him for refusing to seize the opportunity she had created for him. The man was stubborn beyond all reason.

Fearful to trust.

She remained awake late in her chamber, recalling that kiss and the way it had shaken her. She thought of the emptiness within Murdoch and wondered what could replace his losses. He would die at Kilderrick, by Maximilian's command, unless he pledged himself to the Silver Wolf. She could not imagine he would do as much, but she did not wish him to die.

She had urged Alys to visit him, thinking their old bond might give him hope, or that Alys might offer a bargain. Both, though, had been sure of their positions, too certain to compromise.

Maximilian would not compromise either.

Dorcha chortled to himself as he groomed upon his perch in the corner of her chamber, and did as much so long as the candle burned. It seemed he believed his appearance in need of attention. He had soared through the window as soon as Nyssa brought a candle into the chamber and opened the shutters, landing triumphantly on his perch. She'd brought him meat from the kitchens and water, both of which he consumed quickly as she watched. Usually, his antics amused her, but on this night, Nyssa was consumed by other concerns.

She pinched the wick, though Dorcha clucked at the sudden darkness.

She did not think she would sleep readily, but Nyssa both slept and dreamed.

THE FOG CAME from the sea, rolling across the rocky shore and hiding the coast from view. It moved slowly but with persistence, unstoppable in its course. It surrounded the familiar keep on the island, obscuring the water on all sides, then continued to the coast. It flowed across the lowlands and piled against the cliffs, billowing higher and higher until it was immediately below the walls of the keep. Instead of resting on an island in the ocean, the castle appeared to be adrift in the clouds. The wind was still and the sky was overcast, so dark overhead that there might never have been a star in the firmament.

'Twas so quiet that time itself might have stopped. It had been a warm summer day, but overcast, and in the evening, the air so still that the merest sound echoed loudly.

All the world might have awaited...something.

The silence was rent by a woman's scream, the cry echoing from the high tower of the keep. The cry came again, filling the hall with the sound of pain, setting teeth on edge, making others in the keep wince in sympathy.

Aye, Nyssa recalled this night too well. She stirred in her sleep, not wanting to remember these events, but the dream was relentless. It held her fast in its grasp, unfurling with relentless clarity.

The laird sat in the hall, his brother at his side. The pair of them had always been inseparable and now the younger brother was the captain at arms of the elder, the pair of them united in defending the holding that was the windfall of marriage. The laird ate his evening meal with resolve, never sparing a glance to the stairs. Nyssa sat at the board, as commanded, forbidden from the solar as she was yet a maiden. She could only watch the brothers consume their meal, having no appetite herself. Hugh Sutherland, now laird, was not unlike her father, a man who did not swerve from his own satisfaction, regardless of circumstance. Indeed, that was likely why her father had chosen Hugh as his successor, as spouse of his eldest daughter. Hugh's brother, Erik, possessed a savagery beyond that of his older brother and lacked the charm of the first-born, but they complemented each other well in matters of might.

Nyssa gripped her hands into fists under the board and prayed for her sister's welfare. She hoped the babe would fare well, but she feared more for Elsa.

She doubted the laird would welcome a daughter.

She and Elsa had lived this tale before and survived to tell of it.

Elsa had not confided the gender of the babe, which was a concern. Nyssa had no doubt that her sister knew—and that her silence meant she would deliver a girl. What then? What would Hugh do? Nyssa feared she knew.

Elsa's cries of pain repeated with relentless regularity and grew in volume each time. Nyssa was not certain she could bear the sound much longer, then suddenly, there was silence.

Every soul in the hall looked up when the next cry did not come. Several crossed themselves. Others clearly feared to think the worst, while hoping for the best. Every soul held his or her breath, waiting.

Nyssa rose to her feet, looking upward as if her gaze might pierce through the ceiling.

The laird, who was less concerned with his lady's welfare than might have been ideal, finally abandoned his meal. He rose to his feet and strode to the stairs, his brow furrowed. "Remain here," he bade Nyssa and Erik. Erik showed no inclination to move, while Nyssa sat down with reluctance.

Hugh halted, one foot raised to the next step, when a babe's cry sounded with vigor.

The servants laughed and clapped, the women embracing each other in their relief. The laird marched up the stairs with purpose, intent upon knowing the fullness of the tale. Nyssa dared his wrath and ran after him, hoping she would find her sister alive as well as the child. She reached the solar just steps behind him, as the babe's cry fell silent as if in foreboding.

Her heart flooded with relief to see Elsa in the great bed, panting and pale but alive. The lady lay back against a mound of pillows, her fair hair loose and damp with perspiration, her maid bustling to clean the chamber. The midwife, Mary, had just finished washing the infant. The laird frowned down at the swathed infant and did not accept the bundle. A handsome man, he had a fearsome temper and was difficult to anticipate.

He pointed to the maid and midwife in turn, then to the door. The maid *was young and quick to abandon her task, while the midwife, older and more doughty, lingered with the child.*

"Leave it," he ordered. Mary looked to Elsa for guidance, a detail which did not please Hugh. Elsa smiled and opened her arms. Once the child was in her embrace, Elsa smiled. The midwife, clearly discontent, left the solar then by the smaller staircase, the one that led to the kitchens, closing the door behind herself.

Hugh lifted a brow and pulled his dagger. He used it to draw down the swaddling around the babe, the better than he could see the child's gender. Elsa watched him warily.

"A daughter," he said, his view of that more than clear.

"Aye," Elsa agreed, then her tone grew firm. "If you recall, I advised you, my lord, that it might be thus."

His reply was cold and hard. "If you recall, my lady, I advised you that a daughter would not suffice." He moved his dagger in that moment and Elsa cried out as the infant in her arms was fatally stabbed. There was a cry and then a dreadful silence, followed by Elsa's cry of anguish.

And the blood. So much blood.

Hugh retreated, fury still simmering in his gaze. "Your father taught me to be certain," he whispered and Nyssa fled before her presence could be noted, her heart racing in terror.

NYSSA AWAKENED, her breath coming quickly, her heart pounding just as it had that night. The memory was as clear as if the events had just occurred. She lit the lantern with shaking fingers, earning a mild complaint from Dorcha, and wrapped her arms around her knees, shuddering.

Elsa!

She had not dreamed of events at Duncheann in years, and doing so now was no good thing.

Hugh had killed his own child. The memory was no less potent for the passage of time. But why had Nyssa dreamed of that long-ago night on this one? Elsa was dead. That daughter was dead, as was the next one. Though Elsa had planned their names, the infants had not survived long enough to have those names bestowed upon them.

The first would have been Gerda, after their mother, the second Rana after their grandmother. Nyssa wept on this night for those two innocent children, then she wept for Elsa with such vigor that her sister might have passed a day before, not eight years before. Nyssa had left both the Sutherland brothers and Duncheann, once her father's pride, far behind, with no intention of ever returning.

But that dream filled her with such dread that she felt ill.

Surely, she was not destined to return to that vile place? Did Hugh still hold Duncheann as laird? How many wives had he buried? How many children? She shivered at the prospect. For the first time, Nyssa wondered whether she should have pursued justice for her sister rather than fleeing to ensure her own survival.

But only a warrior could exact vengeance, a warrior like Murdoch. She was merely a healer, a power mighty in itself but as naught compared to men of war. And more, she saw no merit in such violence. To kill Hugh in retaliation for the child's death would accomplish little, save earning Erik's vengeful fury. Violence only begat more violence, and that healed naught at all.

Then why this dream and why now? Had it been fear for Michael, another defenseless and innocent babe, that had reminded her of Duncheann?

But Michael was safe for the moment. Her dream provoked her to some deed, Nyssa was certain. It reminded her of some lesson or foreshadowed some future peril. But strive as she might, she could not discern its meaning though she remained awake all the night long.

Somehow Murdoch had stirred her doubts, and convincing him to abandon his quest was the key to her own tranquility.

She would have to talk to him again.

MURDOCH WAS cold and he was hungry. That might have been sufficient cause for another man to abandon his convictions, but he remained resolute.

Let the Silver Wolf do his worst. Murdoch was quite certain he would not survive another day. Though it vexed him to leave his quest incomplete, the sole course would be to deceive Maximilian, to pledge his allegiance to the cur then pivot to slaughter him. Murdoch would not bow so low. His word was his bond and he would not sully it.

He paced his prison, though, disliking that he would die without avenging Rupert. He did not expect to be fed, but the trap door creaked without warning, admitting a beam of light. 'Twas morning then, perhaps time to face his reckoning. He stood tall, arms folded across his chest. He could hear a dispute overhead, one conducted in whispers. He caught tantalizing hints of the conversation but not sufficient to understand.

That there was any debate over him and his future was intriguing.

A rope ladder was cast down and he caught the end of it, more than prepared to leave the darkness. An order was barked from overhead that he should stand back, and Murdoch did as much, wondering at this.

Someone intended to descend into the pit with him.

He backed against the wall, hating that he had no weapons save his hands, though they were not to be underestimated. Even if he overwhelmed his visitor, though, he had to climb the ladder and escape the hall. His path would be blocked by countless mercenaries.

He debated the merit of dying quickly, in flight, but discarded it as an ignoble demise.

"One move and the bolt will be between your eyes," a man warned from overhead, his voice gruff. "This time, there is no good cause for you to survive." Murdoch could see a silhouette on the lip of the pit and discerned the crossbow aimed at him.

He nodded once, then a slender man descended, carrying a wooden pail. 'Twas only when the visitor's boots were on the floor of the dungeon that Murdoch realized this was no man. She turned and he was shocked. The seer herself came to him! He took a step backward and found his shoulders against the stone wall.

Her hair was pulled back into a long braid that he now realized was tucked beneath her dark tabard. She wore chausses and boots as on the night of the new moon, her garb cut with sufficient generosity that her curves were disguised from view. Her expression was inscrutable, her gaze watchful, and she faced him warily as she put the pail down on the stone ledge.

"Bread," she said. "And soup. 'Tis daylight and you must be hungry." Her tone was terse and he understood that she was irked with him. Or perhaps she feared him. Her eyes flashed as she stepped closer and he told himself that her opinion was irrelevant.

His heart skipped, insisting otherwise. That she stepped into the dungeon with him, after he had threatened her raven, when she was afraid of him, kindled an awe within him. She was not fearless, but she confronted her fears for the greater good, and despite himself, Murdoch admired that.

She was paler than before, he noted, and there were shadows beneath her eyes. She had not slept well, he guessed, and he wondered what had concerned her so. She could not have fretted for him, could she?

He was curiously pleased even by the possibility, then forced himself to frown and dismiss that response.

"I thank you, and the Silver Wolf," he said, keenly aware that at least one guard listened overhead. He could smell the soup, a venison broth unless he missed his guess, and one warm enough to be fragrant. He recalled readily how good of a cook Denis was from his time in the Silver Wolf's company, and his stomach growled in anticipation. "I expected to be starved."

"Maximilian does not always fulfill expectation."

"Why would he want me to live?"

She tilted her head to study him. "Perhaps he would speak to you. Perhaps he would reconcile. Are you not half-brothers?"

"By no father of estimation," Murdoch said hotly.

Her gaze sharpened but her voice dropped. "Would Rupert be proud of your choice in this?"

Nay, he would not. Rupert had always been interested in the greater good, the longer strategy, and had never seen the merit of sacrifice, however noble it might be. Murdoch glared at the floor and did not reply.

It had been a long time since he had been chastised.

"What of Gwendolyn?" she asked, her words sending a knife to his heart.

"Why do you bring the soup?" he demanded, knowing his voice was harsh.

"Because I would ask you a question."

"You have asked three."

She smiled. "And you have answered none. Will you reply to my fourth?"

"Why should I?"

She stepped closer, her eyes so bright so that he could not avert his gaze. "Because I do not think you want to die, Murdoch Campbell," she said with heat. "Because I do not believe you need to die. But in order to ensure that end, you have need of an ally. I will aid you, if you answer one question."

He waited, folding his arms across his chest, heart skipping with uncertainty.

She took another step closer, which cast her features into shadow. "What would give you the will to survive?"

"The choice is not mine," he said with impatience. "Look about yourself. I am imprisoned."

"Because of your choice to use me to threaten the laird's son. And so, you will face his justice, unless you give him cause to reconsider. He offered you alliance before and you refused. What would entice you to accept such an agreement now? You wager with your very life and that cannot be so worthless to you."

"It is worth more than the shame of compromising with the Silver Wolf." He lifted a brow. "Would you have me lie to him and make a pledge I cannot keep?"

She shook her head and stepped back, her disappointment palpable. "Of all the deeds you could do, of all the justice you could bring, of all the battles you could wage for truth, you choose instead to die for a vengeance you will not achieve."

There was something about her words that made Murdoch wonder whether he did err in this. She undermined his resolve, as if her kiss had created a crack through which the water would run, opening it to a crevasse. He felt growing doubt since first confronting her, and it seemed to him that his parents whispered to him in the darkness of his folly.

She was right: neither of them would have endorsed this path.

And she said she cast no spells.

"I gave my word," Murdoch said through clenched teeth.

"Then you can rescind it. You can repent of folly. You can change your goal."

"Of what import to you?"

"I would see any person healed rather than condemned, when there is a choice," she said, then eyed him. She licked her lips, a sign of agitation that he thought uncharacteristic. "And you might know someone who will have need one day of a valiant warrior's protection."

He scoffed, though the possibility thrilled him. "You cannot imagine that many would trust me."

"Aye," she said with surprising resolve. "I know it. I think there already are many who do."

Murdoch turned away, determined to protect those who aided him.

The seer waited but he bit his tongue to keep silent, to keep from making a promise he could not keep. She could not know how he yearned to pledge himself to her, much less how vigorously he wished to defend her.

'Twas a potent spell she had cast, to be sure.

He felt the weight of her gaze as she studied him, and knew the moment she turned away. "To cling to a futile quest is less than I hoped of you. Perhaps you are right and you deserve to die."

She caught the rope ladder in one hand and Murdoch felt a sudden surge of despair. She was going to leave and they would never speak again, and he refused to part in anger.

He had made that error once before.

"I do not deserve to die!" he roared and impulsively lunged after the seer. He meant to catch her arm, to pull her to a halt. Instead, the bolt of a crossbow seared across his shoulder and he fell backward, gasping at the sudden eruption of pain.

"You were warned," came the grim voice from above as Murdoch gripped his shoulder. 'Twas only a flesh wound though it bled mightily, yet another sign that the Silver Wolf wanted him alive to face his reckoning. Murdoch did not doubt that the archer could have buried the bolt in his heart instead. Was it the same one as the night before? Did it matter? Murdoch retreated, though the seer hesitated.

"Nyssa," the guard above growled.

"I must tend this wound," she insisted. There was compassion in her magnificent eyes, but Murdoch averted his gaze.

She was not for him. She only offered temptation.

"Nyssa!" called the guard.

Her name was seductive in itself, winding into his thoughts, compelling him to remember it, urging him to whisper it aloud.

"My fate is of no import to you," he said, his tone so hard that she flinched. "Go."

"But you have not yet sealed your destiny," she whispered with quiet heat. "Consider your path before you face the Laird of Kilderrick, I entreat you. The world is rife with violence and this course will only ensure your own destruction."

"What of it?"

"Choose," she urged with soft fervor. "Choose to survive instead."

For a moment, Murdoch was snared by her gaze and tempted by her advice. Then he knew that he could not abandon his quest so readily.

"Go," Murdoch said gruffly. "You have had your answer."

He turned his back upon her, keenly aware that she waited for him to say more. Had there ever been another who believed in him so? Aye, there had been two, both gone from this earth, both responsible in their way for his quest. He stared resolutely into the corner, mustering his composure before he faced her again. She could not know that she had awakened something within him—though he feared she had guessed that truth already.

By the time Murdoch glanced back, the seer had climbed the ladder and he did not know whether to be relieved or disappointed. He saw only the disappearing heels of her boots and stared upward, hoping she would appear in the square of light again. Instead, the trap door dropped into place, making the very walls shake as it fell home.

She confused him, but was that not the way of seers? She asked questions that should not be asked, and expected answers that shook his convictions. She kindled doubts within his heart and made him yearn for what he would never possess. Murdoch knew he had chosen aright, that it was noble to follow his course to its end, whatever that might be.

But she made him wish for more.

Nyssa.

"Nyssa." Her name was on his lips when he had no intention of uttering it. Did he care whether she had enchanted him? Even recalling her name gave her greater power in his thoughts, doubtless by her design. But how could he distrust or despise the sole person who thought his survival would be of merit?

How could he ignore the one who awakened his own desire to live?

No one had cared about Murdoch in so long that he was confused by her concern—and stirred by it, to be sure. Even his few kin in Rowan Fell were reluctant in their support of him, such as it was, though he could not blame them for their distrust.

Why did the seer care? What did she desire of him?

What manner of wager might he make with the Silver Wolf? Could there be one that satisfied them both?

Murdoch ate and he thought, only realizing much later that he did want something more than to fulfil his quest or die in its pursuit—he wanted to taste Nyssa's kiss again.

How much would he surrender for that prize?

THE MAN WAS IMPOSSIBLE.

And now he had another injury, one that he forbade her to tend. Nyssa exhaled in frustration, hoping Murdoch had the wits to clean the wound himself. He had survived as a mercenary for years, so she wagered he had some understanding of the treatment of wounds.

Still, she had never met anyone so stubborn or resistant to good sense. She left the dungeon with both regret and frustration, hating that he had a new injury thanks to her presence, knowing he had not intended her any harm, and infuriated that he had refused her.

She was approaching the hall when she realized that Murdoch had grown up at Kilderrick.

Someone had to have known him as a child.

Someone had to remember him.

Someone had to hold him in affection—which might be reciprocated. Someone might know how best to appeal to Murdoch, to convince him to abandon his quest for vengeance.

Could she find the person in time?

He or she would have to be at Rowan Fell, for the keep and the small village nearby had been abandoned until recent years. Nyssa was not fond of Rowan Fell, for there were those in that village who had in the past tried to take advantage of the vulnerability of the four women in the forest. She did not trust cities or gatherings of men. But even the sheriff's wife Jeannie would not be so bold as to assault the friend of the laird's lady wife in daylight. A man's life hung in the balance and Nyssa's fears were naught compared to that.

She would go immediately.

ALONE IN THE darkness of Kilderrick's dungeon, Murdoch dreamed.

He was in the camp of the Compagnie Rouge, somewhere in the north of the Italian states. He remembered the mountains rising to the north and the dusting of snow on their peaks. The camp had been erected outside the walls of a town besieged at the command of a wealthy baron. The siege had lasted weeks and the rain had been relentless. The mud was deep in the makeshift road that wound through the camp. There were tales of the illness in the camp and the weakness of the sickened men.

Knowing that opportunity beckoned, Murdoch arrived in darkness.

There were no sentries on the perimeter of the camp. He had smelled the fires in the assaulted town and as he entered the camp, he could see the lick of flames amidst the buildings in the distance. He also heard the roar of merrymaking. Those men who were not ill, were abroad, celebrating. From the vantage point of the camp, which had been established on a rise, he could see the breaks in the curtain wall and the frenzy of activity in those areas.

The town had fallen and the pillaging had begun.

A pair of drunken warriors approached him, jesting with each other. The first passed Murdoch a wineskin, pressing it into his hand as he made some comment in a language Murdoch did not understand, then staggered onward. The second snatched it back, grinned, offered what might have been a jest, then followed his companion.

The camp then was strangely quiet.

Murdoch listened, seeking his prey. There was one tent beyond the mire of the camp, a large tent of white silk set on higher ground. It could only be the tent of Jean le Beau. Was that man celebrating within the town walls or with his men? Murdoch wagered not. The notorious mercenary was fond of despoiling women and even he might desire some privacy for that deed.

'Twould be particularly sweet to interrupt the creation of another like himself, no less to ensure that the villain could never repeat that deed again.

Murdoch headed for the tent, stepping into the shadows whenever other men appeared, ensuring that he was seen by no others. It was cooler and quieter near the large tent, as if the company did not dare to disturb their leader. The ground was firmer underfoot and he could discern the rhythmic grunt from within the tent. He circled around to the shadowed side, knowing he was too late to aid this maiden, even as the sound steeled his will. 'Twas a potent reminder of the reason for his quest. Murdoch paused to consider the stars overhead before he gripped his dagger and slit open the silk wall.

Lanterns were lit inside the tent, filling it with golden light. The silk walls of the tent shimmered and there were thick carpets underfoot. Trunks were stacked on every side, undoubtedly filled with plunder, but Murdoch saw only the couple entwined on the pillared bed. He was awed at this luxury in warfare, then knew Jean le Beau had the resources to transport an entire palace and its contents with him if he so desired.

He could see the mercenary's bare back as that man pounded into his partner with vigor. He could see the dark river of the lady's hair, spread across the silken pillows, and the sound of her discomfort sickened him. He eased ever closer, bracing himself to strike the blow.

Then she saw him. Her dark eyes widened. She gasped, and Jean le Beau spun like a viper prepared to strike. The man was on his feet in a heartbeat, his dagger in his hand, his nudity showing that he was not wrought like an old man in the least. He snarled and flung himself at Murdoch, his intention clearly to kill the intruder.

His first blow caught Murdoch in the upper arm, the blade carving a trough into his flesh. Murdoch stabbed the old mercenary in the other shoulder and they spun away from each other, blood running over the flesh of both of them. The woman pulled the covers over herself and whispered a prayer softly, but Murdoch did not look away from his victim. Those blue eyes, so like his own, were filled with malice and fury.

"Who are you?"

"Your destruction," Murdoch said.

Jean le Beau laughed, confident in his own powers, and Murdoch struck. He buried his blade in the mercenary's throat, forcing it downward. Jean le Beau roared and seized Murdoch, lifting him bodily and flinging him aside. They were of a size, but Murdoch was thirty years younger, and he was shocked by the older man's vigor.

Murdoch rolled out of the way as his own blade was driven down toward him. Jean le Beau missed, just barely, but the dagger was driven hard into the dirt, piercing a carpet first. For a moment, Murdoch feared he might be the one to die this night. He bounded to his feet as the mercenary's own dagger slashed through the air, opening the flesh across his chest. The wound was shallow, but it bled copiously.

Murdoch lunged at his opponent before he had finished the strike, and the pair of them toppled backward on the ground. They fought for the dagger, rolling back and forth as they struggled for ascendancy. He heard the woman flee, her footsteps racing into the night and guessed that he did not have much time to finish what he had begun.

When next he was atop the mercenary, Murdoch had no weapon to strike a blow. Jean le Beau chuckled at his plight, but Murdoch bent and bit the older man's ear hard, making him roar with pain. He drove his knee hard into the mercenary's groin. Jean le Beau snarled and cuffed Murdoch so hard on the temple that Murdoch saw stars. Then he felt a knee in his groin, the force enough to steal his breath away and send him rolling backward.

The fury dawned cold within him then, along with his determination to triumph. There could be no rules of fair conduct with this man, and no mercy.

Murdoch drove his elbow into Jean le Beau's wound and leaned all his weight upon it, hearing the older man gasp for breath yet refusing to relent. Indeed, he pushed harder, feeling Jean le Beau squirm like a fish. The older man's grip was loosened on the dagger, and Murdoch seized it, Jean le Beau *flung him aside. Murdoch caught him around the waist and flung him to the ground, ensuring that the older man hit his head hard. He knelt atop his opponent to plunge the mercenary's own blade into his belly. He buried it to the hilt with one savage gesture, then hauled it down toward the groin, watching the older man bare his teeth in pain even as he continued to struggle against Murdoch's weight. The color left his face, he shuddered, then his eyes opened again to survey Murdoch. He bared his teeth, his eyes flashing furiously.*

"Why?" he demanded, even as he strove to seize the weapon.

"Gwendolyn," Murdoch said, waiting for understanding to dawn in those eyes before he gave the blade a savage twist. He pulled out the blade so fast that Jean le Beau gasped aloud, then buried it deep again to finish the deed. He stood then, shaking with his near escape, and watched his victim writhe on his fine carpets in anguish.

Murdoch reminded himself that Jean le Beau's torment could not be sufficient to make up for the pain and suffering he had caused himself.

Murdoch cast aside Jean le Beau's dagger with disgust: He would take no souvenirs of this night. He retrieved his own blade, cleaning it as he watched to ensure the deed was done. It took longer for the demon to expire than anticipated.

Finally, Jean le Beau exhaled one last shaking breath, emitting a long low moan as he breathed his last.

There was only silence, then the thunder of Murdoch's pulse as he realized he might be discovered before he could escape.

This might be his own last day, as well.

MURDOCH'S EYES flew open in the darkness, his heart leaping. He might have been in that tent again, fearful that he would be caught and executed. For years, his sole goal had been to kill Jean le Beau, but once the deed was done, he feared for his own survival.

He had not made a plan, which had been his error and one that might have cost him dearly.

He lay in the darkness, recalling that moment vividly and recognized the lack. He had felt no satisfaction in completing half his quest.

None.

It had been done and it had been foul, and he had nearly paid for it with his own life. Instead of being glad of his own good fortune, he had continued the hunt.

This time, he would surely die for it.

And thanks to the seer, he saw the folly of his choice.

Sadly, he saw that folly when 'twas too late to influence the outcome.

The seer would be content with her influence, were she to know of it. Murdoch would never see her again—or if he did, they would have no chance to speak—and that was a good thing.

Sadly, he could not completely believe that.

No one objected to Nyssa's departure from Kilderrick. Indeed, no one seemed to notice, possibly because Royce was nowhere to be seen. She changed to a plain kirtle and heavy cloak, keeping her chausses and boots on beneath. She took her thickest cloak and heaviest gloves for the wind carried the bite of ice. The ground crunched beneath her feet and the wind slipped cold fingers through her hair.

When would Maximilian judge Murdoch? Nyssa guessed it would be after the midday meal, as that was the usual routine with his courts. She doubted the laird would be hasty in releasing his prisoner, but her steps quickened all the same.

She walked out from Kilderrick, past the gatekeeper who bowed to her, and strode toward the village on the hill to the west of the keep. Many who labored in the keep made their homes in the village, and the stables were there. She heard the smith's hammer and knew Tynan Smith was at his labor. The wind was brisk but not so strong that Dorcha failed to keep pace with her. He landed on the roof of the stables when she went inside to choose a horse.

The ostler was in a talkative mood, for two foals had been born that morning and one had not come easily. Nyssa did not wish to arouse his suspicions, so she indulged his enthusiasm and went to admire the pair. They were both stabled with their mothers, who each watched over their new arrival protectively. The ostler was particularly impressed with the darker of the two, pointing out his long legs and fine features.

Nyssa admired them both, gave apples to the mares, then was permitted to stroke the foals' velvety noses.

A palfrey was saddled for her by the ostler himself. "The laird will be pleased with them both," he said and Nyssa could only agree.

"Has he come to see them as yet?"

"Not this day. There are concerns for him in the hall, 'tis said." The ostler looked toward the keep, evidently more interested in the horses than the fate of Murdoch Campbell. "He will come when he can, though. He always comes to see the newly-born foals and I sent word earlier."

"I mean to ride only to Rowan Fell this day," Nyssa confided. The palfrey stamped and shook her head.

The ostler did not seem to think this as remarkable as Nyssa knew it was. She had no friends in the village but the ostler clearly did not know as much.

He smiled. "If you would go further, Clara will not mind. She has not been ridden for a few days." The ostler patted Clara's chestnut rump. "A good windy day and she could run to Edinburgh, this one." He waved Nyssa off, returning to his tasks with such purpose that Nyssa was certain he would check again upon the foals.

Nyssa's trepidation rose at even the prospect of visiting Rowan Fell. She eyed the open moor between Kilderrick village and Rowan Fell and could not bring herself to ride openly across it. Anyone could witness her choice, and that prospect troubled Nyssa. Instead, she urged the horse down toward the stream, bent upon her task.

CHAPTER 5

The Liddel Water, a broad river, flowed from north to south, carving a valley to the east of Kilderrick's keep on its course to the Solway Firth, and providing an avenue for men and beasts. It had been on that river that Nyssa and her companions had demanded a toll from reiving parties retreating to the north—until the Silver Wolf had arrived to claim Kilderrick.

Few concerned themselves with the smaller stream that ran from west to east and to the north of the keep, joining the Liddel Water to the northeast of Kilderrick's hall. Its course was open in the vicinity of the keep, the scrub and young trees having been cleared away to grant an unobstructed view for sentries. To the west of Kilderrick village, though, the willows and shrubs grew unimpeded alongside the merry little stream, creating a covered passageway used by few. The stream was only sufficiently deep to run in its very center during the winter. On this day, there was ice along each shore, which snapped beneath the palfrey's hooves. The branches were bare overhead, but still Nyssa preferred this path. She knew that beyond Rowan Fell, a number of smaller rivulets descended from the moor and joined to create this stream. Beyond that, she had never ventured. She knew the land to the east and north much better, though it had been years since she had ventured from Kilderrick.

She could not evade that detail, not with her dream still so vivid. Though she could not explain the dream to her satisfaction, it left her unsettled. 'Twas too easy to recall the sense of being trapped or even hunted, and she shivered, striving to forget the past without success.

The wind was diminished along the stream and they made steady progress, finally reaching the rocky section that was closest to Rowan Fell. Water was gathered here by the villagers and on fine summer days, laundry might be done and gossip exchanged. The closest cottage was that of Nerida, the keeper of bees.

The older woman lived with her grand-daughter and had been a friend of Morag's, selling herbs to the woman of the woods. Of all those in Rowan Fell, Nyssa knew Nerida best, which still was not well.

Nerida had two cottages on her allotment, a smaller older one close to the stream, and a larger one within the circle of homes in the village. The beeskeps were alongside the older hut, the structure providing a windbreak, and between the two cottages were Nerida's gardens, a mix of herbs and flowers grown both for the bees and for their healing powers. Even in this season, there were birds active among the deadened flower stalks and seed pods.

Nyssa could see a familiar figure scattering grain for the chickens at the next cottage. 'Twas Jeannie, the sheriff's wife, though she did not so much as glance in Nyssa's direction. She suspected then that Nerida and Jeannie were not allies. Other than Jeannie, Nyssa could not see another soul.

Nerida herself, wrapped in several shawls, was singing softly to her bees, but turned at Nyssa's approach. "I did not think to see any from Kilderrick on this day," she said, her manner less welcoming than Nyssa might have hoped. "Many have gone to the keep out of curiosity as to the fate of Murdoch Campbell. Dara could scarce be kept away."

"The laird will hear Murdoch on the morrow at noon." Nyssa watched Dorcha land on the roof of the smaller cottage, pacing along the crest of the roof and peering down at the beeskeps.

"Do not distress the bees, you rogue," Nerida said to him, and he bobbed his head, cawing back at her, as if he laughed.

Nyssa dismounted, leaving Clara to graze. "You were not sufficiently curious to go?"

Nerida harrumphed. "I have labor to do and no time for such idleness."

"Singing to the bees."

The older woman's expression was defiant. "Aye. You of all people should understand the import of that task." She turned then to walk up the slope to her larger cottage, as if their conversation should end.

Nyssa followed her, not quite convinced of that. "Did you know Murdoch's mother?" The question was bald, asked without preamble, but perhaps surprise would ensure a better reply.

Nerida glanced over her shoulder in surprise. "Why would you ask as much?"

"Someone must have done. He was born here, was he not?"

"And what of that? They are all dead now and nigh forgotten." There was bitterness in her tone that reminded Nyssa of Murdoch.

Dorcha jumped down to the ground with a flap of his wings. To Nyssa's surprise, he went to the door of the hut as if he strove to look within it.

How curious.

The older woman continued her march toward the larger hut as if she would escape Nyssa and her questions.

She had to know some detail to be so evasive.

Nyssa meant to learn what it was before she returned to the keep. She followed Nerida, who moved more quickly than she might have believed possible. "I thought the bees slept in these months."

Nerida cast a glance over her shoulder. "They never sleep, not truly. There is always work to be done in the hive, though they may be slower in the cold months. See the sun? Already the days grow longer and the bees *know*."

"What is in the hut?"

"Honey," Nerida said with a ferocity that did not seem deserved. "And dried herbs. Naught for a raven. Hie!"

Dorcha cawed and took flight.

Nyssa wondered. She spared a glance toward Jeannie, only to discover that the woman she despised had gone into her home. Doubtless, she still watched from a window.

"You are never in the village. Do you come to spy for the laird and lady?" Nerida demanded.

"Nay. I would know more of Murdoch Campbell."

"What of him? He has been gone from Kilderrick since Rupert's demise." The older woman evaded Nyssa's gaze as she said this, bending to break a dried flower stem.

"But he has not been truly gone, Nerida, not since the return of the Silver Wolf."

The older woman flicked a wary glance her way. "And what would I know of it?"

"I wager you remember him as a boy," Nyssa guessed. Dorcha was marching along the roof of the smaller cottage again, as if he would draw her gaze to it.

"Aye, but that is little enough."

"But you *know* him." Nyssa realized that the smaller cottage might be approached from the stream at night, and no one in Rowan Fell would know of it. The hut was in markedly good repair for a place that was unoccupied. "And you must know if he has kin in Rowan Fell, no less whether they have granted him shelter. *Someone* must have aided him. And why not, if they knew him as a boy?"

Nerida drew herself taller and spoke sternly. "'Tis of no import. His parents are dead and he has been gone. Rowan Fell is not as it was. Leave the matter be!"

"Is it Murdoch Campbell's situation that irks you?"

"I am always irked to see an honest man be condemned," Nerida said sharply. "No less to have the village run to watch his condemnation. People should tend to their own affairs." She then shut her mouth so abruptly that Nyssa knew the older woman believed she had said too much.

"You take his side."

"What if I do?"

"I would know something of him, if you would share." Nyssa smiled when Nerida granted her a hard glance, once again reminding her of Murdoch. "I might be able to aid him."

The older woman exhaled and shook her head. "Not now. He is in the laird's dungeon. None leave that hole alive."

"You cannot be certain of that. The new laird has never yet used the dungeon. All might be different in these times."

Nerida raised her brows.

"I will not betray you, Nerida."

The older woman eyed Nyssa for a long moment, then heaved a sigh. "I have known Murdoch many years, all his life, and his father before him. That is not a detail to ignore."

Nyssa guessed that Nerida meant Rupert, not Jean le Beau. "Murdoch did conspire against the laird previously," she noted. "That will not show in his favor."

"And who would not? He blames the laird for Rupert's death, and seeks vengeance for that old crime. The laird himself would do the same in his place."

"But he demanded that I bring him the child, Alys' son," Nyssa confided.

Nerida winced. "And you say he will leave the dungeon alive," she said, shaking her head. "He is doomed, to be sure." She sighed again.

"I would convince him to make peace with the laird, if possible."

"Why?"

Nyssa smiled. "Perhaps I too see his merit."

Nerida studied her for a long moment, then turned aside. She abruptly indicated the sheriff's cottage, interrupting Nyssa. "Does the laird know that his sheriff has left?"

"Eamon has left?"

Nerida nodded wisely. "Jeannie said he was ill, but his pony is gone."

"But where did he go?"

The older woman shrugged. "The truth will be revealed when he returns, whenever that might be." She nudged Nyssa. "You should go back to the keep now and tell the laird of Eamon's absence. No village should be without its sheriff! Take your horse and ride!"

Nyssa understood when someone strove to be rid of her. "I will go when I have done what I must."

"What else would you do? There is no one at home in Rowan Fell this day, no one save me. We have talked. You can go." Nerida laughed a little. "Unless you suddenly have affection for Jeannie's companionship? I recall a time when she sent some men…"

"As do I," Nyssa said tersely, then was struck by a notion of how she might linger in the village a bit longer. With luck, she might then have the opportunity to look in the smaller hut. "I came to talk to the dead, Nerida," she declared, watching the older woman's expression turn to surprise. "I believe they are precisely where they always are."

The older woman looked alarmed, but Nyssa headed for the small church in the village. Nerida stood by her own home and watched, arms folded across her chest.

'Twas eerie to walk through the village when it was so quiet. Rona's goats were secured in a patch of ground behind the cottage, and they watched Nyssa with their curious yellow gazes. Undoubtedly, Jeannie watched as well. The priest was not at home, nor was the smith. Chickens pecked in barren gardens, slate-bellied clouds began to muster in the west, and it was ominously quiet. Dorcha cried out as he flew after her.

An ancient tree grew alongside the chapel, the rowan for which the village had been named, its trunk twisted and its branches stark against the sky. Dorcha landed in its highest branches, bobbing his head with approval while Nyssa surveyed the churchyard.

She sought Gwendolyn and Rupert Campbell. Were they both buried here? She wagered that Gwendolyn was, at the least. How would their resting places be marked? Simply, Nyssa would wager, if at all, though Gwendolyn's grave might be more readily found. She could imagine that Rupert would have ensured his wife was well recalled.

But there were only small stones at intervals in the churchyard, none of which carried any mark. Nyssa entered the chapel and confirmed that all the inscriptions were for the Armstrong family. The priest was not to be found.

What of the dead? Would they aid her?

SHE STEPPED OUTSIDE AGAIN and sat beneath the ancient rowan, noting how Dorcha had claimed a perch at its summit. She closed her eyes and opened her heart, as her mother had taught her, listening to the wind in the bare branches and prepared for more.

. . .

78

As was so often the case when Nyssa was troubled, she dreamed of Elsa.

She smiled when her older sister appeared in her dream, her heart fairly glowing at the gift of another precious glimpse. Elsa was rowing a small boat, laughing as the waves splashed against the side of it. There was mist gathering above the water and clouds dipping low overhead. 'Twould rain shortly, which might have explained Elsa's vigorous rowing.

Elsa wore garments that Nyssa did not recall, though she was young, perhaps eight summers of age. Nyssa would have been six, and they would have been in the custody of the Sutherlands. Her memories of those early days were hazy, not because they had been treated badly but because she and Elsa had often been alone.

The fog meant that Nyssa could not see precisely where Elsa rowed. The way that Elsa's loose hair blew meant that Nyssa did not have a clear view of her sister's face, though she yearned to see it again. Rocks loomed suddenly behind Elsa and she leapt out of the small boat, tugging it onto high ground as her companion called encouragement. There was a cured hide stretched tightly over the wooden frame of the small vessel and Nyssa thought it curious that she did not recall the boat.

Perhaps she witnessed an adventure Elsa had undertaken alone.

Her sister left the boat and climbed the rocky terrain. Did she visit an island, or had she simply rowed to another point on the coast? Indeed, she might have crossed a small lake. Nyssa had no notion of her location. She was laughing and talking to her companion, whose view Nyssa evidently shared in this vision.

A small stone structure emerged from the mist ahead and the children hurried toward it. Evidently it was their destination. Once inside, they whispered in the cool darkness, clearly familiar with it, moving with purpose to one corner.

Together, they moved a flat stone and set it aside, Elsa watching as the other child reached into the darkness. Nyssa was startled by the familiarity of the other child's hands. They were strong hands for a girl but moved with unusual grace for a boy. The fingertips were almost square. Where had she seen such hands before? Did she know this child?

All she could remember was that Elsa feared spiders.

Within the cavity hidden beneath the floor was a collection of treasures. The children examined them and laid them out in a line. First, there was a *very smooth pale grey stone, a little smaller than the egg of a chicken. Next, a dark jagged stone with a gleam upon it, which had to be a piece of obsidian. There were two pieces of polished amber, like the pieces she and Elsa had found on the shore as children, but neither of them ones Nyssa recalled. And finally, a fistful of raven feathers, long and dark, so glossy and blue-black that they could be naught else.*

"Beware," said Elsa, picking up the feather and spinning it between finger and thumb.

"Beware," the other child echoed, then they laughed together.

Elsa spun so that her back was to her companion and that child began to braid her hair, weaving each feather into one braid.

Then a raven cried as if the children had been discovered. The vision faded so abruptly that Nyssa was startled.

NYSSA STOOD in the churchyard and shivered, unable to tell for certain how much time had passed. Had she slept? The skies looked darker.

Dorcha cawed overhead and she looked up to see him bobbing his head.

Beware.

Of what? Of whom? Who was being warned? Elsa or herself?

Who was the other child? No one Nyssa remembered, but then, she might not have done so. It made sense to her that Elsa would have tired of her younger sister's company and found a companion of similar age. Was it one of the Sutherlands? Nay, there had been only the two older boys. It might have been a servant's child, or a child from the village.

And where had she seen such hands before?

Elsa would have remembered. Elsa had always been the confident one, the pretty one, the one who knew what to say and do in every situation—or had the daring to make a guess. She trusted her instincts with a surety that Nyssa could only strive to emulate.

And her powers had been far beyond Nyssa's own, even beyond those of their mother. Elsa been a seer beyond compare. That had not stopped her from striving to change the future, but her view of pending events was often astonishing in its clarity.

Was that why she had dreamed of Elsa?

She looked around the chapel and noted that Nerida had vanished into her cottage. In fact, there was no one within sight, as if the village was abandoned.

This was Nyssa's chance to look inside the hut.

NYSSA HOPED against hope that no one would notice her or interrupt her. She slipped past Nerida's cottage without catching so much as a glimpse of the older woman. Indeed, she might have been a thief creeping between the cottages, striving for silence as she hastened past each window. Once in Nerida's garden, Nyssa bent low, as if she might vanish between the dried stalks of flowers. Dorcha landed on that roof again, but this time, there was no one to shoo him away.

This time, mercifully, he remained silent, simply watching her progress with his bright gaze.

The hair prickled on the back of Nyssa's neck, but she slipped inside the smaller hut, relieved that the door had no latch. The interior space was small, smaller even than Morag's hut had been in the forest. It was also close to empty, giving no sign of having sheltered anyone of late. Dried herbs hung from the rafters, disguising the floor of a loft above. It smelled of sunshine, honey and dried herbs even in this season. There was a hearthstone on the floor but the soot upon it was dry and not of recent use. After all, Nerida had no cause to light a fire in this place in these times.

Nyssa might have turned back, but she spotted footholds in the wall. They were difficult to discern, but once she had noticed them, she could not ignore them. There was a loft! She climbed, convinced that she had found Murdoch's sanctuary when she saw a saddlebag hanging from the rafters, invisible from beneath because of the herbs. The bag was sturdy and had been used well. There was a straw pallet against one sloping roof and a bowl and cup near the saddlebag. A fur-lined cloak hung from a peg and Nyssa ran her hands over it. She caught the scent of someone's skin, of Murdoch's skin, upon the garment. She inhaled deeply of it, recalling his potent kiss, and that tingle was roused deep within her.

She found four apples in the saddlebag and half a loaf of bread, as well as a faint scent of cheese. Did Nerida bring Murdoch food—or simply leave it here for him to discover? Was she unaware of his presence, or did she turn a blind eye?

There was also a bundle of sticks and vines against one wall, the same manner of materials he had used to weave the cage for Dorcha. Nyssa chilled at the sight of it, then had to avert her gaze.

Beware.

Nyssa heard Elsa's voice clearly, though she knew no sound had been uttered. She caught her breath and surveyed her surroundings anew. There was no window or vantage point in the loft, which made her fearful of the approach of another. There was only one way out of the small structure, after all.

She could be trapped in this place, with no means of escape. Nyssa slipped silently and quickly from the loft and back to the stream, her thoughts churning with what she had found.

Murdoch had a sanctuary in Nerida's hut. Nyssa could not believe that the older woman was unaware of his presence there, given her prickly attitude. Nyssa also did not believe that Murdoch would reveal that Nerida had aided him, lest the older woman come under Maximilian's scrutiny for her choice.

Nay, he would be protective of his ally.

There had to be a bond between them, perhaps kinship. Murdoch's mother might have been a friend of Nerida—she had, after all, born her child at Kilderrick. Why? Had she been raised in Rowan Fell, or had Rupert brought her to the village? Where would the pair have met?

Nyssa hesitated beside the palfrey, sensing that she had missed some key detail. Her gaze rose to the sheriff's cottage. Was Eamon truly gone? Where might he have gone? Hidden by the growth, Nyssa impulsively moved further to the west along the stream. Dorcha jumped from branch to branch behind her, as if understanding the need for stealth.

She caught her breath when she spotted dozens of hoofprints in the mud, frozen there. A company had evidently followed the stream and lingered in this place, the closest point to the sheriff's cottage. The ground was too barren at this time of year to discern whether any had walked from this hidden point to the cottage, but there was no other reason to linger in this place.

Who had visited the sheriff? Had he accompanied this large party, and where had they gone?

'Twas all too easy to think of reivers in the valley of the Liddel Water, of their need to find another route once the Laird of Kilderrick demanded a toll from all who passed that way.

Never mind the sum Eamon and Jeannie owed to the Silver Wolf, which was due by the full moon.

What had Eamon done?

If Murdoch had used the hut for shelter, did he know?

There was, to Nyssa's thinking, only one way to find out.

TO MURDOCH'S DISMAY, he could not cease to think about the seer. He recalled her kiss for obvious reasons, but more than that. He saw again the flash of her eyes and knew she was not so demure as he had imagined. He recalled the way a tendril of her hair lifted in the wind and ached with desire. He heard her fury when she feared he might injure the bird, and he knew her soul was kind. He remembered her trepidation when he had touched her, the flutter of her pulse beneath his hand, and was awed again by her audacity in facing her fears.

She haunted him.

In the darkness and solitude, he became aware of how little he knew about her. Where was she from? How had she come to be alone in Kilderrick's forest? Why did she remain here, where she had no family?

Why did she fascinate him? Was it an enchantment—or could it be destiny?

He was ruminating over this endlessly when the trap door was suddenly opened above him. Murdoch rose to his feet, squinting at the square of light. Once again, he saw a figure silhouetted above him and he hoped against all reason that 'twas the seer.

Then he hoped 'twas not. Another encounter might only strengthen her hold over him—or worse, attract the ire of the Silver Wolf. He did not wish for her concern to have repercussions for her.

Still, it would be sweet to see her again.

The figure above studied him in silence and he could not discern that person's features. No ladder or rope was lowered.

Finally, Murdoch could bear the silence no longer. He folded his arms across his chest, staring upward as he raised his voice in challenge. "I am not yet dead, if that is your concern."

"How are your wounds?" the seer asked and Murdoch's errant heart leapt with pleasure. He almost laughed aloud, but he scowled instead, striving to hide his reaction.

"How can I assess them?" he demanded gruffly, wanting more than was wise to desire. He wanted her beside him, her hands upon him, her lips against his, her softness beneath his hands. He wanted her as he had not wanted a woman in years, and he knew that after just one kiss, no other woman would ever suffice. *Nyssa*. "I am no healer."

Would she descend into the dungeon again? Would she touch him? He knew she had the audacity to do as much, and hoped.

"And I am not permitted to approach you again," she replied.

There was a rumble of commentary that Murdoch could discern, and she turned to answer quickly, her face averted. Murdoch understood that Royce or another defender was at hand. She turned back to Murdoch, holding a lamp, and he was glad that he could discern her features better. Her hair was bound back again, her expression solemn. She wore boots and chausses again, a long tunic and a cloak. He wondered whether she had left the keep or intended to do as much. Was it morning or night? It did not matter—she belonged in the wind, as wild and free as her raven. "Touch them," she commanded. "Tell me if they are swollen or inflamed. You can discern as much even in darkness."

"What difference?" Despite his reply, Murdoch found himself following her instruction. "I can die in this place as quickly with healed wounds or nay."

"The laird has decreed that you will remain in the dungeon for three days, then you will face his judgement. If you are to die in that hole, it has not yet been decided."

So, the Silver Wolf would let him stew and simmer. Murdoch was not surprised.

"How much time has passed?"

"One day."

And it felt like an eternity. Could he endure two more such? Did it matter?

She had not left so he spoke again.

"You are a seer. Will you not tell me my fate?" He expected her to say that she had need of payment to do as much, but instead she shook her head. Murdoch did not care what she said. Just her presence lifted his heart, which he knew did not bode well for his future happiness. He need not peer into the future to understand that desiring such a woman was folly.

"Foresight does not work thus," she said.

"How does it work?" In truth, Murdoch wished only to prolong her visit and to hear her voice a little longer.

"I see what I am shown. I cannot guide it so precisely. And worse, what I am shown is often symbolic, if not mysterious. The visions require interpretation."

"It does not sound like such a gift when you describe it thus."

"I would argue that 'tis more of an obligation than a gift."

Murdoch was surprised by that. How was her talent an obligation? And why did she sound so weary?

She shrugged as he studied her. "And matters can change, of course."

"How so?"

"We can make choices. Indeed, each choice we make changes our prospects. You, for example, could repent of your quest and favorably influence the result of your hearing with the laird two days hence."

Murdoch snorted at the unlikelihood of that.

She did not seem to have expected otherwise of him, which proved she was keen of wit. "Your wounds?"

"They seem better." He fingered them as instructed. "More flat and less sore. It seems I might survive to be judged and executed."

"Will you not plea for his mercy?" She sounded curious.

"I will not beg the Silver Wolf for any compassion," he said with disdain. "But if I am to die, I would rather it be quick."

"He may understand that much and plan for it."

"No matter what torment he plans, 'twill be better than sitting in

85

darkness until I starve." His stomach grumbled mightily in that moment, as if to emphasize his point.

"How can you believe as much?" she asked. "Have you seen a man tortured afore?"

He was intrigued by her question. In his trade, it was common, but he would not have expected as much from her circumstance. "Any torment he might devise will be over in hours or days." Murdoch knew as much from his experience of war. The seer evidently was shocked to silence. He raised a hand. "While starvation will take weeks, weakening one to bone and sinew."

Particularly if his captors continued to ensure that he was given small portions of food, amounts that he was not able to resist.

"You should ask his forgiveness and become his ally," she suggested.

Murdoch laughed. "He has no need for my alliance."

"Does he not?" she whispered as if expecting no reply. She said something then to her companion, whoever it might be, and Murdoch heard footsteps moving away. The seer leaned closer, her hair spilling over her shoulder like spun silver. "The sheriff is gone," she confided, though this was not news to Murdoch.

"You cannot lay blame for that at my feet."

"Of course not! But if you know more of this, the laird would be glad to learn of it."

"The sheriff's business is his own."

"Is it? Can it truly be thus if he would bring trouble to Kilderrick?"

"He is sheriff," Murdoch said with care. "One would not expect such a man to invite trouble of any kind."

"Nay, one would not," she said, then paused as if choosing her words with care. "A man who had seen some evidence of the sheriff's choice might be rewarded for confiding as much."

Murdoch's heart skipped. Did she know of his refuge in Nerida's hut? Would she betray him – or Nerida? He could not bear the prospect of the older woman being exposed to the wrath of the Silver Wolf, and spoke quickly. "You know naught of what you speak," he said, his tone dismissive.

He heard the little sound of vexation she made. "You are not the sole one who has endured an injustice, Murdoch Campbell."

"Aye, the world is full of men bent upon vengeance of one kind or another."

"Yet there are far more who learn from the injustice and carry on, declining to demand a toll for what they have suffered."

"I know few such."

"I know one well," she said firmly. She glared at him. "I would know another, but that may not come to be for some men are cursed stubborn."

She moved away from the trapdoor before he could ask for detail and Murdoch was dismayed that he could not see her any longer. He was more dismayed that she had departed without a word of farewell or a promise to return.

Did she call him stubborn? He would choose to call himself loyal!

A familiar servant appeared, lowering a rope and bucket into the dungeon. Having learned the routine—and that denying it left him both dirty and hungry—Murdoch untied the bucket and set it on the stone shelf. He retrieved the other bucket, which held the empty bowl and cup from his last meal, and tied it to the rope. He stood and watched as it was hoisted out of sight, anticipating that the trap door would be closed again. After some interval, another bucket would be lowered, to be exchanged for his pail of slops.

To his surprise, the trap door was not closed. The seer reappeared. "You should eat," she said gently. "The soup is yet warm."

"I will if you linger to speak with me." 'Twas an outrageous proposal and he expected to be declined.

"And what would you have me speak of? The sun and the wind?"

"Tell me of yourself."

She was clearly startled. "Myself?"

"Where did you come from? Why are you here?"

"What difference?"

"None, but I am curious."

She was silent so long that he was certain she could decline him. When she vanished from view, his heart sank. The seer, though, brought a stool and sat upon it, within his view. Her choice gave him enormous satisfaction, though he told himself 'twas natural to yearn for companionship given his situation.

Even so, Murdoch knew that the companionship of no other would suffice.

To his satisfaction, she began to recount a tale.

Her choice made Murdoch smile. He sat on the stone ledge and began to eat the soup, content at the change he had wrought in his own circumstance.

∼

"ONCE UPON A TIME," the seer said. "There was a warrior of great skill, a man who had amassed an impressive amount of wealth and gained both a holding and a title. He was smitten with a woman he believed to be the prettiest he had ever seen, but she declined his offers repeatedly. He was certain that only she would satisfy him as his lady wife, though she was rumored to be a witch. He courted her with vigor, sent her presents, appealed to her, but she always declined him. It might be said that she was the only objective he failed to achieve readily, and perhaps that was what increased his resolve to win her."

Murdoch strove to eat the soup slowly, savoring each warm mouthful as it slid down his throat. Why did she linger? Did she want to ensure that he ate? There was no question that he would finish every drop.

He enjoyed the sound of the seer's voice as much as the words themselves. When she spoke, he thought of sunlight and clear skies, of wind and freedom. The darkness of the prison retreated, even though there was only a small square of light visible above him. When she spoke, he believed he could have sat in that hole and listened to her forever.

"It could, perhaps, have been her reputation that fed his ardor," the seer said, her tone thoughtful. "There are those who believe that binding oneself to a witch can only bring them power and good fortune, that the witch's ability to cast spells will be harnessed by the wedding vow."

She paused.

What was this tale? Why did the seer tell it to him? Murdoch could not understand its relevance, but he loved the sound of her voice too much to protest. He liked also that she bothered to come to him, at the implication that she had some concern for his welfare. It prompted a glow around his heart that Murdoch had not felt in a long a time. Indeed, it had been many years since anyone showed much concern for him. He sat and listened, sipping his soup, knowing himself to be enthralled and unable to regret as much.

"Is it not?" Murdoch asked when she did not continue.

"The matter is not so simple, and this lady was not a witch, in truth. She was a seer, like me, one who might have tired of the obligation of providing insight to her fellows." Her voice dropped so low that he had to strain to hear her words. "I wonder whether, she too, began to feel the price was too high, for she relented to his persistent courtship." She shrugged as Murdoch watched. "But then, perhaps she loved him."

What price did she pay for her gift and why did she find it burdensome? Murdoch wanted very much to know. He let her continue, hoping all would become clear in the course of this tale's recounting.

"The maiden granted the warrior a quest, vowing that she would wed him if he succeeded in it. It was widely believed to be an impossible task. The warrior was not to be put aside and he bent every effort upon achieving that goal. When he did, they were wed with great ceremony and celebration, and despite her lower birth, she was made his lady. The warrior was content beyond all for he had triumphed."

"What was the quest?" Murdoch had to ask.

"'Tis another tale," she chided and he smiled into his soup. "In the early days of their marriage, it seemed that all the warrior touched turned to advantage, for his fortunes and advantages increased by leaps and bounds. It seemed that he had only to utter a wish to have it fulfilled. If his lady was a witch, her powers were only to his benefit and he found no fault with that. In time, his lady wife rounded with child. The warrior was certain that he would soon have a son and heir, and that his happiness would be complete. This was a man who had succeeded in every endeavor, and with his marriage, he had become convinced that his will was indomitable. He was much concerned with his legacy and the future of his holding, with the preservation of all he had earned, so only a son would suffice for him." She paused. "The child, alas, showed the poor judgement to be born a girl."

"Ah," Murdoch said. "Surely her beauty changed his view?"

The seer shook her head. "The warrior was displeased with this situation. He refused to so much as look upon his daughter in his disappointment. He had wished for a son! How dare his wife deny him this desire! How dare the child be a girl! He resolved that he would not compromise, for he saw that as weakness. He wished for a son and he would have one. He ordered the child to be killed, despite his wife's protests."

Murdoch was startled into looking up, but the seer continued, her tone hard.

"The lady wept, but the warrior would not be swayed. Indeed, they two were estranged for some months after his judgement was fulfilled. Her sorcery, if she possessed any, was not turned against him, though, and his advantages continued to increase. In time, his lady conceived a child again, and the warrior's confidence was restored. He was certain that this time, he would have his heir. He was convinced that the odds were in his favor and that soon, his joy would be complete." The seer paused and Murdoch anticipated the result.

"Another daughter," he guessed.

"Another daughter," she agreed, then sighed.

Was this a tale of her own kin? She seemed to place great import in it, as if she had lived it. But the first girl had been killed, and he would wager the second met the same fate. He was so intrigued that he almost forgot to finish his soup.

CHAPTER 6

$\mathcal{J}$ was easy, all too easy, to confide her tale in Murdoch. Nyssa might have been the one beguiled, for the words flowed from her lips as if she had been awaiting this moment all her life.

"Here was another child that the warrior ordered to be killed," she continued, aware of Murdoch's avidity. "He was adamant that he must have a son to inherit his assets, his title and his holding, yet strangely, after the execution of their second daughter, his wife did not conceive again."

From the dungeon carried the sound of a snort of disdain, one so emphatic that Nyssa smiled.

"Women, even those who knew naught of sorcery, oft understood their own bodies," he said gruffly.

"True enough, for 'twas not for lack of effort on the warrior's part," she continued. "The villagers whispered of the wife's sorcery, suggesting that she could cast a spell to ensure that she was not burdened with a pregnancy. There were even those who agreed with her choice, if that had been her choice, in the face of the warrior's cruelty to those infants. Still, his fortunes grew. It appeared that he was to have everything he desired, save a son."

Murdoch emitted a sound of disapproval.

"You think she should have denied him?" Nyssa asked, curious.

"I think this fate better than the cur deserved. Had he desired the lady for his wife solely for what she could bring to him? Did he give no consideration to her own merit?"

"Her beauty, you mean?"

"I mean her counsel and her companionship," Murdoch replied, sounding annoyed. "I mean the satisfaction of having such a woman by his side for all his days and nights."

Nyssa was startled to silence for a moment, then pleased beyond all that Murdoch seemed to think partnership had more merit than the creating of children.

'Twas a mark of his merit as a man, not a detail with any import for her own future.

She cleared her throat and continued. "The years passed and the lady grew older, so that her womb was less likely to bear fruit. Still the lord was disappointed, but he had come to love his lady with all his heart and would not put her aside for another bride. They were happy and affluent, despite their lack of children."

"And despite his deeds," Murdoch evidently felt compelled to note.

"They would not be the sole couple in which the husband makes the choices and the wife must abide by them," Nyssa noted, hearing a sharpness in her tone again.

"Aye, that is true enough, but not all matches must be thus." His conviction surprised her.

"You cannot hold Alys and Maximilian as an example," she said. "For I know you give no credit to the Silver Wolf in any matter."

Murdoch chuckled, a comforting sound. "Nay, I think of my mother and Rupert."

"I thought she died when you were young."

"She did, but I remember them talking each night." There was a welcome smile in his voice. "Aye, back and forth they would worry a matter, though I understood little of any specifics at the time." She heard the wooden spoon scrape across the bottom of the bowl. "I remember how they would confer, relying upon each other, sharing their experience and views, until they resolved upon a solution that both found agreeable."

"That is uncommon in my experience," Nyssa said when he said no more.

"'Tis all I know," Murdoch replied and there was a moment of silence while they both considered this.

Nyssa resumed her tale, for she reached the point of it. "One day, the warrior and his lady were invited to the wedding of the son of the earl to whom the warrior was sworn. There were to be tournaments and feasts, dances and much merriment to celebrate the joyous union. The lady thought the warrior would not wish to attend, for it would only remind him that he did not have a son and heir, but he insisted that they go and make merry with his liege lord. Once there, he watched the dancers and sighed, speaking with regret to his lady wife. 'Look upon those two lovely maidens,' he said to her. 'They would be of an age with our own daughters, if I had not been so wrong as to order their deaths. In my wish for a son, I was blind to all other possibilities, and I owe you every apology, my beloved. The earl has now a daughter in the marriage of his heir. We would have had sons, not by blood, but by marriage when our daughters wed.' He kissed her hand and begged her forgiveness for his folly, his eyes filled with tears.

"The lady, who had hoped and dreamed for this moment for years, took his hands with her own and kissed his cheeks. 'And I must beg your forgiveness, my lord, for my deception.' He expressed astonishment at this and protested, knowing she had been the most loyal, loving and honest of wives. 'I have had a secret all these years, sir, two secrets, for when you condemned our daughters, I could not bear to see the deed done. I defied you and sent them away to be raised by another. These two maidens you so admire *are* our daughters in truth.' When she had convinced him and he had forgiven her deception, they were reunited with their own daughters in joy."

"Did they forgive him for his judgement?" Murdoch sounded skeptical of such a conclusion, and rightly so, to Nyssa's thinking.

"By the tale, they did," she said mildly.

"I would be hard-pressed to forgive any man who had ordered my demise at birth."

"You would not be alone in that, to be sure."

"But you said the lady wife was a seer. Did she not anticipate the result of her pregnancy?"

"Aye, she denied the warrior's offer of marriage because she knew he wished for sons, and knew also that it was her legacy to bear only daughters."

"Did she not foresee what he would do to those daughters?" Murdoch's disgust was more than clear and Nyssa could only warm to him for that.

"I believe she feared only to disappoint him, without knowing the specific results of that." Her voice softened. "She bore a great love and admiration for him before they wed, which may have hampered her foresight of that shadow within him."

"He was a warrior. He had to have cruelty within him."

"Perhaps she did not wish to see that truth, so she did not."

"Aye, but she was taught the truth in a way that could not be ignored. To know her first child condemned for the babe's gender!" Murdoch was outraged, which made Nyssa smile. He was protective, even of those he did not know, even of those in a tale. "Why conceive the second after the fate of the first? What of her foresight then?"

Nyssa bit her lip, then decided to share the truth. "She possessed it no longer."

"I do not understand. How was it lost?"

"Its sacrifice is the price of union with a man."

"What is this?" He was indignant.

"A seer only retains her gift so long as she is a maiden. With carnal knowledge comes another kind of wisdom, 'tis said."

Nyssa managed to say this as if it did not trouble her, as if the detail had naught to do with her and her own circumstance. In truth, she saw it as a terrible choice. To love a man and not be able to lie with him, to know him utterly, potentially to bear his child would be a toll beyond all expectation. Yet to willingly surrender her gift was a prospect she could not imagine.

She both yearned for a child, her own child in her embrace, and dreaded the sacrifice of her gift. 'Twas the conundrum of her legacy, but to date, she had never anticipated the need to choose. Now she listened to Murdoch's indignation, recalled his potent kiss, and realized the choice would be simpler than she had long believed.

"But even without her powers, could she not anticipate the result?" Murdoch demanded roughly. "Even I can see that possibility was there, even that it was likely."

"One cannot blame her for hoping for better of him."

"I can blame her for folly and misplaced trust."

"Aye," Nyssa agreed softly. "You would."

"And the daughters?" Murdoch demanded. "What of them? Did they not avenge themselves upon their father? Did they demand retribution?"

"Their mother had ensured their comfort. They had been raised by a family of some affluence," Nyssa said with care. A family with two sons of their own who, unlike their parents, were less worthy of trust.

"And so, they forgave their father for desiring their deaths?"

"And so, they were glad to be reunited with their mother," Nyssa said. "Perhaps naught else was of comparable import."

"She was a seer," Murdoch recalled. "Were they seers as well? Did she teach them of their gifts?"

"Aye."

He harrumphed. "Then I see their choice well enough. One must oft sacrifice a principle to gain a skill. Glad they might have been of their mother's tutelage, but I would wager that neither turned her back upon her father again."

Nyssa smiled at his insight. "I wager you are right."

"And what became of them?"

"One was wed to a young warrior, giving her father the son by marriage that he desired."

"The mother approved of this?"

"Nay, it occurred after her death."

"When he was assured of his power, to be sure." Murdoch muttered this darkly, as vehemently on the side of the daughters as if they were his own. "Did that warrior also wish for sons? Did she give him daughters?" His voice rose with a fury Nyssa welcomed. "Did this travesty of a tale repeat itself? A babe cannot choose its gender any more than the mother!"

"She bore him a daughter." Nyssa spoke softly, tears pricking her eyes. "But there was no opportunity to learn the reaction of the father for the child died." She fell silent then, needing to compose herself and choose the tale she would tell. Murdoch said naught but simply waited. "When she bore a second daughter, both mother and child died in the delivery. In his desire to keep the holding and title gained by his marriage, the warrior declared that he would wed his wife's sister and the father agreed." This last was confessed in a rush, even the words filling Nyssa with fear.

"But she would only bear daughters to him as well, if the legacy ran true."

"Aye. And so she, having a measure of foresight herself, chose to flee her so-called home."

Murdoch gasped. "You are the younger sister," he guessed quietly. "You confide your tale in me this night."

And Nyssa felt both exposed and relieved, a curious mixture that confused her to silence. How could it be that the sole person in whom she could confide was a man condemned by the Silver Wolf? How was it that the one who understood her so well was a man bent upon vengeance at any price?

There was a bond between them to be sure and Nyssa did not need her foresight to guess that more than understanding would pass between herself and Murdoch before all was done.

THE SEER'S silence told Murdoch all he needed to know.

This was her tale, an outrageous history of a man's abuse against his wife and his daughters, a tale that made Murdoch wish to swear another oath for vengeance. He would tear down the heavens to see Nyssa and her sister avenged, but he guessed that she would not be glad of his pledge to do as much. He bit his tongue, then saw her rise to her feet above him. He wished he could have seen her features, for her tone was cool, giving him little hint of her thoughts.

"And so, I would counsel you to accept that the past cannot be changed," she said quietly. "Your mother was taken by force and you were the result. The man you knew as your father is dead, perhaps unjustly, but he is dead all the same. Vengeance will not change either fact." Her words proved that he had guessed her inclination aright. He felt a surge of panic, knowing she would leave. "The sole detail that can change, Murdoch Campbell, is your choice. Will you be governed by the crimes of the past or by the possibilities for the future? Will you die with a heart full of hate or will you carve a corner within it for forgiveness? I know which path I admire most."

The future. She spoke always of the future!

"How can you fail to understand that there can be no future when the past remains unavenged?" he cried, but she had already stepped back from the opening. "There must be justice!" he added, suspecting that she would not hear him. "Would you not see your sister avenged?" he roared.

His sole reply was the thump of the trap door being dropped back into place, leaving him in darkness again. Murdoch growled in frustration and paced across the cell and back, restless to do more. He was still cold. His belly was still too close to empty for comfort. But Murdoch's thoughts were churning with newfound vigor. He paced the width of his prison again, irked beyond all that the seer refused to see the merit of his quest. There was a fire within him for justice, but 'twas not solely Rupert's death he would avenge—'twas that of Nyssa's sister and her two infant daughters.

Murdoch was intrigued by her tale. He should not have been surprised by the seer's power to turn his thoughts in a new direction, away from his own woes to the puzzle of her past. In a way, she cast a spell with her words, weaving a web around him, conjuring images of a father and his daughters, of choice and tragedy, and her own history.

No wonder she eschewed violence. She had been surrounded by men who seized what they desired and did not care for the consequences. He was impressed again by her courage in not only confronting him, a man of war, but in challenging him. Aye, she had provoked him, alone and without a weapon to hand.

Who was the man who intended to claim her as his bride, simply because she was the sister of his dead wife? Who was this man who chose a woman by what she could bring to him—good fortune, as her mother had brought to her father—and who cared little for the lady's own desire? He was a cur and a fiend, to be sure, a man who deserved to be denied. What other threat had he made that Nyssa had been driven to flee to Kilderrick and take shelter in the forest?

Had he touched her? The very possibility enraged Murdoch. The blackguard could not have claimed her, for then her gift would have been lost, but there was much that could be claimed before the final deed was done.

Again, he thought only of her valor. Nyssa would face any foe for a cause she believed to be right and true. Such bravery was rare and powerful in itself. He was awed by it. Such a woman had need of a defender, a warrior who would be steadfast by her side, protecting her as she followed the cause of righteousness.

Murdoch found himself prepared to volunteer for that task.

Aye, in her place, he would have ensured that there could be no repercussions from her flight, he would have guaranteed that the fiend could not pursue her, but Murdoch knew Nyssa had not done as much. She was not inclined to vengeance. She would simply have abandoned a situation she could not control—which meant she could be followed.

She was not safe. She would never be safe, so long as that cur desired her for her gifts.

Would the villain pursue her? Perhaps he had done as much already and knew Nyssa's location. Perhaps she was already endangered—while Murdoch was trapped in a dungeon, soon to be condemned.

Murdoch shoved a hand through his hair and swore with vigor, before he realized that her tale had done precisely what she had been unable to do otherwise. It made Murdoch think of the future, and more, of his own survival.

It made him think of what he could achieve beyond exacting vengeance from the Silver Wolf.

All because he wanted to defend Nyssa until his last breath.

He threw himself onto the hard stone ledge and shook his head, admiring her easy command of him. Aye, she cast a spell, to be sure, and he was beguiled—but he had no desire to break her spell. On the contrary, he wanted to surrender to it fully.

But surely, she had guessed as much. Surely, she knew what he, what any man, would desire of her. Was that why she had confided the price to him?

Murdoch could not help but recall her kiss, all the more glorious because it had been willingly offered to him. Another man might have taken more.

Did she not fear for the loss of her gift?

Or had she been prepared to sacrifice it in the hope of healing him? The very possibility troubled him beyond all.

Murdoch knew he was not worthy of such a sacrifice.

But he could choose to be.

He knew then that he would make peace with the Silver Wolf when he had the chance. He would vow what was necessary to ensure his own release.

Then he would defend Nyssa from the perils of her past, no matter the cost to himself.

Nyssa fled to her chamber, astonished that she had confided so much to Murdoch. She had not even permitted herself to recall her own history since leaving Duncheann, so determined had she been to forget it. She felt exposed and vulnerable—and revitalized.

And this even without confessing all of the truth. She had told him the tale of her niece's fate, then the tale contrived by Hugh that Elsa had died in childbirth along with her second child. The truth was so horrific that Nyssa could not even think of it.

But her dreams had urged her to remember, and Murdoch's situation had convinced her to share it. Nyssa realized that like Murdoch, she had carried a weight, a desire for vengeance, a need to see a crime avenged. She had no ability to do as much, not as a healer, but she had been unable to surrender her sense of obligation.

Justice.

Surely Elsa deserved justice.

But it had been so long. They might all be dead in these times. Duncheann might stand empty as Kilderrick had, open to the wind and occupied by the birds. Her mother's grave might be overgrown and untended, forgotten even. Much could happen in eight years so many leagues away and Nyssa had been taught that the Fates had a way of correcting what had gone awry.

Perhaps what mattered was that Elsa survived in Nyssa's heart.

Perhaps what mattered was that Nyssa had shared Elsa's tale.

Standing in her chamber, looking out the window, Nyssa felt as if she could take flight, as readily as Dorcha, all because she had confided in Murdoch. The raven swooped through the window with gusto and landed on his perch, calling to her with enthusiasm.

Nyssa smiled at his antics.

Still, she had hidden all these years, fearing retaliation, but she would cling to the shadows no longer. She would live her life fully and if peril found her, she would confront it squarely.

Her thoughts filled with memories of her mother and sister, Nyssa secured the shutters and shed her garments, examining the marks on her own skin in the candlelight. Only Morag had seen them since Nyssa's arrival in Kilderrick, and only once briefly. Nyssa was careful to keep them covered and hidden from view. She even undressed and washed in the shadows, not looking upon them fully herself. They were her secret, now that Morag was gone.

On this night, though, she examined them anew in the candlelight, joyous that her legacy was marked upon her very flesh. She recalled the day at the baron's court in Inverness where they had seen their parents again, though it had felt like an introduction. Their mother, with her silver-grey eyes, had felt immediately like an old friend, their father a stranger. There had been a gleam in his eye even then, though, a hint that grown daughters were assets to be used. Even her mother had taken note of it.

Nyssa remembered the hasty tutelage of herself and Elsa in their legacy from their mother. Those had been thrilling days, filled with lessons and tests, filled with learning and a new awareness of possibilities. She could close her eyes and feel the wind at Tom Fhithich, smell the pines, and feel the turf beneath her feet. She felt the needle again, too, the sharp sting over and over again. She traced a fingertip over the blue marks on her skin, remembering the addition of each spiral and curl, the spells whispered as the marks were made, the flicker of the candle and the smell of the dye before it was pressed beneath her skin.

Elsa's marks had been the same, an echo of her own, though Elsa had another one on her forearm. Their mother's marks had been more extensive, for she had trained all her life, until her marriage, while Nyssa and Elsa had learned for only two years.

All changed when Gerda lost her battle against a cough that could not be shaken. Her demise meant that she had not been able to defend Elsa and Nyssa from their father's ambitions any longer. When Gerda died that winter, their lessons had halted along with their visits to the Raven's Mound—and with the first breath of spring, Elsa had been wed against her will to the oldest son of the Sutherlands.

Nyssa winced at the memory of the Sutherland brothers and their ambitions. Hugh, Erik and her father had been of a kind, and Hugh had been intent upon claiming the same good fortune from a sorceress bride. Duncheann had not been a bad addition to his holdings either.

But that was the past. All these years, Nyssa had feared pursuit, but it had not come. She urged Murdoch to ponder the future, but truly, she should consider her own. If she was not afraid of a man bent on vengeance, what might she do? If she felt sufficiently bold to step out of the shadows, to leave the forest and raise her voice, what might she accomplish?

Was it too late to begin?

Nyssa opened the shutters and gripped the sill, considering the possibilities as she stared toward the western sea. She wanted to journey further to the west, and to the north as well. She would like to see the lands to the south. She might visit Elizabeth at Beaupoint, or better yet, Ceara at Gisroy, if she were not afraid to leave Kilderrick. She might even return home to Duncheann, perhaps in disguise, and leave a flower upon her mother's grave. She could think of a thousand possibilities, but she trusted her gift to show her the one of greatest import.

Nyssa whispered a summoning spell, requesting a dream of her own future, instead of a portent for another. On this night, her gift would provide a hint for herself, not for those who sheltered her and relied upon her counsel.

On this night, she would be shown her path.

JEANNIE NEVER ANTICIPATED that she would miss Eamon as ferociously as she did. The man was not inclined to talk overmuch, and 'twas true that they often argued—particularly of late—but his absence made their hut full of ominous shadows and their future of dire prospects. She slept poorly, her thoughts churning, her confidence fading steadily that all would come aright as a result of his venture.

One night alone and she was convinced that he would be killed in a raid, that his corpse would never be returned to her for a proper burial in Rowan Fell's churchyard. On her second night of solitude, she was convinced that her cousin's son Cedric would meet the same fate or fear to tell her of Eamon's demise, and that she would never hear a word of either of them again.

She lay awake, knowing that meant the Laird of Kilderrick would demand the monies due from her all too soon.

And Jeannie did not have it.

She could not sleep after that.

At first light, she counted the coins secreted beneath the floor, but there were never any more of them than the day before. She was so dismayed that she did not complete her chores; indeed, she forgot to feed the chickens twice.

Meanwhile, all the village was talking of Murdoch's hearing before the laird. It seemed all intended to make their way to Kilderrick to stand witness as Murdoch faced the wrath—or the justice—of the Silver Wolf at noon on Tuesday. After all, Murdoch had planned to abduct and kill the laird's infant son, by endeavoring to compel the seer to aid him. She had refused and he had been captured. He would spend a day and two nights in Kilderrick's dungeon before his reckoning, a situation Jeannie could not have endured.

"But why would he kill the boy?" she asked Tynan Smith, who had brought the tidings from Kilderrick village, as well as the laird's invitation that they all attend the hearing.

"To strike a blow to that father's heart," Tynan said grimly. Jeannie recalled that he and Nathalie now had a child of their own. "'Twas a wicked impulse, to be sure."

Jeannie could not help but think that 'twas a clever one, as well. Aye, the Laird of Kilderrick, that seemingly invincible warrior, had one weakness.

She wondered what the Laird of Kilderrick would surrender to ensure the safe return of his son. She wagered he might offer a great deal.

He might even offer sufficient to repay Eamon's debt to him.

And if the boy was never truly in danger, who was to know that truth?

Jeannie could not push the notion from her thoughts and indeed, its allure grew during her long wakeful night. By the morning of the hearing, Jeannie was resolved. She would secretly seize the boy while all attended the hearing, secure him somewhere, and wait.

She could blame the deed upon Murdoch Campbell and further blacken that man's name. She could insist, if caught, that Murdoch had threatened her in Eamon's absence, that she had unwillingly done as he demanded. Aye, she would not have to feign her fear of another mercenary, and she would insist that it was by her efforts alone that the boy survived.

No doubt the laird would find against him on this day, leaving Murdoch unable to protest any such accusation. An executed criminal could be blamed for all manner of foul deeds, and never defend himself against them. Jeannie could lead the laird triumphantly to his abandoned son on the morrow, and the laird, Jeannie was certain, would be quick to bestow a generous measure of his gratitude upon her.

'Twas perfect.

All she had to decide was where to hide the boy.

She took a great basket to Kilderrick that day, knowing she would need a means to hide the infant and carry it away. To explain the basket, she carried the last of her eggs as a gift to the laird, and even one of her hens that had ceased to lay. Though she would regret the loss of a dinner, 'twas a small sacrifice to see the future secured.

The party of villagers was heading to Kilderrick when Jeannie solved the last detail of her plan. She eyed the small hut on Nerida's allotment, the one that woman used to store honey and dried flowers.

Jeannie would leave the boy there, tucked safely in the darkness until any search of the village was over. No one would hear him, much less find him, and he would be both sheltered and safe from predators. She would have to silence him, but that would do him no injury.

After all, he would not be there long.

NYSSA SAW *the world through the eyes of another, and though she sensed that she knew this place. The woman huffed as she climbed a dark curving staircase, one that might have been familiar with its fitted stones and tight curves, one that might have been at Duncheann save that there had to be hundreds like it in Scotland alone. A swaddled babe was held against her breast, but there was some detail awry. She carried the infant with a measure of carelessness, as if it was a loaf of bread or a bundle of cloth. In her other hand, she held a candle aloft and the shadows fled from the swaying gold flame, infuriating Nyssa as the light disguised too much for her to be certain.*

She could hear the wind whistling through the chinks and the roar of the sea, not so distant. She could nigh feel the chill emanating from the stone and smell the salt-tinged air. It had to be Duncheann.

This had to be the small staircase that led to the solar, the second smaller one that led to the kitchens. Who was the woman? Did Nyssa see past, present, or future? She could not say.

The woman heaved a sigh when she reached the summit of the stairs and hastened through a portal, barely sparing the door a glimpse. Nyssa saw it, though, and recognized the wooden door with its heavy lock. A woman in the chamber caught her breath and called to this one in a whisper. They conferred, their voices so low that Nyssa could not distinguish their words. The darkness was infuriating, the shadows deep especially when the candle was set aside.

What scheme did they hatch? Who were they?

Then the woman who had been in the chamber gasped with vigor. Nyssa caught a glimpse of her fair hair, and saw the familiar embroidery on the cuff of her chemise. Elsa? Did she dream of Elsa?

Nyssa wished she could halt the dream for she did not wish to witness

Elsa's demise. *She had felt it immediately when it had occurred, and her despair had been overwhelming.*

The woman's voice rose in a cry of anguish and the new arrival hastened her to the bed, even as the blood appeared on the floor. Nyssa knew that bed, with its four pillars and its velvet curtains. She knew the deep blue hue of those draperies and the height of the bed, the softness of the mattress and the smoothness of the linens. The woman fetched the candle and Nyssa's heart leapt at the unexpected sight of her sister.

Elsa! As lovely as when she had drawn breath, the sight stole Nyssa's breath away. Elsa had been the older of the two, the beauty, the one who charmed every new acquaintance. She had been the bold one and the gifted one, and Nyssa ached anew with grief at her loss.

She watched as Elsa braced herself on the bed and took short breaths, gathering her strength before the next contraction. Nyssa had not witnessed this. She had not been permitted into the solar when Elsa labored the second time. So much was different from the first time, from Elsa's solitude to the darkness. The second daughter had been born during a winter storm, like a babe summoned out of a tempest. The first had been born on a midsummer afternoon.

There was only Mary to aid Elsa, stout Mary with her loyal heart, Mary the midwife from the village. She pushed up her sleeves, revealing a blue mark wrought long before by Gerda as a mark of her skill with midwifery. Meanwhile, Elsa struggled to catch her breath. The infant Mary had brought was abandoned on a chest as Mary whispered encouragement to Elsa.

Her sister had not labored so hard with the first daughter. Was something amiss?

The labor continued for what might have been hours, Elsa's screams alternating with Mary's murmured reassurance. The laird knocked at the door finally and Nyssa winced at the familiar sound of his voice. "What news?" Hugh demanded, impatience in his tone. "Has my son arrived?"

"My lady battles to bring him forth, my lord, but he is reluctant."

Hugh snorted, then his footsteps echoed on the stairs. The two women looked at the other very still infant and exchanged a nod. Again, Nyssa wondered at their scheme.

An exhausted Elsa lay back panting with her exertions, her fair hair stuck to her skin with perspiration, her face flushed and eyes glittering. A moan gathered in her throat as the next contraction began, then she tipped back her head and roared. She strained, struggling to push the child forth. Mary bent lower, obstructing Nyssa's view, caressing and coaxing, uttering soothing sounds of reassurance while Elsa caught her breath.

"Another," said Mary and Elsa screamed with the power of her next contraction. Her fingers gripped the linens fiercely and she moaned with anguish, her eyes closing when the contraction passed.

Mary became suddenly very still and Nyssa wished she could see. "No pushing," Mary advised then, hesitating only a moment before patting Elsa's knee. "Let the child do the work."

Something was amiss. Mary knew it but Elsa was too tired to care.

"I want it over," Elsa said, her teeth gritted. "I want it done."

"And 'twill be done in its time. A child comes when it will, you know as much."

Elsa opened her eyes to consider Mary, her gaze clear and commanding. She braced herself on one elbow, and pushed away the linens. Mary took a step back and Nyssa stared at the vast quantity of blood. It flowed from Elsa with too much vigor and the two women stared at it for a long moment. Nyssa saw Elsa's belly ripple with the next contraction, then her sister looked at the midwife.

"You must do as agreed," she said with heat.

Mary nodded. "Aye, my lady."

"You must not falter."

"Nay, my lady."

Elsa seized Mary's hand, her eyes wide and her voice low. "Tell no one."

Mary simply shook her head.

Then the contraction was upon Elsa, making her cry out again but with less vigor than before. Nyssa heard the babe come forth and saw her sister shudder with relief. Mary moved quickly then, fetching the other child and smearing it with the blood, ensuring it was between Elsa's thighs when the afterbirth began to emerge. In the meantime, she hastily swaddled the newly arrived babe, not taking the time to wash her completely. She cleaned out the babe's mouth and patted her back, prompting a cough from the infant.

'Twas then that Nyssa noticed Mary's hands, strong, capable and yet graceful, the fingertips blunt. This was where she had seen that child's hands before!

But she and Elsa had not known Mary when they were children. It made no sense, unless Elsa had kept a secret from her.

In the vision, Elsa's eyes were closing, her grip loosening on the linens as her blood flowed from her with terrible speed. Her breathing was shallow and she seemed to fade before Nyssa's eyes. Mary offered her the newborn child, but Elsa shook her head, pressing only the briefest kiss upon that babe's brow. Her tears began to flow then, even as Mary put the other infant in her arms. That child did not move and Nyssa realized it was dead.

Her sister had learned from the birth of her first daughter. Knowing she would deliver a second girl, Elsa had planned to deceive her husband. 'Twas a daring plot, one that showed her sister's audacity. Nyssa feared for its failure.

Though it nigh broke Nyssa's heart to witness her sister's final moments, still it was precious to see Elsa again. Now Nyssa hoped the dream would not end too soon—much less, in the way she remembered.

The midwife hastily extinguished several candles, plunging the room in greater shadows, then shook the newly-arrived babe. The infant gave a healthy cry, then was silenced with a rag and placed in a basket hidden in the shadows.

Footsteps sounded on the stairs and Hugh flung open the door, striding into the solar with obvious expectation.

"A girl, my lord," Elsa managed to whisper as his hand fell to the hilt of his dagger. She was pale and she breathed with difficulty but Nyssa saw the resolve in her. Doubtless she recalled his gesture the previous time, for she eased away the swaddling to show the babe's gender. She rocked it, as well, and Nyssa would not have guessed that she cradled a corpse.

"A girl?" Hugh's eyes flashed. "I demanded a boy of you!"

"And yet, we are blessed with another girl," Elsa said, offering the bloody child. Hugh took a step back in revulsion. "Perhaps your seed has not the vigor to create sons," she added, a hint of provocation in her tone. "Perhaps you will always father daughters."

Hugh's eyes flashed as he drew his dagger and stabbed the child in one savage gesture. Nyssa saw the glint of satisfaction in Elsa's expression and knew she had prodded him apurpose, so he would not look too closely. Mary gasped and snatched at the child, but he granted her a look and stabbed the babe again.

"Sir!" the midwife protested.

"I desire no daughters," Hugh said, his voice low and dangerous as he

waved the stained blade before Mary. That woman retreated with her hands raised. "I made this clear to my wife, but she has chosen to defy me in this matter."

"You must know, my lord, that a lady has no choice..."

"And you must know that my lady wife is a witch who foretold that she would bear only daughters unto me, just as her mother did to her sire."

Mary dropped her gaze.

Nyssa hoped the live child would remain silent.

"Get yourself from my abode with haste. There is no labor for a midwife in my keep on this night."

Mary lifted her chin. "The lady yet has need of me, my lord."

"I die, Mary," Elsa whispered. "Get yourself home to your own kin. There is naught to be done here."

"You die?" Hugh crossed to the bed and looked down upon her, finally making sense of all the blood before him. He covered his nose with his hand. "That resolves matters well," he said with undisguised satisfaction. "But then, you always were one to scheme."

"Let Mary take some of my clothes," Elsa entreated him, stretching out one hand toward him so that he recoiled. "She should be paid, and she has need of a heavy cloak like mine."

"What of your sister?"

"Nyssa already has one. Show some increment of charity, my lord, since you are unlikely to give Mary a coin for her assistance this night."

"For a daughter, born dead," he said with disdain, giving Mary a hot look. "There is no reason for reward in that. Take the cloak," he said with a dismissive gesture. "But swaddle the child first that there are no questions." He paused beside the bed to survey Elsa, who could only be conscious by force of will. "Farewell, my lady. You would have done better to have served my will. Perhaps your sister will be wiser."

Elsa gasped and sat up with dismay, then collapsed from the sudden effort. Her last breath was loud and Nyssa heard that she did not take another.

Hugh was gone.

Mary bent over Elsa, closing her eyes with a gentle thumb, then kissed her forehead. "Blessed be, my lady," she whispered. "Blessed be." The older woman was blinking back her tears as she turned from the bed.

She took the fur-lined cloak that Nyssa remembered well and wrapped it around herself. It was generously cut and so long that it nigh brushed the ground. 'Twas easy for Mary to disguise the satchel with the newly born infant beneath the copious folds of cloth. She stole one last glance at her lady, shook her head, seized the sole burning candle then hastened down the small staircase that led to the kitchens.

Leaving Elsa dead and in darkness.

NYSSA AWAKENED ABRUPTLY, her thoughts spinning. She had no doubt that she had witnessed the truth and though it had been painful to watch Elsa die, she marvelled at her sister's scheme.

Rana had survived.

This then was her path, to find her sister's daughter.

Where had Mary taken the babe?

And what had happened to her in the years since? Rana would be nine summers of age if she yet lived. What was she like? Where was she? She might have favored Elsa too much when she grew up. How far had Mary taken her from Duncheann? *Eight years.* Had Rana's gifts begun to make themselves known?

Or had Hugh found her and finished what he had begun?

The possibility was terrifying, but Nyssa could not believe 'twas so. Nay, she had dreamed of a young girl with fair hair, green eyes and Elsa's smile. She had thought that a vision of Elsa as a young girl—but what if she had dreamed of Rana?

What if Elsa's daughter needed Nyssa's aid?

CHAPTER 7

$\mathcal{M}$urdoch lost track of time. He dozed at intervals then was wakeful, the seer's tale swirling in his thoughts in some moments, the wondrous heat of her kiss flooding through him at others. Far from forgetting her, he was haunted by her.

Yet she did not return to him again.

MURDOCH DREAMED OF FIRE, a fire that ravaged all within sight. It burned so hot that his skin blistered when he was within a dozen steps of it. The wall of flames was all he could see, high and brilliant orange, shooting sparks against the sky. The light of it was blinding, the crackle of it terrifying. It could not be slowed, much less halted, and it steadily, relentlessly consumed Murdoch's surroundings.

He should have fled. He should have made for the sea. But instead, he was filled with an urgency to walk through the flames, to plunge into their depths. He knew that the seer was on the other side, though he could not see or hear her. He knew that the fire sought to annihilate her, and he knew that he was her sole hope.

He lunged toward the blaze, knowing he could not abandon her, and braced himself for scorching pain.

. . .

THE TRAP DOOR creaked as it was opened far above and a beam of light landed upon Murdoch's face, startling him to wakefulness. "Murdoch Campbell, the Laird of Kilderrick would judge with you!" cried a man with a deep voice.

Murdoch leapt to his feet, dazed as his heart thundered in his chest. All was cold darkness around him.

Where were the flames?

What burned to ash?

And where was the seer?

He felt a dread then, that she had not visited him again for a reason. He feared that some ill had befallen her. Just like his dream, he would not be able to aid her, and this filled Murdoch with a sense of failure beyond all else.

'Twas nonsense. He pushed a hand through his hair and stood, prepared to meet the laird, but there was an uncertainty in his heart that would not be dispelled.

THERE WERE VERY few moments when Maximilian de Vries missed his days as the Silver Wolf, leading mercenaries under the banner of the Compagnie Rouge. He was more than content with Kilderrick; he adored his wife, Alys; he was awed by the blessing of their son, Michael; he derived tremendous satisfaction in his ability to improve the circumstances of those beneath his hand. He liked the stability of living in one place. He was proud that he had led his half-brothers Rafael and Amaury to a land where they had found similar contentment.

And then there was Murdoch Campbell, the proverbial thorn in Maximilian's side. He did not blame the man for killing Jean le Beau— indeed, he might have thanked him for that deed—but he did find it irksome that Murdoch declined to be reconciled with him.

On a day such as this, when yet again Murdoch had conspired against him, when Alys was distressed by the prospects for her child-hood friend—even acknowledging his guilt—and the better part of the village of Rowan Fell had arrived to witness whatsoever Maximilian might do, he felt a tiny yearning for his former life. Once, his word had been law. Once, might had made right. Once, he had not needed to balance his own desires, or even his temper, with the prospect of stability and security.

Having Murdoch executed would be the simplest solution for his own peace of mind. But as Maximilian sat in his chair in the great hall and surveyed the faces of his villeins and tenants, he knew that was precisely what they dreaded. Some of them must have known Murdoch as a boy. More than a few of them harbored a fondness for the man. Many, quite likely, also blamed Maximilian for the death of Rupert Campbell, Murdoch's adopted father and a man held in esteem by all. He knew affection for him was not universal in his holding.

He was keenly aware of the counsel Alys had given them years before, that a laird must defend the interests of those beneath his hand, as well as see to his own. He surveyed the villagers who had gathered, seeking a sense of their allegiances. Nerida had come without her grand-daughter and her expression was stern. He would wager that she had sympathies for Murdoch, as did Cormac Smith, that older man fairly scowling at Maximilian. His son, Tynan, the smith at Kilderrick strove to look impassive, but Maximilian guessed that his alliances were torn—his wife, Nathalie, after all, held their own young son. He might have taken Murdoch's side if Michael had not been threatened. Maximilian's perusal of the company gave him the sense that a decided share of older residents of Rowan Fell favored Murdoch or the memory of him—or that of Rupert Campbell.

Maximilian drummed his fingers, knowing he had to choose with care. There was a balance to be struck, to be sure. Perhaps he could see Murdoch banished, though that offered little guarantee that his opponent would not return to finish what he had begun. He could brand the other man as a criminal, ordering the removal of his ear or nose, even his eye, but Maximilian shirked from such a dire choice.

He had offered Murdoch alliance.

He had offered reconciliation.

And in a way, Maximilian respected that Murdoch was steadfast to his vow. Murdoch had sworn to take a reckoning from both Jean le Beau and Maximilian for crimes against his mother and the man who had raised him. Maximilian admired Murdoch's constancy, despite its inconvenience.

Had their places been reversed, he would have done the same.

And hence, Murdoch's quest for vengeance was the perfect collision for Maximilian between the life of a mercenary and the responsibilities of a laird.

There was no winning the situation, so far as Maximilian could see. He watched as the prisoner was brought into the hall, his hands bound behind his back. Murdoch's plaid was dirty, undoubtedly from his night in the dungeon. His auburn hair was tousled and there was dried blood on his temple and his shoulder. Otherwise, he appeared to be unharmed. His lips were set in a grim line, though, and his blue eyes— of the same hue as Maximilian's own—burned with a fury that was both familiar and characteristic.

Maximilian heard Alys catch her breath beside him. She, too, was torn, and had appealed to him again the previous night. Maximilian had not been amused to learn that she had visited his prisoner, though at least she had not entered the dungeon. The man might have seized the opportunity to have an asset for bargaining.

That would have been simpler. Maximilian would have killed Murdoch without remorse if the other man had dared to threaten Alys and no one would have blamed him for it.

Royce left the prisoner standing alone before Maximilian, who had not seen a man so unrepentant in a long time.

"What am I to do with you, Murdoch Campbell?" he asked mildly, uncertain of the answer himself. "You threatened the life of my son and that cannot be dismissed, yet you have history at Kilderrick and there are those who hold you in regard here."

"I suppose you will see me dead, lest I do the same to you."

"What would you do, if our places were exchanged?"

Murdoch smiled a little. "Cut out your black heart and feed it to you." He spoke without hesitation.

There was a rustle of agitation amongst the townspeople at this, but Maximilian smiled. He understood this impulse well. "'Twould not be fair to cut you down while you are bound," he said. "Though our brother Rafael might favor that course."

Murdoch snorted. "Without a doubt."

"I suppose that our other brother, Amaury, would issue a challenge to a tournament."

Murdoch nodded, a gleam lighting his eyes as if he savored the prospect. "Aye, that would be his way."

"Four brothers, similar in skills but varying in methods," Maximilian said. "How interesting that you and I are the pair in complete agreement. I, too, see the merit of abandoning this chair, crossing the hall and slicing out your heart." He touched the hilt of the dagger on his belt, knowing he held the attention of all. "I'm not convinced that I would feed it to you, though. That seems overzealous."

Murdoch chuckled with apparent reluctance. "And perhaps not suitable for this audience," he said gruffly, prompting Maximilian to chuckle in his turn.

How could he end the days of a man so much like himself, and one with a greater right to abide in Kilderrick than he?

"I have offered you alliance," he reminded his prisoner and Murdoch nodded.

"Aye, more than once."

"Did you ever expect Kilderrick to fall to your hand? Is that the true obstacle between us?"

Murdoch shook his head. "'Twas Rupert who spoke of that, when Alys and I were young comrades, but his was the sentimentality of an old man." He spoke with great fondness and Maximilian was reminded of his own affection for Yves, the châtelain who had been like a father to him. That man stood at the far side of the hall, listening avidly. What would Maximilian have done to any man who injured Yves? He knew he would not have rested until restitution was made, and only the death of Yves' attacker at his own hand would suffice.

He frowned. "You were not here that night," he said.

"Rupert sent me away when word came of your approach. There was talk of the army arriving, and of the savage mercenary who led it."

Maximilian nodded. There had been a time when he had enjoyed the cultivation of dread. "I arrived at a keep devoid of sentries or guards."

"They had left Laird Robert long before."

"An unsympathetic man, and one said to dabble in the dark arts."

"He was wicked to his marrow, of that there can be no doubt."

"And yet your father served him faithfully."

Murdoch shrugged. "He reminded me that we had a home, shelter and food, as many did not in those days. It was cause for gratitude." He smiled a little. "And he had pledged to serve the laird. His vow was all to him."

They returned to the merit of a sworn word. Maximilian had to believe there was a solution but he could not yet discern it, so he talked. "And so, you departed, but Alys remained."

"She was bidden to leave, as well."

"Her defiance does not surprise me," Maximilian said mildly and a few in the company smiled and whispered. "But I arrived to find only an old man before the door to the laird's chamber." He held up a finger. "One man, well beyond his most active years."

Murdoch was taut, his jaw tight.

Maximilian considered him. "Would you believe me if I confessed I did not know what to do?"

"Nay," Murdoch said, biting off the word. "You were too young to hesitate before easy prey."

"I cannot blame you for believing as much, but I did hesitate, Murdoch. I had never struck down a man obviously so much weaker than myself. He had a knife but he did not wield it with any authority. He was terrified. I could smell his fear. But he was determined, as well, to serve his master. He was prepared to die in fulfilling his duty."

Murdoch bowed his head.

"In keeping his word," Maximilian added quietly. Murdoch did not look up. "Just as you are on this day. I admire that, Murdoch. I respect your desire to avenge your father, but I tell you that I did not touch him."

Murdoch looked up, his gaze intense in his surprise. "A convenient tale," he murmured.

"He fell before my very eyes. He dropped the knife. He clutched his chest and bared his teeth in agony. Before I could reach his side, he was dead. He died of fright, Murdoch, not by the bite of my blade."

"So you say," that man said beneath his breath.

"So I say, and there is no one to support my tale or surrender another. The sole person remaining in the keep was Robert Armstrong. I did not strike him down either, but I had a greater role in his demise." Maximilian tasted the curiosity of the assembly and addressed them. "I bound him to a chair, intent upon learning the location of his treasury. He ranted and made little sense, and I thought a touch of fire would encourage coherence. Instead, he commanded the blaze somehow and it leapt higher than should have been possible."

Maximilian shook his head, still seeing the sudden fury of the flames and the hall fell silent as everyone listened to him. "The bed hangings were alight, the tapestries, the rug upon the floor, then the wooden room began to burn. He laughed as the sparks fell among us, as the room became a pit of flame, and still he made no sense in his ravings. I barely escaped with my life." He reached for Alys' hand, only to find her scarred fingers cold. "While Alys, hidden in the cellar unbeknownst to me, paid a higher toll. I did not kill either of them, Murdoch, neither the honorable seneschal nor the wicked laird." He studied his prisoner and knew what he would do. "Though you did the world the favor of killing Jean le Beau, and I am inclined to forgive much for that deed."

"I do not understand," Murdoch said when Maximilian did not immediately continue.

"I would seek a compromise with you, a bargain, if you will."

"What manner of bargain?" The prisoner's suspicions were clear.

"You will abandon any intentions toward my wife and son and I will let you survive this day. Indeed, I will release you upon your sworn pledge to do them no harm."

There was a murmur in the hall at this offer and Murdoch frowned. "And what of the dispute between us?"

"I invite you to offer a solution, Murdoch Campbell. If you would fight hand-to-hand, prepared to accept the winner as victor, I will set the date for our battle. If you insist upon your quest for vengeance, I can see you maimed, exiled or executed. You could choose to banish yourself from Kilderrick, abandoning your quest to pursue your fate elsewhere."

"I could do as much and return to assault you."

"You could and I would invite you to try."

Alys caught her breath, her grip tightening on Maximilian's hand.

Maximilian smiled. "But you would not lie and so discredit your honor."

Murdoch straightened.

Maximilian continued. "I will release you thus if you give your word."

Murdoch inhaled, his glare becoming brighter. "And then what?" he whispered, proof that Maximilian was right about the value of his vow.

"If you would reconcile yourself to my place as Laird of Kilderrick and put aside your animosity, I would welcome your sworn pledge of allegiance."

"Why must I choose rather than you decree?"

"You know why, Murdoch. Because my wife is yet fond of you and I would not vex her overmuch." He smiled again and there was another ripple of laughter, though this one did not last long. The atmosphere in the hall was too tense.

Murdoch frowned. "If I pledged to you and Kilderrick, what would I do in this hall?"

"You need not be in this hall, unless it were your preference. I have need of good fighting men at all times. I have need of spies and those who gather tidings for me. Indeed, I welcome your suggestion. What have you to offer me, Murdoch Campbell?"

Something lit in Murdoch's expression, something that Maximilian had not expected to see. It was as if his prisoner had an idea, one he found of great appeal. He turned and surveyed those gathered in the hall, as he had not before, his gaze landing upon Nyssa. She wore a blue kirtle and her expression was wary.

What was her alliance? Murdoch had threatened both her and Dorcha, yet Maximilian knew she had visited the prisoner at least twice. Did she believe she could dispel his anger?

More importantly, did Maximilian imagine that Murdoch's gaze lingered on her, or that the seer's color rose crimson over her cheeks? To be sure, their gazes held for a long moment, then Murdoch pivoted to face Maximilian proudly. His decision, evidently, had been made.

Maximilian was curious beyond all.

"Where is your sheriff?" Murdoch demanded.

Maximilian straightened with interest at this unexpected query. Eamon had not come to the hall on this day. Maximilian had seen Eamon's wife, Jeannie, earlier, but now there was no sign of her. How curious. Jeannie seldom missed any incident. Maximilian had not specifically summoned either of them—he had sent a general invitation to Rowan Fell—but he had been surprised that the sheriff and his wife had not been among the curious come to observe Murdoch's hearing.

"I do not know," he admitted. "Though I would wager that you do."

"I do not, not as yet, but I will find your sheriff, in exchange for my life," Murdoch offered.

How very, *very* interesting.

Nyssa smiled, which was even more intriguing.

"This very day?" Maximilian asked.

Murdoch shook his head. "I demand a week."

"And what of your word to accept me as laird?"

"You will not have it, for I will swear no pledge I cannot keep."

The company whispered at that, but Maximilian had not expected otherwise. He waited, considering his course, as the hall filled with watchful silence.

Murdoch took a breath. "But I will swear that our dispute lies between you and I, that I will not injure either your wife or your son."

'Twas a compromise, but one Maximilian was inclined to accept. He had to gamble in this. Maximilian assessed Nyssa's pleasure, Murdoch's defiance, Alys' concern and wagered that he might triumph on the proposed terms.

A week. Even if Murdoch had no intention of retrieving Eamon, in a week, the other man could be distant. If Murdoch intended to flee, Maximilian had no quibble with that choice. If Murdoch intended to hide and attack Maximilian in surprise, Maximilian would not be surprised. If Murdoch meant to find Eamon in time for that man to pay his debt, that possibility would not be unwelcome either.

The matter could be concluded in seven mere days.

And Alys and Michael would be omitted from Murdoch's quest for vengeance. That alone made the wager worth accepting.

Maximilian nodded to Royce, who scowled even as he stepped

forward to unbind Murdoch's hands. The prisoner had no weapon, but Maximilian was alert as he left his chair and strode toward his former prisoner.

"I accept your terms, Murdoch Campbell," he said and offered his hand.

Murdoch was rubbing his wrists, but he looked at Maximilian's proffered hand, then glanced at the mark on the wrist of the other. Doubtless he recalled the creation of that scar, and the pledge sworn as three of the brothers pledged to defend each other.

"Perhaps there is a better way to seal our alliance," Maximilian suggested and reached for the hilt of his knife, intending to make a blood bond.

"Nay," Murdoch said and offered his right hand, his gaze colliding with Maximilian's. His resolve was clear. "Our current agreement will suffice."

Maximilian smiled. The matter was between they two, Alys and Michael safe, and 'twas better thus. The adversaries shook hands, each with as firm a grip as the other. They were of similar height and build, thanks to Jean le Beau, but Murdoch's coloring had to favor his mother's own—just as Maximilian's favored that of his own mother.

"What was her name?" Maximilian asked impulsively, his voice low.

Murdoch was visibly surprised but his eyes narrowed in understanding. "Gwendolyn," he admitted.

"Is she buried in Rowan Fell?"

The other man nodded once.

"Then I will order masses sung for her soul."

Murdoch was wary. "Why? You need not do as much and I will not be in your debt."

"You must see, Murdoch, that we are two of a kind. I would be allies instead of enemies, and so I begin by honoring what is precious to you, the memory of your mother."

Their gazes clung for a long moment until Maximilian saw uncertainty dawn within Murdoch's eyes.

Murdoch averted his gaze, frowned and nodded once. "Seven days," he reiterated.

"And not one longer," Maximilian said. "For Eamon is due at my court on the full moon, to surrender the balance of the tithes he collected for the laird over fifteen years. Let us say sunset on the seventh day."

Murdoch nodded, their gazes clinging for a potent moment.

Then the other man turned to Royce. He touched a fingertip to the empty scabbard on his belt, and Royce grimaced with displeasure. Maximilian retreated to his chair, keeping an eye upon Murdoch all the while. En route, Alys threw herself at him in pleasure and he caught her close, even as a murmur of conversation erupted in the hall.

"Will he do it?" she whispered, her eyes wide.

"I cannot say," Maximilian admitted, watching his prisoner leave his hall as chatter broke out amongst the company. "But I have been merciful this time, which means that if there is a next time, I need not be." He raised a fingertip to her lips before she could speak. "Know better, my Alys, than to ask it of me." Their gazes locked and she nodded once in agreement.

When Maximilian looked up at the company, he noticed that Nyssa had vanished as well. He missed a detail there and he wondered at its import.

He did not have long to consider the matter, for within moments Alys discovered that Michael was missing. She sought the boy and found his nursemaid struck down. The boy was gone, gone as surely as Murdoch Campbell.

"Maximilian!" she cried, her heartbreak in her voice.

The fiend had succeeded after all! Maximilian roared for his horse, determined to run the villain to the ground without delay.

This time, he would not be swayed from what had to be done.

MURDOCH DID NOT DARE to believe in his freedom, not until he walked through the gates of Kilderrick keep without obstruction, not until he had continued until the keep was far behind him. Villagers were leaving the hall, chatting to each other and marveling at the laird's choice, but he moved with purpose toward the portal. More than one clapped him on the back or insisted that he or she had always believed in his innocence. Tynan Smith offered him labor at the smithy in Kilderrick village, much to Murdoch's astonishment.

Murdoch was touched to realize that any of them cared a whit for him. He glanced back to see Nyssa watching him though she only nodded when their gazes met—as if to advise him again to believe in goodness.

He was not yet certain how much goodness was within himself.

He had no qualms in hunting Eamon, for he doubted there was much innocence in that man's soul. If the price of freedom was Eamon's surrender to the Silver Wolf, that was a price Murdoch could willingly pay.

His own quest had been delayed already, and he could only pursue it if he was out of Kilderrick's dungeon. Compromise was not the same as failure.

But first he had to leave Kilderrick, then he had to allay the suspicions of the Silver Wolf.

The gatekeeper nodded to Murdoch when he approached the gates of Kilderrick, but did not stand or obstruct his path. His heart in his throat, Murdoch stepped through the portal and paused, blinking at the fierce midday sunlight. The sky was a clear blue. The wind was crisp from the north and he could almost hear Rupert's voice, forecasting snow. He took a deep breath, savoring his liberation, then marched onward.

The memory was sufficient to bring tears to his own eyes and he strode down the slope without a backward glance. Rupert had died in this keep, not far from where Murdoch had been imprisoned. If he had been a man to believe in ghosts, he might have felt his father's presence close at hand.

Instead, he thought of the seer—which was folly.

The Liddelwater ran shallow and fast to the east of the keep, and it sparkled as it flowed south. He had meant to follow its course out of Kilderrick, but one glimpse of the water and he realized he was not even as clean as his plaid. He knew of a clearing to the south that would be in the sunshine.

He made for it without delay, ensured that he had not been followed, then stripped down and waded into the water. It only rose to his thighs but the chill was sufficient to steal his breath away. Indeed, it lent speed to his task. He scrubbed his plaid and draped it over the branch of a tree in sunlight to dry. He scrubbed himself with vigor, not just removing the mire of the past month and the muck of Kilderrick's dungeon but feeling cleansed of far more than earthy grime.

Murdoch was cleaning his nails, running the tip of his dagger beneath the edge of each one, when he heard the horses thundering closer. They rode with unholy haste, the sound making him wary. He stood, clad only in his damp chemise, and turned toward the sound. The Silver Wolf, fully armored, burst through the cover of the forest and charged toward him on his black destrier. He pulled the beast to a halt and flung up his helm with an impatient gesture, his gaze burning with fury.

"Where is he?" he demanded of Murdoch, even as he directed the men who accompanied him to search the area. They pulled down his plaid and kicked his boots aside, striding through the gorse with more than a measure of their commander's urgency.

"Who?" Murdoch asked, genuinely puzzled.

The Silver Wolf rode closer, bearing down on Murdoch. The force of his will was considerable, but Murdoch held his ground.

"Michael," he said though his teeth. "My son."

Murdoch shrugged. "I wager he is where he belongs," he said, realizing that he used Nyssa's words. The Silver Wolf's eyes blazed with fury. "In his mother's embrace."

"Nay, he is not," the Silver Wolf snapped. "He has been seized and taken from the keep. He has been abducted and perhaps worse. Where is he?"

"I cannot say. I know naught of this," Murdoch said. "I have been here. Alone." He held up his hands to show that he had been washing himself. He saw that the laird was not convinced. "Before that, I stood before you in your hall," he reminded the Silver Wolf. "When would I have seized the boy?"

"You might have an accomplice," the Silver Wolf said, his agitation more than clear. Murdoch had to avert his gaze. He had never seen the Silver Wolf fearful, not in any situation, and the sight of the man's terror for his son was disturbing. Murdoch could not help but consider how love could destroy a man's defenses better than any act of war.

Ha. Now he thought like the seer! Her influence over him was more than clear and he strove to harden his will against the Silver Wolf.

"You threatened his life just days ago," that man reminded him. "Who else would so imperil my son?" He drew his sword and aimed the point at Murdoch. "Where is he?"

Murdoch shook his head. "I do not know," he said, then seeing the Silver Wolf's doubt, he raised his hand. "I know naught of the boy's situation, I swear it to you."

"Upon what will you swear?"

"My mother's grave. My father's honor. You have shown me mercy and I would not reward that with treachery."

"Even though you still would willingly cut me down."

Murdoch inclined his head. "But not the boy. I have vowed not to touch the boy, and swore as much just moments ago."

Their gazes locked and held for long moments, the company behind the Silver Wolf seemingly not daring to breathe. Murdoch understood that the Silver Wolf doubted his pledge, and in all fairness, he might have done the same.

But he was innocent of any abduction of the child. He did not so much as blink.

Finally, the Silver Wolf sheathed his sword and shook his head. "If you have killed him after I have shown you mercy, I will slice you to ribbons myself and I will ensure that the task is done slowly." He spoke with deliberation, his gaze boring into Murdoch's, then gathered his stallion's reins. The beast cast back its head and whinnied, then the Silver Wolf turned the steed and they galloped away. "To Rowan Fell!" he cried and his guards took up the cry.

Aye, the villagers could be the sole other candidates for this deed.

But why imperil the boy? Murdoch could make no sense of it.

All the same, he had no inclination to linger within proximity of the Silver Wolf after that encounter, so he garbed himself. His plaid was still damp, but it would dry in the sunshine as he walked. The boy would doubtless be found shortly, and he had to discover the location of the sheriff. He would not yet abandon his refuge in Rowan Fell, for it was an ideal place to watch Eamon's abode, but he must ensure that he was not discovered there yet.

Murdoch walked to the south, following the path of the river. He took the track heading west to Langholm, arriving there in the late afternoon. His feet were sore and his plaid was still damp at the hem. Perhaps that was why he felt chilled. 'Twas market day and he mingled with those who had gathered in the square, his belly grumbling at the food for sale. Sadly, he had no coin and he would not steal. He gained a ride in a cart headed north toward Hawick, jumping off it at the bend just before the small track that led into Rowan Fell from the west.

He was thinking of the apples in his saddlebag with great anticipation.

Long before the village was within sight, Murdoch descended to the stream and the cluster of growth that marked its path. The shadows were already growing longer, the days short this time of the year. With his plaid pulled over his shoulders and the gorse surrounding him, he doubted he would be discerned at all. The hoofprints from that party were frozen into the mud, proof that he had not imagined their presence.

When Nerida's small hut was in view, Murdoch waited in the shelter of the gorse to ensure that he was not observed. The sky was streaked with brilliant hues behind him as the sun set in splendor. A light glowed in the window of Nerida's larger hut, and he wagered that Dara was at her sewing beside it. He heard the bleating of Rona's goats as they were urged into her hut. Smoke curled into the skies, rising from fires in the cottages. A light burned in Jeannie's kitchen and her chickens had been secured. He smelled a rabbit stew and his stomach growled, though there would be none such for him.

Content that he was unobserved, he left the stream and moved quickly to the hut, opening the door and slipping into the protective shadows within. Only once the door was secured behind him did Murdoch breathe a sigh of relief. He smelled the honey and the dried flowers that hung from the rafters, felt a welcome sense of homecoming—then, as surely as he knew his own name, Murdoch realized that he was not alone.

Something stirred in the shadows within the hut.

～

Murdoch drew his dagger and eased forward as his eyes became accustomed to the diminished light in the hut. The windows were covered so even during the day, the interior of the hut was always darkened. At this hour, the shadows were deep. He slept in the loft above, but he had to cross the lower level regularly and knew the location of every item within it. He seldom dared to light a candle within the hut.

He found the basket immediately. It was set upon an old table, one that was pushed against the wall. The table was sturdy but too heavy to move easily. Nerida sorted herbs upon it, braiding lavender wands and bundling herbs to hang from the rafters to dry. In his memory, it had always occupied the same place and he wondered whether it had been built there.

As the table was familiar, the basket upon it was not. It was not a small basket, but one of goodly size and covered.

Something rustled within it.

Had Nerida left the basket for him to find? If that had been the case, he would have expected it to contain a meal, and one that did not move.

What could its contents be? A litter of kittens? Rabbits snared in the garden? A stolen chicken? Murdoch could not guess, and he had no notion why any of those items would be here, in this seemingly abandoned hut.

He stood beside the table, intent upon the unfamiliar basket. He watched and he listened, but nothing emerged from it, struck him or lunged toward him.

Its contents simply rustled.

Long moments later, he sheathed his dagger then carefully lifted the cloth.

He stared, for the basket contained the missing son of the Laird of Kilderrick.

The infant's cheeks were wet and his face was flushed. He scowled as he squirmed in the confinement of the basket, his hands clenched in fists. His frustration was palpable. There was a cloth stuffed into his mouth, one that was wet from his saliva but ensured that he could make no sound.

Michael. The boy's name was Michael.

But days before, Murdoch had desired this child to be delivered to him, intent upon ensuring the babe's demise. Now he looked upon the helpless infant, knowing it would be simple to do as he had threatened, but unable to injure a helpless child.

Michael's eyes were as blue as those of the Silver Wolf, as blue as Murdoch's own. Murdoch blinked in surprise at the revelation that should not have truly been one.

Not only was the infant vulnerable, but he was kin. Michael was Murdoch's nephew, a precious addition to his few relations who yet drew breath.

Murdoch gently removed the cloth that silenced the boy, setting it aside as Michael hiccupped and coughed. He wiped some spittle from the boy's cheek with a fingertip and Michael's breath hitched in fear. The boy's skin was so soft, softer than the fur on a hare's belly, softer than the petals of a flower. His gaze fixed upon Murdoch, his expression accusing and his mouth working soundlessly.

Aye, his trust of his fellows must be low in this moment. Michael had to be thirsty and hungry, and Murdoch did not doubt that he was uncertain and afraid. How long had he been in the basket? It had been half a day or more since the Silver Wolf had confronted Murdoch in search of the boy.

Alys must be worried beyond all. Even the Silver Wolf's fear had been clear, and Murdoch knew that warrior hid his emotions with ease.

He might have wagered that the boy had cried himself out of tears, but Michael's lip trembled as he kicked hard, then he opened his mouth to bellow.

Murdoch responded immediately, wanting only to soothe the infant. He lifted Michael from the basket, discovering that he knew how to nestle a child close against his chest. One hand rose to the back of the boy's head, the other supported his back, and Murdoch rocked him as if he had been rocking children to sleep all his life. To his own astonishment, what fell from Murdoch's lips was the beginning of a Gaelic lullaby. He sang the first line without considering the choice, then wondered how he even knew the tune and words.

With sudden clarity, he recalled days when he had run from Kilderrick to Rowan Fell, evenings spent by the fire in this very cottage as Nerida sang to her grand daughter. He had always come without Alys, whenever she had been collected by Morag to visit her father. Nerida's home had been his refuge even then. Murdoch recalled Nerida rocking that child, the child lost to the plague along with both parents. It had been so long ago, and he had nigh forgotten those evenings, as sweet as they had been.

He thought of his cousins, now dead and buried along with their lively child, his cousins whose daughter Dara had never known them. He felt such a well of solitude that he tucked the boy between his elbow and chest, rocking him as he murmured the lullaby. The boy's skin was cool and Murdoch made to tuck the blanket more closely around him.

Michael seized Murdoch's finger so abruptly that Murdoch jumped. That small hand closed around Murdoch's finger like a vice, then Michael put Murdoch's fingertip into his mouth. He suckled hard, his breath slowing and his eyelashes fluttering as if the contact reassured him. Michael's gums were hard though he had no teeth as yet, but his strength was considerable for his size.

Murdoch smiled despite himself. Such fragility and ferocity, both combined in one small being. Aye, this was Alys' son. A tide of protectiveness stirred within Murdoch, an inclination that had long been forgotten, and filled him with new purpose.

A defender of widows and children. Murdoch smiled as the seer's words echoed in his thoughts. He held the future within his grasp, and as Nyssa said, its promise was far more important than correcting the injuries of the past.

Indeed, he was awed by the marvel that was this one small child.

"You must have a fair hunger to favor the taste of that," he told Michael, who bit a little harder on his fingertip and seemed almost to smile. They watched each other warily in the shadows for a long moment, then Murdoch felt the boy shiver.

"You must be cold," he murmured to the child, nestling him closer. The boy's cheek was against Murdoch's chest, where his heartbeat would be loudest. Murdoch hummed the lullaby as he retrieved his fur-lined cloak and tucked it around the boy. He sang another verse, held the child close and rocked him gently. Michael hiccupped and drooled, then settled against Murdoch and kicked his feet contentedly as he held fast to that finger. Murdoch sang another verse softly and the boy giggled.

His trust was complete.

And humbling.

Murdoch watched until Michael dozed, aware of his own intention to destroy this very child, and knew he could not do it. He would never do it. It was as if Michael saw the truth of his heart, just as Nyssa had done, provoking Murdoch to realize that he was not the man he believed himself to be. He straightened and looked around, wondering how Michael had come to be in this place, then knew it did not matter.

There was only one detail of import. Murdoch had to see Michael returned to where he belonged.

In his mother's own embrace.

It was the least he owed his childhood friend.

He suspected that Nyssa would not be surprised by his choice, and that made Murdoch Campbell smile.

CHAPTER 8

*I*t did not take long for Jeannie to doubt the merit of her plan.
She had feared that there might be a search in Rowan Fell
for the missing boy, but she had not anticipated the Silver Wolf's fury.
He might have been an avenging angel come to smite all those who
dared to defy him. Every house was entered by the laird and his men,
every cupboard and trunk opened, every barn examined and every
person questioned. He was a tempest, a man whose fear could not be
mistaken any more than his need to find his child.

He was the man they had once believed him to be, but he became
thus only out of terror for his only son.

His manner struck terror into Jeannie's heart. Nay, there would be
no ransom paid and no forgiveness offered, even if the boy was found
hale. If any dire fate befell the laird's son, if the child had so much as a
bruise upon his return, the person responsible would pay a high fee.
She no longer imagined that relief would result in the laird's kindness.

Yet she dared not retrieve the boy until the Silver Wolf left Rowan
Fell and all the villagers had retired for the night.

Jeannie could only pray that the laird did not find the child's hiding
place.

The man was perceptive, though, cursedly so.

"What is that?" he demanded of Nerida when the village had been turned inside out to no avail. He pointed at the second smaller hot on the beekeeper's allotment and Jeannie's very blood ran cold.

"My former home," Nerida said.

"Why do you have two cottages?" he asked, for evidently he did not know the history.

Nerida's lips tightened. "I came to this one as a bride, then my husband built the smaller one for us when our son married." She swallowed.

"But you have no son," the laird said with confusion.

Nerida lifted her chin. "The plague took them all, my lord—husband, son, my son's wife and their older child, a boy." She placed a hand on the shoulder of her grand-daughter, Dara, who dropped her gaze before the laird. "I moved back up the hill to raise Dara in this house, and here we remain."

"And there is naught within that one?"

Nerida shook her head. "Honey. Dried flowers and herbs. No more and no less, my lord."

To Jeannie's surprise, the older woman held the laird's gaze, almost in challenge. It was sufficient to make Jeannie wonder if there *was* someone in the hut.

But who might it be?

She had seen no one.

If she survived this day, she would watch her neighbor more closely.

"And what of Eamon?" the laird demanded of Jeannie, his gaze locking upon her.

She took a step backward and fumbled over her story, though she had planned for this query. "He visits his kin, my laird, to the west of Hawick. Doubtless he will be home again soon."

"He had best be returned by the full moon," the laird said tartly and Jeannie nodded.

"Of course, my laird."

"He will not evade the repayment of this debt, and I hope he has sufficient wit n ot to even try."

Jeannie nodded, swallowing at this evidence that the laird had no more mercy to spare.

Then he spun away, sending Royce to check the smith's cottage again and leaving two men to stand guard in the village. He mounted his steed to return to Kilderrick, his displeasure evident.

Jeannie waited with impatience for Royce to ride after his laird and for the men guarding the village to accept the priest's invitation to dine with him. She waited until the village was silent, all the residents within their homes. She waited until the darkness had fallen and the livestock had been secured for the night, until only the sliver of moon would witness her deed.

Only then did she creep out the back door of her own cottage and steal down to the stream. Jeannie ensured that she was hidden in the gorse as she made her way closer to Nerida's small hut, almost stumbling in her haste. How she would contrive to return the boy was a scheme she had yet to form. For the moment, she had to retrieve him and defend him.

She dashed to the portal. Once inside, she heard the thunder of her own heart. She willed her eyes to adjust to the darkness as she felt her way toward the table where she had left the child.

The basket was empty, the boy vanished as surely as if he had never been there at all.

Jeannie stood utterly still in disbelief. He had not walked away himself! She ran her hands inside the basket, as if her eyes might deceive her. She looked under the basket and around the hut. She looked under the table and bent to pick up the sole item there. 'Twas the cloth with which she had silenced the child.

Who had found him?

Who had taken him?

Did that person know what she had done? Jeannie quaked in fear and she hastened home, knowing she had to contrive a bold plan in her own defense.

∾

KILDERRICK WAS IN UPROAR.

Nyssa had hoped to follow Murdoch to his refuge and confer with him about Rana, but she dared not leave Alys when all was awry.

The keep had been searched from top to bottom. The stables had been turned out and Kilderrick village had been scrutinized as well. Though Nyssa tended the maid and the lump on her temple, she heard all of the tidings. They two were in the solar, with a very agitated Alys.

"'Tis my fault," insisted the maid yet again.

"Nay, nay," Nyssa replied soothingly. "Lie back and do not strain yourself."

"Who was there?" Alys demanded of the maid once more. She was pale as she paced the chamber, her arms folded tightly around herself. "Who was the last person you saw?"

"I do not know, my lady!" the maid said, then began to weep anew. "I saw you. You surrendered Michael to me then went to the hall. I was alone in the chamber and he began to stir. I did not wish for him to disturb the laird's hearing, so I walked with him. I sang to him. He was hungry, my lady."

"And I was not here," Alys said, speaking through her teeth. Nyssa saw that the milk had stained Alys' kirtle, a sign that she was late in nursing her son, but did not mention as much. Alys seemed oblivious to it.

"My lady, he is always hungry," the maid said.

"You cannot feed him all the time," Nyssa contributed. "You should not blame yourself."

Alys only paced with greater speed and agitation. "I should not have left him, not with so many in the hall." She spun to face the maid. "And you saw no one? No one came to our chamber?"

The maid flushed. "We were not in your chamber, my lady."

"What is this?"

"I took him to the hall, my lady," the maid confessed. "I wished to see the hearing." Her flush deepened as Alys stared at her. "I wished to see this Murdoch Campbell of whom I have heard so much. Someone said he was finely wrought." Her voice faltered. "'Twas only to be a moment, my lady, but I was intrigued and lingered." Her face was crimson now. She swallowed beneath Alys' scrutiny. "I was watching and listening, standing at the base of the stairs, then Michael fussed as if he would cry. I turned and carried him back up the stairs with haste, but I only remember reaching the turn."

"You were struck down there," Nyssa said, her tone soothing.

"He could have been injured when you were struck down," Alys said. "He could be hurt even now!"

"Or he could be hale," Nyssa said firmly. "There was no blood."

Alys granted her a fierce glance, then went to the window and looked out at the falling darkness. Nyssa could hear approaching hoof beats and could only hope that Michael had been found. The maid whispered a prayer.

"Maximilian!" Alys whispered, then raced from the solar. Clearly, she knew the sound of her lord husband's destrier.

Nyssa had to know what he had learned.

Alys hastened down the stairs to the bailey, Nyssa followed immediately behind and the maid in pursuit of them both. They three reached the bailey as Maximilian rode through the gates on his great black steed. He leapt from the saddle, casting aside the reins as the horse stamped and snorted. The ostler caught the reins and murmured to the horse, his face pale and his expression filled with concern.

Maximilian strode to Alys. He was impassive, his entire posture taut.

Naught good, Nyssa guessed.

"Any tidings?" laird and lady asked of each other in unison, then each exhaled, seeming to become smaller. Maximilian opened his arms and Alys cast herself into his embrace. He caught her close and fair lifted her from the ground. He leaned his brow against hers and she caught her breath shakily. "He will be found, Alys. I vow it to you."

She shook her head and buried her face against his chest. "Do not make such a pledge," she whispered. "'Tis beyond your power to keep it and you always keep your word."

"Alys!" he whispered and Nyssa heard his voice break.

She turned away for a moment, powerfully affected by his dismay.

When Maximilian lifted his head, his expression was bleak. He surveyed the others in the bailey as if surprised to find them there, then grimaced as Alys began to weep.

Royce arrived then on his destrier, his expression grim. The other men who had ridden out with Maximilian rode into the bailey, their expressions as somber as if they attended a funeral. Nyssa knew she was not the only one who shivered at the chill in the wind this night. She feared for a small boy exposed to the elements.

"He must be found," she whispered.

Maximilian raised his voice. "The keep has been searched. We have ridden to Rowan Fell and searched the village. We have spoken to every person on the road within half a day's ride. If any of you have a notion of where Michael might be, of where we have not sought him, I entreat you to speak."

Silence greeted his words.

"He cannot have vanished," Nyssa protested, earning a hard look from the laird.

"He has been hidden," Maximilian said. "Has there been a demand for payment to ensure his safe return?"

Alys straightened at that, fire lighting in her eyes. "No one would dare," she said softly, but Maximilian shook his head.

"There is no other possibility." He braced his hands upon her shoulders and fixed his attention upon her, as if he strove to convince her. "And there is some merit in that, for Michael has value to his captor only if he is well-tended."

Alys' lips set in a thin line and she seized a fistful of her husband's tabard. "And when he is safely returned, and you have named the villain, I will decide upon his punishment." Her tone was fierce.

Maximilian smiled wryly. "Aye, Alys, you will have that right, though the villain may well wish that he had faced the Silver Wolf instead." He caught her close, summoning Yves and calling for a meal to be mustered for the men. Ostlers and stable hands came for the horses, taking them to the stables in Kilderrick village, and Maximilian led Alys toward the hall. Nyssa bit her lip, noting how her friend's fury had already abandoned her, leaving fear to take its place. Alys clung to Maximilian, and he spoke to her softly, doubtless offering reassurance.

What reassurance could there be in the absence of Michael or news of him?

Nyssa wondered how much hope Maximilian held for their son's return. There must be those yet who despised him, to be sure, and those who never had forgiven him for the destruction of Kilderrick years before. Murdoch Campbell was the sole one who claimed as much openly, but Nyssa suspected there were others in Rowan Fell with their doubts. There could even be those who had acted out of sympathy for Murdoch in seizing the boy.

She wished she knew that Michael was safe, but she had no inkling of his situation or welfare. She could neither see him nor sense a threat. She wondered whether she should visit the standing stones. 'Twould be unkind to demand Royce's escort after he had ridden most of the day, and might be folly to go alone. She might not have a vision at all, even there.

How she hated to feel so powerless.

The rest of the household returned to their labor in silence, for no one wished to give false hope, yet none wished to speculate on dire possibilities. The maid began to weep again, the sound loud in the silence of the bailey. Dorcha cried overhead, prompting more than one person to shudder at the harsh sound. There were those who saw the raven's cry as a call of doom, but Nyssa recognized the pitch of the call.

The bird recognized someone.

She tipped her head back, watching Dorcha fly in a lazy loop, circling over the keep, then flying out toward the stream that passed Rowan Fell. When he returned to fly over the bailey, he cried out again.

Someone came from the north, along that creek.

Someone Dorcha recognized.

Who would come that way rather than walking the road to the south of the keep? Nyssa neither knew nor cared. She hastened to the portal, her heart filling with hope, then heard a man singing.

She charged through the gate, frowning at the familiar tune. 'Twas a lullaby, one in Gaelic that she had not heard for a long time—save for her dream. The man in her dream had sung this lullaby to their child. Nyssa's heart clenched. The tune was sung by a man with a deep voice, a familiar voice that she had not expected to hear again so soon.

There was a murmur in the bailey as others noticed her movement and Nyssa was followed. The company clustered there, close to the shelter of the keep, peering into the growing darkness to the north as the man's song became louder.

Alys caught her breath and turned, evidently recognizing that he sang a lullaby.

Maximilian stepped in front of his wife, his hand on the hilt of his sword.

A shadow strode out of the night, a man with a plaid wrapped around his hips and cast over his shoulder.

A man with a full ruddy beard who walked with purpose, headed directly for the keep.

A man who sang an old lullaby to the bundle cradled in his arms.

Murdoch!

Nyssa's smile lit all the darkened corners of his heart.

Murdoch saw her first, her hands clasped to her lips, her eyes alight. She stood at the fore of the gathered company and was the first to step toward him, casting out her hands and revealing her brilliant smile. "Murdoch Campbell!" she cried and he nigh laughed aloud that she should be so delighted by his arrival.

Alys made to step forward, but the laird blocked her course, his expression suspicious. The baby gurgled as Murdoch ended his song, and Murdoch found himself smiling down at the burden he carried.

"Again?" he demanded in Gaelic of the child. "Aye, you are a demanding one to be sure."

The babe chortled audibly and seized his finger again.

"Aye, but the next to sing to you will not be me, lad. I wager your mother has a sweeter voice than mine." He nodded to the infant then strode toward laird and lady. "'Tis as if you anticipated me," he said gruffly, eying the pair when he halted before them. He nodded toward Nyssa. "Did the seer warn you?"

"Not I," Nyssa said. "I had no vision of this."

Murdoch studied her and watched her swallow. Was she as aware as he of the allure between them? He would not have been averse to a kiss as his reward, a kiss from this woman who had cast a ray of sunlight into the darkness that had filled his heart. She had saved him, he knew it well, though he could not have explained to another.

He stood in her debt, forever.

"'Twas the bird," the laird said with quiet vigor. "It knew you would come."

There was a chill in his tone, one Murdoch chose to ignore. He could well imagine that this pair had been terrified for the boy's fate, and that their manner would improve once they held him again.

"Someone is missing you," Murdoch said to Michael who grinned at him. Murdoch eased his finger from the child's grip, then offered the boy to the Lady of Kilderrick. "I have been told that his rightful place is in his mother's arms."

Alys caught her son close in relief.

Nyssa looked to be blinking back tears, her delight so evident that Murdoch could not avert his gaze from her.

"Aye, it is," the laird said tightly and Murdoch pivoted to face him. "You should not have dared to take him."

"I did not take him," Murdoch replied. "I *found* him."

The laird scoffed. "I am to believe this, after you threatened his life but days ago?"

"'Tis the truth!"

"'Tis a lie, another lie, and I am in no humor after this day to tolerate this one. Seize him!" The laird cried and his guards fell upon Murdoch. Royce grabbed one arm and another warrior seized the other. A third warrior divested Murdoch of his dagger. Murdoch did not fight them, but stood with dignity, holding the Silver Wolf's gaze.

"You are wrong," he said with heat.

"And you are doomed. Enough!"

"You cannot do this!" the seer cried in dismay. "He found the boy and returned him. You cannot treat him as a villain."

"I will treat those in my domain as they deserve," the laird snapped, then turned slowly upon her. "You knew. Your raven knew that he came. You knew of his deed."

"I did not!" she protested but the laird advanced upon her.

"He had to have an accomplice in this, for he was yet before me when the boy was taken, and you, you, have taken his cause from the first."

Nyssa held her ground and lifted her chin. "I will always defend those judged unfairly."

"Unfairly?" the Silver Wolf nigh roared. "This man has threatened my son, my wife and my life, and on this day, he stole my son. I say you aided him in this. I say you took the boy that he might return him, and thus gain my goodwill."

"Maximilian," Alys said softly and he cast a lethal glance her way. "Nyssa is trusted in this household."

"Perhaps her alliance changes," the Silver Wolf said.

"If gaining your goodwill was my intent, the scheme has failed," Murdoch could not restrain himself from noting.

"Simply because I fail to be deceived," the laird said hotly. He pointed to Murdoch, his eyes narrowed to silver slits. "You will taste my hospitality again."

"I cannot find your sheriff if I am detained."

"Then let my sheriff remain lost. That is the smaller price to pay. This deed negates our wager." The laird pivoted to face Nyssa. "You are a guest in my abode and a friend of my wife, but until your innocence in this matter is proven beyond all doubt, you will not be allowed to meddle in the administration of justice at Kilderrick."

Nyssa lifted her chin. "I have never so dared." She held the Silver Wolf's gaze, her outrage clear in her own simmering gaze.

"You cannot so distrust a lady!" Murdoch protested.

"But I can ensure that no one will aid you," the Silver Wolf said, turning to march into the keep. His fury was evident in the length of his strides, but Murdoch no longer expected his temper to cool and reason to reign. Alys matched her pace to that of her lord husband, the pair of them bending over their son with evident relief.

Murdoch found himself watching the seer, drinking in the sight of her before he was cast into the pit again. "You should have more faith in your own influence," he called after her, gratified when she looked back at him and smiled. A guard tried to hurry her along, but she stood still, resisting his urging, staring back at Murdoch. There might have been a bond between them, so strong was her allure. He felt the weight of Royce's disapproval, but did not care. "Sorcery is not wrought merely with spells and potions."

"I did not realize you knew so much of sorcery," Nyssa said softly.

"I knew little before I spoke with you," he acknowledged. "Though my mother warned me of the power of wise women."

"I am not a wise woman as yet," she said, her manner so modest that his admiration surged.

"Aye, but you have shown me that words alone can wreak change, and that choice is potent. That is a kind of sorcery that cannot be denied." Their gazes held for a potent moment before Royce tugged him hard toward the dungeon. "Nyssa Sutherland," Murdoch cried, saying her name aloud like an invocation. "I will never forget your faith in me."

"Nor will I forget you, Murdoch Campbell," she replied, her words making his heart soar.

The trap door was opened and he was fairly hurled into the familiar darkness of Kilderrick's dungeon. This time, though, the darkness did not touch his soul. It did not fill him with despair. It could not dislodge the radiance of the seer's smile—or the glow she had lit around his heart.

If he survived this ordeal, if he was proven innocent, Murdoch would pledge himself to her defense forever.

He made the vow to himself, in silence, and knew it was one he would keep to his last breath.

NYSSA WAS OUTRAGED by Maximilian's choice. 'Twas clear the man would not listen to reason, for even Alys shook her head when Nyssa would have argued Murdoch's cause with him. Though Nyssa could understand the laird's fears for Michael, she could not respect that fear had prompted him to be unfair.

And Murdoch paid the price. He had aided the laird. He had brought Michael back to Kilderrick, showing the true merit of his heart, but he had been judged unfairly. He had been cast into the dungeon again, with no chance of reprieve.

Worse, Nyssa could do naught to aid him. She could not even speak to him, for her attempts to even approach the dungeon's entry had been repelled. Maximilian had clearly ordered as much.

She retreated to her chamber, aching with the injustice of it all. She was so proud of Murdoch for abandoning his quest, but circumstance —and Maximilian—did not reward his deed.

Would the laird's view soften by the morning? Would it ever soften? Nyssa doubted as much, not without evidence to Murdoch's credit.

The true culprit had to be found.

But who might it be?

Nyssa paced as the sounds in the great hall quieted and faded. She paced as the moon rose higher and the wind slipped through the shutters. She lit neither a candle nor lantern, for she preferred the darkness on this night.

Dorcha sat on his perch, quiet and watchful.

"You did no wrong," she told him. "Of course, you recognized Murdoch. I was glad you told me of his arrival. I was glad that he came." She sighed. "I am glad that he chose to bring Michael home."

He had said her name aloud, cried it like a benediction, and she would never forget the sound of it upon his lips.

She could not bear that he should be suspected of malice when he had done the laird a service.

Where had Murdoch found Michael?

Who had stolen the child?

Only the person who knew the truth could clear the cloud of doubt over Murdoch.

She would visit Rowan Fell in the morn and ask questions.

Maximilian had named one matter aright: Nyssa would be Murdoch Campbell's ally.

MURDOCH HAD no notion of how much time had passed. The darkness was complete within the dungeon and the few sounds he could discern from beyond his prison walls did not have a recognizable rhythm. It could have been midnight. It could have been noon. Neither food nor ale had been brought to him this time. He was ravenously hungry, thirsty as well, too desperate for satisfaction to deny himself whatever was offered.

The Silver Wolf could have sent him food that was poisoned, but Murdoch was so hungry that he would have eaten it up and licked the bowl.

He was dirty and chilled. He ached, not just where he was wounded for his feet were sore from all the walking of his day of freedom. He told himself to be glad that he was alive but could feel little joy in that circumstance for he doubted it would endure long.

He thought of Nyssa and her tale.

Instead, he considered that he had met a woman who could possess his heart forever, but had realized as much only before his own demise. They would never have a night together. He and Nyssa would never share another kiss. He wished he could have done a fraction for her of what she had done for him.

But that, Murdoch feared, was not to be.

He was not a man to despair, but in the darkness of Kilderrick's dungeon on that endless night, Murdoch could not find a morsel of hope for his future.

He had failed, not only in his quest but more importantly, in claiming the promise offered by Nyssa. If that was not cause for desolation, Murdoch did not know what was.

NYSSA LEFT KILDERRICK AT DAWN, ignoring Royce's disapproving glance from the gate. She chose to walk to Rowan Fell, taking the road without any effort to disguise her destination. Dorcha flew over her in lazy spirals, ahead of her for a measure, then trailing behind. The wind was crisp and the sky was overcast.

Her heart was heavy. She had not slept, so great was her concern for Murdoch.

She reached the village by mid-morning to find it bustling with routine. Rona's goats were grazing on the common meadow. Chickens and ducks darted through gardens. Dara was sitting outside Nerida's abode, sewing, despite the chill in the air. Nyssa turned her steps in that direction, pausing to admire the girl's neat stitches.

"The laird himself ordered it as a surprise for his lady wife," Dara confided after they had greeted each other.

"You should not finish it promptly or well," Nerida said with some bitterness. The older woman had emerged from her cottage and braced her hands upon her hips. "The man is faithless, to be sure."

"He will pay well, Nan, and promptly," Dara said. "The coin is always welcome."

"As is justice at Kilderrick," Nerida said and her grand daughter bit her lip.

Silence fell between them and Nyssa sensed that her presence was unwelcome.

"I fear for Murdoch," she confessed. Once again, Dorcha had landed on the roof of the smaller cottage and was sharpening his beak. Her companions did not speak. "The sole way to aid him is to find whoever truly stole the child." Again, her words were met with silence. "Where do you think he found the boy?"

Dara remained silent though Nerida's lips tightened.

"I mean to visit the bees," Nerida said, her tone indicating that Nyssa should leave.

"I know he has taken refuge in the smaller hut at least once," Nyssa said, holding her ground. "I saw his cloak there two days past."

Dara caught her breath.

"Corbies bring foul fortune and death," Nerida said hotly. "There was no corbie in Rowan Fell before yours arrived, and now all has gone awry. Murdoch Campbell will die."

"A single raven means change, no more than that," Nyssa said mildly. "And change may end well. If you know a detail that might aid Murdoch, you should share it with the laird."

Nerida scoffed. "And see myself judged for aiding my own kin?" She nodded toward her grand daughter. "I would not be so foolish as that." She held Nyssa's gaze for a long moment, making her protectiveness of Dara clear.

There would be no assistance for Murdoch here. Nyssa rose to her feet and surveyed the village, wondering who to ask next. Dorcha cried and came soaring toward her. She smiled and raised her hand as he

THE SCOT & THE SORCERESS

descended toward her, landing heavily on her hand and nodding approval.

Perhaps the dead would have some guidance.

Nyssa would have stepped toward the chapel, but was halted by Dara's sudden question.

"Why would Jeannie go into the bee's hut?"

Both Nyssa and Nerida turned to look at her. Dara did not even glance up from her work, but still there was an urgency to her question that implied it was of import. "She would not," Nerida said. "She has no right to do as much."

"But she did." Dara lifted her gaze, serene and confident, to hold Nerida's own.

"When was this?" Nyssa asked.

"When Nan went to hall for Murdoch's hearing."

Nyssa returned to sit beside the younger woman, her curiosity piqued. "But she was at the hall as well."

Dara shook her head and threaded her needle again. "Nay, she returned earlier than Nan, when all were still at Kilderrick. She carried a great basket, until she went into the hut, then she went home without one."

Jeannie. It stood to reason that Jeannie might wish the laird ill, and thence his son. Eamon was soon to be required to repay the tithes he had spent, and there were few who believed he could do as much. The laird had granted the sheriff more time to gather the funds on two occasions, and Nerida doubted he would do as much again. Would Eamon lose his post? It seemed unlikely that he could retain it.

Nerida sat on the girl's other side. "This could be of import, child, but you must be certain before you confide as much in the laird. You are certain that Jeannie left a basket in our hut?"

Dara nodded emphatically.

Nyssa watched Nerida straighten her shoulders, and recognized that Murdoch was not the sole person who was protective of his own.

"Put your work away, then," Nerida said to Dara even as she rose to her feet.

"But the light is good…"

"Never mind the light. We must go to Kilderrick so you can tell the laird what you have seen."

Dara's gaze slid to the sheriff's hut, her thinking so clear that Nyssa did not have to ask for an explanation.

"I will ensure that you can tell him in confidence, not before all." She smiled. "All will be well, and your words will aid Murdoch."

Dara smiled, reassured, and put her work away as bidden.

Nerida eyed the sky. "We will be fortunate to be home by darkness," she said, then gave Nyssa an intent glance. "I shall check upon the bees."

Nyssa was well aware that Jeannie could be watching. There was no sign of activity outside the sheriff's cottage.

"I could tell Rona that the laird wished to see the progress on the kirtle for his lady," Nyssa said to Nerida. "I could confess that he sent me to collect you."

Nerida smiled. "That would be wise."

She strode then down to the other hut, singing to the bees as she went, and Nyssa dared to hope for the best.

NYSSA ACCOMPANIED Nerida and Dara to the keep, not wanting either of them to have second thoughts. She ensured not only that they would have a private audience with Maximilian but that she was included. Alys and Maximilian were surely curious and Maximilian granted her an assessing glance, but Nyssa was adamant that she must hear their tale as well. Maximilian invited them into the small chamber where he kept his accounts. It was a small room on one side of the hall, little bigger than the guard's chamber at the gates. A table filled most of the space, with a simple chair behind it and a locked trunk against one wall. Maximilian sat in the chair, Alys by his side. Nerida and her grand daughter stood facing the laird, the younger woman showing some trepidation. Nyssa remained standing by the door. All were silent until the door was secured behind them, with Yves on the other side to ensure that they were not interrupted.

"Murdoch does not lie about Michael," Nyssa said by way of beginning. "He found the boy and brought him home."

"Perhaps he does not lie," Maximilian allowed. "But neither does he confess the truth. He simply remains silent."

"To protect me," Nerida said, lifting her chin.

Alys frowned. "But why? You disowned his mother, along with all of your family," she said.

Nerida nodded. "I will not deny that harsh words were spoken when Gwendolyn returned home ripe with child and no man by her side. My sister, Anna, never again uttered her daughter's name for shame. She praised God that her husband never had to know of it, for he was dead and buried years before. I took Gwendolyn into my home when 'twas clear that no other would aid her. She and my boy, Ranald, were always close, though I was not happy with her situation either."

"You are Murdoch's relation?" Maximilian asked with care. 'Twas clear he had not known as much. He looked at Alys.

"None of the family accepted Gwendolyn again," Alys said. "I was told that she might as well have been a stranger." She shrugged. "It happened before I was born."

Maximilian, Nyssa realized, would never have believed such a claim without proof.

He frowned now, clearly disliking that he had not anticipated this detail.

Nerida nodded. "I took her in so that she and the babe would not starve. 'Twould have been wicked to deny the child, even if Gwendolyn's choices had been poor ones. We thought then, you see, that she had trusted a man overmuch, granting him more than his due before he wedded her, and that he had cast her aside when she conceived his child. We thought she had been foolish." The older woman frowned. "But one night when she could not sleep for the burden of the babe, when she was coming near her time, she confided the truth in me."

"What truth?" Maximilian asked.

"She was stalked by a foreign mercenary in the very hall where she served as maid to a fine lady. He followed her and he flirted with her, and when he ensured one night that she was alone, he took what he desired of her with cruel force. He rode out the next morn, never to be seen again." Nerida's lips tightened. "She said his name was Jean le Beau and she spat at the ground whenever she was compelled to say it aloud."

Maximilian bowed his head. Nyssa knew he was not surprised for he had already guessed that he and Murdoch were brothers, but he had not known the details. His disapproval of his blood father's deeds was evident. "Where was this?"

"Gwendolyn served the Lady Mary Douglas, sir. They were at Sterling keep when it happened, conferring with the king over the hiring of fighting men to aid the French."

Maximilian appeared to calculate something. "The war had begun between England and France," he told Alys. "In 1340, there were battles at Saint-Omer and Tournai in the low countries. The next group of battles were in Brittany. Jean le Beau had already begun to form the Compagnie Rouge by gathering those fighting men left idle in the wake of battle. He must have been in Scotland seeking a commission."

"Idle warriors did not need to turn to lawlessness," Alys said tightly.

Maximilian's brows rose. "Nay, but you must see their view. They were abandoned by the leaders they had sworn to follow and cast aside like so much offal. Often they were far from home, unpaid and without skills beyond fighting. They were not going to become shoemakers or millers, and they needed coin. The *routiers* were lawless and ungoverned, a menace upon the land. The Compagnie Rouge was a force that could be hired, and my father, for all his faults, ensured discipline within its ranks."

"There were battles on the borders, too, my lord," Nerida said. "There were those as were certain that English counties could be claimed in those days."

"Aye, the Compagnie Rouge could have been hired by the Scottish men of influence either for their own battles or to aid the French in theirs. 'Twould take a heavy purse to bring that force from the continent, though, even at its size in those days." He eyed Nerida. "More to the point, what happened when Gwendolyn's state was revealed?"

"She was compelled to leave the lady's service. I understood that she declined to wed a warrior chosen from the lord's forces as her spouse. She said he was no different from the one who had abused her, so she came home to Rowan Fell alone."

"And thus to your abode, because of Ranald's fondness for her."

Nerida nodded. "I admit that I was vexed with her. She had always been clever and I thought she had been a fool. Once I knew the truth, I could not hold her state against her. She was tiny, that girl, pretty as a flower and would have been easily overcome by a man who cared only for his own desire."

"And then the boy was born?"

"Nay, before that, Rupert Campbell came courting." Nerida smiled a little in memory. "There were those as said that he was too old for her, those who said she could not be so desperate as to wed a man old enough to be her own father, but Rupert was smitten in truth. He was a good man. A kind man." She fixed Alys with a look. "He served your father better than that man deserved, if I may say as much, my lady."

"He did, indeed, Nerida. I will not dispute that truth."

"Gwendolyn wanted no man, so she said, but Rupert was so resolute and so agreeable that she softened to him. When he offered for her, she asked me what to do. As round as could be, she was, and inclined to tears at the end of her time. 'Twas then she told me of the babe's conception, and I reminded her that she had always been a child of keen wit. I told her I would be disappointed if she turned aside Rupert simply because of his age, for never was there a man so enamored of a lady and determined to treat her well." Nerida's gaze flicked over the man opposite her. "Barring present company, of course, my lord."

Maximilian almost smiled. "Of course. And they wed?"

"I told her also that her child might have need of a parent, though she did not care to be reminded that childbirth does not always go well for the mother. I would have taken care of the babe, but I was not young even then. I bade her choose wisely."

"And she accepted Rupert?" Alys guessed.

"Aye, my lady. You never saw a man so jubilant in all your days." Nerida smiled and Nyssa felt a glow of satisfaction that Murdoch had been raised by such a man. "Then she came to live here at the hall with Rupert, so the bond between us stretched thin. Anna preferred that, to be sure. And when the boy was born, you never did see a father more proud of his bairn. They were a fine pair together, an unlikely couple by some accounting but happier than most." Nerida sighed. "And then she died, the poor lass."

Nyssa was not the sole one who gasped.

CHAPTER 9

*H*ow?" Maximilian asked when the silence had stretched overlong.

"'Twas the babe, of course," Nerida said. "The second one. Years it took for Rupert to plant his seed, and who is to say how long it took Gwendolyn to welcome him. But she ripened one spring, and was well with it, as rosy and happy as could be. Murdoch had seen five summers or so at the time." Her expression darkened. "All went awry in the delivery and even the midwife from Hawick could not save either of them. I thought Rupert would lose his wits." She shook her head. "But there was the boy, the boy he loved with all his heart and soul, and they two made their way together. Rupert brought him to me after the funeral, saying the boy must know his kin. After that, Murdoch would come sometimes on his own. He was always intrepid, a quiet lad but kind and clever." She looked up. "Loyal beyond the inclination of most."

Maximilian looked up at Alys, his expression questioning. "I do not recall this," she admitted.

"You could not, my lady. You were born two years later and 'twas another four or five before you and Murdoch became companions. He was patient with you, despite the difference in your ages, and came less often to me then. My house was full in those days, for my Owen was yet alive, Ranald was wed and Eliza had given him four children.

Indeed, Owen built the larger cottage for Ranald and we lived in the smaller older hut together. 'Twas long ago." Her hand landed on Dara's arm for a moment and the younger woman managed a slight smile.

Maximilian looked momentarily confused and Nyssa, too, wondered how so much had changed.

"The plague," Alys said softly. "First you came," she said to Maximilian. "And then the Black Death. Nerida's family paid most dearly. That I do remember, for Morag spoke often with Nerida in those days."

"It took all but me and the youngest of all," Nerida said with a sad smile for Dara. "She was but a babe and never knew her parents and siblings."

"We have each other, Nan," the girl said, squeezing the older woman's hand.

"And now you must tell the laird what you saw yesterday, Dara," Nyssa prompted softly.

Dara gripped her hands tightly together but did not look up at Maximilian. "'Twas the day of the hearing for Murdoch Campbell, sir. I remained at home, for Nan did not wish for me to witness his fate."

"I did not know how swift your justice would be, my lord."

Maximilian looked between them. "You are fond of him."

"He is kin, sir, and we have precious little family remaining. I came the day before, but yesterday, Nan said all might go badly for Murdoch and she did not wish me to see." The girl smiled at Nerida. "I think she feared that I might reveal us."

Maximilian nodded. "I understand. What did you see?"

"I was sewing, sir, upon the kirtle for your lady."

"What kirtle?" Alys asked, but Maximilian raised a hand and she fell silent.

Dara continued at his gesture. "I saw someone return early and alone from the keep, sir, someone who carried a large basket. This person came along the stream, which was why I noticed, for few come that way. I watched this person appear, then vanish in the growth closer to Rowan Fell." She took a breath. "Then she entered our hut. I put aside my work, wondering whether I should challenge her and could not decide. When she reappeared, she carried no basket."

Maximilian straightened slightly. "She?"

"Who?" Alys demanded, but Maximilian placed a hand upon her arm.

"'Twas Jeannie, sir. The sheriff's wife." Dara took a breath. "I did not go to look, for I feared she would see me. I thought perhaps she had brought something for Murdoch, a meal or a heavy cloak, that I was the sole one who did not know." She took a breath. "Nan does not tell me everything, my lord."

"'Tis a fair stretch to imagine that I should conspire in any matter with Jeannie," Nerida said, her tone tart, and the girl flushed.

"I forgot to ask when you returned, for the laird came seeking his son and all was in uproar. 'Twas only this morn that I recalled."

"And you told Nerida and I," Nyssa supplied.

"And I went to see, under guise of singing to the bees. I found this." Nerida reached into the fullness of her skirts, placing a wad of cloth on the table before the laird.

Alys gave a cry of recognition. "'Tis from his bedding!"

"The basket is in the hut, sir," Nerida said. "I dared not take it, lest Jeannie see that she had been discovered, so I hid it that it could not be easily removed in our absence."

"Michael was in the basket," Nyssa said.

Maximilian tapped a finger on the table. "So, Murdoch left the keep and found the child in the hut behind your cottage, left by Jeannie."

"It must have been thus, my lord."

"Why would he go there at all?" He lifted his hands. "The man could have journeyed in any direction after his release, but he went to your hut." He fixed Nerida with a stern look, clearly having guessed the answer.

Nerida flushed. "To be sure, I offered the hut to Murdoch as a sanctuary and swore to tell none that he took refuge there. I could do no less for Gwendolyn's son."

Maximilian nodded, though his manner was not disapproving. "And Murdoch, in his turn, will not tell me that he found my son in that hut, for he would not implicate you." He frowned a little. "Your loyalty to each other is laudable, to be sure. And I have erred mightily of late."

"'Twas your fear for Michael," Alys said, placing her hand upon his shoulder.

He reached up and caught her hand beneath his. "But only Nyssa was sufficiently bold to seek the truth and ask questions. I thank you, Nyssa."

Nyssa bowed her head, feeling her cheeks heat.

"I have been wrong and I have been hasty, and I must make matters right." Maximilian stood with purpose as the village women watched him, some wariness in their expressions. "All this time, I have believed that Murdoch had no kin and no allies, but in truth, he has a grand-mother and a cousin who would dare much on his behalf. Every man should be so fortunate." He inclined his head to Nerida and Dara. "I thank you for these tidings and for offering them to me. If you would linger, you would be welcome to join us at the evening meal. I will see that you are given a wagon ride back to Rowan Fell afterward."

The two seemed uncertain what to do and glanced at each other.

"There is venison and civet of hare this night," Alys whispered. "I would stay."

Nerida smiled at her and Dara smiled a little. Still the pair did not speak and their eyes were filled with shadows.

They cared for Murdoch and feared for his fate, Nyssa knew, and not just because he was kin. He had kept his sanctuary secret to defend them and they knew as much. Though he had been away from Rowan Fell for years and had returned embittered, Nerida knew the truth of his heart—and that fed Nyssa's confidence that she understood him as well.

He was a man of merit, and now that he had put his quest for vengeance behind him, Nyssa knew he was the man to aid in her quest.

She did not doubt that Murdoch would need to be convinced, but the prospect made her smile. Aye, 'twas most satisfactory to surprise him.

Maximilian cleared his throat. "I must speak to Murdoch in privacy, but I believe he might return to the village this night as well." His eyes glinted as he glanced at Alys, who smiled at him.

"Thank you, my lord!" Nerida said with delight and kissed Maximil-ian's ring. Dara for her part curtseyed and flushed, then Alys escorted them back to the hall.

Nyssa for her part fled to her chamber. On impulse, she gathered her few belongings and packed her satchel, Dorcha flying behind her down the corridor and the stairs. Even his cry sounded jubilant.

She halted near the gate when Royce appeared. That man was clearly headed to the dungeon to fetch Murdoch, but he paused when he saw her. She had no doubt that he had noticed her satchel and guessed the import of it, for his gaze swept over her and his expression turned grim. Nyssa feared he would stop her, but Royce simply shook his head and continued on his path.

She watched him walk away, aware of his disappointment, but knew she had a path to follow. Nyssa shouldered her bag and left the keep, walking to Rowan Fell one more time on this day. The sun was sinking and clouds gathering in the west. 'Twould rain on this night but Nyssa knew she would be warm and dry, in Murdoch's sanctuary—and his embrace. She embarked on a new adventure and though her heart fluttered with uncertainty of where her path might ultimately lead, she knew she chose aright.

MURDOCH STOOD before the Silver Wolf, hands by his sides, gaze fixed on the point where the opposite wall met the ceiling of the laird's small chamber. He dared not expect aught good from this interview. Alys sat on a trunk to one side, quiet and watchful, while the Silver Wolf occupied the sole chair, like an emperor prepared to pass judgement. He wrote in a ledger, the quill dragging audibly across the parchment, and there was no other sound within the small chamber.

'Twas diabolical the way that the Silver Wolf compelled Murdoch to wait, to wait for what would certainly be his doom. Murdoch hated that his pulse quickened and his breath caught, his agitation rising precisely as the other warrior had doubtless intended.

And still the quill scratched.

Murdoch's jaw was set with the surety that he had been convicted as soon as he had appeared with the child, perhaps even before the babe had been found. The Silver Wolf had already called him a liar and cast him into the now-familiar dungeon again.

The sole detail he could not explain was that he had been removed from the dungeon so quickly this time. Perhaps the Silver Wolf truly had no remaining patience as he had said. Perhaps Murdoch would die within moments at that man's hand.

In this chamber.

Who would know the truth of it?

Murdoch ran his tongue over his lips, disliking that there was no witness beyond Alys, who was as committed to her husband's cause as ever a woman could be.

He did not have to be a seer to know that this situation did not bode well for his future.

Where was Nyssa? Murdoch might have hoped for her presence in his last moments, but even that wish was to be denied.

As he waited in silence, he felt a trickle of cold sweat slide down his back. A hundred times in his life he had been certain he would die. A hundred times he had lunged into battle, suspecting that he might not see another day. A hundred times he had been prepared to die for his choices, but not on this day. On this day, he wanted to shout his innocence, to shake the Silver Wolf until that man understood that he was not guilty—that he had saved Michael, not imperiled him. He wanted another moment, another day, another month—not to make war or avenge Rupert, but to talk with Nyssa.

Yet he was unlikely to have it. The sorry truth was that had their places been exchanged, Murdoch would not have believed the truth either.

"I have had a guest," the Silver Wolf said finally, setting his quill aside. "Two guests, actually." He blew upon the page in the ledger, then closed it with care, a man with all the time in the world. Finally, he folded his hands together and looked up at Murdoch. As ever, his expression was inscrutable, but his gaze seemed particularly cold.

"Indeed," Murdoch said, for it seemed the laird awaited his reply.

"Indeed. I thought you would find that detail of greater interest, since Nerida and Dara came to argue in your defense."

"Who?" Murdoch strove to keep the surprise from his voice, hoping against hope that the older lady had not paid for her loyalty. He feigned ignorance of the pair as well as he was able, which he doubted was sufficiently well to fool the Silver Wolf. What else could he do, though, other than betray those who had aided him? "Is she from Rowan Fell?"

"You know she is," the Silver Wolf said with a smile. "You know she keeps the bees, and you know she has a small hut upon her allotment as well as the cottage where she lives with her grand-daughter Dara, for you are her kin." He stood up and folded his arms across his chest, looking Murdoch in the eye. "She told me that your mother was her niece, and that Gwendolyn took refuge with Nerida when she returned home from Sterling in shame and was cast out by her kin—at least until Rupert's courtship was successful."

Murdoch's chest tightened and he looked down at the floor. He had no notion how much Nerida had confided in the Silver Wolf and he dared not betray more. He resolved to keep silent.

"She told me also of the loss of her family to the Black Death," the Silver Wolf said softly. "'Tis simple to understand that she would desire to defend any remaining kin, regardless of their actions. I might have thought that she provided a tale for your benefit, perhaps one that was not fully true, but Dara shared one intriguing detail."

Murdoch looked up.

The Silver Wolf produced a piece of cloth, which Murdoch recognized as the one that had silenced the child.

"She saw the sheriff's wife, Jeannie, with a basket, a basket she left within that hut beside the bees," the Silver Wolf confided.

"Jeannie!" Murdoch whispered, his thoughts flying.

"You asked me where my sheriff was," the Silver Wolf said, strolling around the table. He put down the cloth. "I do not know." His cool gaze collided with Murdoch's. "Do you?"

Murdoch shook his head.

The Silver Wolf waited.

Murdoch held his tongue.

"You have been in the hut on occasion. I understand it has been your refuge."

Murdoch looked at the cloth, thought of the frightened boy, and chose his course. "I saw Eamon leave from there. The night of the new moon, the night before I was seized."

"He left Rowan Fell alone?" The Silver Wolf was incredulous and rightly so.

Murdoch shook his head. "A company arrived, riding along the stream at night to hide in the shadows of the gorse. Several of them went to the sheriff's cottage, and he left with them moments later. They rode west, though I know not their destination."

The Silver Wolf paced. "Did you recognize any of them?"

Murdoch shook his head. "'Twas dark beyond all and the rain was fierce that night."

"Did you hear aught they said?"

Murdoch again shook his head.

The Silver Wolf turned to face him. "How many?"

Murdoch lifted his hands. "Half a dozen? I could not say." He felt immediately that this reply was inadequate and shared what little he had observed. "Most on horses, but with ponies as well. At least six ponies," he continued, anticipating the question. "With empty saddlebags."

"A quest, then."

Murdoch inclined his head in agreement. "That would be my conclusion as well."

"Do you know where they rode?"

"Not with certitude. They followed the stream to the west, that much is evident, but beyond that, 'twould be only speculation."

"Speculate then."

"South, I would wager. There are tales of reivers using the road through Langholm at night, now that the route along the Liddel Water has a toll."

"A sheriff should not ride with reivers."

"Nay, he should not."

The Silver Wolf took his seat again, drummed his fingers on the table for a moment, then impaled Murdoch with a fierce look. "I am prepared to release you," he said. "I would have you complete your pledge to find my sheriff, but would also request your vow that you will tell me if and when this party returns to Rowan Fell."

Murdoch folded his arms across his chest in turn, challenging the other man in his turn. "Do you not fear for your son's welfare if I am free?"

The Silver Wolf's eyes narrowed to blue slits. "You would not be so fool as to make that error, I wager."

"He will not," Alys contributed. "Because he did not seize Michael before. He brought him *home*."

"Aye, he brought him home, and I was unjust." Murdoch blinked at this confession as the Silver Wolf rose to his feet. "I choose to trust you in this, Murdoch Campbell." He offered his hand that they might shake upon their agreement as equals. "I would see us allied."

Murdoch was wary. "You have offered as much before."

The Silver Wolf nodded. "And you have declined. Yet I will doubtless offer as much again, if there is opportunity. You are *my* kin, Murdoch, and I value the merit of a blood bond, though you strive to convince me otherwise." The words startled Murdoch, for he had not considered that truth. He found himself studying the Silver Wolf, who steadily held his gaze.

He had never considered that there might be any value in his lineage through Jean le Beau. There was much of merit in this man's deeds, though. What if he had not killed Rupert outright? What if that man had died as the Silver Wolf insisted?

Then Murdoch would have no quarrel with the current Laird of Kilderrick.

'Twas a dizzying prospect.

"Stay for the evening meal," Alys urged, perhaps intent upon creating harmony where none could yet be.

Murdoch shook his head. "I cannot say when Eamon will return. I would not miss it by partaking of pleasure." With those words, he realized he had become a warrior loyal to the laird, by dint of his pledge.

'Twas because of a baby boy.

Nay, 'twas because of a woman who believed in his merit.

And that was both the greatest and the most unexpected gift of all.

MURDOCH SOUGHT Nyssa in the great hall of Kilderrick before his departure but there was no sign of her. Neither Nerida nor Dara had seen her, though both embraced him openly at his release. He could only conclude that Nyssa's efforts on his behalf were completed. Aye, there were many in need of healing—while he had come to care for her, clearly he had been just another person requiring assistance in her eyes.

Murdoch could not blame her for being who she was and doing what she did best. He might wish for one last glimpse, one last touch, much less one last kiss, but 'twas not to be.

Nyssa's absence made her disinterest clear.

Murdoch declined again to linger for the meal, though the scent of it was tempting beyond all. If he could not be with Nyssa, he did not wish to be with any other soul. Alys brought him a basket of provisions and thanked him again, even as the maid brought the babe to her. Murdoch found himself smiling as Alys cooed to Michael and took a seat to nurse him.

He felt the weight of another gaze and found the Silver Wolf watching him. The two exchanged a nod and Murdoch left the hall with purpose. He could not help but look for Nyssa in the bailey and at the gates, even outside the walls, but there was no sign of her. She might have left Kilderrick completely. There was not even any sign of the bird. The realization did naught to improve his mood, though he knew he should have been merry.

He was hale. He had survived the Silver Wolf's dungeons. He had been acquitted of all accusations against him.

Still.

Murdoch made good time on his march to Rowan Fell, sticking to the muddy path along the stream that his arrival at the hut might not be noted. The sky was darkening to the west as a storm gathered and he hoped he made shelter in time. He felt his exhaustion when he climbed the bank under the shadow of darkness to the small hut he had come to consider his home. He wondered what Alys had seen packed for him, and acknowledged his hunger, even as he noticed the silhouette of a raven on the roof of the hut.

Dorcha! Murdoch's heart leapt as the raven cried out. He hastened onward with new vigor and reached for the door quickly, smiling at the surety that—yet again—he was not alone.

She had come to him.

He eyed the gathering tempest and whistled softly to the raven. To his satisfaction, the bird cawed a reply, then flew down toward him, soaring through the door of the hut with grace. Murdoch secured the door behind himself, pleased that the raven showed an increment of trust.

He paused then, savoring the sound of Nyssa speaking to the bird in the loft above.

Though she might have invited herself into his abode, this intruder was not unwelcome. Her scent was sweeter than that of the honey stored in the hut and more vital than that of the dried herbs that brushed against him as he moved to the ladder. He sensed her warmth, like a summer day about to dawn.

Murdoch had never been a man of good fortune, and he dared not trust that had changed until he saw for certain. He had felt since Rupert's death that he was a man doomed to struggle in pursuit of any advantage. That conviction faded with the realization that Nyssa waited for him. He climbed to the loft quietly as if his very presence could shatter the spell and halted at the sight of her, thrilled by her presence and humbled by her trust.

She sat in the growing shadows, her manner both serene and expectant. She was more still than any person he had ever known, so tranquil and trusting that he feared for her welfare in the greater world. She had known little good of men and warriors, yet she awaited him alone in his refuge, in a loft with no escape, her confidence in him giving her a radiance.

Aye, she awakened every protective urge within him and if Murdoch had been a man of any means—if he had possessed more than a single dagger and a heart bent on vengeance—he would have sworn himself to her service forever.

He still was not worthy of her, but he was prepared to do whatsoever was necessary to redeem himself, to follow whatever quest she offered to him, to gather whatever prize she demanded of him. He could serve her, without promising what he could not deliver.

As he stared and Nyssa smiled at him, the rain began to fall heavily against the roof. They might have been alone in the world and Murdoch could desire naught else.

Nyssa had lit a trio of candles, ensuring they were placed low so their light might not be seen through the thatch. The space was filled with a soft golden light that made her look ethereal. She wore the blue kirtle again, and her fair hair was loose, spread over her shoulders like silver. She might have been a goddess come to visit, for her beauty seemed beyond mortal possibilities.

Her boots were at the closest end of the loft, her feet bare where she sat on his straw pallet. Her dark cloak was folded beside her boots and satchel. With her presence, the humble loft had been transformed into a treasury, with Nyssa as the most precious jewel within it.

All the same, despite her composure, Murdoch sensed the uncertainty within her—which only fed his need to defend her. He recalled what she had said about maidenhood and her gift. He would not be the one to steal that prize from her, despite the vigor of his desire.

"He released you then," she said finally.

Murdoch nodded, keeping his distance. "Aye." Dorcha sat on a beam at the far end of the loft, preening. "I am pledged to aid him in finding Eamon and whatever company he joined."

Her smile broadened and lit her eyes. "Good."

"You cannot have waited for me." He had to say it, though there was no other reason for her presence.

"I did. I came here after Nerida and Dara told what they had seen."

"You encouraged them," he guessed.

She nodded.

They eyed each other as the rain grew more forceful. Murdoch dared to ask what he most wished to know. "Why are you here?"

Nyssa smiled. "Because I would make a wager with you." She frowned for a moment, and he waited, content to grant her all the time she desired. If she wished him to slaughter her sister's faithless husband, he would do it without remorse. "I would seek out my sister's daughter."

Murdoch frowned. "There was another, beyond the two killed by her husband?"

"The second was stolen away. I dreamed of it. My sister and the midwife conspired to present a dead infant to my sister's lord husband."

Murdoch understood. "He killed a child that was already dead."

"Aye."

"He must have been beguiled not to know the difference."

This seemed to amuse her. "Perhaps he was. My sister's gifts were considerable."

Murdoch moved closer to her, considering this. "How long has it been?"

"Eight years." Nyssa supplied. "I do not know where she is, but if Hugh finds her first…"

"Aye," Murdoch said so she would not have to utter the words. He looked down, uncertain how to tell her of the folly of her desire. To find a child without an inkling of her location? After she had been hidden for eight years? It could take a lifetime. It might be a quest doomed to fail. The child could have died of natural causes. He was nigh overwhelmed by the possibilities and did not understand her quiet conviction in him.

"I cannot pay you," Nyssa said, mistaking the reason for his silence and his gaze flew to meet hers. "Save in the oldest possible way." She rose to her feet and came toward him, remaining in the middle of the loft where the roof was high enough to allow her to stand. He swallowed as their gazes locked, though he knew he could not accept what she offered.

Her gift would be sacrificed if he touched her.

If she stayed, he would be unable to do aught else.

"You should leave," he said gruffly. "You should go."

She caught her breath. "Will you not aid me? How can you decline so quickly as this?"

"I will aid you, though I doubt the quest will succeed." He ran a hand over his brow, his body taut with the promise of her proximity. "If you will not go, then I will."

"Nay! Not in such a storm as this. I entreat you to stay."

Murdoch's heart skipped when Nyssa stepped forward and caught his face in her hands. He stared down at her like a man struck to stone, snared by her intent gaze. She cared deeply about this, he knew, though he believed that she erred.

"I choose this, Murdoch. I welcome it." She exhaled shakily and held his gaze, her own eyes so vivid a green that he knew she meant every word. "I offer myself willingly."

"Nay," he protested softly, but her grip tightened upon him.

"We are alike in this," she insisted. "You journeyed far to see your mother avenged. I will do whatever I must for Rana."

"You heal others," he whispered. "I only slaughter…"

"Nay," Nyssa said with a smile. "We each in our own way improve the world. Do not tell me that Jean le Beau's demise is mourned by many."

"Nay, but…"

"We are united in purpose, Murdoch." She gave him no opportunity to argue, but touched her lips to his, offering a kiss so sweet that it fair broke his heart in two.

Surely this could not be happening. Surely, he dreamed it all.

Surely, he was a fool to decline what she offered.

She sensed that he was tempted, for she angled her mouth across his and deepened her kiss, flicking her tongue against him so sweetly that Murdoch groaned aloud. She awakened a fire in his blood, a desire to run his hands over her, a need to taste her and bury himself within her softness. He knew that this woman alone could satisfy his every need. He knew that once would not suffice, not with Nyssa, and he feared he might demand too much if he surrendered. He clenched his fists and let her kiss him, not daring to respond lest he could not control the surging tide.

But Nyssa, Nyssa, was always bold when defending another. He knew she would be fearless in her seduction, for she believed it to be right.

Was it wrong to wish that she had desired him for himself, and not to pay a perceived debt?

Either way, she was determined to dismiss his reluctance and Murdoch knew that he would lose to her sweet assault. He could not think clearly, not when her hands eased from his face to his throat, when she pushed her hands through his hair with increasing confidence, when she fingered the length of his beard. She grew bolder as she kissed him with more demand, her surety growing with every moment. She caressed his shoulders and ran her fingertips down his arms, slid her palms over him in a sweeping caress as she fed that fire beneath his skin. Murdoch closed his eyes and she kissed him more boldly, her tongue demanding more of him, until he caught her close with a growl and slanted his mouth over hers.

If he had thought to frighten her, he was not to succeed. Nyssa gasped and wound her arms around his neck, mimicking his every caress, pressing herself against him until he thought he would lose his wits. His fingers were in her hair, his arm locked around her waist, and he was lifting her against him, feasting upon her sweet lips.

When she pulled away, he thought the taste of heaven was over. His heart was thundering and his body taut, even before he saw her smile. Her lips were slightly swollen and her eyes were dancing as she tugged him toward the pallet. Murdoch had to bow his head slightly below the highest beam as she unfastened his cloak, setting it aside.

"I want to see you," she confessed in a whisper that made him catch his breath. "I want to feel you." Then her hands were on his skin, flitting across him so lightly, so beguilingly, that he could only clench his fists and *want*.

"I will take your quest. You owe me naught."

Her smile was impish and utterly alluring. "But I want this, as well, Murdoch. I desire you."

He was lost at that heartfelt confession. His belt was removed next, and then his plaid. Nyssa slipped around him like a will o' the wisp, as graceful and elusive as a firefly, removing the length of cloth from his shoulder and unfurling it from around his hips. She planted a kiss in the midst of his back, immediately over the thunder of his heart, startling him with her sudden touch even though the linen of his chemise was between them. Her hand stole around his waist, her palm flat against him and her fingers spread, and he thought the cloth would incinerate in the heat between them. He looked over his shoulder only to find her watching him with those clear eyes.

"You like to be admired thus," she whispered, her hands moving to his shoulders and back to his waist. Her breasts were against his back, her scent inundating him. She was wet and that made him want to roar.

"I like you," he confessed in a low rumble and she smiled. His mouth went dry as she slid her hands beneath the hem of his chemise and he felt her fingertips against his bare skin, then she pushed the garment over his head. She folded it roughly as she walked around him, just looking. He stood in his braies alone and there could be little doubt what was beneath them. He thought his size might make her falter, but not Nyssa. She never faltered, this one, and he loved her all the more for it.

There was the slightest tremble in her hands as she poured water from a vessel into a large bowl. That small sign of her uncertainty fed Murdoch's protective urge, coaxing it to a tide of demand that would not allow him to see her injured in any way—whatever the price to himself. Again, Nyssa granted him a shy glance, her cheeks turning pink, then she began to wash him.

'Twas strange and yet luxurious to be tended. Murdoch thought he might die of the pleasure, or be overwhelmed by it. He tried to take the cloth from her hands, but Nyssa evaded him.

"Let me," she whispered.

"You are not my servant."

"I would know you," she said again, her fingertips landing across his chest. She watched her own hand flatten against him and slide over his chest in a caress. "I would see what I have never seen before." She smiled a little as she looked into his eyes again. "If I am to learn the shape of a man, I would learn as much from you."

Murdoch could scarce argue with that. A trail of fire was awakened by her light caress and he gritted his teeth. He would not shame her or force her. He would let her choose, even if it destroyed him to show such restraint. He closed his eyes, aroused beyond measure but compelling himself to simply stand and be tended.

Her hands were strong and gentle as she washed his face. Yet again, he was aware that she wove a spell, that the candles and the sound of the rain and his own raging desire were all elements in her sorcery, all woven into an enchantment with Nyssa at its center. She checked upon the scabbed wound over his ear and the second one in his shoulder, her very touch seeming to draw out any pain and set recovery in motion. He might have sworn that his very flesh knitted together at her command. He could smell the soft perfume of her skin and felt the brush of her hair against him at intervals. Murdoch kept his eyes closed, savoring the sense that his welfare was of import to someone— that he might be worthy of this woman's concern was sufficient to humble him anew. He felt a changed man as she washed him, more than cleansed.

He was wrought anew.

If she truly meant to surrender to him, he would ensure she had no regret. He did not have it in his heart to argue with her over her choice. He wanted her too much.

But she did not owe him her maidenhead. He would aid her without payment. He would find her sister's daughter, if it took all his remaining days and nights to do so.

But first, he would grant her pleasure.

CHAPTER 10

$\mathcal{M}$ urdoch's braies were last to be removed and he held his breath as Nyssa untied them. He was larger and harder than he could ever recall, and feared her first glimpse of that truth. He could do naught else but be aroused with this woman. He watched her closely, noting how her eyes widened, then was relieved when she smiled. Their gazes met, then locked and held, and he was certain there was naught to breathe in the small space. Time might have stopped utterly. The loft seemed warm, warmer than he knew it to be, and more of a sanctuary from the world.

Nyssa.

She lowered her gaze, her fingertips brushing across him in a sweet torment that nigh made him groan. She smiled, a bit of mischief in her eyes, and pushed the wet cloth down his belly with purpose. Murdoch closed his hand over hers, gently claiming the cloth. "You must let me finish this task," he said, hearing the strain in his own voice.

She surrendered the cloth for him, then reached for the ties at the sides of her kirtle. Murdoch watched hungrily as she unlaced them. She flicked a glance his way but did not falter, nor did she turn away. She pulled the loosened garment over her head with a swift gesture and set it aside. Her chemise was white and sheer, so finely woven that it might not have been wrought by mortal hands. He recalled his mother's tales of lengths of linen so fine as to be drawn through a ring, of Fae cloth woven of spider's webs, of all the marvels beyond mortal ken.

She might have been from another realm, a Fae queen come to capture his heart, a woman of smoke and moonlight and beauty beyond his own experience. He could see shadows beneath the fine cloth, mysteries hidden from view, and could only stare.

He did not blink as she untied the lace at the neck of the chemise, then loosened it, baring her shoulders to view. Murdoch's mouth went dry and he dropped the cloth back into the bowl, not wanting even to blink lest he miss a detail. Nyssa smiled, then rolled her shoulders so the chemise dropped to the floor, baring the perfection of her to his view. She was fair and slender, so finely wrought that he could only shake his head in wonder.

And her skin was marked with blue designs. This detail was unexpected and yet, they suited her perfectly. There was a spiral around her arm, one that began at her left wrist and wrapped around her arm to her shoulder, a spiral like an ornamental snake. He had seen similar designs on the ancient stones in the north. On her right arm was a jagged line with a circle in the middle and on the inside of her left wrist was a three-pointed design, not unlike a small sharp flower. The marks were blue and formed of little pricks in the flesh. It only made Nyssa seem more ethereal to him.

Then she lifted her gaze to his, her eyes wide with uncertainty. When he saw her shiver, he knew. She feared this union, though she would not back down.

Murdoch retreated a step and reached for his braies.

"I cannot claim you," he whispered, wondering even as he spoke how he would evade the temptation. "I will not do as much, not when your gift is the price."

She smiled. "You remembered what I said."

"I remember every word you uttered, and I always will."

"But what if I desire this?" she asked, placing her hand upon his chest again. "What if I would know this truth?"

Murdoch raised a hand to her cheek, beguiled by her beauty and her boldness. "Your sister's husband, did he claim you?"

She shook her head. "I am yet a maiden. I fled before Hugh could force our nuptials." He saw the shadows in her gaze and again, his urge to defend her leapt to the fore. If that man had done her injury, Murdoch would hunt him down and demand a toll...

"I am glad you escaped that fiend." He dropped a hand to her shoulder, feeling the softness of her. "I am sorry about your sister, but in your place, I could never have forgiven the father."

Nyssa smiled at him. "I know. You are disinclined to compromise," she said lightly, her tone almost teasing. Her eyes shone, though. "But I like your need for justice." She blinked back sudden tears. "I would like for Elsa to have justice."

Murdoch understood suddenly how she had named the grief in him. Nyssa, too, mourned the loss of her mother and sister, and that loss had shaped her life, stealing its promise and sending her away from all she had known before. She, too, had left her home, and carried her grief alone.

"You would see her death avenged?" He cupped her shoulders in his hands, feeling a new communion with her, a common understanding, lifting her closer and deepening his kiss. They both had lost. They both needed to believe in new promise.

Murdoch was prepared to pledge himself to that quest, but Nyssa shook her head.

"I would see her daughter defended. Hugh will find his own reckoning, if he has not done as much already. I would find Rana, and teach her, and defend my legacy." She said this with conviction, her eyes shining, and Murdoch felt pride flood his heart.

Aye, Nyssa would choose the course of peace. Of course.

Murdoch found himself smiling down at her in the surety of what he had to do. "I will aid you in the search for Rana. You have saved my life and I stand in your debt. I will aid in this endeavor, I swear it to you."

"Thank you," she whispered.

He folded his arms around her to draw her closer, then speared his fingers into her hair, awed and honored by her trust. He bent to capture her lips beneath his own, knowing that this was right beyond all.

He would teach Nyssa of the pleasure that could be found between man and woman.

He would help the healer to recover from whatever she had endured in the past.

NYSSA NOTICED that Murdoch moved slowly, granting her the time to turn him aside if she so chose, and that alone was sufficient to dissolve any uncertainty. She trusted him and knew him to be protective beyond all. This fierce warrior, with his strength and power, treated her as if she was as fragile as a butterfly. She knew he would step back if she asked as much, and that emboldened her as naught else could have done.

His kiss was as sweet and potent as their first embrace had been, and she closed her eyes, welcoming his touch. He was warm and strong, so vehemently male, his touch stirring a response within her that was right and good. She surrendered to sensation with a confidence that came from her chosen partner.

Murdoch kissed her tenderly, his fingers in her hair, his heat but an increment away. He was patient, granting her time to respond, not hastening her onward. Nyssa leaned against him, loving that she could feel the thunder of his heart against her own. She was not the sole one enjoying this, to be sure. She let her hand slide down the length of him and closed it around his strength, hearing him catch his breath, feeling his heart leap.

He deepened his kiss yet more, one arm locking around her waist to draw her ever closer and Nyssa stretched to her toes, inviting more. When he growled a little with pleasure, nipping at her lips with his teeth, she found herself arching against him. She loved that he caught his breath, that he exhaled as if to compel himself to continue slowly, that she could feel the rising tension in him. She caressed him with ever more boldness, liking her power in this encounter. His kiss turned hungry and hot, demanding a response that she was only too happy to provide.

They were lost in each other, feasting on each other's mouths, hands roving over each other's bodies, exploring with a joy that made Nyssa's heart sing. She found herself on his pallet, his cloak spread beneath them, and Murdoch looming over her. For a moment, her audacity faltered, but Murdoch bent to gently kiss her nipple as if paying homage to it and she smiled in her relief.

Then she caught her breath at the sensations he awakened from that one point. A tide of pleasure surged through her, filling her with a liquid heat that was seductive beyond all. She lay back and tangled her fingers in his hair, feeling the brush of his beard on her skin, savoring his kiss. She heard herself moan when he flicked his tongue across her taut nipple and gasped in wonder at the sudden graze of his teeth. She felt him chuckle, then his hand cupped her breast, his broad smooth palm running across her nipple as he bent to tease the other one in similar manner.

When he had tormented her to the point of dizziness, Murdoch braced his weight on his elbow, his other hand sweeping down the length of her, his eyes glowing in the shadows. The sight of his slow smile, the hint of his satisfaction, was enough to make Nyssa's heart race. He caressed her, tracing the lines on her arms with a warm fingertip so slowly that time might have stopped.

"Tell me of them," he invited as if they had all the time in the world.

"They are traditional. My sister's were the same, though she had several more." She watched his fingertip, transfixed by his slow steady movement. "Each denotes a lesson learned or a skill conquered."

"Do you know where your sister rests?"

"At Tom Fhithich."

"The raven's mound," he translated, stealing a kiss that was all too quick.

"Aye, near Duncheann, my father's holding." She studied him, noting that his eyes were a vehement blue. "What of Gwendolyn? Where does she rest?"

"She sleeps in the shade of the tree near the chapel in Rowan Fell."

"And Rupert?"

Murdoch smiled a little. "He lies beside her, as he would have wished." He swallowed. "I carried him from Kilderrick so it could be thus."

Aye, he would. This man's code of honor was strict, but he was most relentless with himself. Nyssa raised a hand to his cheek, her heart filled with admiration. "I insisted that my sister lie beside my mother," she said, wanting him to know that she understood his impulse. "I think of them together forever."

His eyes glinted with humor. "Sending you dreams?"

She smiled back. "Watching over me." She considered his words. "Though my mother could dispatch dreams."

"Perhaps she sent you the dream of Rana," he suggested and Nyssa turned to him with surprise.

"I had not considered that she could yet do as much, but perhaps she did." The very idea gave Nyssa great pleasure.

"Perhaps your dreams will tell us where to find Rana," he murmured, bending to kiss her anew. There was a hunger in his kiss, a purpose that Nyssa welcomed. She knew that with Murdoch's aid, she would find Elsa's daughter—and in his company this night, she would find a new satisfaction.

Murdoch's hand swept down the length of her as he kissed her, and he cupped her breast in his hand once more. He ran his thumb across the nipple so that Nyssa gasped in pleasure, then caught the peak between finger and thumb, pinching it so that she squirmed with delight. She felt his smile, then his hand eased lower. His touch awakened an army of sensation, well beyond all she had ever known before. Then his fingers slid between her thighs and she caught her breath at his bold touch—and the surge of pleasure that rolled through her like a tide.

A heat was roused within her, one that made her pulse race and her body demand a satisfaction she could not name. She felt an ache for something, and Murdoch's every touch only increased her appetite for more. Her nipples were taut and tingling, her skin was flushed, her pulse was racing, and her hips moved of their own volition. When she thought she could endure no more, he caressed her more boldly. Heat raged through Nyssa, enflaming her senses and feeding her need. She felt as if her very soul was afire, then his fingers eased inside her, his thumb sliding across the most sensitive part of her so that she caught her breath.

"Speak to me," he murmured against her throat, kissing her ear and her neck. His thumb teased and tickled her, driving her wild with need, even as his breath made her shiver. "Tell me what you want, Nyssa."

That he used her name made the moment all the more potent.

"More," was all she could say and he chuckled. To her dismay, he moved his hand away just when she felt on the cusp of…something. But he eased down the length of her, trailing kisses over her belly and the tops of her thighs. She felt the brush of his teeth and the heat of his breath, then his mouth closed over her so that she moaned aloud.

She gripped his shoulders, needing to hold on to him, but not wanting him to stop. He tormented her anew, his understanding of her needs so much greater than her own. The tumult rose within Nyssa quickly, catching her between the desire for release and the wish for more pleasure first. Murdoch drove her on, ever higher, caressing her with surety until she was certain she could endure no more. When she was on the cusp of release, he retreated, letting her heartbeat slow then building the tension within her again. 'Twas a dance of unspeakable pleasure, a tease that she began to fear would never reach its culmination. On the other hand, it would be bliss to be snared in such a web of pleasure forever.

When finally, he moved with purpose against her, she guessed that this time, he would not halt. She held on as he drove her higher and higher, urging her toward a precipice much higher than before. It seemed impossible not to perish of such pleasure, but Nyssa trusted Murdoch, surrendered to the sensations he was determined to kindle. She rose higher and higher, then was cast into an abyss of joyous release.

Nyssa heard herself cry out in ecstasy as fire filled her veins, as her entire body was consumed in a conflagration of delight. She fell back against the pallet in wonder, striving to catch her breath, slick with perspiration.

She smiled as Murdoch leaned down beside her and gathered her into his embrace. He braced himself on one elbow and washed them both. There was a glint in his eyes, one that spoke of pride, and Nyssa reached out to touch his unexpected smile with a fingertip.

"Thank you." She traced the curve, watching her hand, and felt his smile broaden.

"You were pleased?"

"Aye. I have never known such a marvel." Their gazes clung for a long moment, one in which she could scarcely take breath.

He surveyed her with undisguised pleasure, then cast the cloth over his erection before he pulled her into his embrace. He buried his face against her neck and inhaled deeply, his hand sliding down the length of her with a proprietary ease that she found thrilling. She felt the press of his manhood against her hip.

"But you…" she began to protest but Murdoch kissed her to silence. His embrace was a little rougher and more demanding than before, but exciting for that. She realized that he touched himself and she put her hand upon his, loving how he eased his thigh between hers. She felt the tumult rise within him with remarkable speed, then he became taut and roared as he found his release.

"Not fair," she whispered as he leaned his brow against her shoulder. "You should have been tempted thrice before your satisfaction."

Murdoch lifted his head, his eyes nigh indigo as he smiled at her. "I was tempted more than thrice," he murmured. "For your pleasure was mine as well."

Nyssa smiled and they stared at each other for a long moment. The rain was still beating on the roof and there was a chill in the air. One candle went out, stirring Murdoch to look away. Nyssa studied his profile, admiring how he had contrived their mutual satisfaction without claiming what she had freely offered. He was a man of principle and she admired that.

He rose and cleaned himself, then fetched her chemise for her. He donned his own, glanced toward Dorcha—who already had his head beneath his wing—then extinguished the remaining candles. He lay down beside Nyssa, locking an arm around her waist and holding her fast against his side. He pulled his cloak over them both and she nestled against him as her eyes drifted shut.

She felt safe as she never had before, and that was because of Murdoch.

He would have her think him a rogue and a mercenary, a man who cared only for his own pleasure, but no such man would cajole a woman's satisfaction so ardently. She trailed her own fingertips down his cheek and he caught her hand in his, turning it to plant a kiss upon her palm. Then he placed her hand on his chest, the beat of his heart beneath her palm, and closed his own hand over top.

"Sleep," he advised then pressed a kiss against her temple. "I take the first watch."

Nyssa's eyes closed even as she smiled.

Just as in her vision, this wolf had been tamed.

'TWAS WORSE THAN A SPELL.

'Twas a dream Nyssa offered and one that tempted Murdoch mightily. She might have peered into the recesses of his heart, the better to name his one deepest desire, then offered it to him as if there was naught remarkable in all of that. He wanted what she offered, wanted it more than he had ever desired anything before in his life. 'Twould be easy to succumb to this temptation.

But it would all go awry.

A home, a family, a life with a woman he admired beyond all—aye, aye, and aye again. 'Twas all Murdoch could do to keep from snatching the prize with both hands, ensuring that opportunity did not escape him.

But how could that vision come to be? A home required funds to build and maintain. He had never learned to read well and was even less accomplished with sums, despite Rupert's efforts. He had never been interested in books and tallies when the world was outside the door. He was no smith, no baker, no brewster, no ostler. Murdoch possessed no skill save that of making war.

He could only earn coin on the battlefield, which meant either joining a company of mercenaries and offering his blade for hire, or serving a laird of import. The sole one of those who knew aught of him was the Silver Wolf, and Murdoch doubted either of them would be hasty in entering such an arrangement. Alliance from afar was one matter, but even Maximilian de Vries would not be so confident as to invite a man to sleep in his abode who had sworn to kill him. He certainly would not pay such a man in hard coin. Nor would Amaury or Rafael, and the Silver Wolf's lack of reference would give the King of Scotland doubts as well. He might as well apply at the court of the English king, where Scots warriors found little favor. Nay, he would be in France again, either way.

And what of Nyssa? He would not take her into those camps of fighting men. Murdoch had never thought to find merit in Jean le Beau with his lusty appetites, but at least that old cur had savored one woman at a time. Any woman who managed to remain a favorite was pampered, though the situation seldom lasted. After a battle, though, Murdoch had seen one woman taken by a dozen men or more in rapid succession, sometimes while her spouse was compelled to watch. He would die rather than let Nyssa face any such indignity.

So, they would remain here, impoverished, hungry, destitute. And he would watch the admiration die in her gaze. He would watch her come to regret her sacrifice. He might witness her start to despise him for failing to be all she had envisioned he might become.

Nay and nay again.

Murdoch rolled from the pallet with vexation, leaving Nyssa nestled in his cloak. He would not do it. He dared not succumb.

What then?

He eyed her, his chest squeezing at her perfection even in sleep. He had a quest unfulfilled, to avenge Rupert's death. He had made a vow to the Silver Wolf to find Eamon the sheriff of Rowan Fell. And he would take Nyssa's task to find her sister's child, though he feared that also might be a dream doomed to disappointment.

'Twas more than sufficient to occupy him. And when 'twas done and he had no cause to linger in Scotland, he would ride south to blood and battlefields and perhaps an early demise.

How curious that the inevitable solution became less appealing with every passing day.

Because of the marvel of Nyssa.

The sound of the falling rain filled the loft as Murdoch struck a tinder and lit one candle. He opened the satchel that Alys had given to him and examined the contents. There was a crockery vessel with a narrower neck, its top sealed with a piece of hide and a length of cord, which contained stew that was still warm. There was bread, and dried meat, along with cheese and apples. He set it all on the small table at one end of the loft, not truly surprised that the raven appeared out of the shadows. Dorcha hopped down to the table to peruse the offerings.

"I thought you slept," he murmured to the bird, which made a sound in its throat that sounded like a question. Murdoch broke off a piece of bread and offered it to his companion, uncertain whether the creature would accept an offering from him, given past events.

Dorcha eyed him for a long moment, then snatched the bread and retreated to the beam he had chosen as his perch. He held the bread against the beam with one claw and tore bites from it with gusto.

"No doubt you would prefer the meat," Murdoch said and the bird considered him with such interest that it might have understood. Murdoch took a small wooden bowl and put an increment of stew within it. The raven abandoned both perch and bread to land on the table again. He marched to the bowl and nudged through its contents, then seized a piece of meat and retreated to the perch to consume it. In moments, he was back for another. When the chunks of meat were gone, Murdoch tore another piece of bread and ran it through the bit of gravy in the bowl.

The raven took it from his very hand, then tipped his head back and swallowed it, without leaving the table. He cocked his head then and eyed the vessel of stew with such obvious expectations that Murdoch found himself chuckling.

"It appears we also are allies now," he said and the raven cawed.

"He will befriend anyone who shares meat with him," Nyssa said. Murdoch glanced over his shoulder to find her watching him, her smile making his heart leap. She rose smoothly to her feet, pausing to wash before she came to his side. Her hair was loose and it brushed against his arm, making everything clench within him. It hung to her hips, all silvery-blond with a slight wave, like a river of moonlight. Had he ever seen a maiden more beautiful?

Murdoch turned back to the table, deliberately averting his gaze from the temptation she offered. "I thought they ate carrion."

"In the wild, they do. He has been with me long enough to have learned to prefer venison stew." Nyssa's smile was wry and Murdoch found himself smiling in turn. Aye, he could imagine how readily one could become accustomed to goodness in her presence. She halted beside him, setting his every sense to tingling, and inhaled with appreciation. "That smells good."

"Alys granted it to me."

Nyssa cast a sparkling glance up at Murdoch and his heart lurched. "Shall we eat now?"

His belly growled then, so he could tell no tale of being sated. He took a bowl and put stew into it, tore another piece of bread from the loaf and offered both to her.

"I thank you," she said, pressing a kiss to his cheek as she accepted it. Her caress sent a quiver straight to his toes and he clenched one fist lest he touch her. She touched him so readily that they might have been intimate a hundred times, a couple who had lived together for years— but his body stirred with the vigor of novelty. He dared not imagine years with Nyssa, or even of months, but he doubted his reaction to her presence would fade soon.

If at all.

Not that it mattered. Their paths must part and soon.

Murdoch served out more stew, granting an increment more to the watchful bird, then took it and a piece of bread when he returned to sit on the pallet. Nyssa brought hers and joined him. The rain was coming down hard, pounding on the thatch overhead, and a few familiar leaks were making themselves known. He pointed one out to her so it did not drip upon her and she moved a little closer to his side. He swallowed and stared at the bowl, convinced that he was his own worst enemy in this.

"You did not finish what we began," Nyssa said finally. Oh, how he liked the low timber of her voice and the softness of it. The sound of it alone could make him tingle with desire, no matter what she said. When she spoke of intimacy, it lit a fire within him.

"I did not intend to do as much," he acknowledged.

"But I did."

"And I have no desire to be the man who eliminates your gift."

"Not even if I surrender it willingly?"

He frowned. "I cannot imagine that you would, or that you would not subsequently regret the choice. 'Tis a rare skill and a potent one."

"Perhaps the wager is a fair one, in my view."

Murdoch stared straight ahead, that he not lose himself in her gaze. "I have already pledged to aid in your search for your sister's daughter. You need make no sacrifice to ensure my aid."

"Is my view of no import?" She put her hand on his arm and Murdoch had to set the bowl aside as his desire raged, threatening to overwhelm his principles.

The raven was not one to overlook opportunity. Within a heartbeat, the bird was perched on the side of Murdoch's bowl, eating the two pieces of meat remaining.

"He will sleep three days after this feast," Nyssa said with a smile. She slid her hand up Murdoch's arm and he closed his eyes against the tide of need. "Are you not curious?"

"Nay, I can guess what a marvel our union would be." He spoke more curtly than was his intention and her hand halted. He shook his head, then swallowed. "But I fight temptation to the last."

"Why?" She insisted on tracing her fingertips across his skin, a most distracting and beguiling caress.

"A hundred reasons, including those already mentioned."

"There are more?"

"You might conceive a child, for example."

The notion did not trouble her. "I should have a daughter of my own, then."

She was so untroubled that Murdoch considered her with astonishment. "But you cannot wish for that. You cannot wish to be despoiled and abandoned with a child in your belly, as my mother was."

Nyssa shook her head. "There would be no similarity with what your mother endured. You will not forcibly take my maidenhead from me, and you will not abandon me."

The first was true, but Murdoch shook his head about the second. How could she be so certain? "But I might be compelled to leave your side. I might be killed. I might fail to fulfill my word to the Silver Wolf to his satisfaction and pay the price. Even if I would not leave you by choice, you could still be left alone."

"Even if?" she echoed softly.

He took a breath, bracing himself to say what had to be made clear. "I will not pledge to you. I will not take your maidenhead and I will not commit to any future between us."

"Whyever not?"

"Because it cannot be!"

"No one can fully predict the future. I would take the risk."

He felt the weight of her gaze but did not look at her. He spoke with resolve. "You have more wit than that. I have no means to provide for a wife or a child. I have no coin, and if I consider a future as you have urged, I can only see my return to the Compagnie Rouge or a similar company. That is no place for a wife, and less of one for a child. More, you have a gift, and your skill should not be cast aside for mere satisfaction."

"I suspect there would be naught *mere* about it."

"And you would be wrong. Desire comes and goes. Satisfaction is fleeting. You would be surrendering much for a small reward and I will not be a part of such a sacrifice." He spoke with conviction, wanting to persuade her beyond all doubt, and feared he had been too fierce for there was a long moment of silence. Did she weep? Her head was bowed, her hair hiding her features.

Aye, he was a cur and a blackguard. Even in doing what was right, he stepped awry.

"But I have taken your quest," he said gruffly. Here was an opportunity to gather detail, and also to break the silence between them. "What of the girl's appearance?"

"In my vision, I thought she was my sister. I thought 'twas a memory at first. Her hair is long and fair like mine, and she is slender and tall as Elsa was." She shrugged. "But there were raven feathers woven into her hair, an adornment Elsa never would have chosen."

"You and Elsa looked alike?"

"Aye, but Elsa's eyes were blue."

He nodded once.

Nyssa frowned. "There was another child in my dream, one whose hands resembled those of the midwife, Mary Gunn. She came to aid with Elsa's first pregnancy and remained. A most sensible woman, and kindly, too. Her fingers were blunt and strong. This child's hands were similar."

"That makes sense," Murdoch acknowledged. "If the midwife ensured Rana's escape from Duncheann, she might have raised her along with her own children."

Nyssa's expression brightened. "I was thinking of Rana alone and abandoned, but you speak aright. She might have been raised with a family, one that offered more affection than the Sutherlands granted to Elsa and I."

"You fostered with them?"

"Aye. My mother paid them but their favor of the situation lasted only so long as the coin." There was an increment of bitterness in Nyssa's tone when she continued. "Then when we were reunited with our father and returned to Duncheann, their oldest son, Hugh, realized his abiding affection for my sister." She shook her head. "My mother would not accept his suit, for Elsa did not desire it, but once she died, my father made the agreement without delay."

Once again, Murdoch saw evidence that Nyssa's father had been less than kind to his children. 'Twas a marvel that Nyssa had any ability to trust a man at all. "And Rana was born at this Duncheann?" He watched her nod, wishing she would raise her gaze to his but knowing his resolve would be lost if she did. "Where is that?"

"East of Inverness on the north coast. The keep is built on an island, though the holding includes a village and its fields."

"That is a mighty distance," he felt compelled to note.

"I managed to travel it." Her tone was sharper than expected.

"I have no doubt that I will, as well." Murdoch frowned. "You must consider that if Rana is only in the village and shares your coloring, she has likely been found by now."

"Mary may have taken her to kin. I do not know where she was from. 'Twas not Duncheann."

All the same, Murdoch feared the prospect of a good result less than promising. He did not wish to disappoint Nyssa, so he kept silent.

She cleared her throat finally. "You say there is no place in your life for a wife and child. Does that mean you will deny yourself forever?"

Murdoch pushed a hand through his hair. "I might indulge myself with a whore, for such women know the price of their trade and have means to address any such cost."

Her eyes narrowed slightly. "You might pay a whore for satisfaction but will not accept what I freely offer?"

"Nyssa, I cannot. The price to you is too high. Such women have no expectations."

Her hand slid to his thigh and thence to the power hidden beneath his plaid. She touched him, gently at first, then with greater boldness. He closed his eyes, taut as an archer's drawn bow, and felt himself shudder. "It seems you desire me," she whispered.

"Aye, but I should not. I have not the right."

She shook her head. "Desire is not a right to be earned."

"It should be," Murdoch insisted, the ghost of Jean le Beau at his very shoulder. "I am not a man to follow my prick, whatever its counsel or however much it insists," he continued with resolve. "I will only beget a child when I have a wife, and I will only have a wife when I have a home and a means of supporting such a woman."

"I do not care whether I am a wife."

Murdoch rose to his feet so abruptly that he hit his head on one of the low beams. He winced and ducked, sparing Nyssa a hot glance. "Enough! I will not take what you offer," he said with heat. "And you will not persuade me otherwise. This suggestion you make cannot be!"

Nyssa rose smoothly to her feet, her chemise swirling around her ankles, her hair loose and a thousand beguiling shadows visible beneath the cloth. Aye, she was an enchantress, and she held him in thrall. But there was a fire in her eyes when she raised her gaze to his, a reminder that she was not wrought of mist and moonbeams. Nay, she had a will like forged steel and he felt only admiration of that.

"But if ever you decide to take a wife or father a child, will you seek me out?" she asked and Murdoch caught his breath.

"Of course not," he said. "For if I vowed as much to you this day, you would wait upon me."

She smiled. "Aye, I would."

Murdoch shook his head, dazzled by the reward of her smile, uncertain how he might convince her. "You cannot," he protested. "You should not..."

"But I *do*. You are the sole man I desire, Murdoch Campbell, and that will never change." Before he could express his astonishment, Nyssa caught his face between her hands and kissed him with such demand that his every thought was banished.

There was only Nyssa and her sweet demand, Nyssa and her surety, Nyssa and her confidence that all would come aright. For a man who had seen so much go awry and had learned to expect as much, he found her conviction almost as compelling as her touch.

Indeed, he wished he had the folly to accept this woman who challenged all he knew to be true. Murdoch would not be the one to disappoint her, not so long as he drew breath.

But one final kiss was too much temptation to resist.

CHAPTER 11

*B*ut how could you return without Cedric?" Jeannie demanded again. She had been startled to wakefulness by a noisy intrusion into her cottage, then alarmed by two shadows looming over her in the darkness. That one had proven to be Eamon had done little to dismiss her fright.

For his sole companion was the dark-haired warrior with the shadowed gaze. That man had retreated to stand with his back against the door, and had yet to speak. His arms were folded across his chest and he watched them with the avidity of a hawk.

Jeannie's hands shook as she lit another lantern and brought it to the table, as she put bread and ale in front of Eamon. He had lost weight during his absence. His garments were soiled and he looked to be exhausted, but worse, she knew he feared his companion.

Though she could understand that view well enough, she would hide it with all her might.

"Where is Cedric?" she asked when she had no reply to her query. The silent one raised a shoulder, either because he did not know or did not care. She sat down hard facing Eamon. The man would not meet her gaze, which was no good sign.

"I do not know," he confessed heavily.

"How can you not know?" Jeannie demanded. "He is my cousin's son. You rode out as his companion. How can you return without him, with no explanation and no notion of his location?"

Eamon granted her a hostile glance and began to eat. "This is all your doing," he muttered.

"Oh, there is an explanation," the stranger said. He straightened from the wall and strolled across the hut, taking a seat beside Jeannie. She fought her urge to pull away from him and instead met his gaze steadily. "But you will not like it." He smiled, which was scarce better than when he scowled.

Jeannie's innards trembled but she reached across the table and seized Eamon's hand. "Tell me," she insisted and he sighed.

He pushed the bread and ale away. "Our party was divided in Carlisle," he admitted. "After matters went awry."

Jeannie's breath caught at that. "Awry?" she asked, her voice rising in concern.

Eamon frowned. "Cedric had a notion that we should raid the home of a known moneylender."

Jeannie felt her lips purse. She supposed the best place to seek wealth was where it was gathered, but she would also expect a man in the habit of keeping large quantities of coin might ensure its defense.

"I see that you disapprove," Eamon said and flung out his hands. "But you must agree that such a man would have coin."

"And you must have anticipated that such a man would see his treasure defended," she snapped. She noticed how the stranger's smile broadened and turned upon him.

"We were not unprepared for that," he said softly. "Our numbers were such that we had a good chance of success, given what was known of the household."

That sounded ominous to Jeannie.

"And we learned on the way that he had been collecting debts and tithes for the king," the Eamon said.

"The venture sounded most promising," the stranger agreed.

Eamon looked grim. "And so, we charged his gate in the midst of the night and forced our entry, overwhelming the guard and the man himself. His treasury might have been that of a king, for it overflowed with abundance. I have never seen such quantities of coin!"

Jeannie felt her lips tighten and folded her arms across her chest. "Yet with only two men to defend it."

Eamon granted her a dark glance. "A pity then that you did not embark upon this journey, with your greater wisdom to share."

"'Tis only good sense!"

"Continue the tale," the stranger urged and Eamon did.

"We filled our sacks with as much as we could carry and hastened to depart. I was last, by dint of my burden, so was caught by the guard. The man revived as I stepped over him, and seized my ankle. The others ran. I fell. He shouted for aid and panic struck me when I heard the footfalls of more guards approaching. I could not be caught in the act of thieving!" Eamon passed a hand over his face and fell silent.

"What did you do?" Jeannie asked softly, fearing his reply.

"I drew my blade," Eamon said and swallowed. "And I escaped." He raised his gaze to hers, his eyes so dark that he looked haunted. He pulled his dagger and placed it on the board.

There was blood upon the blade. Jeannie's mouth opened and closed as she stared.

Eamon continued, his tone bitter. "I fled, abandoning my sack of coins. I have never been so frightened in all my days and nights."

"Were you injured?"

Eamon flicked a hot glance her way. "Nay."

Though she was glad of that detail, Jeannie could not feel relieved. "And then?" she prompted.

"There was a hue and cry," the stranger provided.

"'Twas Cedric's suggestion that we should divide, the better to evade detection," Eamon continued. "They were nigh upon us by that point, bells ringing and men shouting. Cedric led half of the party to the east, while Erik here led the rest of us north. We then divided again to leave the city by different gates, so that Erik and I rode on together." He gestured toward the stream. "The boy, Angus, is with us and the coin."

Jeannie considered the other man who steadily held her regard.

This Erik would be relentless in pursuit of his goal, whatever it might be, and she could not help but think it of import that they guarded much of the reward. "And where is your share?" she asked, distrusting how Eamon grimaced. "Surely all would divide the spoils, even though you had to leave some behind?"

"Surely they would," Eamon agreed heavily. "But since I abandoned my claim, the sum was less. I knew my share would be insufficient to pay the laird." He cast a dark glance at Erik. "Erik offered a wager over dice last night when we took shelter from the rain, and I seized the chance to double my gains."

He fell silent then and Jeannie guessed the result. "And you lost," she said with disgust, pushing to her feet. "First you spend the coin that is not yours to spend—"

"You had a share in that, Jeannie!"

"Then you ride out with reivers to steal—"

He shook a finger at her. "At your instigation, Jeannie."

She leaned her hands on the board to glare at him. "Then you *killed* a man—"

"In defense of my own self," Eamon said sullenly. "'Twas him or me."

"And *then* you gambled away your meagre gains, so that you are returned with less than when you departed." She shook her head. "I cannot believe that I am wed to such a man as this. Perhaps you should have sent the guard home in your place."

"You are not without guilt in this matter, Jeannie," Eamon growled.

"I did not strike a man dead!" she shouted and Eamon sat back, his expression mutinous.

"How unfortunate that you have naught to sell," Erik said finally, his manner too smooth to be trusted. Jeannie turned to look at him, sickened by their situation, and the cur smiled. "I would surrender my entire share, for example, and that of Eamon, too, for a tale."

"For a tale," Jeannie echoed, skeptical beyond all.

Erik rose to his feet. He strolled around the hut, peering at this empty shelf and that bare cupboard. "I seek a woman I once called sister," he said softly. "Who left our family abode alone."

"Why did she leave?" Jeannie asked.

He raised a hand. "Who can name the whim of a young girl? Perhaps she was in love with a man of whom we would not approve. Perhaps she had a yearning for adventure." He pivoted to face them, his eyes fairly glowing. "Perhaps 'twas because she was declared a witch."

When he stood thus, Jeannie was struck by the unfathomable darkness of his eyes. He was taller than Eamon and wrought more slender, though she had no doubt of his strength. She could not hold his gaze, which she found chilling.

Aye, he might have been the one to name her witch.

Though Jeannie had been unafraid to name a witch when she knew of one. She thought of what she had seen earlier in the day, a sight for which she had no explanation, but a detail that might prove highly useful.

"Was she a witch?" she asked.

"I suspect so." Erik shook his head sadly. "Yet we grew up together as siblings. Her older sister wed my older brother. Do you know the fear of not knowing the fate of a loved one? I fear for her alone and undefended." He sighed. "I have sought her ever since her departure, fearing to find her dead or abused." He shook his head with apparent concern, though Jeannie was not convinced of his fears. "A maiden alone can find herself in great peril."

Jeannie wagered this maiden might have had good reason to flee her family home, if all her kin were like this man.

"From whence do you come?" she asked.

"Far to the north. I have searched near our family home without success. And some months ago, I heard a tale that there had been four witches known at a ruined holding south of Galashiels. It took me some time to learn the holding was Kilderrick, too much time, for those witches are said to be gone." He feigned dejection, but his eyes glittered.

He knew.

"Not gone," Jeannie said. "One wed the laird himself."

"Is that so?" Erik returned to his seat beside her, his attention fixed upon her.

"Aye. A second wed the Lord de Beaupoint and the third wed the Baron of Gisroy," Eamon supplied.

"How remarkable. And all witches?"

"Nay, there was only one true witch among them," Jeannie said.

"There were said to be four." Erik's gaze locked with hers as if he had read her very thoughts, as if he would will a confession from her lips. Jeannie could not so much as blink.

On the one hand, she did not wish to be this man's ally in any matter; on the other, what matter if she surrendered a witch to her own kin, in exchange for the coin to pay the laird and their own future security? Witches invariably earned their due sooner or later.

And she had to have seen what she had seen earlier for a reason.

"Her name is Nyssa Le Cheyne, though once she was Nyssa Sutherland," Erik continued quietly, his gaze compelling. "And I would pay a great deal to be able to escort her home again. My brother lies ill and would be much comforted by the return of his wife's sister."

Jeannie did not even look at Eamon. She did not wish to be swayed by sentiment. Sentiment had no merit in this situation. A witch was a witch, and the world was better with fewer of them.

Jeannie took a breath. "How much?" she asked and Erik smiled so that his teeth were bared.

Though it felt like someone walked over her grave, she refused to shiver in dread.

MURDOCH KNEW he was a fool beyond all expectation. He had touched Nyssa again, finding a primal satisfaction in her joyous release, and now watched her sleep, discontent. She was nestled in her own cloak on the pallet, the raven making a noise that might have been interpreted as amusement. Murdoch refused to even approach her again, for proximity only undermined his resolve.

He would depart upon her quest at first light.

Alone.

He straightened when he heard horses, relieved of the distraction. He stood in darkness, even the raven silent overhead as the rain slowed its onslaught.

Not horses. Ponies. Whoever arrived did as much in stealth, which fed Murdoch's conviction that they arrived for no good purpose.

Could Eamon have returned with his companions? Where had they gone and why?

His thoughts raced. If 'twas the same party, they had been gone five days, which limited the possible distance to less than three days ride. Considering that they might have travelled only at night, that they rode ponies instead of horses and that a larger company always journeyed more slowly, Murdoch concluded that they could readily have reached Carlisle. They might even have ventured a little farther south and returned in the elapsed time.

That sounded like a reiving party.

Perhaps his pledge to the Silver Wolf would be fulfilled this very day.

Murdoch went to the end of the loft closest to the river. Here, he had made a gap in the thatch and a panel that could be removed to grant him a view. As he looked through it, he wished the moon might have been brighter and larger. The skies were overcast, but he could discern movement by the stream. A pony nickered, and then another. He saw at least one silhouette moving through the gorse.

Murdoch dressed quickly, glad that Nyssa was no longer wrapped in his cloak. She would never know he had been gone. He saluted the bird, which bobbed its head, then descended from the loft in silence. He donned his boots, then unfastened the door and peered into the darkness before he left the hut. He was struck by the stillness of the night. Then he heard someone cough. Murdoch eased into the shadows on the downhill side of the hut and made his way into the scrub.

If the sheriff returned from reiving, there would be evidence in his belongings. A pony nickered, followed by a crack of ice and a slight splash. No one chastised the beast or advised it to silence. If they had left the ponies hidden along with their spoils, this was his chance to gain evidence of Eamon's deeds for the Silver Wolf.

Murdoch could guess the location of the ponies by the steam that rose from their hides, a sure sign that they had run hard. There were also far fewer creatures than previously. He saw three, nay, four. Had only a fraction of the party returned? Where were the rest? These ponies were burdened with bulging saddlebags, still harnessed and tethered to the trees, a sure sign that their riders would not pause in Rowan Fell for long.

Here was the chance to learn what they carried.

Murdoch waited and he looked, but he must have imagined that one fleeting shadow. The ponies appeared to be tethered and left, perhaps while the party made a visit to Eamon's hut. They would not linger.

He eased forward quickly, placing a hand on the flank of the closest pony. He murmured something and the beast exhaled, flicking its tail with disinterest. Murdoch opened the closest saddlebag and the contents gleamed in the shadows. Murdoch reached into the bag. His hand sank into a saddlebag filled with silver pennies, their chill considerable and shape unmistakable. His fingers were buried within them and he could not feel the bottom of the bag as yet. There was a veritable fortune in just this one bag, and even this beast carried a second.

A second pony was similarly burdened. Murdoch took a step to confirm the contents of its saddlebag. His hand was buried in silver coins again when Murdoch realized he was not alone.

He spun to defend himself, but too late. He saw no more than a menacing shadow before he was punched in the face. Murdoch staggered backward as blood spurted from his nose. He had a moment to close his hand around the coins that he grasped, then he was struck in the temple and knew no more.

∾

GONE.

Murdoch had vanished.

Nyssa sat in darkness, at first with patience and then with growing annoyance. He had made his view clear, but she had never expected him to simply leave without saying farewell. He could not have embarked on her quest. His satchel was yet in the loft. Surely, he would have packed all his belongings before such a journey.

As time passed, though, his absence seemed more portentous.

Was this the price of disagreement? Did the man walk away from any who refused to be persuaded to his view? She would not have expected such a vexatious choice from him, but he was gone all the same.

There was no sound from beyond the hut. She could not be certain how much time had passed—every moment seemed an eternity—but she was certain that he should have returned by now.

If he had intended to do as much.

Nyssa fumed as she rose to her feet and dressed with savage gestures. She had chosen him. She knew they belonged together. She had faith in the merit of their future, but Murdoch not only disputed their prospects with her, but when she disagreed with his view, he left.

That was a coward's choice, to be sure, and one she would never have expected of such a valiant warrior.

Perhaps he had done her a favor in this, then. Perhaps she misunderstood his nature.

Nay!

Another might have said 'twas better thus, but Nyssa could not agree.

Though truly, she had never been so vexed with another. She would return to Kilderrick at dawn. Perhaps Royce might aid her to find Rana. She doubted as much, though. That mercenary was more likely to list the reasons why such an endeavor was folly.

Perhaps men were all the same.

Nay, again. Nyssa refused to believe as much.

She was tugging on her boots when she had an unwelcome thought. What if something had befallen Murdoch? What if he had left the hut for some earthy reason, and fallen? What if he had been assaulted?

Nay, not in Rowan Fell.

She bit her lip, though, recalling the party he had heard on the night of the new moon. Had that been the truth or a tale? If 'twas truth, they might have returned.

Murdoch might have ridden away with them.

The silence seemed ominous to her now. Nyssa descended from the loft. She opened the door with care, halfway thinking she would see

Murdoch striding toward her, that he would chastise her gruffly for her concern.

Naught. She stared into the shadows of the gorse that lined the stream and listened. She heard only a trickle of water.

Was that the nicker of a pony hidden in the scrub? Nyssa leaned forward in the same moment that she thought she heard a splash.

Silence followed that sound.

Had Murdoch stumbled in the darkness? Was he injured?

Nyssa left the hut, needing to know for certain. She darted across the small gap between the hut and the stream, glad to reach the protective shadows close to the water. The stream was almost silent here, its flow so diminished in the winter, and ice cracked loudly beneath her boot.

Moments later, she halted. She could see the silhouettes of ponies, steam rising from their coats as they stood by the stream. She counted three. They were saddled as yet, their saddlebags open.

In the middle of the night.

What was this?

Nyssa had a bad feeling. She moved quickly to the closest pony, noting that the saddlebag was unfastened, as if it had been opened. The hair pricked on the back of her neck, but she reached within it.

She touched cloth before a man's hand landed abruptly upon her upper arm. She might have screamed but a heavy hand was clamped over her mouth. She was hauled roughly against her assailant and raised her hand to pull away his hand. She felt a ring beneath her fingertips and heard him chuckle when she froze.

Nyssa knew that ring.

Her heart sank to her toes.

She had been found.

"Well met, sister mine," her captor murmured, his tone mocking. Nyssa's very innards writhed. "Promise your silence and I will release you."

Nyssa knew she would not be truly released. This man would happily cut out her tongue if she defied him, but she did not wish to be close to him. She nodded once and he removed his hand from her mouth, spinning her to face him though he did not relinquish his grip on her arm.

Aye, the man with the unfathomable dark gaze was familiar beyond all.

His appearance had changed little, from what she could discern. His heart, she knew, would be blacker than ever. His expression made that clear.

"Erik," she whispered. They were not siblings by blood, but she knew he would readily use her in pursuit of his ambitions. Even as a child, he had been wicked, more wicked than his older brother, Hugh. Erik might have sought her at his brother's behest, but the glint in his eyes warned her that he would not surrender her willingly to another.

Nyssa struggled against her urge to shiver.

Erik inclined his head as if they met at the king's own court. "Nyssa."

"Where is Murdoch?" Panic rose within her—and new understanding for Murdoch's absence. He had not vanished by choice. She peered into the shadows, unable to see him. "What have you done to him?"

'Twas just as he had forecast, that he might be compelled to leave her alone. How she hated for his words to come true, and so quickly.

"Who?" Erik raised a brow. "If he is a defender of yours, you must learn to choose more reliable protectors, for there is no living man here but you and I." He jerked his head even as Nyssa's heart sank. Murdoch was dead. "And Angus, of course."

She noticed a silhouette in the trees, the shape of a man with a hood drawn high.

Two of them against her, and no prospect of assistance.

Nyssa lifted her chin, striving to hide her fear. "Why are you here?"

Erik laughed, as bold and merciless as ever. "Seeking my fortune, as all errant younger brothers must do. You may rest assured that I have found it. A witch for my own! What splendid good fortune."

His words made no sense to Nyssa. "What do you mean? Why are you even in Rowan Fell?"

"Ah! I heard a tale of four witches in a distant holding called Kilderrick." He lifted his brows. "Despite my skepticism, it seems I have found the only one of import."

Nyssa tugged at her arm, but his grip was unshakeable. "I am no witch and you know it. I am a seer."

"Yet the sheriff's wife does not make the distinction."

"Jeannie!"

"Jeannie," Erik agreed. "A harridan I will be glad to leave behind, to be sure. Fear not, I have paid a mighty price for her confession, so she has been well compensated."

Nyssa was sickened by his claim. Those funds would ensure that Eamon could repay the Silver Wolf, thereby protecting his post as sheriff. 'Twas wicked and wrong, but there was little Nyssa could do about it with Erik holding fast to her arm. Indeed, his fingers dug into her flesh.

"I have sought you far and wide, Nyssa." Erik gave her a little shake, then urged her toward a pony. "Let us hasten home."

Home. Duncheann had never been home for Nyssa. She considered the merit of fighting Erik but knew she would need the advantage of surprise. She wondered whether she could surprise him here and ensure her escape, then he said the sole words that could have changed her thinking.

"And truly, Rana will be glad to see you."

"Rana?" Nyssa turned to stare at him.

"Surely you recall Elsa's youngest daughter?"

"But, but she died."

"Nay, she did not. We were deceived." Erik's conviction sent shivers down Nyssa's spine. "But in my search for you, I found the child some months ago. She is now *safe* at Duncheann."

Did he lie? Nyssa hoped as much but she dared not guess. If Rana was at Duncheann, she had to be captive there—or she had been deceived. The very possibility that Rana survived in Hugh's custody gave Nyssa new purpose.

She had to find out for certain.

"Hugh is unwell these days, I fear," Erik continued. "Though I have no ability to glimpse into the future, I suspect my brother's state will worsen shortly after our arrival at Duncheann." He patted his purse and chuckled, though Nyssa could make little sense of that. His eyes shone. "I have a gift for him, one he will not be able to resist, to his own detriment."

"And you will claim my father's holding in his stead," Nyssa guessed.

Her foster brother's smile flashed. "With the seer's surviving daughter as my bride. It gives such a measure of legitimacy to wed the daughter of the former laird. Fear not, Nyssa," he dropped his voice to a whisper. "I will not be so fickle as my brother, not when you ensure our good fortune with your arts."

"And what of daughters?" she had to ask.

"I might welcome one, though truly, a son is always best." He winked at her. "You might keep that notion in mind when you conjure a child."

He lied about the fate of daughters and Nyssa knew it. She would be trapped in her father's keep, captive like her sister, and any daughters would be doomed. She realized then that he was the ravaging wolf she had feared, the one who would devour all to ensure his own gain.

But if there was any chance that he spoke the truth about Rana being at Duncheann, Nyssa had no choice but to accompany him. She could not hide at Kilderrick any longer. She had been found, as she had long feared, and her future, whatever it might be, would be determined at Duncheann. And without Murdoch by her side, there was no reason to remain at Kilderrick.

Her path led to Duncheann.

"And so, you have a choice, fair Nyssa," Erik said, his grip tightening upon her again. "Make no mistake, you will accompany me this night. The decision is yours whether you will ride as a member of my company or arrive at Duncheann bound as a captive."

"You know I would prefer to ride," Nyssa said. "And truly, I welcome your tidings. I have missed Duncheann, but have always feared Hugh. That holding will be more hospitable without him." She shivered, watching Erik's eyes narrow.

"Aye." Erik was skeptical but his grip loosened slightly. He urged her toward a pony and a younger man stepped out of the shadows, casting back his hood. This had to be Angus, and his expression revealed that he would be of no aid to her—in fact, Nyssa would be certain that she was not left alone with him.

Wolves had a tendency to conspire with other vermin.

But she would conquer against these brothers, inspired by Murdoch's resolve to see justice done.

The reins of Nyssa's pony were held fast by Erik, a sign that she was not to be trusted much. They rode west along the stream, just three ponies, Erik, the younger man and herself. There were no sounds of pursuit, though Nyssa had not expected otherwise. She wondered whether she would be missed at Kilderrick and could not imagine that it would be easy to track their route, by Erik's design.

Then she heard a raven cry and the sound lifted her heart. Dorcha would follow her. Who could say—she and the raven might find and free Rana where a more doughty warrior might fail.

Nyssa had to believe in the best outcome—and do whatever she could to bring it about.

Patience would be the key.

~

"MAKE HASTE!" Someone hissed the words into Murdoch's ear, someone who shook his shoulder roughly at the same time. He was wet and cold, his head ached and the light was dim. It was just before the dawn, he decided when he opened his eyes, a mist rising from the stream and the light pale.

For a moment, he could not understand how he had come to be lying in the muck on the far side of the stream, then he felt something cold and hard in his grasp. He opened his hand to find silver coins there, their impressions dug into his palm, and remembered.

Nerida gave a sigh of relief. "God in Heaven, lad, I thought you would never stir," she said in an urgent whisper. "You must hasten back to the hut to hide before Jeannie feeds her chickens."

"How did you find me?"

"I came down to the bees and the portal was open." Her tone turned scolding. "You should not ever leave it unlatched."

"I did not." Murdoch sat up, which made his head thunder. He pushed his fingers through his hair and winced when he found the lump. "I was struck down."

"Aye, looking where you should not. Up, boy!" The old woman urged him to his feet, her manner anxious. "I followed the tracks."

Murdoch looked around, but the ponies had vanished, along with their riders. He had been pulled away from the stream, further from the village, on the far bank where the growth was thicker. Nerida had followed the two troughs left by his boots in the mud.

He looked at the silver coins again. In daylight, he could see that they were English coins. All from the same mint and all newly struck, by their gleam. 'Twould be uncommon to find a large hoard of similar ones in a single place. He strode back to the stream where the ponies had been and stared into the water.

"Ha!" To his satisfaction, there were more coins spilled there. They would have been difficult to see in the darkness and rain, but Murdoch could see them now. He gathered them all, while Nerida fussed beside him, much like an agitated chicken herself. Now he discerned the hoof-prints of the ponies in the wet bank.

Reivers, to be sure, and Eamon likely amongst them.

He looked up, confirming that the sheriff's cottage was the closest. He could see the rump of the sheriff's pony in the lean-to behind the cottage.

Eamon was back, and had returned on the same night that the party with the coins had arrived.

"Hasten yourself!" Nerida whispered and Murdoch followed her back to the small hut.

Nerida gave Murdoch a shove when they reached the hut, sending him over the threshold with a strength he had not known she possessed. Then she braced her hands on her hips and scowled at him. He strove to look meek, though in truth, he fought the urge to laugh at her. She was so outraged and so tiny. He could have tipped her over his shoulder with little effort and carried her off, but she shook a finger at him.

"Never ever leave the door unlatched." She shook her head, continuing in a fierce whisper. "Any manner of vermin could come for my honey. I trust you to defend my interests and my livelihood, otherwise I should never have let you linger here. You may be nigh the last of my kin but there is a limit..."

Belatedly, Murdoch realized the stillness in the hut and guessed who had left the door unlatched. He spun and climbed to the loft, knowing before he looked that Nyssa was gone. Her cloak and boots were missing, though her satchel was yet there.

Had she gone back to Kilderrick? Nay, not at night and in the rain, not without a word to him. Not without her satchel. Murdoch heard the raven cry, then hurried back outside, lunging past a sputtering Nerida. The bird circled over the hut and cried, then flew hard to the west.

Murdoch understood. Nyssa was with the reivers. He doubted her departure was by choice. She must have sought him and been over-come. He caught his breath, sickened by her prospects. How long had it been? Was she already despoiled? How could he have been such a fool as to let himself be assaulted?

"What is amiss?" Nerida asked.

"Did you see her?" he demanded of Nerida and she sighed.

"You would be a fool to lose your heart to a witch," she said gently, as if she knew it was already too late for such advice. "I saw her arrive yesterday, but not depart."

"She was here when I left," Murdoch said. "And now she is gone."

Nerida's eyes widened even as dread grew in Murdoch's heart.

"They have taken her," he said and she nodded agreement.

"Reivers only ride west from here, because of the Laird of Kilderrick," she said and pointed. "Once 'twas otherwise, but now they ride from here to the road, then north to Hawick or south to Langholm."

"Aye." Murdoch thought of the raven, even as he packed his satchel with haste. Would the bird lead him to Nyssa? He could only hope.

"You mean to pursue her." Nerida looked skeptical of this.

"Aye. I vowed to aid her in finding her sister's daughter," he confessed, then pressed the silver coins into Nerida's hand.

The older woman gasped when she realized what he had given her. "How did you come by such a fortune, lad?"

"There were four ponies last night, in the stream, the saddlebags of at least two loaded with coins. *These* coins. I had found them when I was struck down."

Nerida was turning them in her hands, and they looked even brighter than before. "They are all the same." She looked up. "No hoard of coins is all the same."

"Save if they are newly minted," Murdoch said and her eyes widened. "And therein lies a hint, for if Eamon is returned—"

"His pony is there this morn." She spoke with authority. "He is back."

"And he pays the Silver Wolf with coins like these, then he was part of that reiving party." Murdoch held up his fingers. "They were here on the new moon, then again last night. Five nights. They could ride to the south of Carlisle and back, but not much further."

Nerida inhaled sharply. "I will keep these for you."

"Nay, Nerida, you must take them to the Silver Wolf without delay."

"Because you vowed to aid him?"

"Because he can discover if there was a theft in Carlisle two nights ago. Tell him what I saw and when. 'Twas on the new moon that I saw them first, and the party was much larger. I would guess a dozen ponies that night."

"But only three or four last night? Where are the rest?"

"Something must have gone awry for them to separate."

Nerida nodded. "Perhaps they were caught."

"Perhaps Lord Amaury knows more of this matter."

"Aye." Nerida's fingers closed over the coins. "I will tell the laird this very day."

"Be sure that Jeannie does not become suspicious."

"Dara will have to take the kirtle to Lady Alys this day," Nerida said with conviction. "I am certain of it."

Murdoch smiled in his relief. "Aye, there is a scheme."

"You mean to follow the reivers alone, lad," the older woman guessed, her tone turning stern. "No sooner are you free of one trouble than you take up another…"

"We both can guess what Nyssa's fate will be if no one comes to her aid. And no one else even knows she has been claimed." He pushed belongings into his satchel even as he spoke. "How can I not ride in pursuit?"

Nerida, he thought, seemed to swallow a smile, but there was naught amusing about the situation. She was sober when she spoke. "But how will you find her?"

"I have tracked men before." Murdoch smiled. "And the raven calls to me. I will follow the corbie and find the seer."

Nerida shook her head. "You cannot do this alone. They are a company..."

"And they will never expect a single man to come after them."

"Then you will return?" Nerida asked and Murdoch was compelled to shake his head.

"I vowed to Nyssa that I would aid her with her own quest. Her sister died in the delivery of a daughter and she long thought the daughter dead, as well. That was why she left her home years ago, only halting when she reached Kilderrick. But she has dreamed of late of the girl and wishes to find her."

"Aye. She would." Nerida patted his arm. "She may have need of a warrior's aid, though. You must help her."

"I will, Nerida, even if we must search as far as Nyssa's home."

"Where was her home?"

"A keep called Duncheann, to the east of Inverness, upon the coast. You must tell the Silver Wolf where I have gone, lest he believe that I have abandoned my pledge to him."

"You speak aright that he may learn more of the reivers' deeds from his brothers." Her gaze became worried. "But you must show care."

"I will." Murdoch caught Nerida's shoulders in his hands, then kissed her cheeks. He smiled down at her, well aware of her concern. "All will be well, Nerida, I vow it to you."

She smiled. "And you always keep your pledges, lad. You were always thus."

"Rupert insisted upon it. Now, sing to your bees, lest Jeannie become too curious this morn."

"You cannot mean to embark upon this quest on foot."

"Nay." Murdoch chuckled. "I will borrow a pony." He opened the door and glanced toward the sheriff's cottage. "I know which one it shall be. Do you think they will blame the reivers for the loss?"

Nerida covered her mouth with her hand as she chuckled. "Mind you are not caught," she scolded gently. "You have spent time enough in the laird's dungeon of late."

Murdoch eyed the quiet cottage. "I wager they are sleeping well this morn and the pony is close at hand. Otherwise, I should have to go to Kilderrick to obtain a steed, and even I would not dare to borrow a horse from the Silver Wolf."

"There you are again," Nerida said with a contented sigh. "The lad I remember." She ruffled his hair as if he were no more than a wee boy and seemed to be blinking back tears. "Godspeed to you, lad." She hugged him fiercely, wiping away her tears, then began to hum to her bees. The coins had vanished into her skirts but he knew she would take them to the Silver Wolf.

Murdoch was filled with purpose. The sun was just rising above the horizon, painting the morning with pale silvery light. The mist was rising from the river and he had a quest of merit to fulfill. The raven cried far overhead, a silhouette against the bright morning sky, and Murdoch knew he also had an ally in this endeavor.

Aye, it had been Nyssa who had told him to defend those who found themselves vulnerable. She had mentioned widows and orphans, but he was much more content to come to the aid of a maiden and seer.

ERIK RODE hard that first night and every night afterward, so hard that Nyssa was sore whenever they finally halted. Still, the smaller creatures did not cover ground so quickly as horses might. Their respite was short, and their accommodations humble. Such was her state that she was glad of a piece of bread and a bed of straw in a farmer's lean-to.

It seemed she had scarcely wrapped herself in her cloak and resolved to remain awake than Erik was shaking her shoulder. Dusk was falling and the chill growing in the air, but the ponies were already saddled. They left that town in darkness, establishing a pattern that would prove both predictable and relentless.

Each morn, they halted and Erik strove to ensure that no one caught a glimpse of her. Nyssa cast back her hood in defiance when they entered any town, hoping that the hue of her hair would be noted. Perhaps someone would follow, and though the chance of it being Murdoch was slender, she still wished it might be. She heard a raven cry at intervals, sometimes in the night, sometimes during the day, but could not be certain it was Dorcha.

The only mercy in their furious pace was that Erik did not touch her. Angus kept his distance, though he watched her with gleaming eyes. Nyssa chose to believe that she would be safe, at least until they reached Duncheann.

At this rate, 'twould be all too soon.

CHAPTER 12

*E*amon stood in the great hall of Kilderrick keep, garbed in his best, striving to hide his fear. He was certain that he would not succeed when the Silver Wolf looked upon him. Jeannie was fast behind him, her breath coming quickly. He could fairly taste her terror.

On this day, they faced the final reckoning. By the time the sun set, his fate would be known. Eamon could only hope that this day, and events leading to it, would one day become a jest.

He licked his lips and tried to quell the tremor in his belly. The hall was crowded with villagers, many of whom speculated in whispers as to the outcome of the first court of the year. Not only the villagers from Rowan Fell but those from Kilderrick village had gathered, along with seemingly every soul who labored in the keep itself.

Eamon wondered how many hoped matters would go in his favor and how many would rejoice if the opposite were true.

A door at one side of the hall opened and Eamon's heart nigh stopped. The Silver Wolf, Laird of Kilderrick, strolled into the hall from that small chamber as if unaware that all had been awaiting him. Perhaps he did not care. The assembly immediately fell silent and the sound of his footfalls echoed loudly.

He was armed for battle, his armor glinting beneath his black tabard, a veritable arsenal of knives hanging from his belt along with his sword. That could be no good sign. He moved like the dangerous warrior he was, garbed in black like a demon, his fair hair shining like a crown of gold. Cast over his shoulders was a dark cloak cut full, a considerable volume of expensive cloth, one that swept to his ankles and was lined with glossy silver fur. Wolf, no doubt. The pin that held the cloak to his shoulder was large and silver, worth a veritable king's ransom, but no more than an ornamental bauble to this man. His gaze, so clear and blue, swept over the company, his expression inscrutable, his lips a hard line.

Eamon swallowed and held his ground, knees trembling.

The laird nodded to the villagers and sat on his great chair, facing the company. Eamon thought perhaps he counted their number, or took a tally of those in attendance. He gave a minute nod, then removed his black leather gauntlets, one finger at a time, and laid them with care over the arm of his chair.

His lady appeared then, descending the stairs with their infant son in her arms. She, too, was dressed formally, wearing a kirtle of so deep a blue it might have been black, with silver embroidery upon the hem and cuffs. Her dark hair was wound up tightly, a more severe style than was her custom, and she wore both a wimple and headdress on this day. Her expression was inscrutable and 'twas too easy to recall that her father, Robert Armstrong, had been so merciless a rogue.

Eamon heard Jeannie shift her weight behind him.

Who could have imagined that this fine lady was the wayward child, Alys, scarred and abandoned, raised in the woods, a wild unkempt child of seemingly no merit whatsoever. But the Silver Wolf smiled at the sight of her, his admiration and affection clear, then raised his hand to her. Her expression softened, but only for her spouse, then she stood beside him, as tall and straight as a shield maiden. He braced his elbow on the chair and she held his hand, their son dozing in the nook of her other elbow. They were regal, indomitable—terrifying.

At the laird's nod, an older man with silver hair stepped forward. Yves, too, had a particularly severe manner on this day, and Eamon feared they all knew that his fate had been decided.

Worse, that 'twas not good.

"And so, we gather this day for the first court of the year of the holding of Kilderrick," Yves began, his voice booming to every corner of the hall. He spoke in Norman French, as was his custom, but Tynan the smith had evidently been granted a task on this day. That man—tall, dark and broad, no less imposing than the laird himself—stood beside Yves and repeated his words in Gaelic.

They ensured that all understood. Eamon thought this was no good sign.

Yves consulted a scroll, though 'twas unlikely he needed to do as much. "The first matter before the laird's court is the repayment of monies owing to the laird by the sheriff, who gathered such fees in absence of the laird and owes them to the laird's treasury. Said sheriff has been granted additional time to repay the debt on two former occasions and must surrender it in total on this day." He looked at Eamon with expectation.

Eamon stepped forward, reminding himself to show no concern. He lifted the trunk he had brought to the keep with no small effort—that faithless fiend Erik having stolen his only pony, a matter he could neither report nor dispute since the villain was gone, and was never acknowledged to be in Rowan Fell in the first place—and presented it to the castellan.

Eamon bowed, a trickle of perspiration on his temple from the weight. Yves nodded at Tynan, who accepted the burden. He carried the trunk easily to the laird, who opened it and glanced inside. The Silver Wolf took a single coin between finger and thumb, and examined it closely—it flashed when he turned it in one hand—before returning it to the trunk with a flick of his fingers. He then gestured to a large trestle table to one side of the hall, undoubtedly provided in anticipation of this payment. Tynan placed the trunk upon it and returned to Yves' side. The laird's expression did not change, and Eamon was irked. He had expected some praise in his fulfilment of this deed.

He bit his tongue, though, and prayed that Jeannie did the same.

"It must be counted," the laird decreed.

Yves bowed, then went to the table. He began to empty the contents, counting the silver coins as he removed them and arranging them in stacks of five coins each. All watched him for several moments and

Eamon thought the wait might be the death of him if they were compelled to watch Yves count it all.

The laird cleared his throat. "I thank you for this settlement of an old debt, Eamon," he said, his tone uncommonly hard. "If 'twere a smaller sum, it might be counted more quickly. As it is, we must wait to be certain that you do not intend to deliver short of the measure."

"Aye, my lord."

The silence stretched long, only the light click of coins interrupting it. Eamon heard a whisper or two from the company, but he was most aware of the weight of the laird's gaze. Did the man not even blink? Eamon began to wish that he had counted the coin a fifth time. What if there was a small increment missing? What if he had erred?

"How fares the count, Yves?" the laird asked finally.

The older man turned and nodded. "It all seems to be in order, my lord, though I will know for certain in moments."

"Do my eyes deceive me, Yves, or are the coins all similar to each other?"

Eamon closed his eyes for a long moment.

"Some are soiled, my lord, but the overwhelming impression is that they are of an age, as if, truly, they had all come from a mint and recently so. None are nicked and few are scratched. Even those that are dirty may have been soiled deliberately, for the marks upon them are the same. They were struck at the same time, I believe."

The laird was watching Eamon, his stare unblinking. "Can you discern the mark, Yves?"

"They are from the royal mint at York, my lord."

The laird smiled. "And that is not so strange, is it, Eamon? That would be the closest mint to Kilderrick, the mint at Carlisle being closed in these days. It only stands to reason that most people in this vicinity would have coins minted there."

"Aye, my lord." If he survived this day, Eamon would never dare to cross the Laird of Kilderrick again. If he survived this day, he would fall on his knees in this very hall and praise God for his mercy. If he survived...

"The count is complete, my lord," Yves said after half an eternity had passed and Eamon dared to release the breath he had been holding. "And the entire sum has been remitted."

"Excellent," the laird said and inclined his head. "I congratulate you, Eamon, on the successful discharge of your debt."

Jeannie made a little squeak of delight, one that almost prompted the laird's smile.

"I thank you, sir," Eamon said, bowing low.

"I wonder, though, if you are aware that we welcomed visitors to Kilderrick last evening."

Eamon could not imagine the import of that, though he dreaded any mention of any detail at this moment. "I was not, my lord."

"I suspected as much. 'Tis a fair distance to Rowan Fell, and even the arrival of these two companies might not be discerned."

Eamon waited, his suspicions rising.

The laird raised a hand and another knight entered the hall. Eamon's heart sank. 'Twas the brother of the laird, who had ridden away from Kilderrick the year before.

"I was very interested to learn from my brother, Amaury d'Evroi, now Lord de Beaupoint and Lord Warden of the March on the English side, that they sought the killer of a guard, employed by a moneylender in Carlisle."

Eamon fairly groaned but strove to hide his dismay.

Amaury had been a hunter in his days at Kilderrick, though 'twas well known that he was a knight. He had his spurs, after all, that mark of knighthood, and had ridden a fine destrier, with three hounds running alongside and a hawk on his fist. On this day, he wore finery beyond those former days and his armor had been polished to brilliance. He was accompanied by his wife, an auburn-haired beauty who had once been one of the supposed witches living in the wilds of Kilderrick. She would not be mistaken as a woman of the woods any longer, to be sure. The pair might have been a king and his queen, garbed in black and gold, as regal and glorious a couple as Eamon had ever seen.

It could be no good portent that Lord Amaury was Lord Warden of the Western March, no less that he had ridden to Kilderrick to seek a villain.

"Indeed, sir," Eamon managed to say.

"Indeed. The unfortunate man was slaughtered while at his duty, on January fourteenth, between the new moon and the first quarter," the laird continued, his tone conversational. "'Twas said that a company of reivers attacked his employer's abode and he paid the price."

"How tragic," Eamon said, a lump in his throat.

"More than tragic," Lord Amaury said. "Murder is a crime beyond theft and one that cannot be left unpunished. A hue and cry was raised when the crime was discovered. There was a tale that the company had divided when pursued, half riding east and half to the north."

"Indeed," Eamon fairly whispered. How had the Silver Wolf known?

That man raised his hand and another warrior strode into the hall. This one was dark of hair and dark of eye, tall with a confident gleam in his eye. Jeannie caught her breath sharply and Eamon reached back for her hand, startled beyond all to see another half-brother of the laird appear. A familiar woman with fiery hair was by his side and the triumph in her smile could not be mistaken when she glanced at Jeannie.

Jeannie whispered a prayer, holding fast to Eamon's hand.

This pair were garbed in green and gold, and on the lady's shoulder was a cloak pin that sparkled with garnets. "You might also recall my brother Rafael, now Baron of Gisroy, and his lady wife, Ceara MacRuari," the laird said, as if a trap was not closing around Eamon with surety.

But what could he do? He could not flee with any success. He would not manage three steps before he was felled.

Perhaps he might yet brazen it out.

"Aye," Eamon said and forced a smile. "What fortune that you should have such guests at this time of year."

"Ah, but my brothers did not come to make merry, Eamon," the laird said, as a man shouted in outrage from another part of the keep.

"You cannot do this to me!" that man roared in Gaelic, his voice familiar beyond all. "I demand to be released. I demand *justice*. I told the truth and you lied to me! I demand a hearing from the laird or the king with all haste…"

"Cedric!" Jeannie cried with delight, even as the cold trickle of sweat down Eamon's back became a rivulet.

"Silence," Eamon said sharply and his wife granted him a look that could have curdled milk.

She bit her tongue, though, though Eamon thought that might be a miracle.

Cedric appeared in the custody of two guards. He was dirty with his hands bound behind his back and his knees tied together. The two guards aided him as he hobbled onward, ignoring his tirade—which halted when he spotted Eamon and Jeannie.

He paled and Eamon knew the younger man had contrived some lie that would not be to his own advantage.

Then he realized that the laird had risen from his seat. The assembly watched rapt as he strolled toward Eamon.

The laird gestured to Cedric. "This man, Eamon, whom your wife has called Cedric, was arrested within the Barony of Gisroy."

"Cedric is a good boy," Jeannie said hotly. "You had no cause to detain him for riding through Gisroy on his own affairs..."

"Ah, but I did," Rafael said smoothly. He hefted a trunk and poured its contents onto the table, disturbing Yves' careful piles. At a glance, any soul could tell that the coins were the same as those Eamon had offered. "He had these coins in his possession."

God in Heaven. 'Twould all come out now.

"These coins did not belong to him," the laird said. "In fact, they had been stolen from the moneylender in Carlisle. Charged with both the theft and the murder of the guard, this man confided that one of his companions had dealt the fatal blow." Rafael smiled at Cedric with amusement. "He even had the audacity to protest his own innocence. Evidently, he was dragged into the moneylender's abode by his unworthy companions."

"Innocent," Cedric insisted. "I am innocent..."

"Silence!" the Silver Wolf said with such force that Cedric did as instructed.

Eamon found the laird immediately before him, that man's gaze piercing.

The Silver Wolf spoke softly. "He charged you, Eamon, with the murder of the guard. Should I believe him?"

Eamon opened his mouth and closed it again. "I meant no harm to anyone, my lord."

"And yet harm was done." The laird extended one hand. "May I see your knife, Eamon?"

His knife? Eamon held that cold blue stare and his heart fluttered. What was this? He dared not disobey, though, so pulled the knife from its scabbard and offered the hilt to the laird. He even bent his knee, bowing his head as he held out the blade. It could not hurt to show deference, though he feared 'twas too late to matter.

The laird plucked the weapon from his hand, offered a slight nod, and then examined the blade closely. What did he seek? Eamon watched as the laird turned the blade in the light, then slid his thumbnail along the edge where the blade met the hilt. His two brothers came to stand beside him, all three men looking keenly at something on the laird's thumbnail.

They were unsurprised by whatever they had found.

Eamon's heart began to thunder. He had cleaned the blade. He had polished it. He had ensured that there were no signs of what had happened. The blood was gone, every increment of it, scrubbed away...

But the coolness of the laird's gaze indicated that he had missed something.

"Dried blood," the Baron of Gisroy murmured. "How interesting."

"I...I killed a hen this week. I thought the blade was clean..." Eamon's protest fell silent as the three knights smiled in unison and shook their heads.

The laird showed the blade to Cedric. That man inhaled sharply, clearly recognizing the knife. Eamon prayed that the boy would not betray him, but he knew 'twas a futile hope.

"Aye," Cedric said. "He used that weapon."

The laird beckoned to his squire standing at one side of the hall. The dark-haired lad was familiar to Eamon and responded with characteristic haste to the laird's summons. "Reynaud, see that the sheriff's blade is sharpened, if you will. A man of his standing must keep his weapon in good repair."

What was this ploy? Eamon could not guess. The boy bowed and took the knife, vanishing from the hall with it in his possession.

Eamon wondered whether he would get it back.

He found the three knights before him, his judgement clear in their expressions. "Have you any explanation to offer for your actions of January fourteenth?" the laird asked. "You are believed to have departed from Rowan Fell with a party of reivers, to have participated in a theft from a moneylender, and to have killed a guard charged to defend those premises. Or is there another explanation for your possession of these coins, all from the same delivery, all stolen from the same treasury?"

Eamon sighed and bowed his head. "I was afraid, sir. I feared your justice and I was determined to do whatever was necessary to regain the coin."

"Surely you did not think that a sheriff could be rewarded for theft and murder?"

"I did not mean to kill him, sir, but he grabbed for me and..." Eamon fell silent when Jeannie jabbed her elbow into his ribs. He lifted his gaze to that of the laird, dreading that man's next words. "I chose badly, my lord."

"Aye. You did." The Laird of Kilderrick rose to his feet and raised his hands, preparing to make his final judgement. "I was fortunate in this matter, for Murdoch Campbell first alerted me to Eamon's absence from Rowan Fell. He then witnessed the sheriff's return and sent several of these coins along to me, with his observations. 'Twas he who suggested that my brothers might know the rest of the tale, and so I consulted with them, to much edification."

The company of villagers nodded approval of this course.

"Lord Amaury intends to take both Eamon and Cedric to Carlisle to be judged as reivers and killers," the laird continued. "Myself, I see no justification for the expense, but you will both remain as my guests until Lord Amaury's departure."

"Guests?" Jeannie asked and the laird granted her a chilling glance.

"In the dungeon," he said softly. "Where all guests of their merit abide."

A heavy hand fell on Eamon's shoulder and he glanced at it, only to realize that every finger bore a ring save for the one that was missing. He looked up, way up, to the hard gaze of the mercenary Royce, and knew his fate well.

"'Twas Jeannie's fault!" Eamon cried. "She summoned Cedric, for he is her cousin's son. She contrived the scheme for me to accompany the reivers. She..."

"She has much to answer for, herself," the laird said, interrupting him smoothly. He considered Jeannie from his great seat. "And yet, and yet, the evidence against her is less compelling. I have only your testimony, Eamon, and to be sure, it might be influenced by your current situation. Similarly, I believe that Jeannie was responsible for the abduction of my son, yet I cannot prove as much. A laird, as you all know, must be fair in his dealings with those beneath his hand and refrain from punishing those whose guilt cannot be proven. You are not in that company, Eamon, though your wife, as yet, is."

Eamon heard Jeannie exhale with relief.

"You must make a choice, Jeannie," the laird said, his voice soft and silky. Eamon saw him offer his hand, with the signet ring of Kilderrick upon it. "You may swear your allegiance to me and return to Rowan Fell this night, or you may join your husband and nephew. I have no proof of your deeds, but I have doubts, and the option to reassure me is entirely yours."

Jeannie raised her chin, fire in her eyes, and Eamon was certain she would remain by his side. Instead, she stepped past him and fell to one knee, touching her lips to the offered ring.

Eamon involuntarily emitted a sound of shock.

The laird raised a brow. "Aye, Eamon. I share your response, but my offer has been accepted and I will not break my word."

He turned to the assembly of villagers and raised his voice. "The post of sheriff is vacant in Rowan Fell as of this moment. I ask for your patience as I seek a suitable candidate. In the meantime, I encourage you to bring all complaints to my hall for resolution. You need not wait for the monthly court."

The villagers nodded approval of this course and several applauded the laird.

He inclined his head. "We have no other matters before the court on this day, and I would invite you all to partake of the meal prepared to celebrate the visit of my brothers and their ladies." He waved a hand and the two guards seized Cedric and Eamon, hauling them toward the dungeon.

Jeannie, the faithless wretch, watched, silent for once in her days.

Eamon realized in that moment how much he had come to despise her. He turned his back upon her, refusing to entreat her for any favor.

Cedric was dropped into the pit of darkness and roared with pain, evidently when he hit the ground. "My ankle!" he cried but the mercenary Royce looked down upon him without mercy.

Indeed, that man only shook his head with mock dismay.

"Alas, we have no healer in these days," he said, then fixed Eamon with a look. "I suppose you know naught of Nyssa's disappearance?"

Eamon thought he would be ill.

Royce then gestured to the open trap door. Having no desire to be flung into the dungeon, Eamon hurried toward the gap and jumped. He landed hard but missed Cedric. The two of them stood, looking upward, as Royce chuckled. Something flashed in that man's hands, though Eamon could not guess what it was.

"Your skill improves daily, Reynaud," the mercenary said with admiration. "This edge will draw blood with ease. Well done!"

"I thank you," the boy said, his voice deeper than it had been upon his arrival at Kilderrick.

Royce brandished the blade over the open trap door, a hint of his intention. "I bid you pleasant dreams," he said, then dropped Eamon's knife into the dungeon. The blade caught the light before the trap door above fell shut, plunging them into darkness. There was a clatter as the knife landed on the stone floor and both of them dropped to their hands and knees, seeking it in the darkness.

Eamon wondered which of them would be alive in the morning, then guessed that had been the laird's plan.

Nay, 'twas the solution of the former mercenary known as the Silver Wolf, chosen for its expediency. Eamon's hand closed over the cold hilt and he dared to hope that he would survive to face Lord Amaury's justice instead.

Then Cedric tackled him with a snarl, and their battle began.

~

JEANNIE WAS QUIVERING when the Laird of Kilderrick turned his cool gaze upon her. The man might have had ice running in his veins for all the compassion he had shown Eamon and Cedric. She stood, hands clasped together, fearing his wrath.

Nay, she feared his composure yet more.

The laird had only to straighten in his chair for the hall to fall silent. "You have been accused, Jeannie, of abducting my infant son, on the twelfth of January and abandoning him in the small hut on Nerida's allotment." He conjured a rag from the folds of his cloak and held it out on his outstretched palm. Jeannie licked her lips at the sight of the rag she had used to silence the boy. "Do you recognize this?"

A thousand possibilities flitted through her thoughts. Should she lie? That certainly was her inclination, but if she lied, could she convince the laird of her sincerity? If she lied and he knew as much, she feared her fate would be all the more dire.

And yet...and yet, to confess to this man before dozens of witnesses that she had seized his only son was a folly she could not commit.

"Nay, my lord," she said.

"I could not discern your reply," he said, his gaze boring into her own.

"Nay, my lord," she fairly shouted.

"And what do you know of Michael's abduction?"

"Naught, my lord, save that I have been told of his recovery." She managed to force a smile. "Indeed, he looks most hale. Whatever occurred, for whatever reason, the lack of injury to him is surely of the greatest import."

"I am glad, of course, of his happy state," the laird said. The babe gurgled then as if to reassure his father, and Jeannie watched both parents smile at him. "But that does not remove the fact that his very survival was in question, by dint of someone's choices."

"You cannot know as much, my lord. The person in question might have meant no ill."

The laird's brows rose. "By abducting an infant and leaving him untended?"

"It might have been solely for a moment, my lord."

"To what purpose?"

"Perhaps to gain your goodwill, my lord."

He shook his head. "My goodwill would never be gained by imperiling my son."

"But it might have been won by his safe return."

The laird leaned back in his chair to regard her, one elbow braced on the chair as his fingertip stroked his chin. "But then, the person who returned the child could not be the one who seized him—or at least, I could not have realized that they were one and the same. I would not reward a thief for returning a stolen prize."

"Perhaps they two were not the same person, my lord."

"But Murdoch Campbell returned my son, so who seized the boy? He said he found the boy in the hut when he returned there after being released from my dungeon. The boy was taken while Murdoch stood before me."

"Perhaps he had an accomplice, my lord."

"One might believe as much of any other man, Jeannie, but Murdoch Campbell, a warrior who relies upon himself to the exclusion of all others." He raised a finger. "I would suggest to you that someone wished me to believe that Murdoch was responsible for the abduction, when in fact he was not. He brought Michael home because he discovered the boy and chose to ensure his welfare. I believe he had no part in the abduction."

"He had sworn to kill the boy before."

"And so, if he had seized him, he would have done as much. By the time he found the boy, he had changed his view." The laird straightened again. "Which makes me wonder who else might have desired to injure my son? Or, if we consider the alternate view, who would have hoped for reward from me for Michael's safe return?"

"I could not say, my lord."

"Could you not, Jeannie?" The lord rose from his chair and strolled toward Jeannie with dangerous grace. "This day of reckoning for my treasury has been arranged for a long time. Eamon even chose to go reiving in the hope of making the payment due." He halted before her. "I suggest that you had the notion and the opportunity, and that you hid the infant in Nerida's hut when I came to Rowan Fell to seek him. That your plan was a poor one does not mean that you did not make it."

Jeannie lifted her chin. "You have no proof, my lord," she said with all the confidence she could muster.

"Not as yet," he said with a smile, then pivoted. He strode to his lady wife and lifted the boy in his arms, cooing to the child as he returned to confront Jeannie. Michael kicked and gurgled, as merry a child as there could be. The laird lifted his cool gaze to hers and offered the infant. "Hold him," he said softly.

Oh, this she could do. If this was the test, Jeannie would excel at it. She smiled in relief and reached for the boy. But she did not even have him in her arms, for the laird had not released him, when the boy turned his gaze upon her.

His eyes widened. He made a choking sound and struggled in his father's grasp. Then he screamed in terror, a sound fit to deafen every soul in the hall, his gaze locked upon Jeannie's face. He howled and he wept and the laird pulled him close to his chest, rocking the boy as his fright subsided.

"I find you guilty, Jeannie, by the testimony of one who cannot yet speak for himself, and consign you to the dungeon to await sentencing at my leisure."

"But you must tell me when…"

"My son had no notion when relief would come to him. You will savor the same sense of uncertainty."

"But my lord, I will pledge myself to you…"

The laird stopped and turned, no less imperious for the fact that he carried a babe in his arms. "You have just lied to me, in my court and before witnesses, Jeannie. Only a fool would take your pledge now, and I, alas for you, am no fool." He did no more than glance toward the guards, who came to seize Jeannie.

She struggled against them, though she was no match for two tall and sturdy men trained for war. "You cannot do this," she protested. "I am the wife of the sheriff. I am respected and honored in this holding. You cannot treat me with such indignity…"

"You stole his son, Jeannie," called Cormac Smith. "Even you cannot have imagined such a deed would go unpunished."

215

Jeannie stared at the older man in outrage, but her own dismay grew as his sons nodded agreement beside him. The wives clearly concurred, and one, the wife of the youngest, began to clap as Jeannie was fairly dragged away. The applause grew as others joined to show their approval of the laird's choice, and Jeannie sputtered with fury at their ingratitude as she was inexorably dragged away. A trap door was opened in the floor ahead of her, that big ugly mercenary who lacked an eye standing over it.

"There may be only one left," he said, which made no sense to Jeannie at all.

Then she was cast into the prison, screaming with indignation. She only caught a glimpse of Cedric, a knife in his hand, then the door was dropped back into place and the darkness was complete.

"Your fault," Cedric whispered. "I should never have answered your summons."

AFTER THE MEAL, the hall was swept and the tables moved away. The villagers returned to Rowan Fell and also to Kilderrick village, all undoubtedly with much to discuss. Alys retired to the solar with Michael, accompanied by Elizabeth and Ceara, the three women still endeavoring to catch up with each other's tidings. Maximilian waited until the hall was empty, save for himself and his brothers, then cleared his throat.

Rafael grinned. "I knew you had more to say," he said with quiet confidence. "You are not so inscrutable as once you were."

Maximilian might have smiled in return if his thoughts had not been sober. "I continue to wrestle with the challenge of Murdoch Campbell," he said, then told his brothers of his thoughts on the matter. "I would trust him, but he will not trust me."

"Is it you he refuses to trust, or does he distrust all men?" Amaury asked. "For in the time of my acquaintance with him, he has always kept his own counsel."

Maximilian shook a finger at Amaury. "You speak aright. He always labors in solitude. Either he has been betrayed or he never learned to rely upon others."

"Did he not grow up alone in the keep, with his parents?" Rafael asked. "I would think a young boy in such a situation would be beneath the attention of the laird and lady."

"Aye, Alys has said that the servants fled her father's service, save for Rupert."

"And the village at Kilderrick was abandoned," Amaury said.

"And 'tis far to Rowan Fell," Rafael added. "Particularly for a young boy to go alone."

"'Twould seem he had few friends in his youth, then he took the vow against me when he was barely grown to manhood."

"Then he pursued his vengeance alone," Amaury noted.

"And now he would aid Nyssa in the search for her sister, without aid."

"Do you know this Duncheann?" Maximilian asked Amaury, who shook his head. "'Tis evidently east of Inverness, on the north coast, a fortress on an island."

"Yet he means to steal a young girl away, with only the aid of Nyssa?" Rafael asked, his doubt of that scheme's success more than clear.

"With Ceara, he might have a chance of triumph," Maximilian said. "But Royce has oft despaired of Nyssa's inability to strike a blow, even in her own defense. He has urged me more than once to insist that she not carry a blade at all."

"Why?" Amaury asked.

"I would guess that she is so readily divested of it, that she simply provides a weapon to any assailant," Rafael said and Maximilian nodded.

The three warriors fell silent, and Maximilian knew they were united in their concern, not just for Nyssa and her sister's daughter, but for Murdoch.

"Your challenge might be resolved in the failure of his quest," Rafael said grimly.

"But he is another of our brethren," Maximilian insisted. "I would not have it be so."

"And so, you have a scheme," Amaury guessed.

Maximilian leaned forward. "What if he has never learned the might that comes in numbers? What if he has no inkling of the gains of alliance, of having other warriors at his back? What if we could show him such, ensure his victory, save Nyssa and her sister's daughter, and convince Murdoch to swear himself loyal to me."

"So long as you are not too ambitious in your schemes," Amaury said, his doubts more than clear. "You might wish for the moon to tread upon the earth while you are making such plans."

"Nay," Rafael said softly. "Nay, I think there is merit in this notion. If you contrived his success when he feared opportunity lost, he is the manner of man who would be loyal to you forever."

"This, too, is my conviction," Maximilian said. He raised his hands. "And I have need of a sheriff with Murdoch's strong desire for justice, as well as his refusal to compromise or be compromised."

"Sheriff?" Amaury echoed. "By dint of our arrival here, I am Lord de Beaupoint, while Rafael is Baron of Gisroy, thanks to your influence. Why would Murdoch be content, as another of your brothers, to merely be Rowan Fell's sheriff?"

"I think he has little interest in a title or more formal duties, and I believe his passion for truth and honor would serve him well in the administration of justice. He has no qualms in meting a lesson himself and is much concerned with character and reputation. He listens and he remembers, and I am convinced that he would excel in the post."

The brothers considered this as Yves filled their cups of wine, then left them alone again.

"How would you contrive to ally with him when he is so distant?" Rafael asked, then his eyes glinted. "Or shall I guess that you intend to ride in pursuit of him?"

"He rides a pony, by Nerida's tale, as did the reivers. When he ensures Nyssa's escape, they both will ride his pony north to Duncheann to seek tidings of her sister's daughter. They will not make such rapid progress as a trio of warriors riding destriers. I wager we could reach this Duncheann shortly after them, though we depart later."

"We?" Amaury echoed.

Maximilian inclined his head to that brother. "I do not see this as an errand appropriate for a man of your repute. Would you remain here at Kilderrick and ensure its defense in my absence?"

"You mean to go?" Amaury asked.

"I must be among the party to win Murdoch's favor," Maximilian said.

"If it can be done," Rafael added.

"Aye. I would ask you to accompany me, along with your supplies," Maximilian said to Rafael, who grinned. "There is naught like a dragon in the ranks when assailing a keep."

"Naught at all," Rafael said. "Then we two are to ride at dawn?"

"Three," Maximilian said. "I would ask Royce to join our company." He counted on his fingers. "Three destriers, three palfreys, the three of us, two squires, and a journey north with all haste. Reynaud should be in the party, for 'tis time he saw more of warfare. What say you?"

"Take Oliver," Amaury said. "He has trained diligently this year."

Rafael smiled and offered his hand to Maximilian. "I say we ride."

"And I wish you both Godspeed," Amaury said, shaking their hands in turn.

Well satisfied with the result of the discussion, Maximilian finished his wine then strode to speak with Royce. Rafael headed for the stables to make preparations for their departure, while Amaury climbed to the solar to inform the ladies of their plans.

All without a word. Maximilian smiled at the accord that had grown between the brothers and knew he would be well content when the fourth, Murdoch Campbell, was his ally as well.

The dawn could not come soon enough to suit.

CHAPTER 13

*N*yssa *dreamed of a rolling sea of a thousand hues of silver and blue, the waves crested with white foam. She stood on a coast that was familiar and yet strange, one she might have visited long before, or one that was similar to places she had known. Mist rose from the sea and a fog rolled across the land, obscuring all from view. Nyssa heard the approach of another and turned in place, striving to pierce the veil of the fog.*

Then a woman stepped out of the mist before her, a woman so familiar that she gasped aloud.

Her mother smiled and raised a fingertip, raising it to Nyssa's lips in a command for silence. 'Twas then that Nyssa noted how insubstantial her mother was, how the mist seemed part of her undyed kirtle, how her hair flowed into the fog and became a part of it.

Beside her mother then appeared her sister, Elsa, as ethereal as their mother. Nyssa understood that their ghosts visited her in this dream. One took each of her hands, leading her to the east, though she could feel only coolness against her hand. They followed a familiar path, one worn by many footsteps, an ancient course to a familiar destination.

They passed through a pine forest, each tree as well known as her companions, then climbed a small rise. At the summit was a circle of worn stones, each leaning at its own angle. Like the Ninestang Ring near Kilderrick, there was one larger stone standing upright, though this one had a spiral etched upon its face.

Her mother crouched beside a bowl, though Nyssa did not know from whence it had appeared. The dark dye was mixed within it, then Elsa offered that sharp tool to her mother. They conferred together, then turned to Nyssa, their manners expectant.

Nyssa bared her arms, knowing what would happen next. Her mother touched the dots on the inside of her left wrist, two of them, one for each daughter born. Each was a dot surrounded by smaller dots, like the center of a flower surrounded by petals. Elsa turned her wrist, displaying that she too had one such collection of dots. There was a shadow of a second set, a hint of a mark that should have been there but had not been made before Elsa's early death. 'Twas a potent reminder of the child Nyssa sought.

Elsa took Nyssa's left wrist and turned it upward. Her mother pricked the skin to indicate a daughter born. Nyssa strove to protest for she had no daughter, but she was unable to make a sound. Had her mother silenced her with that touch? Why?

The mark was made, and Nyssa counted eight dots surrounding the central one. Her mother whispered a blessing, then the blue dye was rubbed into Nyssa's skin, the color forced into the pricks made by the sharp tool. Her arm was cleaned and her sister kissed her cheeks as if to congratulate her. Her mother smiled with familiar serenity, and kissed her cheeks in turn.

"But I have no child," Nyssa managed to say. Her mother and sister shook their heads, untroubled, then faded steadily from her view. As she watched, the mist seemed to consume them both, their very essences turning to fog and air.

When they had vanished, she felt more alone than ever she had. Nyssa looked at her wrist. She considered the Raven's Mound and ached to be there with her mother and sister in truth. She ached that she might be compelled to wed Erik and bear his child, and she feared that daughter would share the same fate as Elsa's first-born. 'Twas cruel beyond all that the tale must repeat itself over and over again, always at Duncheann.

And then she heard a child's cry.

In that same moment, Nyssa felt the heat of another close behind her. The weight of a man's hand landed upon her waist and she smelled the sweet scent of the infant he carried. She closed her eyes and simmered with satisfaction when he pressed a kiss against the side of her neck, his beard tickling against her skin.

Erik had no beard. She could not imagine he would grow one.

She knew one man with a beard and scarce dared to look over her shoulder lest her hopes be destroyed. She felt his breath against his skin. She heard his low murmur of pleasure as his arm closed around her waist, drawing her back against his strength.

Aye, his touch was familiar, his gentle power and his tenderness. Tears pricked her eyes at the familiar breadth and warmth of Murdoch behind her.

Her companion began to hum a tune. 'Twas a Gaelic lullaby, one she heard very recently at Kilderrick, and the familiarity of both the song and the man's voice made her smile.

Murdoch!

Nyssa turned in his embrace and met the steady blue of his gaze, watched the smile dawn slowly on his lips and thought her heart might burst with joy. She took the child from him with ease, as if she could do naught else.

Nyssa's heart filled with wonder and awe at the infant's slight weight. The babe was swathed in furs and wool, its gender hidden. Its eyes were clear blue, as deep a sapphire as a summer sky. Its hair, while short, was deepest auburn, and its smile warmed every corner of Nyssa's soul. The infant made a small cry of discontent and Nyssa felt the milk rise within her breasts, her body recognizing the babe as her own daughter. She saw the man's strong hand as he caressed the child's head and she knew in her heart that she and he had wrought this babe together.

In this vision, Nyssa had a daughter, a beautiful healthy child. She had a man, a strong and valiant man, determined to protect them both. She bared her breast to nurse her child and watched with joy, feeling the absence of her gift less keenly than she might have anticipated.

'Twas time for her legacy to continue.

With this conception, with this surrender to sensation, Nyssa had paid a price, but there was not an increment of regret within her. She was no longer a seer. She was a mother and a wife and a partner to this man. Her path was no longer solitary, but joined to his and that of their child.

Better, she would become a teacher. She would entrust this child with all the lessons she had learned and she would mark her daughter's skin with the

222

proof of each lesson. The wisdom of her forebears would be passed to another, that it might be preserved and used for the good of all.

When she considered that legacy, there was no sacrifice made at all.

NYSSA OPENED her eyes that morning, filled with newfound hope that Murdoch survived. Over a week had passed since he abduction and still they rode on.

The dream lifted her spirits. She could only believe that Murdoch would come to her aid, or that they would encounter each other again. There was a future for them together, one that made more of her gift than would come of it in solitude. She looked at the inside of her wrist in the morning light, unsurprised that there was no mark upon it.

But there would be.

Which meant she had to find both Rana and her mother's tools, still hidden in the solar at Duncheann—and survive Erik's scheme.

IF NAUGHT ELSE, the coin—though twice stolen—facilitated Murdoch's pursuit of Nyssa and her captors. That the coins were all the same aroused no suspicion when he spent only one or two in each town. He did not have to forage for food or seek shelter, which hastened his pursuit. Each time he halted to rest, he simply paid for what he needed. 'Twas a luxury beyond his experience and a welcome one in this situation.

For the party he followed made haste. They did not linger, regardless of the weather, and only allowed the minimum time for their ponies to rest. Murdoch was beyond glad that they did not ride horses, for he would have been left far behind them.

The advantage was that in their desire for speed, they did not pass unnoticed. 'Twas easy to find tidings of a beautiful woman with fair hair who had recently passed through any village. Murdoch learned that her companions were two, a man of an age with himself, a warrior and one seemingly disliked by all those he encountered. The second was a youth of less than twenty summers, one who said little. They never confessed their names.

On impulse Murdoch had shaved off his beard after leaving Rowan Fell, not wanting to be recognized by Nyssa's captors. They might have had only a glimpse of him and that at night, but he would expect them to recall his beard and his plaid. He packed away his plaid and wore the garb of a mercenary instead.

If Murdoch had no time for queries, still his route would have been evident. Dorcha was perched nearby each morning when Murdoch awakened, and the bird showed him the direction to follow. Within days, Murdoch could anticipate it with ease: they rode north. He soon suspected that this was no reiving party, but that Nyssa's past had found her. Murdoch could not imagine how it might be, but their course proved it true.

Their destination was Duncheann. He would have wagered his soul upon it.

And that realization filled him with dread. Naught good awaited Nyssa in the keep where her sister had died. He had to contrive a plan to see her rescued, but feared that once she was within the walls of a fortress, any opportunity would be lost. No matter how hard he rode the pony, though, they never caught more than a glimpse of Nyssa's party on the road ahead. Did they know of his pursuit? What was their scheme?

Murdoch was not inclined to dream but, on this journey, he dreamed most nights. Worse, he dreamed of Nyssa surrounded by flames, and his own inability to free her. He awakened with a racing heart, his fists clenched and cold sweat on his skin, tasting his own powerlessness.

He had to reach Nyssa before 'twas too late.

Never had a man been so driven to achieve a goal than Murdoch as he followed the small party north.

DUNCHEANN WAS as forbidding as Nyssa remembered. The keep looked cold and grey from the shore, surrounded by the sea and buffeted by wind. She clearly recalled how trapped she had felt there, in her father's abode, and how no amount of clothing had ever been able to dispel the damp. The home of the Sutherlands had been more humble but warmer. It had not been a happier place for herself and Elsa, though, keenly aware that they were a burden that had become unwelcome. Her mother had settled a sum of coin upon the family for fostering each daughter in turn, but the funds had been quickly spent and nigh forgotten, leaving Elsa and Nyssa as an obligation that was resented.

The reunion with their father should have been a more joyous moment, but as Murdoch suspected, neither of the sisters had ever trusted him. They had been certain that only their mother cared for their welfare, and when she died, they were without a defender. It had not taken long for their father to show the truth of his nature.

Nyssa was not glad to see those walls again and wished anew that Erik had never found Rana. She was tired and sore from riding long days. She was hungry, for the fare had been limited, and she yearned for a hot bath with unholy vigor. She doubted her captor had any interest in her views.

She distrusted Erik's jubilant mood, knowing that whatever gave him such satisfaction was sure to come at her own expense.

She could not fail to note that the village on the shore close to the keep was nigh abandoned. Cottages were clearly empty and the fields did not look as if they had been tilled in recent years. There were no chickens or goats to be seen and she did not glimpse a single villager. Once the village had prospered and children had run through it. Now it was silent, occupied solely by ghosts. Nyssa understood that Hugh was no kind laird, and concluded that he was even more harsh than her father had been.

That was no good portent.

Erik did not linger in the village, even though the tide was rising—perhaps because night was falling. The western sky was turning hues of orange and gold as the sun sank low. Erik barely slowed the pace of the party, making directly for the road to the keep. Water was closing over it already, disguising it more with each wave, and feeding Nyssa's unease. Erik gave his heels to his pony, holding fast to the reins of Nyssa's own. The water lapped at the ponies' hooves, rising with troubling and relentless speed. The beasts did not have to be encouraged to run, to be sure.

There was a moment when Nyssa feared that Hugh would command the gates to be secured against them and that there would not be time to retrace their steps to the shore again. She had seen others drown on this road when denied admission and had never wished to be in their number.

To be sure, as they rode closer, she saw that the gates were already closed. Erik cursed under his breath, a hint that all was not well between brothers, then forcibly hauled back her hood when they were within sight of the gatehouse.

"Hugh!" he roared, though the wind snatched at his words. "I bring your bride!"

Nyssa realized that the setting sun would reveal the hue of her hair, the sole key they needed to guess her identity. All the same she held her breath as they raced ever closer to the closed gates. She knew that Erik lied—had Hugh guessed as much?

Finally, the gates creaked open to admit the small party, doing so in the last moment possible. They were then slammed with vigor behind the arrivals. The force of the gates closing echoed through the keep, setting the very walls to shaking, and Nyssa realized they had been fortified yet more. She shivered at the roar of the wind and the crash of the waves, at the chill emanating from the stone.

How she despised this place.

She despised even more the man who stood in the midst of the bailey, arms folded across his chest. Hugh Sutherland had aged, to be sure, and it seemed that Duncheann suited him well. He was much thicker through the middle, a sign that he could afford to indulge his appetites, and his garb was rich. His gaze was as steady and merciless as that of his brother, though, and the line of his mouth as uncompromising as ever.

"My reluctant bride, at last," he said, offering her a plump hand. Nyssa did not accept his aid and his lips tightened at that. She also saw the flash of Erik's eyes and wondered which of the pair was less worthy of trust. When they had been children, it had been Erik, a deceptive and unprincipled boy. Hugh had always been more interested in his own pleasures than aught else, but truly, he would have sold his mother for a morsel he desired.

She had been brought to a veritable den of vipers and could only hope that Murdoch would appear before 'twas too late for herself and Rana.

Her father's coin was being spent to secure the keep, for there were more sentries pacing the summit of the walls than ever before. No less than six men guarded the gate and a dozen more were in the bailey, all of them heavily armed. An ostler came to them, but even he appeared to be a warrior and showed none of the friendly joviality of Kilderrick's ostler. His expression was grim and his eyes narrowed as he moved with economy to take the ponies to the stable. Nyssa doubted the creatures were well-tended or granted more than was strictly necessary for their survival. She wondered at the state of the treasury, for her father had been affluent but frugal as well. Did Hugh have a source of income beyond Duncheann?

The stable was located within the one great wall to the right, as ever they had been, barracks in the one to the left and the laird's abode in the tower before them on the ocean side. The great hall was on a level with the bailey with the kitchen on the right, three smaller chambers above it for guests and servants, with the laird's solar at the summit. The dungeon was carved from the rock beneath the great hall and routinely filled with seawater.

She looked up at the tower, remembering the solar on the highest floor. Was it possible that the sole item she desired from this keep was still secreted there? Duncheann was a cursed place, every stone emanating with the cruelty of those who had commanded its construction. Nyssa shivered despite herself her father's legacy should yet survive.

"Aye, the wind is brisk at Duncheann," Hugh said, leading her toward the hall. "I am certain you remember it well."

"Aye," Nyssa agreed.

"And you look just the same." His gaze flicked over her, lingering on the small mark visible at the left cuff of her kirtle. He scarce restrained from curling his lip at the sight and she remembered how he had criticized her sister's marks. "The Lord of Badenoch takes an interest in

Duncheann and its succession," he said, his tone so amiable that Nyssa was warned. "Some fool told him of the survival of my daughter."

"Elsa's daughter," Nyssa whispered.

"He seeks reason to award this keep to another, perhaps more loyal to his causes. If he learns of your survival, I must fear for my own future prospects. Blood is so much more compelling than mere marital vows. I will invite him to visit, now that we are finally to wed and set his concerns to rest. Another daughter of Reginald Le Cheyne shall ensure my claim."

"He will attend the nuptials?" she asked, thinking there might yet be time to escape with Rana.

Hugh smiled. "He will arrive to find the nuptials celebrated and consummated, with no possible alternative in view." He kissed her hand within the hall. "Sleep well, my lady." He surveyed her. "Your sister's garments should fit you well enough. At midday on the morrow, we will wed." He pivoted then, his cape swirling out behind him as he left her there. Venison was brought to the board, the scent of the stew so rich and inviting that Nyssa might have willingly accepted him for a bowl of it, so hungry was she.

But Erik led her to the stairs, his grip upon her elbow ensuring that she had no choice but to accompany him. "Home again," he said with false cheer. "You will notice the lack of meat, wine and other comforts, no doubt. The crops have been meagre of late and spoilage high. Duncheann has need of a lady witch to bring blessings to its door once more." He smiled at her, his gaze cold. "I am certain you will be glad to oblige."

Nyssa chose not to make any such guarantee. "But the laird eats venison."

"Bite by bite, he savors it all each time a deer is taken." Erik grimaced. "All others must be content with salted eels and hard bread." He urged her up the familiar stairs, which seemed colder, darker and dirtier than before. Even with the poor light, Nyssa could see that the strewing herbs had not been changed in recent memory.

"I must see Rana," she said when Erik halted outside the middle door. Behind it was the chamber she and Elsa had shared, but the door now was graced with a doughty lock. There was a small door cut into it, one that could not have been as large as Nyssa's hand, with a flap secured on the corridor side.

This would be her prison.

"You will see her soon enough, to be sure."

When Erik opened the portal, Nyssa understood.

The chamber had been stripped bare of all comforts and there was only a straw pallet against the outer wall. Two windows still faced the north, giving views of the sea, but the shutters that had covered them were gone. The great bed had vanished as had the draperies that had kept the cold at bay. The shadows were deep and the chill penetrating, for there was neither lamp, nor candle nor brazier.

A woman straightened at the sound of the door opening, her features familiar and her expression guarded. "Mary Gunn!" Nyssa said, recognizing the healer who had ensured the survival of Elsa's daughter. She stepped into the chamber as Mary's eyes lit with relief, then Erik gave her a push so hard that she stumbled. Nyssa spun around, but he had slammed the door behind her. She heard the key turn in the lock before she even reached it.

"You cannot mean to keep me prisoner?" she said, guessing that he did indeed.

"Not for long," he replied. "You have an appointment at midday, after all." Erik chuckled then and the sound of his fading footsteps echoed in the corridor.

Nyssa tried the door, fighting against the lock to no avail.

"Bread and ale at dawn and sunset," Mary said, her words crisply uttered. "Slops out the window, nights huddled together for warmth."

Nyssa turned to consider the midwife at this horrific prospect. She saw the lines of strain in Mary's features. "How long have you been here?"

"Since he found us," she said bitterly. "'Twill be three months with this moon. I knew he awaited something, but I am sorry that 'twas your arrival, my lady." She curtseyed then, and Nyssa saw that the other woman's boots were worn and her kirtle was faded. Mary only had a plain cloak, which would not suffice here at night in winter. Once sturdy, Mary was much slimmer than Nyssa remembered.

"I am sorry you had to endure this, Mary." Nyssa removed her own cloak and cast it over the other woman's shoulders. Mary was shorter than her and the hem brushed the floor, but she closed her eyes at the feel of the fur lining and fairly purred with satisfaction. Then she spun briskly and opened her arms to the two other occupants of the room.

One came to her immediately, a young girl whose features carried an echo of Mary's own. Nyssa knew that her hands would be like Mary's own.

"My sister, Catriona," Mary said, wrapping her arms around the girl and holding her close. Catriona buried her face against Mary and visibly shivered.

The other girl lingered by the window, her eyes wide, her uncertainty clear. Her fair hair revealed her identity, as did her features, so similar to Elsa's own. As in Nyssa's dream, Rana's hair was loose and there were raven feathers braided into it at intervals. Nyssa took a step closer and the girl retreated so that her back was against the wall. Her expression was wary.

"She does not often speak," Mary supplied, her tone matter-of-fact. "She can but she does not. She confers with the birds, if you can believe as much."

"I can," Nyssa said, smiling at Rana. "My mother's mother was said to have that gift." She watched Rana tilt her head to listen. "She spoke to the ravens, with ease. 'Tis a rare and wondrous gift and one you are fortunate to possess."

Rana almost smiled. She went to the window and called, emitting a sound precisely like one of Dorcha's cries. A raven came immediately at her summons, landing on the sill and surveying the interior of the chamber with obvious curiosity. It was a larger bird than Dorcha and one with bushy feathers that looked like brows above its eyes. It also carried something in its beak that snared the light. It reminded Nyssa of an elderly man and she halfway expected a pithy comment from it.

She also feared for Dorcha in that moment, and hoped that he fared well. They would tend him at Kilderrick, if he had returned there without her.

The bird made a sound and Rana answered in kind. The raven bobbed its head, then offered her the trinket in its beak. She stretched out her hand and the bird dropped the prize into her palm, then cawed and took flight. Rana smiled as she turned the item in the light, examining her newfound treasure.

"They bring her bits all the time," Mary said, indicating one corner of the chamber. "Sea glass and pebbles. A silk ribbon once, though I know not its origin. A button even and a small hook."

"All items that shine," Nyssa said, knowing Dorcha's fondness for any trinket with a gleam.

"Aye. They could bring a key, to my thinking, but that is evidently not to be."

Rana sang softly to herself as she considered her prize, as if she was unaware of Nyssa. Nyssa guessed otherwise. "Why does she not speak?" she asked Mary.

"Who can say?" the midwife replied. "My mother used to say that she had been changed twice: once here with the stillborn child to save her from that fiend, and once again, between here and my family abode, by the Fae. She might as well be one of them, a changeling who will laugh at death and see us all cursed."

"Do you think the same?"

Mary pursed her lips. "I do not believe in the Fae," she said flatly. "But there is aught different about this one." She eyed Nyssa, her gaze flicking to the mark barely visible on her wrist. "Perhaps she has need of her own kind."

"Then I am glad to be here."

"What does Lord Hugh intend?"

"To wed me, so that Duncheann will grow in power again, as it did when my mother was at my father's side."

"And what do you intend, my lady?"

Nyssa felt a resolve grow within her. "To leave this place forever, one way or the other, with my sister's child. I will teach her all I know, but not within this cursed place."

Rana looked up at her at that.

"Then I can only entreat you to take us with you, my lady." Mary spoke with vigor.

"Aye. Will you return to your own kin?"

Mary shook her head and Catriona made a muffled sound of dismay. "He killed them all when we declined to leave with him," she said and Nyssa knew she meant Erik. "Killed them all and razed the cottage to the ground." Mary swallowed. "I will never return there, my lady, and I will never abandon the child entrusted to me." She stroked her sister's hair. "Catriona survived because Rana protected her. He laughed, but he let her live and brought us all here. I think he expected you to know of it and follow."

"Have you a knife, Mary?"

"Of course not, my lady. Have you?"

"I am left with only my wits," Nyssa said. She went to each window in turn, eying the drop to the sea which was no less considerable than she recalled. There would be no escape that way. There was no one she could heal and no one to aid them…her skills were wasted in this place. Would that she had been born a warrior!

Nyssa realized that Rana watched her. There *was* one who could be healed in this place. Nyssa paused beside the window that admitted the last light of the setting sun. Rana touched her own hair, twirling a strand between finger and thumb as she studied Nyssa.

Nyssa unbraided her own hair and shook it out over her shoulders. She mimicked the girl's gesture, picking up a strand and twirling it between finger and thumb. "You are right," she said to her. "Our hair is the same color. Your mother was my sister."

"Elsa," Rana said and Nyssa's heart leapt that she said the name.

Mary caught her breath.

"Elsa," Nyssa agreed. "She died in the delivery of you, here in this keep, and I ran away because I thought I was alone. But I was wrong. Mary had saved you and I did not know. If I had known, I would never have left you. You are my only kin." She touched her chest. "Blood of my heart."

Rana mouthed the words. *Blood of my heart.*

Then she turned away hastily, retreating to the corner with her treasures, sorting them with such agitation that Nyssa wished all could have been otherwise. She had to teach her. She had to create trust between them. She knew what 'twas like to be betrayed and abandoned, but she would never leave Rana again.

How could she begin to convince the girl?

On impulse, Nyssa unlaced her kirtle and eased down the woolen sleeves. She shivered but pushed up the sleeves of her chemise, aware of Rana's surreptitious scrutiny as she revealed the marks on her skin.

Mary caught her breath. "Like my lady's," she whispered. She smiled as she drew near and reached out a finger to the swirl on Nyssa's wrist. "Just like Lady Elsa."

Rana watched the midwife. Her eyes widened and she drew closer, seemingly fascinated by the marks. How much of a gift did she possess? Rana's fingertip hovered over the spiral on Nyssa's left forearm, tracing its path without touching Nyssa's skin. Her fingertip moved toward Nyssa's shoulder, following the path of the spiral until she froze. Her fingertip hovered over a bare increment of skin. She frowned, then met Nyssa's gaze with her puzzled one.

She made a sound in her throat, the same kind of quorl that Dorcha made in inquiry.

She *was* gifted! She knew the mark that Nyssa did not have, the one that her mother had possessed, the one that indicated Rana's own gift.

Rana dreamed.

Rana *knew*.

Relief flooded through Nyssa, along with a new sense of purpose. "I never gained that skill," she admitted. "I cannot understand the birds, not fully, so I do not have that mark. My mother's mother had it." The girl watched her as she listened. Nyssa indicated the same spot on Rana's arm. "You should have it, here." She outlined the shape of the mark in question, a swirled line reminiscent of a feather. Her finger was just above Rana's skin as she drew the mark in the air. "Did you see it in a dream?"

Rana glanced over her shoulder. She retreated quickly, huddling over her treasures, and Nyssa feared she had made all the progress possible in one interval. Then Rana came back with something in her hand and shyly offered it to Nyssa. Nyssa could only see the end of the stone and the edge of the hole in its midst.

"You have a witching stone," she said with delight, then reached into her own purse for the one she always carried. Erik had not taken it from her, since he believed it to be worthless, and she was grateful for that. "My mother granted this one to me." She placed it flat on her hand so Rana could see it.

Rana touched the stone with her fingertips and caught her breath as if she could feel its power. Then she opened her hand to reveal her stone more fully to Nyssa. It was dark with a pink line through it, a stone that Nyssa recognized well.

"Is this Elsa's stone?" she asked, glancing to Mary.

"She made me take it for the babe," Mary said with a shrug. "Though 'twas of no import to me."

"She knew that you would have skills, even without anyone to aid you." Nyssa smiled at Rana. "Your mother was my sister."

"Blood of my heart," Rana whispered and tears rose to Nyssa's eyes.

"And now we two shall be each other's blood," she said, delighted when Rana smiled.

MURDOCH WAS TIRED BEYOND ALL, but the journey must come shortly to its conclusion. He nigh despaired that he had no plan for when they reached their destination.

He determinedly followed the small party when they trailed along the coast to the east of Inverness. When a fortified keep on an island came into view, its walls surrounded by the sea like an enchanted castle in a tale, he guessed they had arrived. The keep matched Nyssa's description of Duncheann. The others were so far ahead that they were as specks on the coast and he knew he would not catch them before they were secured within the walls. Perhaps they made haste for a reason.

As he rode closer, he discerned a road, one that would undoubtedly be covered by the sea at high tide. There was a village, though, on the headland, which was encouraging. In a village, there were always tidings to be gathered, particularly for a stranger with coin in his purse. Murdoch slowed his pace, watching the sun sink toward the horizon, and planned to seek lodgings in the village that night.

But he was doomed to disappointment. Contrary to his expectation, there was neither lodging nor tidings to be gathered in this village: 'twas abandoned. He walked through it twice, unable to believe that there was not a single soul surviving within it. He did not find so much as a stray hound.

Night had fallen and the tide was in. The road was submerged and the dark sea surrounded the keep of Duncheann. 'Twas not far from the shore, but the sea made assault impossible for much of each day and night. To fortify a small island thus had truly been clever.

It also complicated his quest. He would have to approach the gates when the tide was out and escape with Nyssa before the sea reclaimed the road again. Without a clear notion of what awaited him within the walls, the possibilities of success seemed meagre.

Murdoch sat in the shadow of the closest empty structure and finished the last of his food, letting the pony graze. He watched the silhouetted sentries march along the parapet and counted too many for one man to overwhelm. He noted the many torches lit at windows and in the bailey, and wondered if he was a fool to even contemplate an attack.

One man against many.

No chance of entering the keep unobserved.

And if he were to die in this endeavor, who would ensure Nyssa's escape? Who would aid in the search for her sister's daughter? Who would avenge Rupert against the Silver Wolf? Murdoch did not like to leave matters incomplete, but he feared he might soon do as much.

But Nyssa was held within that fortress against her will. He could not abandon her, no matter the price.

He heard the cry of a raven and looked up, watching the silhouette of the bird against the darkened sky. Was it Dorcha? The bird flew directly toward him and landed on a rock nearby, tilting its head to regard him in a familiar and expectant manner.

Murdoch offered Dorcha the last piece of bread. The bird hopped toward him and claimed the bread, throwing it back with similar enthusiasm to its consumption of the stew.

"Not so good a stew," Murdoch noted and the bird cawed, as if in agreement. It studied him for a moment, then took flight again. He could just barely discern it as it made a course toward the fortress, then he lost sight of it in the darkness.

He wished he could see whatever the bird saw, but that was not to be. Murdoch was considering the merit of presenting himself as a warrior in need of a post when he heard the rustle of wings again. Sure enough, the bird appeared out of the darkness, making a path toward him.

Dorcha landed on a rock near Murdoch then hopped closer, tilting its head and lifting its beak. It carried something, something difficult to discern. Murdoch stretched out a hand and the bird placed the prize within his palm.

There was a feather, a glossy black one that could have come from the bird's own plumage. He thought of the one he had offered to Nyssa so long ago, hating that he had been so furious, then lifted this one. Did the bird make an accusation or a reminder?

'Twas then Murdoch saw that the feather was knotted to a long fine blond hair.

"Rana," he said in surprise. "Nyssa said that Rana had raven feathers bound into her hair in the dream."

The bird cawed and bowed his head repeatedly.

"Rana is at Duncheann?" Murdoch guessed. The bird cried and nodded, then strutted toward Murdoch's satchel. Again, the creature had expectations, but they would both be hungry on this night. Murdoch turned the bag inside out, showing the bird that there were little more than crumbs within it. Dorcha ate every one of them, even as Murdoch twisted the long hair between his finger and thumb, watching the feather spin.

If Rana was within the keep, he might resolve Nyssa's search for the girl, as well. That meant, though, that both of them had to escape along with Murdoch himself. Aye, he might even find that the midwife was captive as well, since she had been custodian of the girl. Had there not been another child, as well? Murdoch pushed a hand through his hair, uncertain how he would guarantee the safety of four women on his own.

He had to try, though.

In the meantime, he planned the timing of his arrival at the gates. Though the tide would recede during the night, he would not approach the keep in darkness. The tide would rise again by midday, and he must be within the walls by then. Though he chafed to find Nyssa with haste, he knew his welcome was likely to be warmer in daylight.

He would go at dawn, and he would walk, leading the pony. The water would have receded by then. A single warrior alone, walking, would not be considered a threat. Murdoch sat back against the wall, impatient to begin, but knew that he had to choose the right moment for success. The moon was waning to its last quarter overhead. He wrapped himself in his cloak, hoping he might sleep a little before this challenge.

Murdoch watched the sentries walk the high walls of that keep and wondered just how much one man alone might do.

CHAPTER 14

*T*he sky had only brightened an increment when the key was
turned in the lock of Nyssa's prison. She had not slept,
though she had huddled with Mary and the girls. Her thoughts had
churned, her fears growing in the darkness, her doubts growing. Even
if Murdoch pursued her, what could he do against so many foes? She
stood, fearing the worst, her heart in her throat.

Erik was framed in the open portal, dressed so richly that Nyssa
blinked. "You," he said, pointing to Mary. She followed him with some
reluctance as Nyssa remained with the girls. It seemed an eternity
before Mary returned but it could not have been long in truth. There
was considerable noise outside the chamber, then Mary returned
bearing red cloth in her arms.

It had been Elsa's kirtle, ordered for her own wedding. Mary had
the shoes and stockings, the fine chemise and a collection of ribbons
for Nyssa's hair.

A tub was rolled into the chamber and a number of discontent men
carried buckets of steaming water from the kitchen. To a one, they
granted Nyssa and the girls dark glances as they dumped the water into
the tub, then stomped from the chamber. The air was soon filled with
warmth and steam.

"We have need of a lantern," Mary said.

"Nay. 'Tis a hazard," Erik argued.

"How shall I see to braid her hair with no light?" Mary asked. "How can I ensure that the bride looks her best?"

"There is naught to burn in this chamber," Nyssa noted and they won their way.

All four of them bathed then, though the others had no clean garb to wear. 'Twas a marvel to scrub her skin, though Nyssa believed the bath was more for Hugh's preferences than her own comfort. She stroked the red kirtle, remembering the day of Elsa's nuptials, and resolved that her wedding would not be the same.

Somehow, she would thwart this fiend.

Somehow, she would teach Rana all she deserved to know.

Mary braided her hair and tied it with ribbons, then laced the sides of the kirtle. Nyssa felt her sister's ghost as she donned the fine leather slippers and knotted the wide silk girdle around her waist. She put her fur-lined cloak around Mary's shoulders, kissed Rana, then knocked upon the door. When Erik opened it, his gaze lit with appreciation.

"They must witness the nuptials," she said, indicating the three others behind her.

Erik's gaze flicked over them, his disdain clear, then shook his head. "Nay," he said. He seized Nyssa's wrist and led her from the chamber and she hated the sound of the key as the portal was locked behind her.

There were two guards outside the door, both of them wearing helmets that disguised their faces. They might have been wrought of stone for all the interest they showed in her passing, but Nyssa noticed where the key was hung on the wall.

Erik led her to the great hall, where Hugh sat at the high table, watching with approval as a bowl was placed before him. The air was redolent of a savory stew, perhaps one made of chicken. Nyssa was keenly aware of the emptiness of her own belly but she would not ask this man for anything. Erik escorted her to the board, offering her a seat between the two brothers as if she was a guest and not a captive.

A servant brought her bread and some honeycomb. A cup of ale was poured for her and another for Erik, who was also brought a bowl of that savory stew when Hugh's bowl was refilled. 'Twas some manner of fowl in that stew, spiced with saffron, the gravy rich and creamy. The brothers began to eat with gusto while Nyssa nibbled at her own offering.

"This is a fine stew," Erik said when he had eaten close to half of it. "Though it would be much improved by a spice I had the opportunity to obtain on my journey."

"A spice?" 'Twas clear that Hugh was interested.

Erik removed a small pouch from his purse. "'Tis a most enticing combination from the East, both rare and expensive. There is pepper within it, along with cardamom and anise."

"I have never tasted cardamom," Hugh confessed, craning his neck to look around Nyssa.

"A most unusual flavor and one highly prized by heretics," Erik said. He opened the pouch and made a motion as if he took a pinch of the content and sprinkled it upon his stew. Nyssa was close enough to see that he did not actually take any. Setting the pouch aside, he took another bite of the stew and clearly savored it. "All the difference in the world," he said with satisfaction, then filled his spoon with another bite.

Nyssa could not fathom it. His stew was no different than it had been before.

Hugh was restless beside her. "And we have not had pepper for some months. 'Tis an important spice to consume in the winter months." He cleared his throat, when Erik simply continued to eat. "What does it taste like?"

"Oh, bitter at first," Erik said. "But it is a flavor one grows to find quite alluring." He reached for his pouch and pretended to add an increment more.

The light was dim in the hall and given the distance, Nyssa doubted that Hugh knew his brother teased him.

"Anise is a fine flavor," Hugh said. "One of my favorites." He eyed the pouch when Erik did not offer him a taste.

Indeed, Erik cleaned his bowl and pushed it away with a sigh. "Now there was a meal fit for a king." He patted the little pouch. "I am fortunate indeed to have acquired this spice. 'Twill make a feast of even the simplest of fare!"

"I would like to try it," Hugh said finally.

"Oh, but I do not have very much," Erik protested.

"But you are a guest in my abode," Hugh insisted, his tone turning petulant. "You are hosted here at my pleasure, and 'twould be my pleasure to taste that spice."

Erik looked skeptical. "I am not certain I could spare it."

"I will pay you for it!"

"'Tis beyond price, brother. I would have to journey to York to find more of it, if even it could be found, and I have only just returned home. Nay, you must simply trust my assessment."

"Give it to me!" Hugh cried, but Erik lifted the pouch and made to tuck it away in his purse again.

"I will not! 'Tis mine!"

"'Twill be mine!" Hugh roared and stood to his feet so quickly that the bench tipped backward. Nyssa fell backward, striking her hip, but Erik bounded to his feet, as if he had anticipated his brother's action. He apparently did not anticipate the two guards who caught his arms, nor the one who plucked the pouch from his hand and delivered it to Hugh with a bow.

That man smiled as he opened the pouch. He sniffed delicately at the contents, then reached into it to pinch a measure. He sprinkled it on his stew, considered it for a moment, then added a fistful more.

"Mind the quantity, brother," Erik said, something in his tone making Nyssa study him with suspicion. His eyes were shining with what she might have called malice. "It has an uncommon bite."

Hugh clearly did not take well to being warned of anything. He held Erik's gaze with defiance and tipped the pouch so that all of the spice poured into his stew. He stirred it in, his manner resolute, then took a hearty bite. He caught his breath, but chewed and swallowed, consuming another mouthful with a haste that was unseemly.

Erik began to smile. "I hope you do not mean to waste my prize, brother," he said, his voice silky.

Hugh granted his brother a furious look and shoved stew into his mouth, chewing audibly.

Nyssa eased away from the board, anticipating that matters would soon go awry. Erik, released by the guards, resumed his seat at the board and locked one hand around her wrist. He smiled at her, an expression so chilling that her blood ran cold.

What was in the spice mixture?

"An unusual combination," Hugh said even as he ran a piece of bread around the bowl to catch the sauce. "Hot and yet savory. Intriguing."

"How unfortunate that I did not anticipate your affection for it," Erik said smoothly. "I might have brought you a present of it."

"You must get more," Hugh said. "I must have everything that is fine and rare." He gave Nyssa an appraising glance before pushing another spoonful into his mouth. He swallowed six mouthfuls before his face reddened. He continued to eat, demanding another bowl of stew from the castellan even as he finished the one before him. Erik was lounging at the board, looking so confident that Nyssa knew Hugh had erred.

Halfway through the next bowl, Hugh caught his breath. His face was flaming red at this point, his eyes wide. His mouth fell open and he stood up, evidently unsteady on his feet. His entire body heaved, then shook. He fell back, crashing onto the bench and into the wall. He made an incoherent sound, gripping at his chest, before collapsing on the floor.

He did not move again.

"I would not waste your skills attempting to heal him," Erik said, sauntering around the board to crouch beside his brother's corpse. Hugh's eyes were wide and staring, and 'twas evident to Nyssa that he no longer breathed. "'Tis too late."

"What was in the powder?" she asked.

Erik glanced up at her, eyes alight. "Can you not guess?"

"My art is to heal not to destroy."

"But you must recognize its effect."

"I would guess it was wolfsbane," she said, thinking of wolves and their appetites again. 'Twas an apt choice for Erik, a poison that was quick and fatal, fierce in its power.

Erik smiled. "I shall have to watch my step with such a clever bride," he said, then reached for the signet ring on Hugh's finger. He tugged it from his brother's hand and placed it upon his own, granting Nyssa a smile. "And so, it is done," he said, offering his hand to Nyssa. "You may be the first to kiss the ring of the new Laird of Duncheann."

"While Hugh's warmth still clings to it," she said, unable to suppress a shiver.

"As much warmth as Hugh possessed. He was a viper, my brother, whose blood ran cold."

Nyssa thought that to be true of both brothers but did not say as much.

"'Tis the best way," Erik continued easily. "Any delay in the succession only creates doubt and uncertainty. There would have been questions if he had chosen to wed his dead wife's sister." He winced and shook his head. "Simpler is far better." When she did not touch her lips to the ring, he caught her hands in his, urging her to her feet. "And now I shall wed the daughter of the former Laird of Duncheann, the better to secure my claim before the Lord of Badenoch's arrival."

He led her to the stairs, hauling her up them even as a commotion rose in the bailey. Nyssa wondered what was happening, but Erik moved with haste, fairly hauling her to the solar. He shoved her into it and locked the door behind her, then raced back down the stairs. The windows in this chamber also gave a view only of the sea.

What was happening?

Had Murdoch come?

Nyssa could only hope.

~

"WRETCHED BIRDS," was the greeting of the gatekeeper when Murdoch arrived at Duncheann. It seemed he was more concerned with the raven that followed Murdoch than the arrival of another warrior at his gates. "They are a plague upon us," he continued, eying Murdoch through the opening in the gate. "What is your errand here?"

"I have none. I am but an honest warrior in search of labor," Murdoch replied. "I was told in Inverness that there is always a place for a man of my ilk at Duncheann." He tipped back his head, realizing only then that a flock of birds had gathered above the keep. Was this typical? They circled, black dots against the blue sky, a veritable cloud of birds.

"Have you fought?" the keeper demanded.

"I spent seventeen years on the Continent, many with the Compagnie Rouge."

The man's brows rose. "Why did you not remain?"

Murdoch shrugged. "I yearned for home."

The gatekeeper hesitated, surveying Murdoch from head to toe, then nodded once. "Albert died last week. There might be room for another." He vanished then and Murdoch heard the bar being lifted from the gates. One swung open, creaking on its hinges, granting a view of the courtyard beyond.

Murdoch led his pony through the opening, surreptitiously studying the construction. The solar would be the chamber at the summit of the tower before him, and the hall might be on the same level as the bailey or the next level. He would guess that the guards were housed in the chambers between the walls.

Where was Nyssa? She had to be somewhere within the tower before him, perhaps secured in a chamber for which he had to find a key. He could not seek her with so many watchful eyes, and he was aware that the tide was steadily rising.

He had need of a distraction and Murdoch understood what it could be. Would the birds above follow Dorcha? He could only try. He whistled to Dorcha, tipping back his head to try to locate the raven amongst the flock overhead. He had time to count ten guards on the parapets before the birds swirled down from the sky like a purposeful cloud.

Then they attacked. Murdoch had never seen the like of it, but he welcomed their arrival.

"Wretched creatures!" shouted the gatekeeper, swinging his sword at a raven that dove toward him, talons outstretched. The bird cried out and evaded the blow, then attacked the man again. Its claws dug into the man's outstretched hand and he roared with pain even as the blood flowed.

Dozens of birds descending upon the keep, if not hundreds, their numbers ever increasing as they attacked the guards with their talons and beaks. Blood flowed from hundreds of tiny wounds as men shouted and strove to strike the birds down. The air was dark with fluttering wings and the sound of rustling feathers, and no one was watching Murdoch.

This was his chance!

Murdoch pulled up his hood and ducked into the main tower of the keep, recognizing that he stood in the great hall. A man dressed in rich garments lay on the floor beside the high table, obviously dead.

Murdoch hastened to the stairs, not wanting to be implicated in that deed. Had Nyssa killed her captor? He could not imagine that she would do as much. Even if she had struck him down, she would have fled for the gates. There was no sign of her and he reasoned she was yet captive.

Murdoch took the stairs three at a time, slowing only when he reached the second floor. There were three doors in this narrow corridor, but the middle one had a guard on either side of it. Murdoch strolled toward them with feigned nonchalance, aware of the ruckus arising from the bailey, which was not visible. There were no windows facing the bailey in this corridor.

"What is amiss?" one guard demanded of him.

"We are attacked, but by birds," Murdoch said, with a snort of derision. "The laird would summon all of us to wage a war against them." He shook his head as if amused by such whimsy.

The pair exchanged a glance. "I will go," said the one furthest from Murdoch.

There was a key hanging on the wall behind the man.

"Fool!" said the first. "I will not abandon a post without permission in this keep."

"A wise warrior knows of his surroundings," argued the second. The first shrugged, and this one turned to Murdoch. "Remain in my place, if you will. I would know what transpires."

"Gladly," Murdoch said, taking that man's place against the wall. "I have no quarrel with *birds*."

The guard left with crisp steps, his footfalls echoing on the stairs, and they stood in silence for some moments. There were obvious sounds of battle in the bailey and several men screamed.

"Birds?" asked the first guard finally.

"Ravens," Murdoch supplied. "Hundreds of them."

The man shivered. "Corbies."

"Aye. Harbingers of death, my gran always said," Murdoch lied, then chuckled. "Do you think we will all die from this assault?"

"'Twill more like be due to lack of provisions," his companion said. Murdoch nodded wisely. "Like poor Albert."

"Aye! If I never see another salted eel, 'twill be too soon."

"Aye!"

There was a moment of convivial agreement then the other guard turned to study Murdoch. "I do not recall you," he said, suspicion in his tone. "Who are you?"

"The ladies' salvation," Murdoch said, granting the man a moment to puzzle over that before he attacked. Two swift punches and a kick in the groin and the man was down. Murdoch hesitated a moment over doing more, but then his opponent straightened, a knife in his grasp, and the matter was decided. Murdoch twisted the blade from the guard's hand, swung the man around hard, slammed him into the wall, then cut his throat.

He kicked the corpse aside and claimed the key, unlocking the portal and shoving it open. A trio of women greeted him, one of an age with him, her expression fierce though she had no weapon, and two girls behind her.

One had fair hair with raven feathers knotted within it.

Murdoch pulled the hair from his purse, letting it spin in the light. "Dorcha told me you were here, Rana," he said. "I came to aid Nyssa."

"Did you then?" asked a man behind him and Murdoch spun to find a nobleman behind him, flanked by three guards. A signet ring glinted on the man's hand and his expression was triumphant. "You were right to summon me, Gunther," he said and Murdoch's heart sank in recognition of the guard who had abandoned his post to him. "This man is not in our service." His gaze swept over Murdoch, then lit. "He must be the one who killed my brother," he said, his tone hinting to Murdoch that the man in the great hall had met his fate by this man's hand. "Seize him!

Murdoch was not in a hurry to see so little gained from his efforts. He drew his sword and lunged at the nobleman, who retreated with haste, typical of his kind. Murdoch bounded after him, clashing blades with one guard and forcing the party out of the chamber and away from the stairs. As he had hoped, the woman charged forth with the girls, the three of them fleeing toward the stairs. Where could they go?

The tide had turned, so they would have to hide themselves within the keep until it receded again. Murdoch could only grant them as much time as possible and hope they knew of a safe corner.

"Stop them!" roared the nobleman and one man ran after the woman and the girls. Murdoch cut down one guard, but the nobleman seized the fallen man's sword. He wielded it with a competency that was disappointing, given the circumstance. Murdoch fought hard in an effort to grant time to the woman who had to be the midwife, Mary Gunn.

'Twas only a matter of time before he was defeated, but he would make the interval as long as possible. Battling against three men, Murdoch steadily backed into the chamber where the women had been confined. He fully expected that the door would be closed against him, but the nobleman dropped the tip of the blade against the opening of Murdoch's jerkin and leaned closer.

The sword nicked Murdoch's skin so that he felt a trickle of blood but his opponent smiled coolly at him. "I remember you, even without your beard," he whispered, undoubtedly keeping his voice low so the guards would not hear. Murdoch gave no hint of the chill this man's words sent through him. "And I will take no chances against such an enterprising adversary. You will be found guilty of poisoning my brother, Hugh Sutherland, Laird of Duncheann, and you will not leave this holding alive. You certainly will not have so much as a glimpse of the lady destined to be my bride."

His eyes were cold, colder than a winter night, but Murdoch did not so much as blink.

At least one of the brothers was dead. That diminished the task before him.

"I knew she was here," he said. "And I will guarantee that you never possess her."

The nobleman laughed and stepped away, casting the sword aside with a disregard for the blade. "Perhaps I will grant you a glimpse after all," he taunted, then turned to his men. "You know what to do with him," he said as he left the chamber. "My nuptials will be celebrated at noon and the great hall must be cleaned."

MARY RAN.

She held Catriona's hand in her own right and Rana's in her left. She fairly hurtled down the stairs, halfway fearing she would stumble and they would be lost. She could not rely upon any mercy this time. She could hear the guard behind her, but also a ruckus in the bailey.

How many had arrived with their liberator? She hoped 'twas an enormous army. She reached the great hall and raced through it, sparing the merest glance to the fallen man beside the board. The cook was bent over what might have been the laird's corpse, the castellan fast beside him. Mary darted past them, diving toward the kitchen.

Catriona made to speak, but she cast the girl a look. They had to hide until nightfall but all she knew of this keep was the chamber where they had been imprisoned. There had to be storage chambers near the kitchen, places where they could secret themselves between casks and sacks. Her heart was leaping in terror but faltered when Rana gave a cry.

Before she could anticipate as much, the girl tore her hand from Mary's grip and ran for the bailey. Cook and castellan glanced up in that moment and shouted at Rana.

"Mary!" Catriona whispered as Rana vanished into the bailey with a cry of delight.

"God in heaven," Mary whispered, then had to choose between her own kin and that of her lady. She caught up Catriona and lunged into the darkness beyond the kitchen, hoping with all her might that Rana would be well.

MAXIMILIAN STOOD on the headland opposite the keep he now knew as Duncheann at midday. A man had joined their party on the journey north, insisting that the Lord of Badenoch would wish to know the intentions of a company of warriors in the territories that man governed. Maximilian was aware of the need for diplomacy, once again the result of his position as a man of repute, so agreed to let the man accompany them so long as he kept the pace. The Lord of Badenoch, one Alexander Stewart, was a favored son of the king and any insult rendered to him was likely to have repercussions.

Maximilian might hope for fewer days in which the need to act within his rights—instead of choosing expediency by force—chafed as much as it had of late.

The man, whose name was Iye, had told them of the Lairds of Duncheann once learning of their destination, including the warrior who had built the keep, one Reginald LeCheyne. The tale was one of women forcibly wed or their executions ordered, and said little good of the men in question. It also went far in explaining Nyssa's flight from her home.

In this moment, Iye pointed out the locations of stables, barracks and kitchens within the walls of the keep, even as Maximilian considered the way the sea surrounded the island. If the tide was nigh at midday, 'twould be high again at midnight and at its lowest ebb halfway in between. He knew this keep to be Murdoch's destination, not just by Nerida's tale but because they had seen a lone rider on a pony ahead of them this past day or so. There was nowhere else that rider could have vanished so completely as Duncheann.

"You have not explained your interest in Duncheann," Iye noted and Maximilian turned a cool glance upon him.

"We believe a woman of my holding, a companion of my wife, has been taken there against her will."

Iye pursed his lips and surprised Maximilian with his next words. "She would not be a seer, would she? One with fair hair and marks upon her skin in blue?"

"Nyssa is a seer and her hair is blond." Maximilian knew naught of marks on Nyssa's skin, though he realized that he had never seen her arms bare. He had assumed she was modest, perhaps more modest than most, but perhaps she hid distinguishing marks.

"Nyssa? That might well be the daughter of Gerda, the one who vanished from these parts some eight years ago." Iye nodded at the keep. "The father, Reginald LeCheyne, wed his oldest daughter to Hugh Sutherland, who became laird after Reginald's demise. The lady died in childbirth delivering her second daughter, 'twas said, the infants as well. The Lord of Badenoch thought to reclaim the keep, which is a doughty one, but Hugh vowed to wed the other daughter to secure his claim." Iye shrugged. "Then she vanished, and the pair have been at odds ever since."

"Why does the Lord of Badenoch simply seize Duncheann?" Maximilian asked.

"'Tis not a fortress readily overcome, and not one worth the loss of an army," Iye said.

Maximilian smiled. "We may be able to be of assistance to your liege lord," he said smoothly. "Though be aware that we will take Duncheann apart, stone by stone, if necessary to retrieve the lady in question."

Iye considered him. "Those seers have a powerful lineage, to be sure. The Lord of Badenoch's wife, Mairead Eachainn, oft consulted Gerda, and 'twas said that she brought wealth to Reginald LeCheyne after their marriage."

"I thought the Lord of Badenoch's wife was Euphemia of Ross," Maximilian said, no longer truly interested. He was planning their assault, taking the tides and the light into consideration.

"I mean his other wife, the one who has given him bairns," Iye said. "Some call her mistress, but they have a handfast."

Maximilian doubted that Euphemia shared this view of Badenoch's second partner, but any dispute was not his affair.

Iye looked back over the small company that had journeyed north with Maximilian, his skepticism clear. "But you are too few to take Duncheann, to be sure."

"Are we then?" Maximilian turned to Rafael, who adjusted his trebuchet. "Begin with the barracks," he instructed in Norman French, aware that Iye might betray them, and Rafael nodded. "End with the tower, for Nyssa may be imprisoned there. Leave long intervals between each assault, for 'twill be hours before we can approach the gates." He turned then to Royce, Oliver and Reynaud. "Rest while you can. The sun will set early, then the tide will be out. We ride under cover of dusk, though Rafael will begin as soon as he chooses." Then he smiled at Iye, who was clearly puzzled. "Perhaps you would like to make a small wager upon our success," he invited, watching Iye's eyes light in anticipation of a ready gain.

AGAIN, Murdoch found himself in a dungeon, though this one showed less merit than that of Kilderrick. Unlike that holding's lairds, who wished a man to have time to appreciate his incarceration and suffer, whoever had planned this prison was intent upon eliminating the condemned, perhaps without the trouble of a trial. The water was waist-deep when he was cast into the cell and it continued to rise quickly. There was sufficient light that he could see evidence of sea creatures to the very ceiling and knew the dungeon flooded fully twice a day.

He could hold his breath, but not for so long as it took for a tide to recede.

Nyssa would be claimed within the hour.

There was a single barred window through which the seawater flowed. Any hope that the bars might have weakened was a false one, for they were well-secured. He shook upon them with all his might, but to no avail.

The water continued to rise. He continued to fight against the door, not knowing what else he might do. He bellowed for help, but no one heard him—or no one listened. The water crested his shoulders, relentless in its progress.

Murdoch was floating, his head tipped back in the last increment of space against the ceiling when he heard a key turn in the lock. He almost thought it was a trick.

The trap door was abruptly swung open and light fell into the hole. Above him was the midwife, who glanced over her shoulder with evident fear. A smaller figure was beside her and Murdoch recognized the other girl who had been held captive. "Nyssa is locked in the solar, and Erik means to forcibly wed her," Mary said, reaching a hand to aid him.

Murdoch swore as he climbed out of the hole, shivered then smiled in relief when he saw that they had brought him dry garb. 'Twas from a warrior in service to the laird, and would ensure that he blended in with the others.

"They cast the dead into the kitchen," she supplied. "But I could not get the hauberk. There was no time."

Murdoch could have kissed her for her foresight, even with the blood stains upon the tabard.

"Thank you!" he said as he changed and she covered her sister's eyes. He laced his wet boiled leather vest over his chest and fastened his belt over it. His braies and wet boots would have to suffice, but he felt warmer already.

A twinkle lit Mary's eyes as she offered him a dagger. "We found this and thought you might have use for it."

At that, Murdoch did kiss her cheek.

"Hurry," Mary urged in a whisper, but Murdoch had no need of encouragement.

"Hide," he said to her and Mary nodded agreement before their ways parted.

Nyssa had run her hands across the floor of the solar twice, seeking the old hiding spot by feel, but she had not found it. She knew her mother had hidden her treasures from her father. She knew the hiding place was in the solar, and she recalled that it was in the floor. Why could she not find its sanctuary? She began again, working from one side of the chamber to the other.

Birds cried and shadows fell across the window so repeatedly that she finally rose to look. The solar offered views in every direction and she looked over the sunlit bailey, only to see a multitude of ravens attacking the guards there. Birds cried and swooped, talons tore into skin, men screamed and swords flashed. The ravens called to each other all the while, evading swinging swords and waving hands. Chaos reigned, blood spattered against the ground yet the veritable cloud of black birds did not disperse.

But why would the birds attack? She had never seen the like and could not explain it.

She noted that the road beyond the gates was flooded at high tide and her chest tightened with the certainty that there was no chance of escape for some hours yet. She imagined she would see the waters rise and fall many more times before she left this wretched place.

'Twas then Nyssa noticed a shadow in the distance, as if a party mustered on the headland by Duncheann village. They were not as numerous as she might have wished, but they had not been there before. Could Murdoch have led a party to their aid? Nyssa could only hope.

But in that moment, she was distracted anew by a shout in the bailey. A small figure appeared far below, darting out of the great hall, and Nyssa caught her breath in recognition. She gripped the sill and leaned out for a better look. Rana ran into the midst of the bailey, her hands raised high in the air. She spun in place, hands stretched toward the ravens, and cried out as one of them. The birds swooped and swirled around her, and Nyssa feared the worst, but they were seemingly answering her summons. They flew around her in a spiral and Nyssa saw the girl laugh with delight. How had she escaped the chamber on the floor below? Were Mary and Catriona free as well?

She could only wonder whether the ravens *had* brought a key to the captives.

A pair of guards stepped toward Rana with purpose, evidently thinking that a child would be easy to subdue, but the ravens cried as one. The sound was deafening as the guards were swarmed by large screaming black birds. Rana stood and watched, her expression impassive, as the birds tore apart both guards. She then pivoted and fled, vanishing into the stables with remarkable speed.

Nyssa called after her, but her cry was snatched away by the wind.

"Someone will have to do something about that child," Erik said and Nyssa spun to find him behind her, watching. He smiled. "I look forward to the resolution of a persistent problem." He stepped away from the door then and beckoned. The priest followed him into the chamber then, at Erik's gesture, he moved to secure the door behind them. "We shall exchange our vows here, rather than be distracted by events in the bailey. It will be more expedient."

"But the keep is attacked…"

Erik shook his head. "I do not fear *birds*, Nyssa."

She thought of the two men who had just been killed, but did not make him aware of what had occurred. Perhaps he would err and the birds would claim him. He was turning the key in the lock and the bed was all too close. Nyssa had time to fear that all was lost, then there was a thunderous crash from beyond the window. She smelled fire and heard men shouting in consternation.

The roof of the barracks was ablaze, the flames flowing down the interior wall in a way she had never seen before. It might have been liquid fire, spreading with fearsome power, setting all alight in its path.

Erik crossed to the window, fairly shoving Nyssa out of his path. "What madness is this? Who dares to assault Duncheann?" He peered at the distant party on the headland, scowling at them. "There will not be sufficient water within the walls. They will have to lower buckets to the sea." He then ran from the chamber with the priest, leaving Nyssa locked within it as the fire hungrily spread across the roof of the barracks. Smoke was rising in a dark cloud from the conflagration and Nyssa surveyed the solar again.

The entire keep might burn before the fire was extinguished. She had to find her mother's tools before they were lost forever!

ROYCE MISSED A GOOD BATTLE, where the fiends were numerous and his allies clear. Peace was all good for daily life and a sound night's sleep, and Kilderrick was a fine holding. He had no quibbles with his current life. All the same, it did not disappoint him to be headed into battle once again, uncertain whether he would survive to see the dawn, knowing he would do his worst before he breathed his last. His sword was sharp, his axe was sharper, he had two knives hidden in his boots, two in his belt and one inside his hauberk.

Rafael's trebuchet was positioned on the headland, three volleys having already damaged the keep considerably. The Silver Wolf's company watched, unchallenged, as the roof of the fortress before them burned and a flock of birds inexplicably attacked those in Duncheann's bailey. The man who had joined them was fascinated and impressed, muttering to himself of sorcery.

Royce respected the damage wrought by the birds and wondered whether that detail was due to Nyssa. It mattered little. All was in chaos within the stone walls, and he could only welcome any circumstance that shifted the odds in favor of their success.

The sun set early, the fires seeming brighter when the sky was dark. The tide ebbed, the moon rose, and the wet road shone in the light of the last quarter of the moon.

At Maximilian's nod, they prepared to ride. Royce heard one of Rafael's missiles whistle as it soared through the air and saw its trail of fire burn against the night. The missile struck the roof of the high tower, the first to land there, and exploded in a burst of flame. Even from this distance, Royce heard the shouts of dismay. 'Twas like old times! He was mounted and prepared when the signal was given, then granted Nuit his spurs. The destrier was born for war, for he never shied or hesitated, never bolted or turned aside. Aye, this beast had fire in his veins—they might have been wrought for each other.

Royce rode hard toward the gates of Duncheann beside the Silver Wolf—a warrior he could not even think of as the Laird of Kilderrick on a night such as this, let alone Maximilian de Vries—wanting to cheer aloud when the next missile found its mark. There was a crash and a roar as the flame found purchase, then a roar like thunder. They truly might have loosed a dragon upon their adversaries.

The Silver Wolf's destrier, Tempest, was a creature as black as midnight that might have been spawned in Hell itself. That destrier tossed his head and nickered, his black mane and tail flowing behind him as majestically as the Silver Wolf's dark cloak.

Oliver and Reynaud rode hard behind them, fairly chafing to prove themselves in battle. Flames rose from the keep ahead of them, licking the night sky with their great orange tongues, sending plumes of dark smoke toward the stars. The tide was already rising again, the road to the keep disappearing beneath the water even as they raced closer.

Archers appeared along the parapet, their intention clear. The Silver Wolf led them onward, without halting, trusting in their plan. Rafael's next missile of Greek fire struck the wooden gates in the best possible moment. It poured a plume of flame across the barrier, setting them alight. The guards cried out and Royce knew he was not the sole one to expect chaos within the walls. The gates burned with startling speed, then gaps appeared as the planks of wood broke away and fell into the sea.

Oliver leapt to the back of Reynaud's palfrey as they galloped closer. Oliver cast Royce the reins of his own steed, and Royce snatched them out of the air. The pair clearly had a plan of their own, for Reynaud charged toward the gates, passing Maximilian and Royce.

Maximilian reined in Tempest, raising a hand to stay Royce.

Aye, they would have their chance.

The guards roared, but Oliver stood behind Reynaud and jumped for the wall in the last moment before the horse was compelled to turn. Reynaud slipped from the saddle, sending his palfrey back to Maximilian and Royce with a smack to her rump. Royce grinned at the way the two younger warriors flattened themselves against the very walls. Doubtless they had anticipated that the guards would not fire upon the steeds, and they did not. The palfreys exhaled mightily and tossed their heads when out of range of the archers, stamping in the water that rose almost to their knees. The tides did not delay in this region, to be sure.

"No lack of valor there," Royce said with satisfaction.

"An impetuous choice. Foolhardy, perhaps, but unanticipated to be sure." Maximilian loosed a bolt from his crossbow as he spoke, striking one archer in the chest so he fell out of sight.

Royce followed suit and injured another. They continued their assault, giving some protection to the younger warriors. Meanwhile, Oliver had climbed over what remained of the gate and vanished from view. Reynaud lunged through a gap in the wood and there was a clash of steel on steel from within the walls.

"Enough," Maximilian muttered and gave Tempest his spurs.

Royce was immediately behind him.

Oliver and Reynaud were visible, back-to-back, battling their way toward the entrance to the great hall.

"Together!" the Silver Wolf roared and they charged into the bailey in a clatter of hoofbeats. Royce planted his sword in the chest of one of the gatekeepers, then pulled it out and kicked the man's corpse backward. The water was rising behind them, a reminder that they would be soon sealed within the keep until the tide ebbed again. That only filled Royce with purpose.

Royce roared at Oliver's assailant and that man glanced up in time to be sliced down by a swing of Royce's axe. He fell and did not rise again. Guards fell upon them on all sides and Royce laughed aloud as he sliced down a pair of men.

"Murdoch Campbell!" the Silver Wolf roared. "The Compagnie Rouge rides at your back!"

"Nyssa the seer!" Royce bellowed. "Know that Kilderrick rides to your aid!"

The four arrivals cheered in unison and set to fighting the defenders with gusto.

Aye, Royce was glad of another taste of this life.

CHAPTER 15

*M*urdoch could see no way into the solar to aid Nyssa. Four guards stood in the corridor outside it, and he quickly retreated down the stairs to the hall. He heard his name shouted in the bailey and could not believe his ears.

But then, he had confessed it to the gatekeeper. He would not be distracted from his task.

The sound of fighting carried from the bailey, which meant that Murdoch was unobserved for the moment. Four guards. How might he distract them all at once?

He suddenly realized that Rana stood close by him. She was so quiet and still that he had not noticed her. When he met her gaze, her eyes lit.

Aye, at closer proximity the resemblance to Nyssa could not be denied, though this child's eyes were as clear a blue as a summer sky. Still, she might know more of this keep than he did.

"I would aid Nyssa," he said softly, and she moved an increment closer.

"Blood of my heart," she whispered so quietly that he scarce could discern the words. When he realized what she had said, Murdoch nodded.

"Aye." He touched his chest with a fingertip. "Mine as well."

She frowned at him, though, and he wondered whether she did not recall him setting them free from the chamber. Abruptly, she reached out with one hand and touched his chin, rubbing her fingertip against his whiskers in apparent confusion. Was she a seer, as well? Nyssa had said the gift was inherited.

Had his beard been full in her vision?

"I cut it off," he said as she held his gaze. He was not certain she understood. "I was there when Nyssa was captured. I did not wish to be remembered." And he gestured with his hands, indicating how long and wide his beard had been, then made a slicing gesture.

Her confusion seemed to clear.

"Nyssa," she said.

"Nyssa," Murdoch agreed, wondering what more to do.

Rana then abruptly seized his hand and spun away. She tugged him into the darkness, moving with such speed and purpose that Murdoch hastened to keep up with her. She flitted from shadow to shadow, moving soundlessly and with confidence. She led him into the kitchens, where corpses had been piled already. Rana led him to a dark alcove, then urged him into a nook. He had a moment to fear that some dark fate awaited him in the darkness, then he smelled the fresh air from the sea. He stretched out a hand and felt the space, finding a low doorway on one side. There were steps there, steps in a tight spiral that led upward.

There was another entrance to the solar!

He squeezed Rana's hand to show his pleasure and she scampered up the stairs ahead of him. The steps were smaller and followed a tight curve, the space small for Murdoch's breadth. Rana flitted up them with ease and familiarity, though he followed with more caution, the dagger in his hand. There was one window, a small square that granted a view of the sea. He took a breath of fresh air and kept climbing, not sparing the time to look.

Rana awaited him at the summit. A low door filled the end wall, a sliver of light leaking from beneath it. Murdoch could not hear a sound. There was a small space to one side of the door, just sufficient room to put down some item while opening the door. Rana climbed into it, folding herself small, giving clear indication that she would not enter the room beyond the door.

Murdoch tapped her shoulder, then the floor. "You stay here," he said so softly that only she would hear him. He felt rather than saw her nod.

Then he straightened and reached for the door. It was secured on the stair side with a heavy bolt.

Who would say what he would find on the other side? Murdoch knew there was but one way to find out. There could be no hiding in the laird's solar, so he had best surprise his foe. He gripped his dagger, drew the bolt, nodded to Rana, then kicked open the door.

"Behind you!" Oliver cried and Royce spun to jab an assailant in the chest. He kicked the man's corpse aside and caught his breath. The bailey was filling with the fallen, though more emerged from the keep with every passing moment. The wooden roofs were all aflame and the heat even in the bailey was considerable. They soon would be sealed on the island as the road would be covered by water. Royce might have bidden Oliver to release all the creatures in the stables, but a woman emerged from a shadowed doorway. She led a young girl and clearly fled from someone, terrified.

The girl favored her so strongly that they could only be related by blood.

The woman surveyed the combatants, then cut a decisive path toward Royce. "Help me," she said, and Royce appreciated her brevity. "He will kill us all." Both were pale and looked chilled, their garb insufficient for the season. Royce guessed that they had not eaten well of late, for they were unsteady on their feet. The woman seemed to be upright by force of will alone.

"Nyssa?" he asked, and relief filled her expression.

"Secured in the solar by Erik Sutherland, who swears to make her his bride." She indicated the summit of the tower.

"Has a man come to aid her?" Royce demanded.

"Aye, but he was in the dungeon." She pointed to the ground below the tower. "I saw him freed, but I had to save my sister." Her eyes filled with tears. "Rana fled from us. I do not know what happened to her."

"You have done well," Royce said. "One must do what one can and not regret a choice to survive."

"I do, though," she confessed. "I *do*." Her dark eyes widened the barest increment in warning and Royce spun to slice down a guard who had intended to attack on his blind side. Another blow and the man would never move again. No other dared to attack in this moment, the others in the bailey granting Royce a wary space. He seized the opportunity to swung off his cloak and wrapped the girl within it, gathering her up with one arm. He felt her tremble when caught against his chest.

"This one," he bade the woman, turning his hip toward her so she could take his smallest dagger. She did, her grip upon it confident and purposeful. Royce understood that she not only knew how to use it but would do as much.

"Follow me and hold my belt," he bade the woman. "I shall know immediately if you are no longer with me." She nodded and did as instructed, the press of her hand against his back unmistakable. He was glad that she was evidently not one to weep in moments of challenge. He pivoted and could not believe how many more men had appeared in the bailey. "They breed like rats," he said through his teeth, watching Maximilian dispatch another. Oliver and Reynaud fought on with impressive skill and gave no sign of faltering.

"We shall not get through them all," the woman whispered.

"We will carve a path," Royce told her. "I vow it to you. Hold fast."

Ten paces through the midst of the bailey, then another half a dozen to Nuit. Progress was hampered by the number of corpses in his path. Royce planned to send the woman through the gates on the destrier without him.

Aye, he would send her in the midst of a veritable herd of steeds.

"Oliver!" he roared. "Stables!"

He saw the boy nod and duck, dispatching a final blow to his assailant, then vanishing into the heavy wall on the far side. Royce heard the anxious nickering of the horses.

A guard lunged for him, again from his blind side, but Royce heard the man. Royce swung his great blade and sliced that warrior down, stepped over his corpse and cut down the next. The girl hid her face against his shoulder, but he steadily cut a path through those who would oppose him. He heard the woman grunt and felt her movement as she jabbed at their pursuers.

Suddenly her grip vanished. Royce roared and pivoted, nigh laughing aloud when she elbowed the man who had seized her then ducked in anticipation of his own move. Clever woman! Royce sliced down the man without delay. The woman was on her feet in a heart-beat, his dagger at the ready and her hand latched onto his belt again. There was a gleam of triumph in her eyes that he understood well.

"A veritable shieldmaiden," Royce told her. "You do well."

"I will *not* die in this wretched place," she said through her teeth.

Aye, this one could seize his heart and make it her own, to be sure.

"You will not have to," Royce promised as ponies and horses surged into the bailey from the stables. Some fool was attempting to steal Nuit, but the destrier would have none of this plan. The beast stamped and snorted, kicked and tossed his head. Royce did not doubt that the would-be thief had been bitten as well as kicked. He whistled and the destrier turned immediately, trotting to his side proudly then holding his ground. Royce dispatched the villain, sheathed his blade and spun to lift the woman to the saddle.

"Tell me you can ride," he demanded of her. She smiled and swung her leg over the horse for a better seat, her confidence atop a horse more than clear.

"Tell me you will collect your horse later," she countered.

Royce laughed then lifted the girl, placing her before the woman. "Do I look like a fool who abandons a prize?"

"Do I?" she asked, her smile lighting her eyes, and Royce was confused. "I am Mary Gunn," she said, holding his gaze steadily. "A midwife."

"Royce," he said inclining his head slightly, before the Silver Wolf shouted for him. "Before the village is a rise where the Dragon launches his fire," he said quickly to her. "Tell him you are with us, and he will defend you."

Mary nodded once and gathered the reins, eying the distance to the gates.

Royce could aid in clearing the way for Nuit—and the horse would be sure-footed. "All clear for the lady!" he roared, then lifted his axe, cutting three men down in rapid succession. Mary let out a cry and gave the horse her heels, the destrier lunging forward with such purpose that Royce did not manage to smack the horse's rump before he had passed. Ponies and other horses milled in the bailey, and Royce smacked every rump he could reach, sending them charging through the gate after Nuit.

He saw that beast vanish through the remains of the gates but did not dare to watch Mary's flight. There were too many opponents close at hand. Would he see Mary again? Who could say? He might not see the dawn. Royce knew better than to have expectations of women. He might have been useful, but a pretty midwife had no interest in a man of his ilk.

Aye, there was labor to be done. He roared and continued to dispatch those who defied him with sure strokes.

NYSSA CRIED out in fear when the missile struck the roof above her and the wood began to burn with fearsome speed. She was soon on the floor, smoke filling the chamber above her as the roof of the solar burned. She watched the fire leap to the great bed and begin to consume it, as well. She could not see the night sky overhead for the great dark plumes of smoke, and she feared she would breathe her last in this chamber.

Just as Elsa had done.

Just as her mother had done.

She pushed to her feet, prepared to jump from one of the windows to avoid that fate, when she heard the key in the lock. She backed away from that door, even as it swung open. A man was silhouetted there and she knew an increment of hope before Erik strode into the solar.

"Why?" he demanded as he marched toward her. "Why are they so determined to save you? What treasure is hidden on your person? What secret do you know?"

"Who?"

"I would ask you the same! A force beyond measure descends upon

Duncheann, determined to slaughter all within its walls and raze it to the ground." He caught her arm and hauled her to her feet. "Why?"

"I do not know."

"Liar! You are all liars, you witches. You are all faithless women who care only for your spells and charms."

"I am no witch," Nyssa insisted.

"Yet a flock of ravens led the assault," he said with disdain. "What unholy force have you brought upon us?" He dragged her toward the open door. "And what will they do to ensure your survival? I will know the truth of it and soon."

"You would release me?" Nyssa asked, unable to believe that might be true.

Erik chuckled. "I will show you to them, and perhaps they will retreat. If not, I will sacrifice you, and then there can be no cause for their continued assault." He leaned closer, his eyes glinting. "Tell me, seer, what future do you forecast?"

"Flames," she whispered. "I see only flames."

He nodded. "I would have expected you to see water," he said, pulling her toward the portal. "For your champion must have drowned by now. The tide has risen sufficiently to fill the dungeon so you need not fear his timely return."

Murdoch *had* come!

"And what of Rana?" she asked, for she could not think of Murdoch in the dungeon.

Erik spat at the floor. "Another witch dead, which can only be for the good of all. Your line ends this day, Nyssa, and the moment cannot arrive soon enough. I was as much a fool as my brother to think that aught good could come of an alliance with witches."

Another missile struck above them, crashing through the damaged roof. A river of flame flowed down the wall, igniting all in its path, and Nyssa watched it in horror. She had never seen fire flow like water before, never seen it burn so avidly and so hot. The floor caught fire in that corner and she feared they would be plummeted to their death.

"Witchery," Erik hissed. "You are allied with demons."

In that moment, the door to the small staircase, the one that led to the kitchens, was kicked open. Nyssa gasped aloud at the sight of

Murdoch and her heart thundered with relief that he yet lived. He had only a dagger, but his expression was grim and he moved with purpose. His beard was gone, he had abandoned his plaid, but she would have known him anywhere.

"Demons," Erik repeated, drawing his sword. "Who defy death beyond expectation."

"'Tis the merit of the cause," Murdoch said, his manner grim. "The lady's very life is in peril, and I am sworn to the defense of those in need of such service."

Nyssa thrilled to hear that he had taken the cause she had suggested to him.

"Fool!" Erik cried. "You should have ensured your own survival first."

Murdoch shook his head. "Impossible, when this lady is at risk." His gaze flicked to her, his eyes so dark and filled with intent that Nyssa could not take a breath.

Erik flung Nyssa away from him, his gesture so emphatic that she stumbled.

"Run," Murdoch said to her, speaking with quiet heat as the pair circled each other.

But Nyssa would not flee before she was certain that Erik drew breath no longer. She eased away from the pair of combatants, hoping the smoke would disguise her deeds, and discovered a small bucket of water, brought for washing. It was not clean and likely had been forgotten in the events of the day. There was not much water within it, but it might be sufficient for her needs.

Meanwhile, Erik lunged toward Murdoch, striking for his chest. Murdoch evaded the blow, stepping aside, then struck at Erik, the dagger blade nicking Erik's shoulder. That man swore and they circled anew. They stepped closer, blades clashing. Nyssa cast the contents of the bucket at the burning floor while Erik's attention was diverted.

The flames hissed as they were extinguished, leaving charred remnants of the wooden floor. Nyssa seized one and wrenched it free of the structure.

Something had been hidden beneath it. She spied the small box and recognized it immediately. She snatched up her mother's treasure and jammed it into her girdle, then turned the length of wood. The charred end was in her hand, still damp from the spilled water.

The other end was dry. Nyssa stuck it into the flames and it burned with vigor. She spun, watching Murdoch deflect a blow from Erik, then lunged forward when Erik's back was turned to her. She shoved the burning length of wood against him, fairly pushing it beneath his tabard and he screamed as his garments caught fire. He spun to face her, cursing vehemently, and she saw Murdoch step toward his foe. She did not avert her gaze as Erik leapt toward her, not wanting to alert him to his peril.

She closed her eyes with relief when Murdoch seized Erik's head and slit his throat from behind. He cast the villain aside so that his corpse fell into the flames, and Nyssa rushed forward to ensure that his own garments did not burn.

"Are you hale?" he demanded, one hand rising to her chin. Nyssa nodded, then her mother's box fell from her girdle. Murdoch scooped it up without hesitation and jammed it into his purse. "We must flee!" he said as one end of the roof came crashing down and flames consumed the solar. They raced down the stairs, hand in hand, feeling the heat of the inferno behind them and the roar of the flames.

She caught her breath when they reached the bailey, for so many dead were scattered across it. Maximilian was alone there, seated astride his black destrier. The horse stamped, its nostrils flaring at the proximity of the flames, but Maximilian clearly awaited Murdoch.

His relief was nigh tangible when the pair burst into the bailey. Murdoch caught Nyssa around the waist and lifted her to sit behind Maximilian.

"Make haste," Maximilian said. "The others have retreated. The tide will make the road impassable within moments."

"The woman?" Murdoch asked. "Mary Gunn?"

"Ashore," Maximilian said. "With her young sister."

Murdoch's relief was palpable.

"What of Rana?" Nyssa and Murdoch asked in unison.

Maximilian shook his head and shrugged. "Your sister? I know not," he said, his gaze flicking to the fire that would soon consume the keep.

Murdoch looked suddenly stricken, then spun to study the tower.

"God in heaven," he whispered softly. "I bade her remain there." His horror was clear—and so was his purpose.

He pulled the box from his purse and shoved it into Nyssa's grasp, then slapped the destrier hard. "Ride!" he cried and Maximilian let the destrier charge forth.

"Nay!" Nyssa cried. "Murdoch!"

But Murdoch vanished into the burning keep without acknowledging her. Nyssa would have relinquished her grip on Maximilian but he seized her wrist.

"Do not even think of pursuing him," he said sternly. "He risked all to aid you."

"But he will be killed!" Nyssa twisted to look, though there was naught to see but flames.

"I think not," the Laird of Kilderrick said with soft assurance. "Murdoch Campbell has a remarkable ability to survive." He shook his head as the horse cleared the gates and plunged into the water that flowed over the road. 'Twas nigh as high as the beast's belly, prompting Nyssa to wonder if this horse could swim. "If you follow, you may turn matters against him."

"How?"

"You will add to his duties, for he will feel obliged to ensure your welfare, too. You might even distract him from his task. Do not risk as much, Nyssa. Let him be confident of your safety, so that he can find the girl. 'Tis the best of an array of poor options."

Nyssa feared that Maximilian's confidence was misplaced, though, and stared back at the keep even as they rode to the shore, hating that she could do naught to aid Murdoch.

THE SMOKE WAS POURING down the stairs, blinding Murdoch to what was before him. He heard the stones creak and crack around him and guessed that the fire had found its way between them to the wooden framework behind the stones. He strove first to enter the smaller stairway from the kitchen, knowing the solar had to be consumed in flames, but the kitchens were a conflagration. There would be no passage that way.

He raced up the stairs to the solar again, and found the sky only above him, masked at intervals by the billowing smoke. The door of the solar had burned away. The floor of that chamber had burned through in places and he could see the chamber below, where the women had been captive. Around the perimeter of the room, sections of floor remained, even as they burned.

He had no rope to bind about himself and secure to any stronghold. The sole course was across the burning floor.

"Rana!" he called, but his voice was snatched away by the roar of the fire. He dared not abandon the girl. She might have fled and saved herself, but given the state of the kitchens, Murdoch doubted as much. She was likely crouched as close as possible to where he had left her.

He started across the floor, choosing each step with as much care as he dared, moving quickly. A beam collapsed beneath his weight and he jumped to another in the nick of time, pressing onward when he might have lingered to catch his breath. The smoke stung at his eyes and surrounded him, obstructing his vision and making his choices half-chance. He reached the opposite side of the solar, heart racing, and flung open the door to the staircase.

Rana looked up at him, her eyes wide with fear.

She had remained, exactly as he had bidden her.

He caught her up with one arm and she huddled against him, trembling in her relief. But Murdoch was not relieved as yet. They had to cross the solar again. Even in those short moments, more of the floor had fallen through and orange flames leapt high. The floor of the chamber below was burning now, the hot flames licking the inside of the stone walls. The creaking grew louder and Murdoch feared that the entire structure would collapse. He could not even see the sea in the darkness and the smoke, but it was perhaps better to be unaware of every obstacle before them.

He would take them in succession.

He stepped onto the solar floor and on his second step, another section of floor broke and crashed into the space below. The flames leapt bright and hot around them and he shielded his face for a moment. One of the feathers in Rana's hair caught fire, the smell of the burning feather sharp and unpleasant, but he crushed the flames in his hand. He considered the burning floor and hesitated to take a step, uncertain where he might find security.

"We are lost," he whispered without meaning to do as much. His greatest disappointment was that he had failed Nyssa in this quest.

To his surprise, Rana lifted a stone to her eye, one like the witching stone that Nyssa used but of a different shape and color. She surveyed the solar through the hole as if considering a pleasant view, then glanced up at him with confidence. She pointed to a board that Murdoch would never have placed his weight upon and nodded with surety.

He trusted her and took the step.

The board broke immediately beneath his boot. He clutched Rana as they plummeted through the floor, struck the floor below with force, then crashed through it to land hard on the stone floor of the great hall. The wood above them cracked ominously and Murdoch ignored his pain, gathering Rana close and lunging into the bailey. As he stood, striving to catch his breath, the entire structure fell in upon itself, each floor crashing into the one below. All that remained was a pile of burning timber on the floor of the great hall, the flames rising all the way to the stone summit of the tower. His face burned from the heat of that inferno and he saw the flying sparks against the night sky.

There was no question of waiting for the tide to recede. Murdoch turned and ran for the gates, considered the dark mirror of the sea between himself and shore, then plunged onward, hoping for the best.

To ROYCE'S RELIEF, Mary and her younger sister were near the fire set on the headland, secure in the company of Rafael. 'Twas enough, he told himself, that they were safe.

He nodded in Mary's direction but she came toward him with purpose, smiling. Women did not look at Royce with favor, much less with encouragement. They invariably regarded him with fear or wariness, perhaps with an increment of respect mingled with caution. But Mary's expression was one of welcome and wonder.

She regarded him as women routinely regarded the Silver Wolf.

Royce glanced behind himself but Maximilian was not there. Nay, Royce stood alone on the shore, with this woman. His heart skipped a beat, but he said naught.

"I thank you," Mary said. "Your horse is a fine one."

"Aye, he is."

"They said his name is Nuit."

"Aye. French for night."

She placed her hand on his arm and Royce stared at it, amazed that she would make such a move. She was neither slender nor robust, but a woman of pleasant proportions—all the same, she was considerably shorter and less powerful than him. "We would have perished without your aid. I thank you, Royce, with all my heart."

Then, marvel of marvels, Mary stretched up and touched her lips to his cheek in a chaste kiss. Royce was so stunned that he could not utter a sound in reply. He simply stared at her as warmth spread through him from the point where her lips had pressed briefly against his skin.

And his innards quivered with the certainty that he had met a woman of remarkable merit.

Mary's eyes began to sparkle as she watched him and she smiled. The change gave her a mischievous air. "Trust me to find a man of few words," she said. "But it has been said that I can chatter enough for two."

Royce strove to recover his wits. He pushed a hand through his hair, then bowed before her, wishing he might have been more finely garbed —or at least not had the blood of several dozen men on his hide. "'Twas my honor to be of service," he said, discovering that he had an inclination to speak formally when overwhelmed. "You may call upon me at any time."

She laughed. "Yet even with that promise, I would not wish to find myself in similar circumstance again."

"I can understand as much."

Mary tilted her head to regard him. "I have been invited to come to Kilderrick village, for they lack a midwife and I lack an abode."

Royce nodded at the good sense in that, and guessed that it had been Maximilian's solution. "'Tis a fine holding and an increasingly prosperous one," he managed to say, wanting to encourage her choice. "With a laird who is fair."

"Good," Mary said with such vigor that he blinked. Her hand slid up his arm. "You can have no notion, Royce, how long I have hoped for a man of both sense and skill to cross my path."

"Aye, I wager I do," he replied in a low growl. "For I suspect I have waited just as long for a fearless woman."

Their gazes locked and held, hers sufficiently dark to hold a thousand mysteries along with their ability to sparkle so merrily. A midwife would see much of life and death, just as Royce had, and yet she was neither saddened nor burdened by it. She was practical. She could ride a horse and wield a knife. Aye, he would answer her summons any time.

"I was the one who saved Elsa's daughter, Rana," Mary informed him. Her voice softened. "Never have I seen such villainy as a man who would kill his own children when the blood of delivery was still upon them." She shuddered, but her gaze was resolute when she looked up at Royce. "I had to foil his plan. I had to aid my lady. I hated to leave her when I saw that she would die of the delivery, but she bade me go. And then, and then, his brother Erik found me." Her eyes flashed. "He killed my family, who had given us refuge. He cut them down before my very eyes and I knew then that I would not rest until I saw him dead." She held his gaze. "You and your fellows did what I could not, Royce. You avenged me, my kin and my lady. If ever you desire aught from me, it is yours."

Royce was humbled by both her confession and her honesty. He frowned and cleared his throat. "I did not..."

"Aye, you did," she said, placing her hand on his chest and he fell silent. Indeed, he thought his heart might stop. "You rode north for no reward of your own. Your company saw that wretched place and the men who governed it destroyed forever, and I thank you."

Unable to hold her gaze for long, given the response she stirred within him, Royce eyed the girl who looked like a younger version of Mary.

"My sister," she supplied, guessing his question. "She was the sole survivor of my family."

"Your sister," he echoed, unable to think beyond the fact that Mary Gunn evidently had no man.

"I told you that I have sought a man to suit me," she chided, her gaze as bright as that of an inquisitive sparrow. "And what of you?"

"I have no desire for a man," he said, pleased beyond measure when she laughed.

"Will I find you in the vicinity of Kilderrick, Royce?"

"Aye. I am sworn to the service of the laird there, a man I served when he was the Loup Argent and one to whom I remain pledged. He is now Laird of Kilderrick." He gestured to Maximilian who strode toward them now, his dark cloak flaring behind him, and feared belatedly that Mary would be captivated by the other man.

"Then I will be happy at Kilderrick," she said firmly, her hand landing upon his arm again. "I could not bear the prospect of never seeing you again, Royce, now that we have found each other."

'Twas there in her dark eyes, a welcome beyond all expectation, a conviction that made Royce's heart thunder with possibilities.

And Royce grinned back, for he could find no fault with that.

NYSSA STOOD ON THE HEADLAND, watching the smoke rise from Duncheann in a dark column. The flames licked against the night, blazing brilliantly, as she desperately sought one glimpse of one precious man and an equally precious child.

There was none.

The tide rose with relentless speed, ensuring that all upon the island would be compelled to remain there until the keep was no more than smoking ash. She thought she heard a splash but could not be certain and feared that she had imagined as much.

Once his missiles had all been loosed, Rafael had searched the abandoned town and had found a cask of ale that had been left behind. He had lit a fire as a beacon for those returning from Duncheann and they were gathered around it, sharing tales of their adventure and savoring the ale. The wind was rising, though Nyssa knew it could not extinguish those flames. The sky was clear overhead, the stars shining brightly.

Nyssa was blind to all of it. She could not bear that Murdoch had been lost in keeping his pledge to her. She would not think of a world without his grim resolve to hold fast to his principles. She would not weep either, not until she was convinced of his demise.

Someone came to stand beside her, offering a cup. She took it blindly, disinterested in its contents.

"There," Maximilian said softly, then pointed. There was no more than a glint of silver against the dark surface of the water, no more than a ripple of movement, but Nyssa caught her breath when she heard a man's voice rise in song.

Murdoch.

He sang that lullaby.

And a small childish voice sang along with him.

Nyssa caught her breath as tears blurred her vision. All the same, she discerned the pair emerging from the sea, Murdoch soaked to his shoulders and Rana no drier than he. Their expressions were jubilant, though that could not compare with the joy in Nyssa's heart. She raced toward them, flung herself upon them and kissed Murdoch with all her heart and soul.

To her dismay, he retreated a step, then put Rana into her arms. "You have a calling, Nyssa," he said, his gaze dark and his manner solemn. "While I have a quest."

Nay! He could not deny her now!

But he did. His conviction was unshakable. He nodded to Maximilian and strode toward the fire, welcoming the cloak that Royce offered to him and stepping close to the blaze with evident relief. He did not look back and Nyssa understood.

He had kept his pledge to her.

He would not take her gift.

And thus, their adventures together must come to an end. Hers had been another quest for him, a task to complete, an obligation he would see satisfied.

No more than that.

"A plague upon men of principle," Nyssa said with heat and Maximilian snorted with surprise. She turned to find him watching her, consideration in his gaze. "I should ensure that all who are wounded have been tended," she said, her tone more formal.

Maximilian inclined his head. "Your assistance would be most appreciated." When she turned away, his voice dropped low. "Do not despair as yet, Nyssa. You are a woman of remarkable resources after all."

What did he mean? She turned but the Silver Wolf was returning to the company of his men. And she had only one resource, the gift of dreams. Thanks to Murdoch's refusal of her, her gift of foresight would have to suffice forever.

CHAPTER 16

*A*fter all this, you do not linger with Nyssa," the Silver Wolf said, taking a place beside Murdoch who had been sitting alone. He had decreed that they would rest until the next morning, then return to Kilderrick at a more leisurely pace. There was not much to eat, but Murdoch expected the party to hunt upon their return to remedy the lack. He had heard of some emissary from the Lord of Badenoch who had ridden with the Silver Wolf, but that man had been dispatched to his liege lord with tidings of the conquest.

Nyssa was tending the injuries and Murdoch had kept his distance from her by choice. He still had naught to offer her, though he yearned to pledge himself to her forever. Rana followed Nyssa and he watched the pair of them, noting how Nyssa explained matters to her sister's daughter with patience. Now that she had an apprentice, he knew that any sacrifice of her gifts would be unjust. He loved her, and wished to be with her, but he wanted her to find joy as well. His love meant that he would defend her ability to pursue her own path and preserve her legacy.

"She has labor on this night," he replied. "I would only be a hindrance to her task."

"Is that what she says?"

"I did not ask her."

"Aye, I know." The Silver Wolf handed him a cup. "'Tis ale of a sort, not very good but better than none at all."

Murdoch smiled at the dubious recommendation and accepted it. He turned the cup in his hand, the ale untasted, knowing he had an apology to make. "I thank you for coming to my aid," he said and the Silver Wolf nodded once. "I know you rode north for Nyssa..."

"We rode north for both of you. Did you not hear our call?"

So, he had not imagined that, and it had not been the gatekeeper. Murdoch faltered before continuing, though he could not doubt his companion's conviction. "But I could never have ensured her safety without your aid. I thank you."

The Silver Wolf smiled. "And you are most welcome. You did not lack for valor in entering that keep alone. I salute that." They bowed slightly to each other and both made to sip of the ale.

Murdoch halted his gesture, knowing he had to say more. "You cannot have ridden north for me."

"Do you call me a liar?"

"Nay. But you are a man of good sense. Such assistance would be unexpected if not undeserved, given my quest for retribution. You knew well of my intention."

"I also know myself innocent of your charge against me." The Silver Wolf smiled. "I see that you have not lost your conviction of my guilt. Might we consider a truce on this night?"

"Aye," Murdoch said with relief. "More than this night, until we are returned to Kilderrick."

"And whither thence for you?"

Murdoch glanced toward Nyssa, knowing the sole choice he could make. "The Continent," he said with a conviction he did not feel. "I will swear myself to another and make my way thus."

The Silver Wolf nodded. "If your thinking changes, I would yet treat with you." He waited a moment, but Murdoch did not reply. He lifted his cup instead and they sipped of the ale of one accord.

They also grimaced in unison.

"You may be wrong about the ale," Murdoch felt compelled to note.

His companion laughed. "I am told it improves." They exchanged skeptical glances. The Silver Wolf offered his hand and Murdoch shook it.

"Until Kilderrick," he said and the Silver Wolf nodded.

Murdoch watched the other warrior walk away, yearning for what he dared not accept. He knew his strengths and his weaknesses and the merit of his vow. Still, he was discontent when he cast himself down near the fire.

All the same, Murdoch slept immediately, so great was his exhaustion.

∾

NYSSA DREAMED.

A plume of dark smoke rose in the distance, and she realized with a start that the view was from Kilderrick's tower. The sun was setting, the sky darkening. There were no stars visible overhead, though, for clouds churned overhead, the wind wild. Two men stood together at the window, the older one standing slightly behind the other in deference. They wordlessly watched the smoke rise and billow dark to the south.

Then there came the sound of distant hoofbeats and the men exchanged fearful glances. The older one fled the chamber, which had to be the laird's solar—though it was different from the one Nyssa knew. The furnishings were heavy and dark, the bed hung with dark draperies and the stones stained with soot, as if many more fires had been burned in that chamber than the one she would have recognized. A brazier was lit, the flames leaping with dangerous vigor. Nyssa thought she saw something flit through the smoke rising from the brazier, though that made no sense.

The view from the window, though, could only have been from Kilderrick, for 'twas as familiar as her own name. She could not explain the difference.

Not until her view followed the older man down broad stone stairs. "Where is Alys?" he demanded of a young boy with reddish hair. Nyssa caught her breath, seeing Murdoch in the gangly youth with his steady gaze.

"With Morag, I think. They meant to gather herbs this day."

"Good," the older man said. The man, Nyssa knew, had to be Rupert. He placed a hand on the boy's shoulder, urging him down the stairs. "You must go with haste. You must give warning."

"Warning of what?"

Rupert hesitated for a heartbeat and Nyssa knew he would tell a falsehood, just as she saw Murdoch's eyes narrow with the same understanding. "Rowan Fell is at risk of attack. Mercenaries ride toward us hard, and they will burn the village. You must warn them."

Murdoch did not move. "Surely they will attack the keep."

"But all know there are no women within these walls. Take a horse, take the best horse, and make haste to the village. Tell Connor."

"I should remain here," Murdoch said with resolve. "I should aid in the defense of the keep."

Rupert seized his shoulders, his gaze boring into that of the younger man. "You must go. Think of Nerida and Ranald. They must be warned!"

"Then you should go, and I will remain to aid the laird." Murdoch's jaw set. "I have trained. I can aid in the defense."

"Nay!" Rupert said. "We have no time to argue! You must go immediately."

"I will not leave you or the laird." In happier circumstance, Nyssa might have smiled at the familiarity of Murdoch's manner. "Father, you make no sense."

Rupert drew himself taller. "I am not your father," he said so firmly that his claim could only be the truth.

Murdoch's surprise was evident. "But you always said..."

"Aye, I lied to you."

Murdoch's eyes flashed.

"Time and again," Rupert said. "I was selfish. I wanted to have a son, though I never did. There was no one to tell you otherwise, so I lied."

"But I would remain with you..."

"Nay, you will be killed with ease. You are young and green, no match for men of this ilk. You can do no good here." Rupert's surety made Murdoch frown. "Go! Go to Nerida and Ranald. They are your kin, not me. Defend your own blood."

Murdoch hesitated, then the sound of the approaching company became more clear. "You should have told me sooner," he said with quiet heat.

"Perhaps." Rupert waved a hand. "Begone, for you are no son of mine."

"And you are no father of mine," Murdoch said bitterly. He pivoted and leapt down the stairs without a backward glance. Rupert stared after him though, and Nyssa saw that he blinked back tears. There was both love and pain in his expression, along with a resolve.

He had been willing to say whatever was necessary to send Murdoch from harm's path.

She saw then where Murdoch had learned such a lesson.

Now, Rupert took up a sword and even Nyssa could see that the weapon was unfamiliar to him. He returned to the door to the solar, which was now closed and likely barred from the inside. A man shouted within the solar, calling to some imp and seemingly raving. Long moments passed and she hoped that Murdoch was gone to Rowan Fell.

The thunder of hoofbeats sounded in the bailey, then a man swore with such gusto that Rupert gasped. Nyssa heard departing hoofbeats again, followed by a man's solid tread on the stairs. Rupert caught his breath and backed against the door, his terror clear in the way the sword shook in his hands.

A warrior came into view, a fighter with fair hair and a grim expression, one who was all the more terrifying for his youth.

Maximilian de Vries.

His smile was mocking as he surveyed the older man, who shook so that his teeth might chatter. The Silver Wolf laughed and swung his blade with a flourish. "So, you think to stop me, old man," he taunted. "I invite your worst." He bounded up the last of the stairs and Rupert gave a little cry. He jabbed with his sword in a most feeble manner, dropped the blade, then fell back gasping against the secured portal. He paled, his mouth worked soundlessly, then he collapsed on the floor. The Silver Wolf stepped forward with caution, clearly thinking this was a feint, and his shadow fell over Rupert as that man exhaled shakily and stilled.

He was dead, untouched.

The Silver Wolf looked over his shoulder, surveyed his surroundings, then kicked open the door to the solar. A silvery thread of smoke wound out of the solar, and swirled around the Silver Wolf. He watched it warily, then shook his head, his expression turning grim. He stepped over Rupert's corpse as the chanting from within grew louder.

The laird cackled. "Come Redcap, make a feast of this one!"

"Surrender, old man. Grant to me the treasury of Kilderrick!"

The laird shrieked and ranted, his words falling so quickly that they were *indistinguishable. The Silver Wolf shook his head and entered the solar, kicking the door shut behind himself. Nyssa saw that curious flicker of smoke spiral over Rupert then slide through the crack just before the door was secured.*

And she shivered, disliking that wisp of smoke with intuitive fervor.

NYSSA'S EYES flew open and she caught her breath with the import of what she had witnessed. Maximilian had not killed Rupert. The older man had died before he was touched, just as Maximilian had insisted.

Which meant that Murdoch had no need to demand a due of the Laird of Kilderrick.

Nyssa's relief was less than it might have been, for she had no notion of how to share this revelation with Murdoch. If she told him, he might not believe her any more than he had believed the Silver Wolf. She lay awake, her thoughts spinning, until she recalled the skill her mother had not had the opportunity to teach.

Gerda had been able to share dreams.

Could Nyssa dispatch this vision to Murdoch?

She did not know, but she would try.

MURDOCH AWAKENED ABRUPTLY in the quiet camp, a vision of Kilderrick vivid in his thoughts. The fire had burned down to embers and most of the party slumbered around him. He could hear the horses nickering to themselves, and saw that the flames at Duncheann were dying as well.

He marveled at what he had witnessed in that dream. Strangely, he knew without doubt that 'twas true. No one else knew of the final words he had exchanged with Rupert. No one else knew they had parted in anger. No one else would have felt such anguish in one final glimpse of his foster father.

And yet more, the Silver Wolf had not killed Rupert.

The Silver Wolf had not lied.

Murdoch's vendetta against that man was undeserved and he could only close his eyes with relief that he had not succeeded in harming the infant Michael in his fury.

Nyssa had saved him from that error.

And Nyssa, Murdoch was certain, had sent him this dream. She had freed him from his hatred and his quest for vengeance, and she had perhaps unwittingly resolved the question of his future.

For if the Silver Wolf had not killed Rupert or lied to Murdoch, then the Laird of Kilderrick was a man to be trusted. And that meant that Murdoch could accept Maximilian's offer of alliance. He could pledge himself to the service of his half-brother without a qualm, which meant he could earn his way *without* joining a company of mercenaries abroad.

He could remain in Scotland. He could take a wife and have both home and family.

He could have the future Nyssa urged him to pursue. And he could do it with the woman who had healed him and claimed his heart.

The dawn had not even arrived, but that future could begin this very day, if Murdoch dared to seize the opportunity. He could hear Nyssa's influence in his thoughts, but to be sure, a fresh start would be welcome. He had been wrong about the Silver Wolf's deeds and glad of that man's assistance in this quest. He had long believed he had no kin remaining, but he had three half-brothers, none of whom were like their father.

'Twas time to leave the past behind.

Murdoch rose with purpose, seeking the Silver Wolf with all haste.

MAXIMILIAN WATCHED the smoke rising from Duncheann diminish to a slender wisp. He had sipped his wretched ale, unable to sleep, and watched the flames extinguish themselves after they devoured all that could burn in that keep. He had noticed the brightness of the stars and the darkness of the night, and knew the eastern sky would lighten soon. He had spent over a week journeying to this distant land with his company, and could not fail to be reminded of what his past life had been as leader of the Compagnie Rouge.

Though they had succeeded and done what was right, Maximilian yearned for the hall he now knew as home. He longed for the comfort of his solar, the plump mattress there and the warmth of the braziers, the solace of good hot meals at regular intervals, and security beyond the walls.

Mostly he wished for Alys, though, her sweet curves against his side, her quick wits and her ability to challenge his convictions. She made him smile. She made him proud. She filled his days and nights to bursting with a joy he had never known he lacked.

Maximilian wanted to go home.

He was surprised when a man came to sit beside him, for he had believed all others to be asleep. Murdoch was both agitated and resolved, his manner changed from the night before, which was intriguing.

He nodded a greeting, then waited, content to let Murdoch have his say.

"I owe an apology to you," Murdoch said without preamble. "I have realized that you spoke the truth and that you did not strike down Rupert, which means I was mistaken in my desire to avenge his death."

Maximilian could not hide his astonishment. "How could you have realized this? I know I did not persuade you."

"Nyssa dreamed of that night."

"Indeed?"

"And she sent the dream to me."

The claim was whimsical, yet Murdoch clearly believed in its truth. "I had no notion she had such an ability."

"Nor did I. I believe 'twas a new feat for her."

"And 'twas done for you. That is not a favor to overlook."

"Nay, 'tis not."

Maximilian watched Murdoch swallow, then flick a glance to the place where Nyssa had retreated to sleep. Aye, they would make a good pair. "I am glad to set our dispute to rest."

"As am I." Murdoch shook his hand, then frowned. "What if we *were* allied as brothers?" he asked, his gaze rising to Maximilian's. His sincerity could not be doubted, much to Maximilian's pleasure. "You have offered such before and I have declined. What if I swore to you this day that I was your enemy no longer?" He turned his left palm up and touched the inside of his wrist with a fingertip, inviting Maximilian to remember.

As if he would ever forget. Maximilian bared the inside of his own left wrist, revealing the scar upon it. He readily recalled the night it had been made, when Rafael, Amaury and Maximilian had each willingly shed their own blood and mingled it, leaving a mark of their pact upon their own flesh.

"That I would accept, and gladly," he said, rising to his feet. He took his own dagger and sliced open his healed wound again, grazing the skin with his blade so that blood beaded along the cut like a line of rubies. "Our path forward is together, bound by blood and fury," he continued with quiet vigor, repeating the words he had uttered years before to Amaury and Rafael.

He had not included Murdoch that night, but he had not known of their shared blood then.

All was different now.

All was better now.

"I propose a union, between blood brothers newly found," Murdoch said, his voice filled with resolve.

Maximilian was aware that someone drew near to watch, but he did not look. He turned the dagger in his hand, offering the hilt to Murdoch. "Two together," he said and raised a brow.

Murdoch took the dagger and cut his left hand with the same confident gesture. "Sworn to each other," he said. "First of all men, pledged to..."

Here he faltered and justly so, for Kilderrick was reclaimed already.

"To the pursuit of justice at Kilderrick and in its environs," Maximilian supplied.

Rafael stepped forward with purpose. "I will make that pledge of three," he said, his smile flashing at Murdoch's evident surprise.

"I have heard you are a better ally than foe," he said, as one brother might tease another, and Rafael laughed.

"I have heard the same said of you, brother," he replied and they grinned at each other, much to Maximilian's satisfaction. Rafael sliced his wrist and Murdoch seized Rafael's hand, mingling their blood together.

"Three so sworn," Maximilian said, clasping Murdoch's wrist. He locked his hand over Rafael's who then gripped Maximilian's wrist.

"Three together," they said in unison.

"Bound in will and in act," the Silver Wolf said.

"Brothers," Murdoch agreed. "I vow I will not break this pledge before I die."

"Nor I, nor I," declared Maximilian and Rafael in unison.

There was a moment's silence.

"And I might wish for a celebratory cup of some beverage that is better than swill," Maximilian said, prompting the other two to chuckle.

"Yet that is not the sole lack. One of our number is without a post," Rafael noted. "Maximilian, we cannot allow our brother to starve for lack of coin."

"Nay, we cannot," Maximilian said, welcoming the opportunity to make his suggestion.

Murdoch raised his hands. "I have no expertise to govern a barony like Rafael, much less a holding like Amaury. I am a simple man…"

"Aye, an honest man who prefers to see justice defended by his own deeds," Maximilian said, content that his impulse had been right. "I have need of a sheriff in Rowan Fell, and I believe the post would suit you well."

Murdoch was visibly pleased. "But…"

"But naught. You have a passion for justice and there is honor in your word," Maximilian said. "I should be honored to have such a sheriff, Murdoch."

Murdoch's eyes glinted with satisfaction. "Then 'twill be so, Maximilian, Laird of Kilderrick," he said.

'Twas in that moment that Maximilian became aware of Nyssa, standing behind Murdoch. He watched that man realize her presence and fairly felt the heat rise between them. Murdoch nodded to her, then dropped to one knee and kissed Maximilian's ring. He swore himself to Maximilian's service and to the preservation of justice in Rowan Fell.

"Rise, Murdoch, and know that I will grant the seal of office to you upon our arrival at Kilderrick. I wager I shall have the most efficient of sheriffs in Rowan Fell."

"I guarantee as much," Murdoch said. The pair grinned at each other then, after the merest hesitation, they embraced like the brothers they were in truth. Rafael offered his congratulations, but 'twas clear that Murdoch cared only for Nyssa and the shine of triumph in her eyes. He offered his hand to her and she slid her hand into his, her features alight with expectation.

"I would speak with you," he said and her smile broadened.

"And I would show you something," she replied, then led him away from the company.

Maximilian watched them go, aware that Rafael still stood beside him. "Another wedding?" that man asked and Maximilian smiled.

"'Twould not be a disappointment to me, to be sure." He nodded to the other man, even as he yawned. "Will you take the watch until dawn? I would sleep a little this night."

THE SKY WAS FILLED with stars as Nyssa led Murdoch along a familiar path. They might have been alone in the world, so quiet was the night. There was only the rustle of the wind. Nyssa had not visited this place in years, but she would never forget the way.

She had never taken it with such joy in her heart as on this morn, and that was because of the man beside her.

They passed through a forest of pine trees, approaching a mound hidden within its shadows. It might once have been the site of a fortress, the earth mounded high. There was a circle of roughly cut stones at the summit, much like a crown. Nyssa did not hesitate. She led Murdoch to the top of the mound, through the moss-covered stones to a refuge with turf so thick that it might have been a carpet. The growth was verdant green despite the season and she closed her eyes at the sure sense of this place's power. Then she tipped her head back to survey the sky.

Murdoch reached up with his free hand. "I could gather a fistful of stars," he said with an awe she shared.

She turned to face him, taking his hands within hers. His eyes were vehemently blue, his smile held all the promises she wanted to fulfill. "I did not know if you would come."

"Naught could have kept me away." He glanced around them. "Is this Tom Fhithich?"

Nyssa nodded. "The women of my lineage slumber here, all around the circle of stones."

"Like gems on a diadem," he said in a low rumble. 'Twas a gift beyond all expectation that this man honored her, without hope of reward, without any fear of her gifts, without making any demands or promises that she could not make. Nyssa knew how rare that was, and it made her love him all the more.

"And we came here to be marked," she admitted. "If there is time, I would like to make Rana's first mark here before we ride south."

"I am sure it can be arranged. The Silver Wolf does not mean to make haste."

Murdoch's very presence calmed Nyssa, even as his touch thrilled her. 'Twas a beguiling combination, one that cast a potent spell. She smiled at the direction of her own thoughts. "I am beyond glad to be here with you."

"I am honored to be here with you."

Nyssa reached up and traced his lips with a fingertip. Her gaze roved over his features, and she ran that fingertip over his brow. "Your fury is gone," she said.

"My passion for justice remains."

"Aye, for you have a future, not only a past."

He smiled, his eyes glowing. "Thanks to you."

"We are meant to be one, Murdoch Campbell," she said with utter conviction. "I have always believed as much."

He caught his breath. "Even at such a price for you?"

"'Tis not a price. 'Tis a journey."

"I do not understand."

"Because the wisdom will be lost otherwise unless I teach another of my lineage what I know. I should have surrendered my gift to the greater good. I should have chosen a man and borne a daughter."

"I am glad you did not," he said so emphatically that she smiled.

"You are not the sole one who has neglected to think of the future, Murdoch." She smiled at him. "And so, the warrior has mended the healer."

"And so, we have healed each other," he replied. "I like that." He looked down at her hands, his brow furrowed. "You heard that the Silver Wolf—Maximilian—has granted me the post of sheriff of Rowan Fell."

"Aye. You will fulfill the responsibility well."

"It also means I can remain at Kilderrick and make a home there. I know you have no care for convention," he continued, his expression earnest. "Or even for marriage. But I love you, Nyssa."

"And I love you, Murdoch."

"I would wed you and honor you, but what of Rana?" He was so concerned for her legacy that Nyssa's heart warmed yet more. "How will you teach her if you surrender your gift?"

"The same as my mother taught Elsa and me. If my foresight vanishes, I will yet have other gifts. I am still a healer and always will be."

His relief was visible. "Then I entreat you to make a handfast with me."

Nyssa eased closer to him. "Nay. I would have more than a year and a day with you by my side."

Murdoch raised a hand to her cheek. "I would not have you feel trapped, Nyssa. This way, each year, you have the choice to leave me or remain." He smiled. "Be warned, though, that I will do all in my power to convince you to renew your vow each year and be mine forevermore."

"You have already succeeded in that," she confessed, then leaned against him. "I love you, Murdoch Campbell. I am not trapped while by your side."

"Then I am blessed beyond all expectation."

"I could argue that I am the one blessed to know such a love," she whispered, her eyes shining. "Let us handfast here this night, beneath the stars and in the presence of my ghosts."

"There is a request I cannot deny," he said, pulling her into his embrace.

"And then we will wed in the chapel at Rowan Fell once we are returned to Kilderrick." Nyssa was resolute.

"Both?" Murdoch said, his brows rising.

"Both," she repeated with conviction. "I would have all know that you are mine forevermore, Murdoch Campbell. None shall doubt the name of my daughter's father, a warrior of honor and esteem."

"And I can only do my best to ensure that you never regret your choice," he said in a low rumble, then captured her lips in a triumphant kiss.

MURDOCH STOOD with Nyssa beneath the stars as he took her right hand in his right hand. She could feel the presence of her sister, of her mother, of her mother's mother, and tears rose to her eyes with joy. Murdoch kissed her fingertips, then took her left hand in his left with a reverence that made her heart soar.

"I have no ring," he confessed, his eyes dark.

"Nor have I one for you," she admitted. "Surely such details can be addressed later."

He smiled crookedly at her. "Surely the truth in our hearts is of the greatest import."

Nyssa smiled, her heart leaping.

"I pledge unto you, Nyssa, to love and honor you for a year and a day, to do all in my power to bring you happiness, to defend you with all my might, to honor you with my touch and my words."

Nyssa could imagine naught better.

"I vow to protect any child from our union, to raise that child with kindness and to ensure his or her welfare for all the days and nights of my life. I vow to respect your gifts, to confer with you and to accept your counsel, to strive for agreement in all choices we might make for our life together. I am yours to command and to claim, and I enter this bond willingly, with every hope for a lifetime together."

Nyssa gripped his hands tightly, repeating the words with fervor. "I pledge unto you, Murdoch, to love and honor you for a year and a day, to do all in my power to bring you happiness, to defend you with all my might, to honor you with my touch and my words. I vow to protect any child from our union, to raise that child with kindness and to ensure his or her welfare for all the days and nights of my life. I vow to respect your gifts, to confer with you and to accept your counsel, to strive for agreement in all choices we might make for our life together. I am yours to command and to claim, and I enter this bond willingly, with every hope for a lifetime together." His grip tightened on her hands.

"I love you," he said with heat.

"And I love you as never I imagined I might love another."

"For this day, and for every day I draw breath, forevermore."

"Forevermore," Nyssa echoed and reached for him. He kissed her with such sweet possessiveness that Nyssa could only respond in kind. Her body was afire, her knees melting, her need for him enflamed beyond all. On this night, they would become one.

Murdoch cast his fur-lined cloak on the ground and Nyssa threw hers atop it. This time, they removed their garb in unison, each watching the other, their hands moving with haste. It was apt, in a way, that she wore Elsa's red kirtle, the garment made for her sister's wedding, on this night, for her own pledge to Murdoch. The difference was that Elsa had been compelled to wed Hugh against her will, while Nyssa pledged herself to the man who would always possess her heart. She knew that the difference could only please her sister as much as it pleased Nyssa herself.

The red slippers were kicked aside, the laces down the sides of the kirtle loosened. Murdoch removed his leather jerkin and his belt as she watched, setting his weapons aside with care. She was not surprised that he ensured they were yet within reach. His boots were next and then his chemise, and she caught her breath at the sight of his broad chest. He waited then, clad only in his brais, as she stepped out of the kirtle. This chemise was even more sheer than her own and she knew he had to be able to see both her body and the marks upon it through the cloth. Murdoch came to her side and reached for the ribbons in her hair, carefully loosening them so that her hair fell over her shoulders. He stole a kiss, his fingers sliding into her hair, and she touched his chin.

"Will you grow it back?" she asked, referring to his beard. He had only short stubble on his chin and cheeks.

"I leave the choice to you," he said with a wicked grin, then loosened the tie of her chemise. The gossamer garment fell to the ground when he eased his hands beneath the neckline, and the warmth of his palms closed over her shoulders. Nyssa let her fingertips trail down his chest to his waist, then she loosened his brais, feeling bold beyond all. He smiled when they both stood nude beneath the night sky, then offered his hand to her. When she placed her hand in his, he kissed her fingertips then escorted her to the cloaks that would be their bed this night. He knelt there and she knelt before him, parting her lips in anticipation when he caught her close and bent to kiss her sweetly. Nyssa ran her hands over his shoulders, loving the feel of him beneath her hands, then found herself being lowered to the ground, even as Murdoch's kiss fed the unruly fire within her.

Murdoch bent over her, his kiss making her passion rise with ease. His hand swept over her and he cupped one breast in his hand, teasing the nipple as he had done before and Nyssa surrendered to sensation. She gasped aloud when his kisses trailed along her cheek to her ear, then down her throat, his whiskers prickling a little and leaving her skin aroused. He replaced his fingers with his mouth, teasing her taut nipple with teeth and tongue as she writhed beneath the weight of his hand upon her waist. When both nipples had been coaxed to peaks, he moved lower again, his hand moving between her thighs and his caress so bold that Nyssa moaned aloud. He eased between her thighs then, his hands beneath her as he lifted her and his mouth closed over her with surety.

His tongue might have been wrought of sorcery, for Nyssa had never felt such desire as he conjured. With every caress, the fire within her veins burned ever hotter. There was only the cool night air on her skin, the stars in the firmament above, the soft fur of the cloak beneath her and Murdoch's wicked tongue, driving her mad with need. She writhed in his grip but he held fast to her hips, determined to inflict yet more pleasure. This time, though, he did not tease her as he had before. He urged her steadily toward the summit, making her heart pound and her breath catch, until she was certain she could endure no more. Then he touched her boldly, casting her into an abyss of pleasure so that she nigh shouted with satisfaction.

Then he was above her, his eyes glinting, his pride in his feat so clear that she could only smile at him. He stretched out alongside her, his hands sliding over her, his kiss tasting of her own delight and surprisingly thrilling for all of that. She rolled against him, kissing him with all the ardor she felt. He smiled at her, though she knew that his desire was as commanding as hers had been just moments before. Aye, his eyes were nigh as dark as midnight, his intensity such that his arousal could not be mistaken. She touched his strength with her fingertips, noting how he caught his breath.

"Nyssa," he whispered when she caressed him more boldly, a delicious strain in his voice, and she repeated the feat. He inhaled sharply, then caught her around the waist, lifting her above him. He lowered her slowly so that she knelt above him. "Never trapped," he murmured. "Never captive." Nyssa understood that she was to ride him, a most exciting prospect. With his guidance, she took him inside herself, her eyes widening at the sensation. She moved lower slowly, gradually taking more of him, noting how taut he became. When she was sitting on him, she exhaled, knowing she had never felt such a sense of unity before. Her hair flowed around them and the cool air made her nipples bead as much as his hot gaze.

She smiled.

Murdoch smiled.

Then he gripped her waist and lifted her up, slowly lowering her back atop him. He rolled his hips and Nyssa gasped at the press of him against that most sensitive part of herself. She smiled then, knowing that they could cast another spell of enchantment, one that would see them both beguiled. She moved with greater surety each stroke, varying her movements so that their mutual pleasure was prolonged. She moved slowly and then quickly. She rolled her hips and discovered what she liked best—she had a suspicion that Murdoch liked it all. She raised her hands to the sky and rocked back and forth atop him, hearing him once again whisper her name with urgency. He eased one finger between them, touching her more boldly and she felt the tumult rise within her again, this time with greater demand. She held his gaze as they moved together, the heat fairly rising from their skin, as they each bewitched the other in a timeless dance.

Once again, she was certain she could bear no more. Once again, he touched her boldly in that very moment. Once again, Nyssa felt as if the stars had filled her very veins and was cast adrift in a sea of pleasure from which she never wished to escape.

This time, though, Murdoch rolled her to her back and drove himself deep within her. She gripped his shoulders, loving the feel of his power atop her, savoring his roar of satisfaction when he found his release. They remained thus, locked in each other's arms and utterly in each other's thrall for long moments.

Then Murdoch lifted his head and smiled at her, his hand rising to cup her cheek. "My Nyssa," he said, his voice husky.

"My Murdoch," she replied, then kissed him with all the sweetness that filled her heart.

Dorcha cried then and circled in the sky overhead, landing beside them with a flourish and a curious glance. The bird, Nyssa saw, had something in its beak that glinted.

"I have no meat for you," Murdoch said, his tone teasing and the bird eyed him as if to challenge that. "Though we made good partners all the same," he continued and offered his hand. Dorcha jumped onto Murdoch's outstretched finger and bobbed his head with satisfaction.

He then dropped the signet ring before Nyssa, giving a caw of jubilation.

She picked it up with surprise. "My father's signet ring," she said, raising her gaze to Murdoch's. "'Twas on Erik's finger I saw it last."

"And that fiend has no use of it now." Murdoch took the ring and turned it in the light, examining it.

"I must give it to Maximilian," Nyssa began.

"Must you?" Murdoch gave her a look. "This is your other legacy, Nyssa."

"But you cannot wish to remain here at Duncheann."

He shook his head. "Nor, I imagine, can you."

"I cannot wait to leave this place behind me."

"But what of this place," Murdoch said, gesturing to their surroundings. "Tom Fhithich is precious to you and part of Duncheann."

She considered the ring, seeing his point.

"We will ask Maximilian," he said, kissing her brow. "He has a talent for ensuring that all gain their desires."

"Then we might visit here again?" Nyssa asked.

"I would make the journey with you whenever you desire to do as much."

'Twas a gift beyond expectation, and Nyssa knew herself to be fortunate beyond all. "I will begin Rana's tattoos today," she said, envisioning her future with Murdoch readily.

"You have an apprentice," he noted and she nodded.

"While you, sir, have a future."

Murdoch smiled with undisguised satisfaction, then he laughed aloud. "Because of you, my Nyssa," he said, kissing her soundly.

And Nyssa's heart filled with joy. She was glad, gladder than she had ever been of any situation in her life. Indeed, each event in her life might have been a step toward her destination, a life with Murdoch in Rowan Fell, her sister's daughter by her side, and a future beyond compare.

Aye, she was fortunate to be sure.

And so it was that three weeks later, Murdoch Campbell wed Nyssa LeCheyne in the chapel in Rowan Fell, surrounded by friends, family and neighbors. Nyssa's eyes were full of stars, her hair flowing over her shoulders like moonlight, her beauty and strength such that he would cherish her for every day and night of his life. If anything, Murdoch loved her more with every passing day and night.

Amaury and Elizabeth had lingered to witness their vows before returning to Beaupoint. Rafael and Ceara had also stayed to celebrate the day. Maximilian and Alys attended with Michael, and had arranged a feast at Kilderrick keep to celebrate both the new union and a new sheriff. Royce and Yves and Denis had come from the keep, and even the chicken Odette strutted in the common of Rowan Fell. Nerida and Dara stood near Murdoch, the older woman beaming with joy, while the rest of the villagers from Rowan Fell and Kilderrick village crowded into the chapel. There were new arrivals, too, in Mary, Catriona and Rana.

Beyond the living who gathered that sunny winter day, Murdoch was keenly aware of two ghosts beneath the rowan tree in the church-yard. He could almost see Gwendolyn's joyous smile and Rupert behind her, fairly glowing with pride.

Because of the woman who held his gaze so steadily, Murdoch had all he had ever desired and more. 'Twas a gift beyond all expectation, a dream fulfilled that he had not even dared to imagine. If this was a spell that filled his life with such purpose and joy, Murdoch had no desire that the enchantment ever be broken.

He had never been one to believe in sorcery, but Nyssa was welcome to beguile him for the rest of his days and nights, indeed, forevermore.

EPILOGUE

It was Samhain, by local tradition, and the anniversary of Royce's arrival at Kilderrick in the company of the notorious Silver Wolf. He walked to Rowan Fell from Kilderrick's keep, admiring the clear skies and the crisp wind from the west, amused at the magnitude of change in that comparatively short stretch of time. His pace was steady but unhurried, for he intended to remain the night in the village, if all proceeded well.

Two years before, Maximilian de Vries had led the remnants of the Compagnie Rouge to a ruined Scottish keep, claiming it as his birthright and home. Royce shook his head in recollection of that journey and the greeting they had received on that stormy night. He smiled at the memory of the mischief made by Alys Armstrong and her fellows in defiance of Maximilian's claim, and nigh chuckled that a mere two years should have changed her hatred to abiding love.

To be sure, it had taken only months for that shift to occur.

That couple's son, Michel, was as hale a child as ever had been and they were united in their adoration of him. Royce knew that Michel would have a sibling in the winter, though he was sworn to secrecy in that matter. He smiled and increased his pace slightly.

He was not a man to put much credit in the notion of destiny, but the fortunes of the four half-brothers, all sons of Jean le Beau, might have been fated to rise in this land of rough beauty.

Royce thought of Elizabeth, so shy and fearful in those early days, and now not only the wife of Amaury, but as regal and confident a lady as ever he had seen. That couple's daughter was a beauty already, and he could not be the sole one who anticipated a line of suitors to form at the gates of Beaupoint in future years.

Ceara, as fierce as any warrior of his acquaintance, had not been a maiden Royce expected to succumb to the appeal of love or marriage. Yet she was Baroness of Gisroy in these days, an equal partner to Rafael, and mother to what she insisted was their first son of many. Francis with his dark hair and blue eyes clearly took after his father, though Royce imagined that there would be at least one of their brood with Ceara's fiery hair. Francis already showed a resolve much like his mother, a clear hint that he was her son even though he did not favor her. Aye, Royce did not envy that pair the raising of a dozen such determined children but he wagered they would enjoy the challenge.

Finally, Nyssa, the gentle healer with her conviction in the goodness of the world, had found her match in the most unlikely of men. There had been a time when Royce would not have turned his back upon Murdoch Campbell in daylight, but Nyssa had proven his suspicions wrong. Perhaps because she had fearlessly confronted Murdoch, she had healed that man's wounds so that his devotion to her was complete. In the end, Murdoch was the perfect complement to Nyssa, and Royce was glad that she would have a warrior to defend her for all her days and nights.

There was, however, one circumstance from which Murdoch could not protect Nyssa. Royce hastened his steps at the notion.

Those four women had been nigh feral, to Royce's thinking, living in a hut wrought of vines and trees, an abode that was nigh part of the forest itself. He recalled Maximilian's outrage when Alys had bitten him, then chuckled at the first visit of Maximilian and Rafael to the sheriff's hut in Rowan Fell. There had been old trouble between the sheriff's wife Jeannie and the four maidens in the woods, but none of them had known as much then. Now Murdoch was sheriff, Eamon and Jeannie were no more, Rowan Fell and Kilderrick prospered, all of the 'witches' were wed and three had children of their own. Nyssa was so ripe that she would join their company soon.

He reached the perimeter of the village to find Catriona loitering outside Mary's abode, her manner more solemn than usual. She was a healthy and sensible child, as skeptical of whimsy as himself, and Royce liked her very much.

"Do not tell me you fear the ghosts who will be abroad this night?" he asked gruffly, his tone indicating his view of that.

"'Tis Nyssa's time," the girl said. "Mary has gone to her."

Royce hastened to the hut that Murdoch had been building with the help of the other men in Rowan Fell. One large chamber was complete and the rest of the roof had been thatched since Royce's last visit. He had no doubt that Murdoch had made haste to complete that, not just to be finished before the winter but because Nyssa's time drew near. 'Twould not be fitting for a babe to be exposed to the winter wind, and Murdoch was protective beyond most.

That man flung open the portal at Royce's knock and ushered him inside. Murdoch was pale with concern, his agitation clear.

"'Tis your first but not Mary's," Royce said by means of encouragement, but the other warrior simply shoved his hand through his hair. His heard had grown back, though 'twas not yet as long and thick as it had been previously.

Nyssa gave a cry then and Royce thought Murdoch would be ill.

"Sit down, man," he said, pushing Murdoch onto a bench. "You have done your part. Now, you must be silent and strong for the lady." He caught Mary's glance when she looked up and welcomed her little smile of greeting. The woman could express all with a glance or a touch, and Royce knew she was glad of his arrival.

Doubtless she had sufficient to attend without an anxious father to reassure. He poured Murdoch a cup of ale and bade the man drink it down, then went to Mary, setting a hand on her shoulder. "What do you need?" he asked quietly.

"Another cloth," she said immediately. She lifted her shoulder so his hand brushed against her cheek, her hands being busy. "And you here," she added in a whisper.

Royce bent and kissed the top of her head, noting how Nyssa struggled to catch her breath. 'Twould not be long now. "And so I am," he said, moving to get the cloth. He found her satchel on the table, the one she always had packed, and knew which kind of cloth she desired. He took it to her and another cup of thin ale, which he held to Nyssa's lips at Mary's instruction. "You will need to learn a lullaby soon," he teased and Nyssa flashed him a smile.

"Murdoch knows the best one," she managed to say before another contraction made her catch her breath.

Royce turned away, not having the fortitude to watch the arrival of children and rejoined Murdoch at the board. Catriona had entered the hut, likely at Rana's invitation, for the two girls sat together with Murdoch. 'Twas clear that Rana was concerned for Nyssa, and Royce could readily understand why. She had lost her mother in childbirth, and though she would not recall that night, she knew the tale well enough. She had only just found Nyssa, her sole remaining kin, and she would be feeling uncertain during Nyssa's ordeal. That was all natural enough, but as a seer, she might be more sensitive.

There was a new mark on her left forearm, a blue spiral not unlike the one on Nyssa's skin. "Aye, you have passed a test," he said, as much to distract her as aught else.

Her smile was fleeting. "Nyssa said I did well."

"And she would know the truth of it. Is that why you went north at midsummer?"

Rana nodded, her gaze flicking toward Nyssa.

Royce poured himself a cup of ale. "Might you explain a matter to me? Is there any import in a child being born on Samhain?"

Rana's brow puckered. "'Tis said that the date and time of birth influence the future of any child, as does that of conception. I might guess that a child of Samhain would be able to pierce the veil between the worlds more readily."

"Seeing the dead, then?" Royce lifted his cup and winked at the girl. "There is a suggestion to make me glad I was not born on Samhain."

"You do not even believe in ghosts," Catriona reminded him.

"When were you born?" Rana demanded.

"On the darkest night of winter."

"The Yule?" Rana asked, a smile curving her lips. "You were born on the Yule?"

"Aye, what of it?" Royce raised a meaty hand. "My mother said I was the light in the darkness."

The two girls laughed at this, surprised into it. "You are more likely the rock that blocks the sun," Murdoch teased gruffly. "For no one can move you before you choose to do as much."

The girls enjoyed this charge, as well.

"I provide shelter from the storm," Royce said, referring to his considerable size. "And shade from the sun."

There was a cry then before his companions could reply to his comment and the girls raced to Mary's side. She was cooing as she always did to a new arrival, and the sound—combined with a cry from the babe—made Royce smile in relief. Rana hugged Nyssa tightly and the new mother smiled at the girl.

Rana's relief was naught compared to that of Murdoch. He had taken Nyssa in his arms and kissed her with ardor as the girls circled around.

Royce kept his gaze fixed upon Mary. As practical as ever, she saw to necessary details with ease. She had aided hundreds of women in their time and he knew she would aid hundreds more. She was kind and competent and utterly reassuring. He smiled at her monologue.

"Look at you," she said to the infant, busily washing her skin as she squirmed. "As hale and hearty as ever a babe might be. And those eyes! So blue. So big! You will see through the shadows of this world to the next, I wager, and thence back again." The infant gave a little cry and Mary soothed her as she had soothed so many before. "A girl," she said to Royce, swaddling the child in clean linen.

"There could have been no doubt," he said, then was startled when she handed the babe to him.

"You will not shatter her, to be sure," she chided, winking at him as he accepted the tiny burden with care. "You had best get used to bairns, if you mean to linger with me," she added in a mischievous whisper.

"I *do* mean to linger," he said, holding her gaze. "I came this night to ask…"

She wiped her hands, tilting her head to study him. There was laughter in her eyes, this woman who saw the best and the worst but never lost her merry manner. Like Nyssa, she believed in goodness. Like Royce, she believed in defending and aiding it. "Aye?"

All the words that Royce had planned to say were lost when she smiled at him thus. "Wed me, Mary," he said simply.

"Or?" she invited.

"Or I will be a much less happy man."

She laughed at this blunt assessment. "And I, without you in my days and nights, would be a very unhappy woman," she said. "I will wed you, Royce, with pleasure."

"And ideally with haste."

She laughed again. "Aye. But you had best rock that child a little lest she begin to cry."

"One detail first," Royce said. He bent down first and stole a sweet kiss from Mary, one that sent heat to his toes and filled him with a conviction that all had come aright.

Then she stepped away, her satisfaction evident. He rocked the babe, as instructed, taking a seat at the board and sipping at his cup of ale, well content. Mary bustled around the hut, ensuring that Nyssa was settled and all was prepared for the night, the fire stoked, the soup warmed, the girls dispatched to stay this night at her own abode. Finally, Mary nestled the newly arrived girl into Nyssa's arms, while both parents stared down at her adoringly.

"She is like to be fair like you with that down on her head," Mary said. "'Tis like moonlight."

"And eyes of blue like Murdoch," Nyssa said with pleasure.

"They may yet change," Mary warned.

"They will not," the seer said with conviction. She bent to kiss the infant's forehead. "Welcome, Gwendolyn," she whispered. "Blessed be."

Murdoch caught Nyssa close and Royce found himself smiling at the trio before the fire. Mary gathered her belongings, including the stained cloth, and spared one last glance around the cottage. She had returned all to rights and ensured that their night would be an easy one. She might have spoken but Murdoch put a finger beneath Nyssa's chin and murmured something that made her smile. She replied in kind and they kissed with a fervor that prompted Royce to look away.

"Do not tell me that you will be shy as a married man," Mary whispered as he secured the door behind them. The girls ran ahead of them toward the cottage that had formerly been that of the sheriff and which Mary had made her own. The stars were emerging, shining with a brilliance overhead. He put his arm around Mary, pulling her warmth against his side.

"Do you not think that man and wife should simply sit together in silence?" he asked solemnly.

Mary laughed. "Nay, I do not. I think man and wife should have a merry time together, and do as much as often as possible." She gave him a poke, as fearless as ever. "You have shown sufficient reticence for three men."

"I was courting a lady."

"And now you have won her, heart and soul." She paused at the threshold of her own abode and met his gaze, her own bright with challenge. "What do you intend to do about that, sir?"

Royce felt his smile dawn slowly. "I would ensure that she has no regrets in her choice."

"There is a sound plan," Mary replied, easing closer. "Perhaps you ought to begin with haste, so she has no opportunity to reconsider."

"I most certainly will," he murmured, then caught her close, framing her face in his hands as he bent and kissed her as if he would never stop.

Indeed, he had no intention of ceasing to kiss Mary any time soon.

∽

AUTHOR'S NOTE

I found inspiration for one elements of Nyssa and Murdoch's story in fourteenth century Scottish history, in the tale of Reginald Le Cheyne and his daughters.

It begins with Duffus Castle, a holding that was granted to Freskin, a warrior who built the original motte-and-bailey keep in the twelfth century. By the thirteenth century, his descendants were calling themselves de Moravia ("of Moray"). The holding was subsequently held by Reginald le Chen (or le Cheyne, le Chain or Cheniot), Baron of Inverugie, as a result of his marriage to Mary de Moravia (a descendant of Freskin) in 1270. Reginald built the keep on the holding, a stone tower, indicated by a grant in 1305 to harvest timber (for roofs and floors) for the construction. Reginald died in 1307, and the work was continued under his son and heir, Reginald le Chen (also Baron of Inverugie). (It is possible that the younger Reginald ordered the stone construction.) Nicholas, 1st of Duffus, married the younger Reginald's daughter, Mary/Mariot, thus bringing the holding back into the de Moravia family.

There is a story about Reginald (the younger) that is reminiscent of fairy tales and which I found irresistible. Evidently, he had a great desire for a son to inherit his holdings etc., but his wife gave birth to a daughter. He ordered the daughter to be killed, and similarly commanded the second daughter delivered by his wife to be killed, too. The couple had no more children. Years later, Reginald admired two beautiful young women at a festival and bemoaned his earlier choices, noting that these two maidens would be about the same age as his own daughters. His wife confessed that she had sent the girls away instead of allowing them to be killed—she was able to introduce their father to them and reunite the family. The wife, whose name is not recorded, was the daughter of the Marshall of Esslemont, so Reginald then named his daughters as heirs to Esslemont. Reginald died in 1345 and the records seem to indicate that his daughter Mary/Mariot married Nicholas after that, passing the holding of Duffus to her husband and thence back to the de Moravia family.

I chose to create a fictional holding of Duncheann and place it on an island off the northern coast, but its imagined location is not far from the site of Duffus Castle. Also, the girls were fostered by the Sutherland family in my version of the story, though I did not find the name of the foster family in the fourteenth century tale.

ABOUT THE AUTHOR

Deborah Cooke sold her first book in 1992, a medieval romance called **Romance of the Rose** published under her pseudonym Claire Delacroix. Since then, she has published over fifty novels in a wide variety of sub-genres, including historical romance, contemporary romance, paranormal romance, fantasy romance, time-travel romance, women's fiction, paranormal young adult and fantasy with romantic elements. She has published under the names Claire Delacroix, Claire Cross and Deborah Cooke. **The Beauty**, part of her successful Bride Quest series of historical romances, was her first title to land on the *New York Times* List of Bestselling Books. Her books routinely appear on other bestseller lists and have won numerous awards. In 2009, she was the writer-in-residence at the Toronto Public Library, the first time the library has hosted a residency focused on the romance genre. In 2012, she was honored to receive the Romance Writers of America's Mentor of the Year Award.

Currently, she writes contemporary romances and paranormal romances under the name Deborah Cooke. She also writes medieval romances as Claire Delacroix. Deborah lives in Canada with her husband and family, as well as far too many unfinished knitting projects.

http://DeborahCooke.com
http://Delacroix.net

~

MORE BOOKS BY CLAIRE DELACROIX

MEDIEVAL ROMANCE

Blood Brothers

THE WOLF & THE WITCH

THE HUNTER & THE HEIRESS

THE DRAGON & THE DAMSEL

THE SCOT & THE SORCERESS

Rogues & Angels

ONE KNIGHT ENCHANTED

ONE KNIGHT'S RETURN

The Champions of St. Euphemia

THE CRUSADER'S BRIDE

THE CRUSADER'S HEART

THE CRUSADER'S KISS

THE CRUSADER'S VOW

THE CRUSADER'S HANDFAST

The Rogues of Ravensmuir

THE ROGUE

THE SCOUNDREL

THE WARRIOR

The Jewels of Kinfairlie

THE BEAUTY BRIDE

THE ROSE RED BRIDE

THE SNOW WHITE BRIDE

The Ballad of Rosamunde

A Most Inconvenient Earl

Time Travel Romance
ONCE UPON A KISS
THE LAST HIGHLANDER
THE MOONSTONE
LOVE POTION #9

Short Stories and Novellas
BEGUILED
An Elegy for Melusine

~

Printed in Great Britain
by Amazon

32567249R00180